MW00852242

'NAMWOLF™ Volume One Published by Albatross Funnybooks, PO Box 60627, Nashville TN 37206, United States. 'NAMWOLF™ & © 2017 Fabian Rangel Jr. & Logan Faerber. All contents and related characters ™ & © 2017 Fabian Rangel Jr. & Logan Faerber. All rights reserved. No portion of this product may be reproduced or transmitted, by any form or by any means, without express written permission of Eric Powell. ALBATROSS FUNNYBOOKS™ and ALBATROSS FUNNYBOOKS Logo™ & © 2017 Eric Powell. Names, characters, places, and incidents featured in this publication are fictional. Any similarity to persons living or dead, places, and incidents is unintended or for satirical purposes.

This volume collects issues 1-4 of the Albatross Funnybooks series 'NAMWOLF.

ISBN- 978-0-9983792-2-7
(Printed in Canada)

**www.albatrossfunnybooks.com**

# 'NAMWOLF
## HEART OF DARKNESS™

Created by:
Fabian Rangel Jr. Logan Faerber

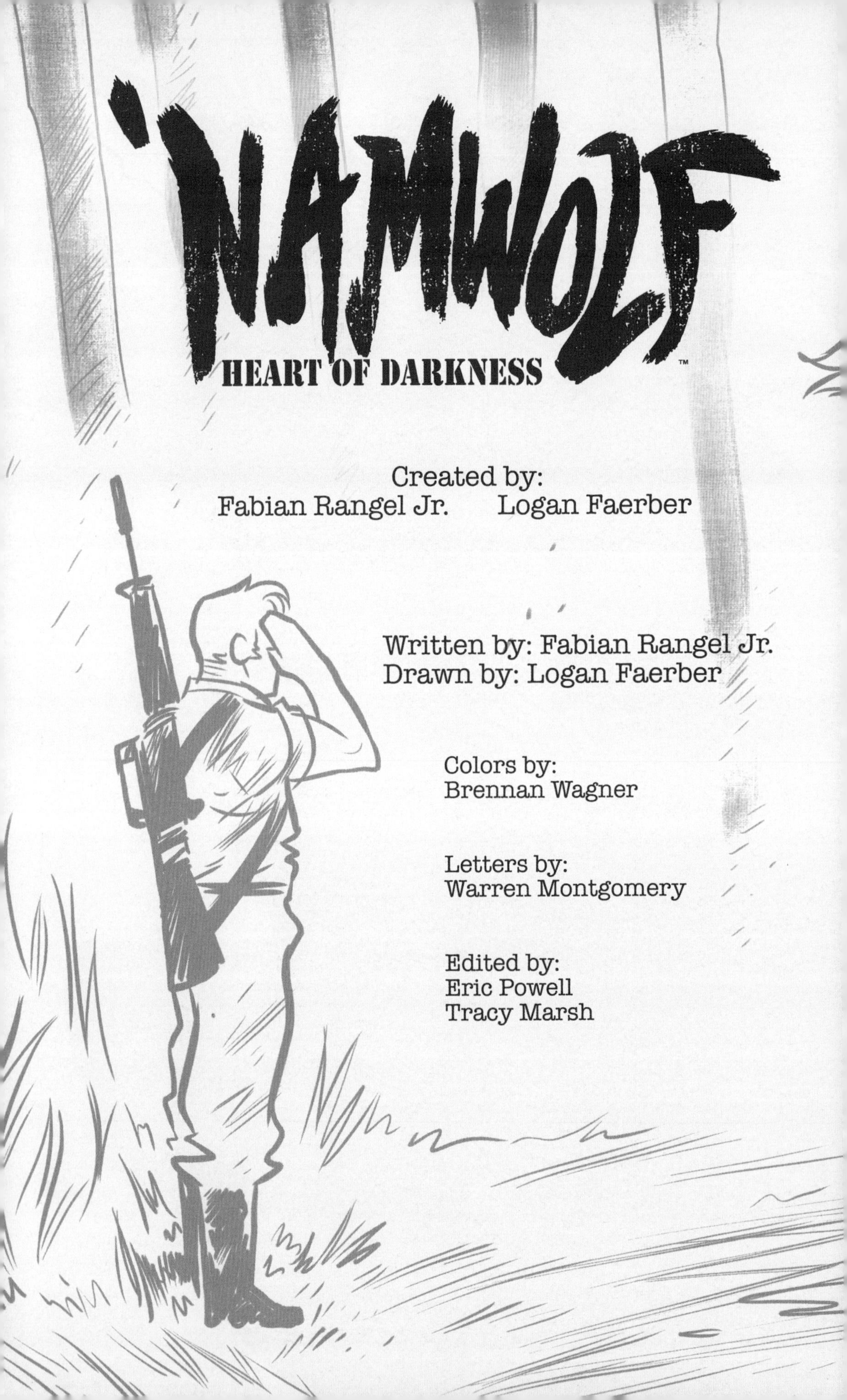

Written by: Fabian Rangel Jr.
Drawn by: Logan Faerber

Colors by:
Brennan Wagner

Letters by:
Warren Montgomery

Edited by:
Eric Powell
Tracy Marsh

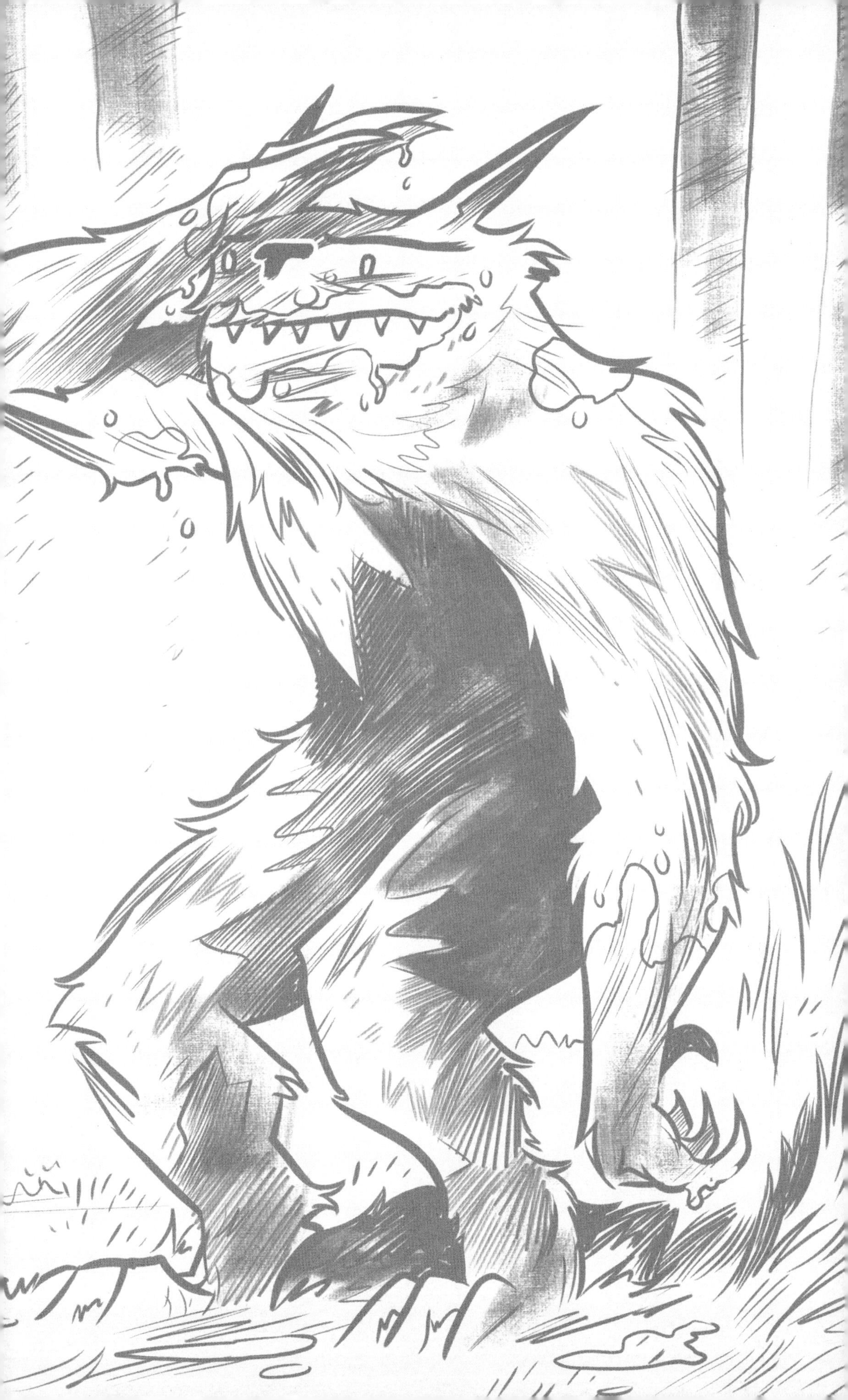

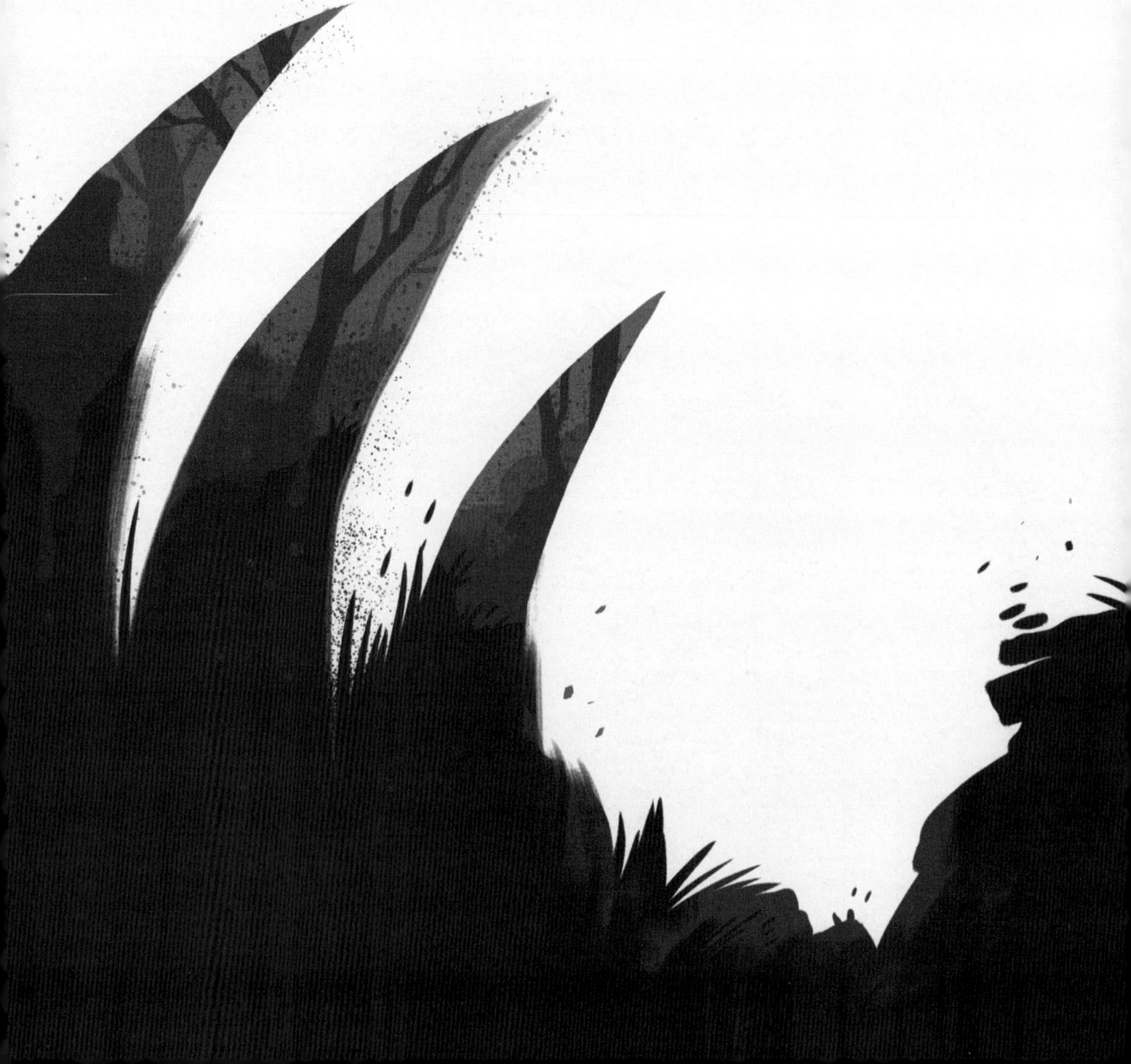

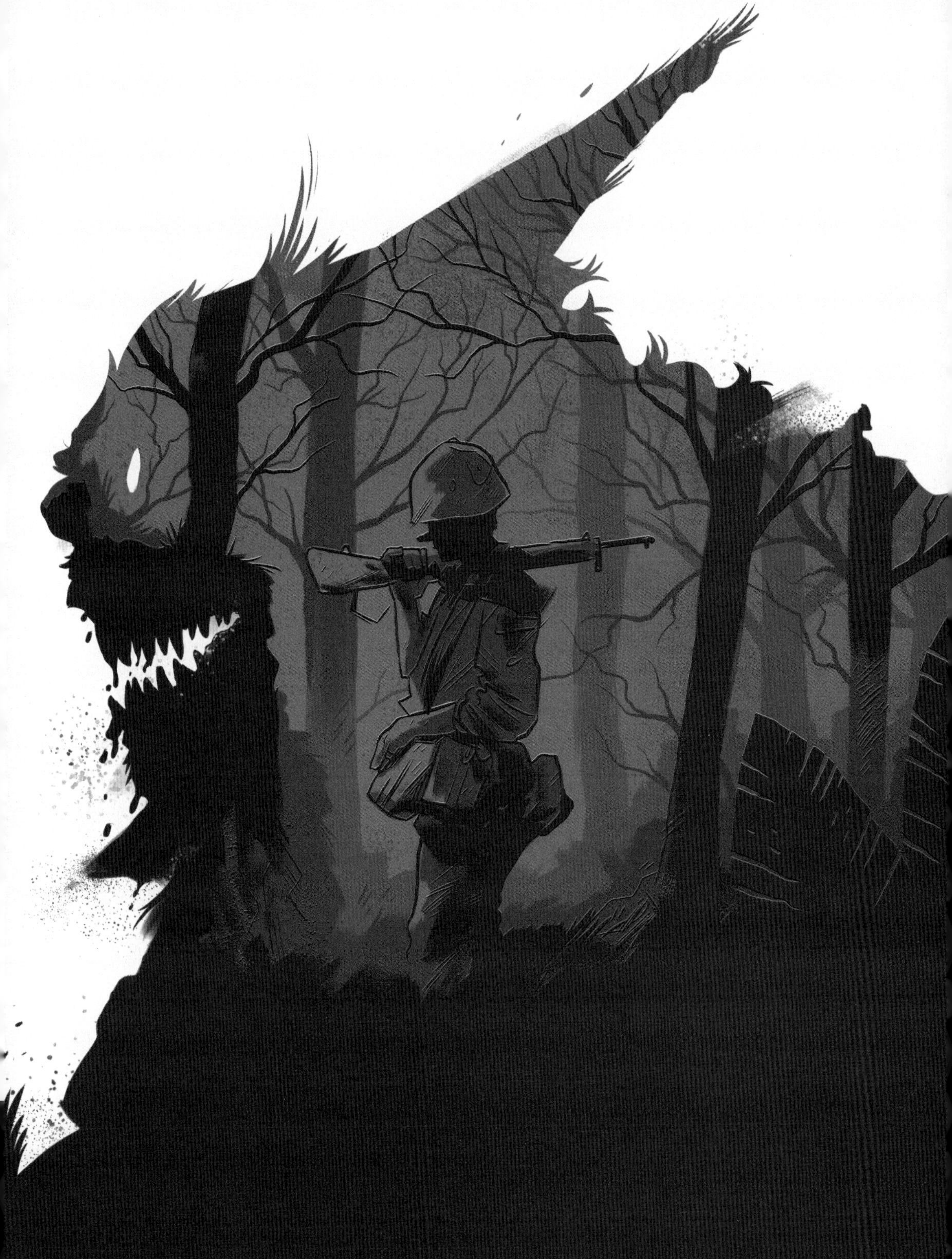

# CHAPTER ONE

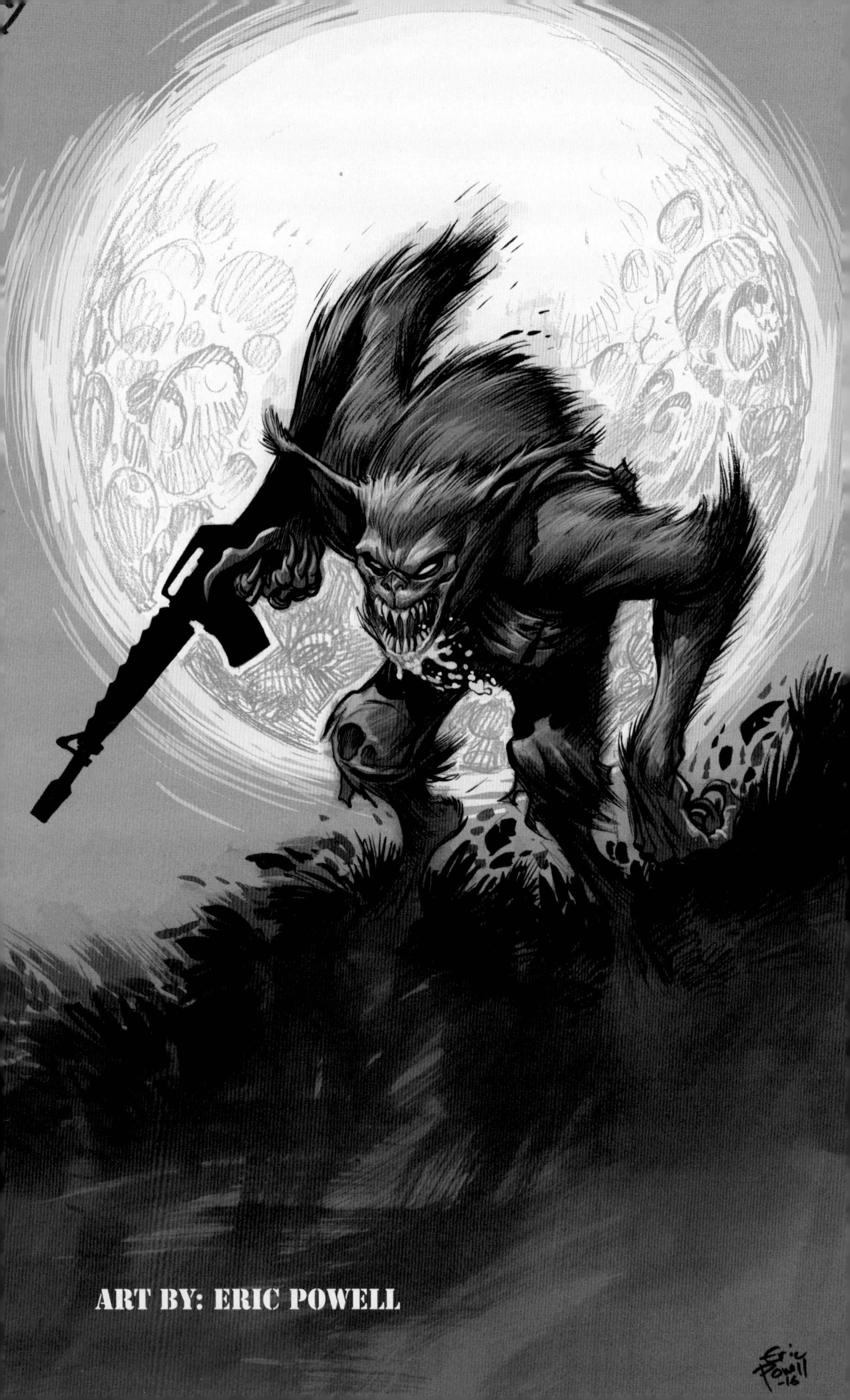
Eric Powell -16

ART BY: ERIC POWELL

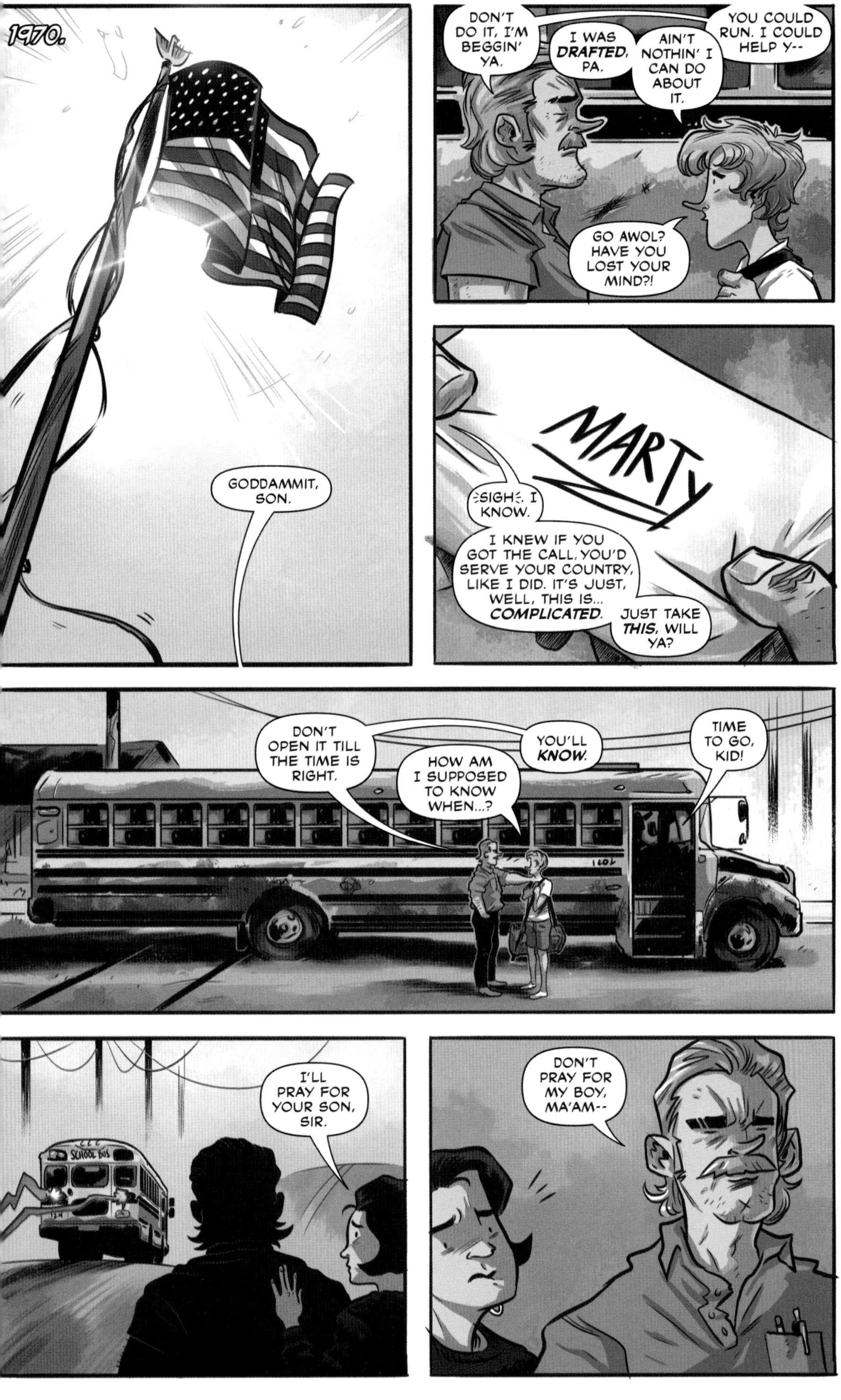
1970.
GODDAMMIT, SON.
DON'T DO IT, I'M BEGGIN' YA.
YOU COULD RUN. I COULD HELP Y--
I WAS DRAFTED, PA.
AIN'T NOTHIN' I CAN DO ABOUT IT.
GO AWOL? HAVE YOU LOST YOUR MIND?!
MARTY
SIGH I KNOW.
I KNEW IF YOU GOT THE CALL, YOU'D SERVE YOUR COUNTRY, LIKE I DID. IT'S JUST, WELL, THIS IS... COMPLICATED.
JUST TAKE THIS, WILL YA?
DON'T OPEN IT TILL THE TIME IS RIGHT.
HOW AM I SUPPOSED TO KNOW WHEN...?
YOU'LL KNOW.
TIME TO GO, KID!
I'LL PRAY FOR YOUR SON, SIR.
SCHOOL BUS
DON'T PRAY FOR MY BOY, MA'AM--

"--PRAY FOR EVERYONE ELSE."

THE 'NAM.

IT WAS THE SUMMER OF *MARTY SPENCER'S* 18TH BIRTHDAY WHEN HE SET BOOTS ON THE 'NAM.

HE WAS ONLY ABOUT A BUCK 25 SOAKIN' WET.

HE HAD NO BUSINESS BEIN' IN THAT JUNGLE, BUT THAT DIDN'T MATTER TO UNCLE SAM.

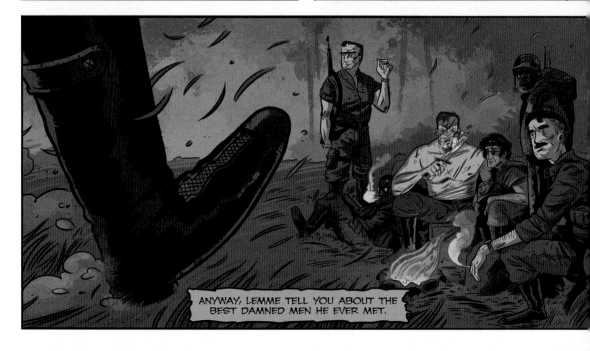

ANYWAY, LEMME TELL YOU ABOUT THE BEST DAMNED MEN HE EVER MET.

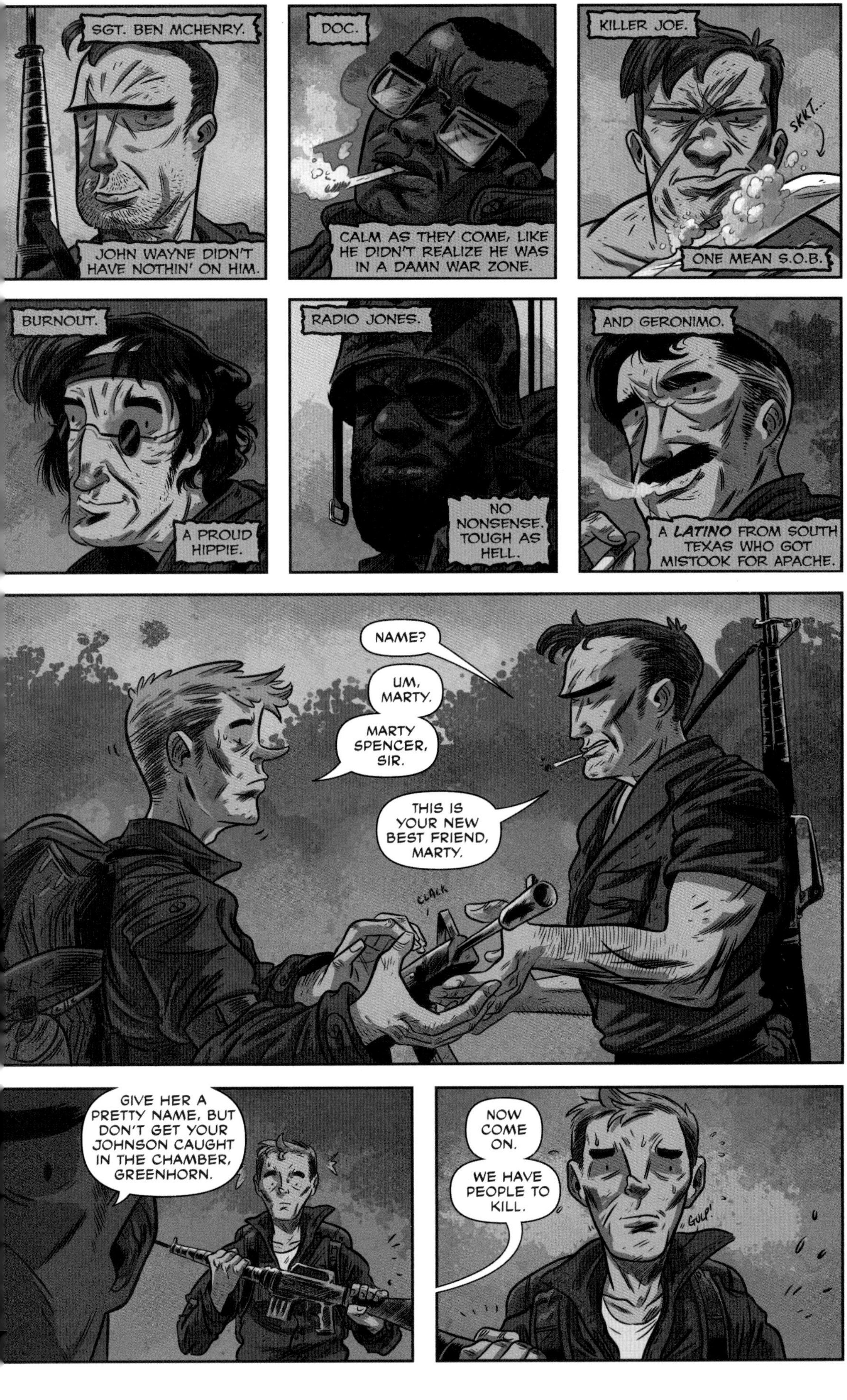
SGT. BEN MCHENRY.
JOHN WAYNE DIDN'T HAVE NOTHIN' ON HIM.
DOC.
CALM AS THEY COME, LIKE HE DIDN'T REALIZE HE WAS IN A DAMN WAR ZONE.
KILLER JOE.
SKKT...
ONE MEAN S.O.B.
BURNOUT.
A PROUD HIPPIE.
RADIO JONES.
NO NONSENSE. TOUGH AS HELL.
AND GERONIMO.
A *LATINO* FROM SOUTH TEXAS WHO GOT MISTOOK FOR APACHE.
NAME?
UM, MARTY.
MARTY SPENCER, SIR.
THIS IS YOUR NEW BEST FRIEND, MARTY.
CLACK
GIVE HER A PRETTY NAME, BUT DON'T GET YOUR JOHNSON CAUGHT IN THE CHAMBER, GREENHORN.
NOW COME ON.
WE HAVE PEOPLE TO KILL.
GULP!

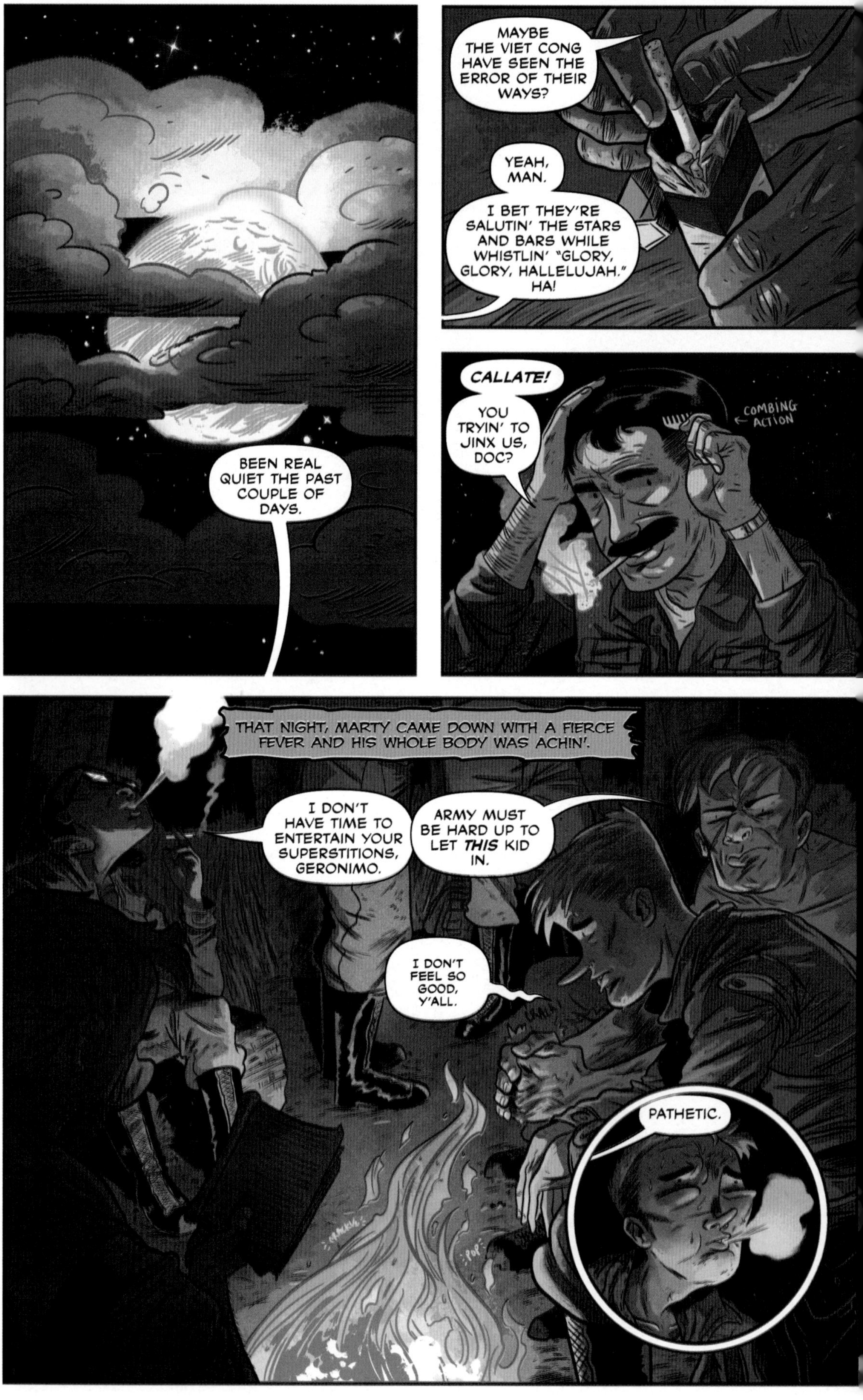
BEEN REAL QUIET THE PAST COUPLE OF DAYS.
MAYBE THE VIET CONG HAVE SEEN THE ERROR OF THEIR WAYS?
YEAH, MAN.
I BET THEY'RE SALUTIN' THE STARS AND BARS WHILE WHISTLIN' "GLORY, GLORY, HALLELUJAH." HA!
CALLATE!
YOU TRYIN' TO JINX US, DOC?
COMBING ACTION
THAT NIGHT, MARTY CAME DOWN WITH A FIERCE FEVER AND HIS WHOLE BODY WAS ACHIN'.
I DON'T HAVE TIME TO ENTERTAIN YOUR SUPERSTITIONS, GERONIMO.
ARMY MUST BE HARD UP TO LET THIS KID IN.
I DON'T FEEL SO GOOD, Y'ALL.
PATHETIC.

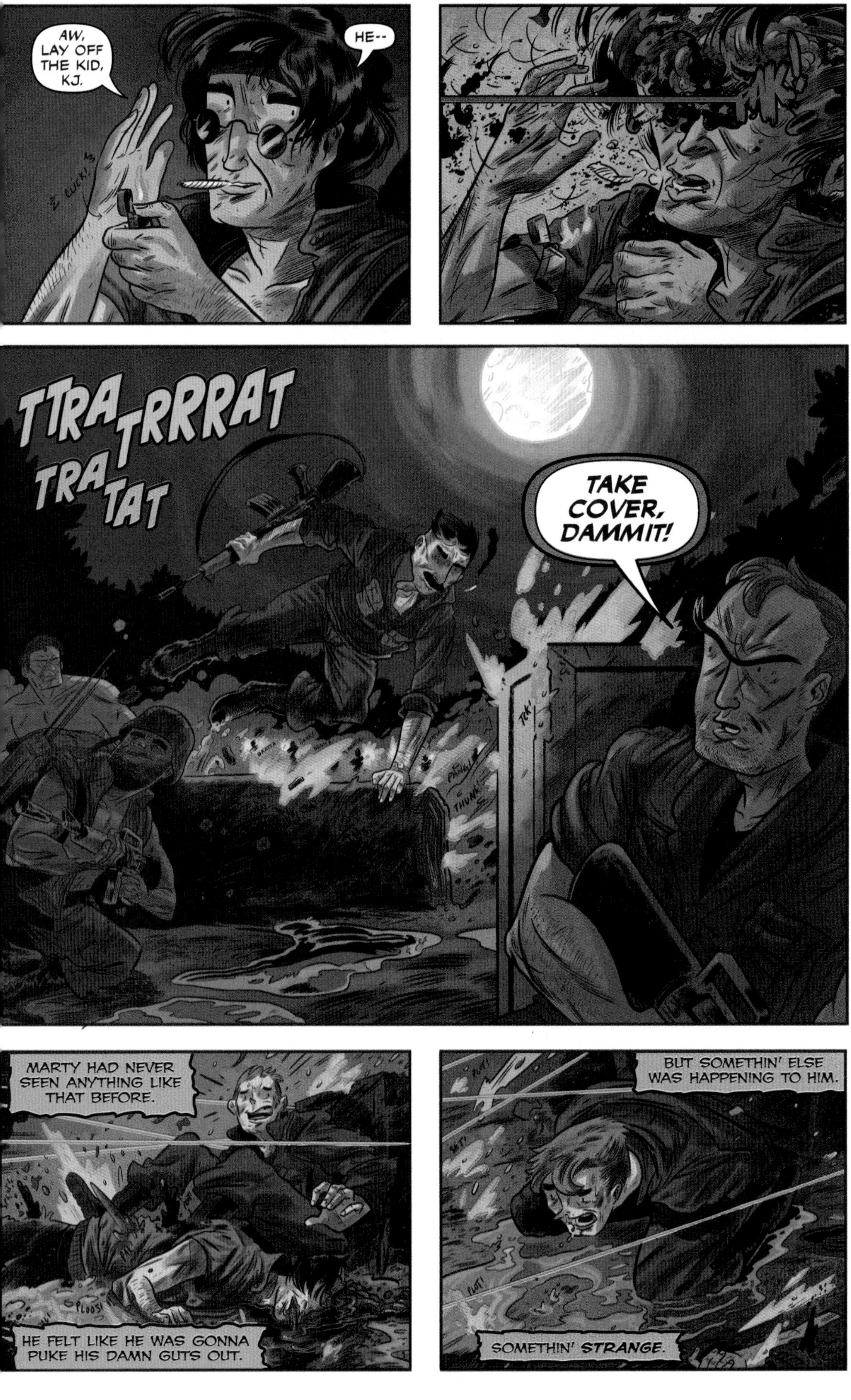
AW, LAY OFF THE KID, KJ.
HE--
TTRA TRRRAT
TRA TAT
TAKE COVER, DAMMIT!
MARTY HAD NEVER SEEN ANYTHING LIKE THAT BEFORE.
HE FELT LIKE HE WAS GONNA PUKE HIS DAMN GUTS OUT.
BUT SOMETHIN' ELSE WAS HAPPENING TO HIM.
SOMETHIN' **STRANGE**.

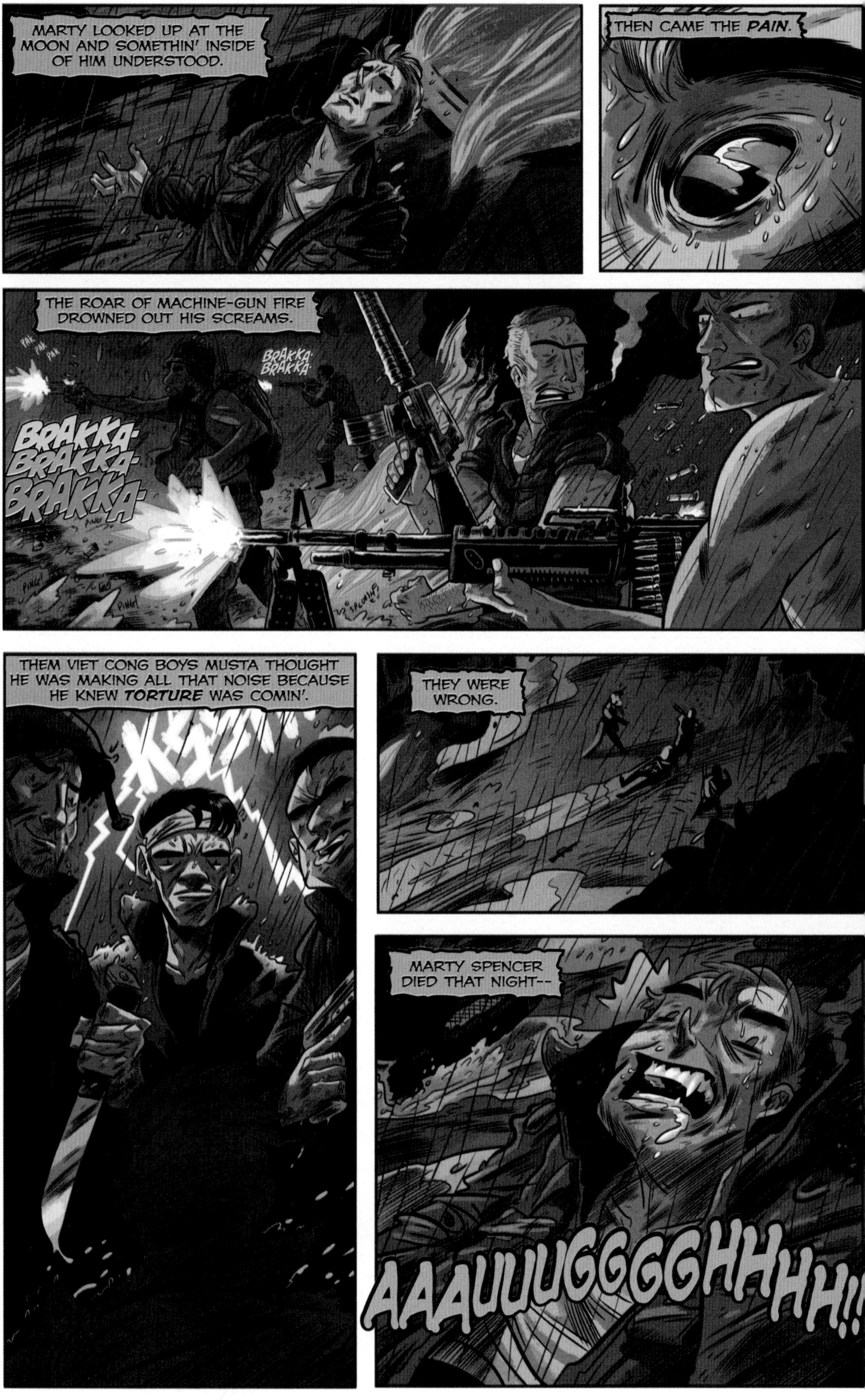
MARTY LOOKED UP AT THE MOON AND SOMETHIN' INSIDE OF HIM UNDERSTOOD.
THEN CAME THE PAIN.
THE ROAR OF MACHINE-GUN FIRE DROWNED OUT HIS SCREAMS.
PAK PAK PAK
BRAKKA-BRAKKA-
BRAKKA-BRAKKA-BRAKKA-
PING!
PING!
PING!
SPLOOSH!
THEM VIET CONG BOYS MUSTA THOUGHT HE WAS MAKING ALL THAT NOISE BECAUSE HE KNEW TORTURE WAS COMIN'.
THEY WERE WRONG.
MARTY SPENCER DIED THAT NIGHT--
AAAUUUGGGGHHHH!!

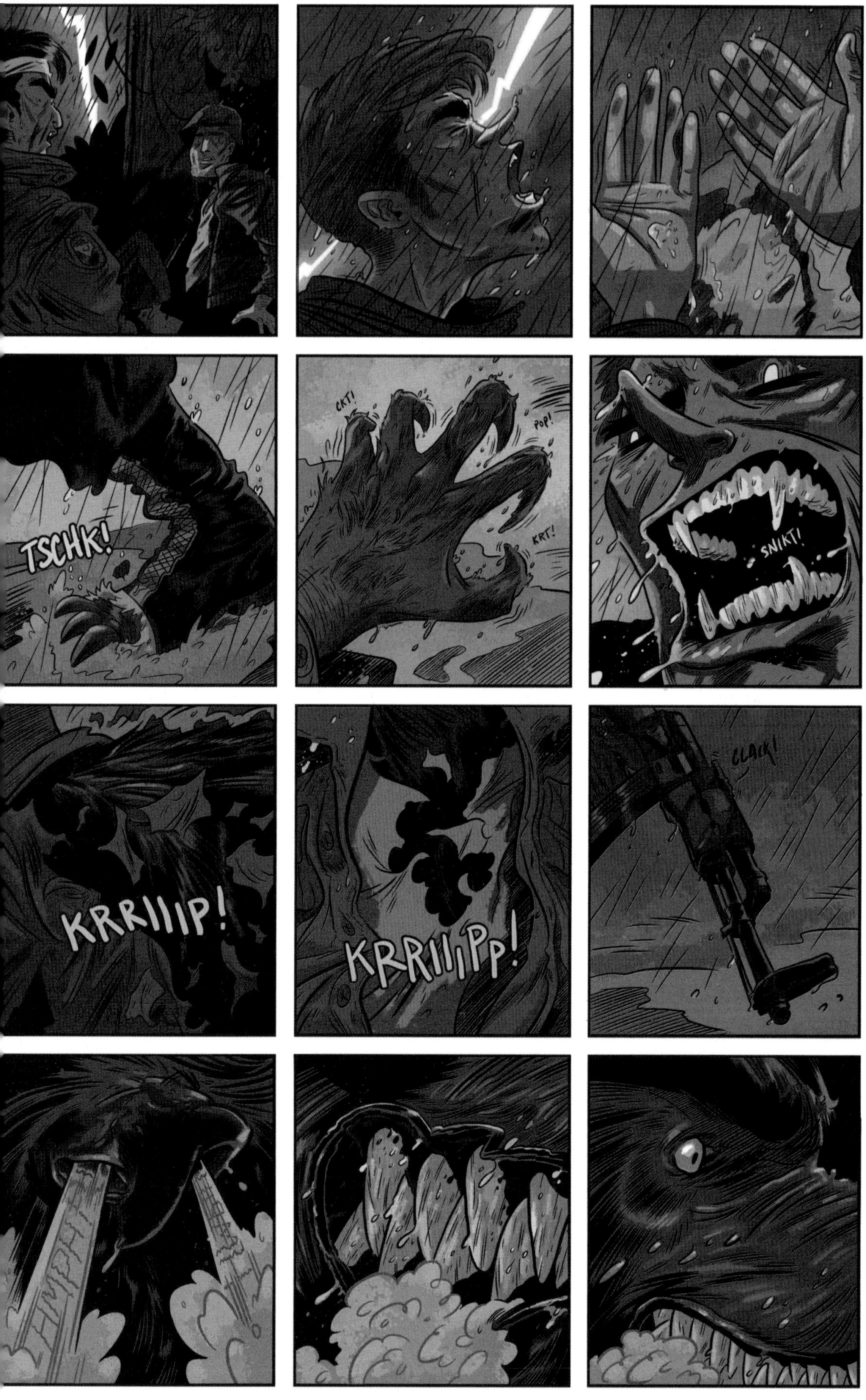
TSCHK!
CKT!
POP!
KRT!
SNIKT!
KRRIIIP!
KRRIIIPP!
CLACK!

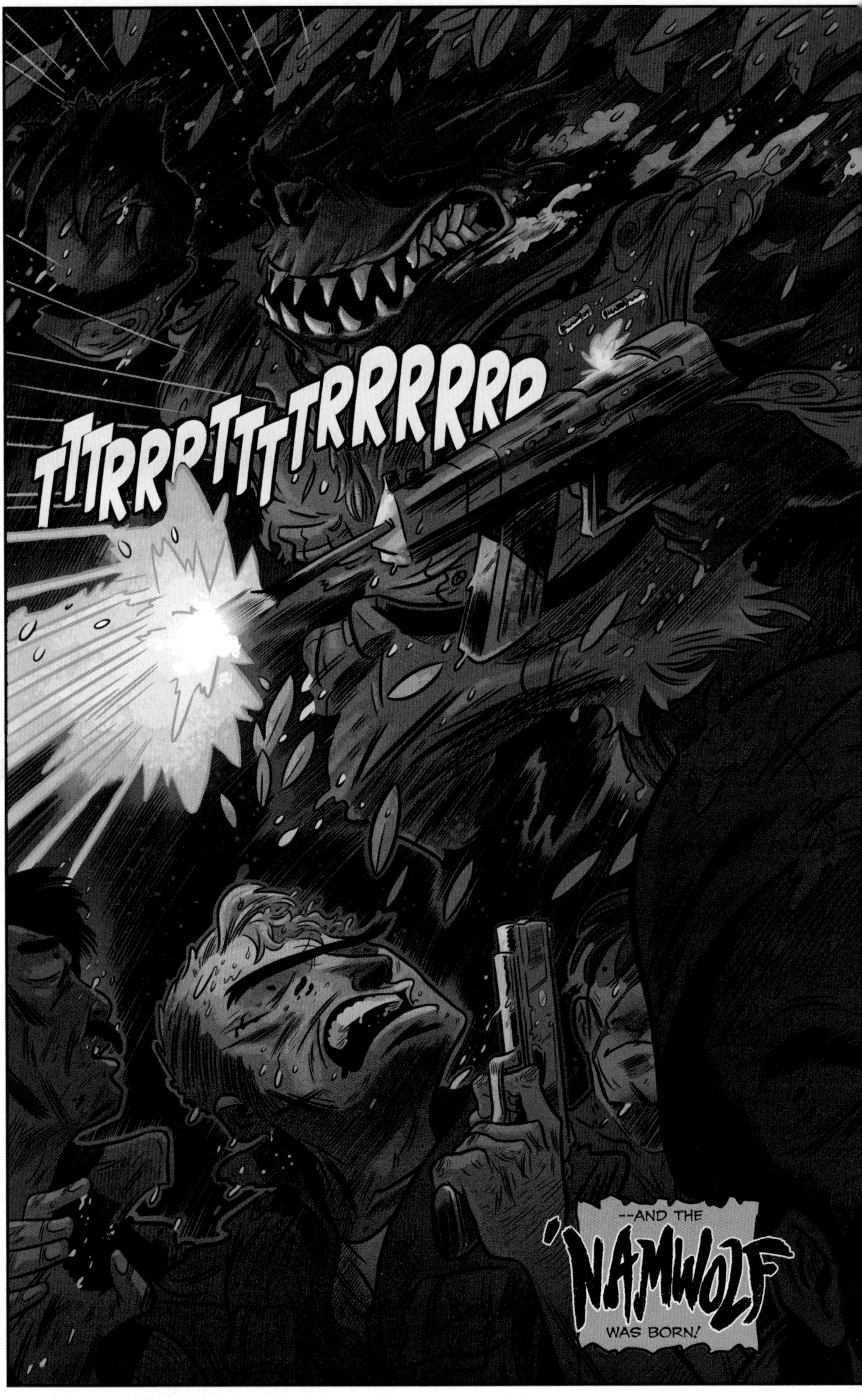
TTTRRPTTTTRRRRRD
--AND THE
'NAMWOLF
WAS BORN!

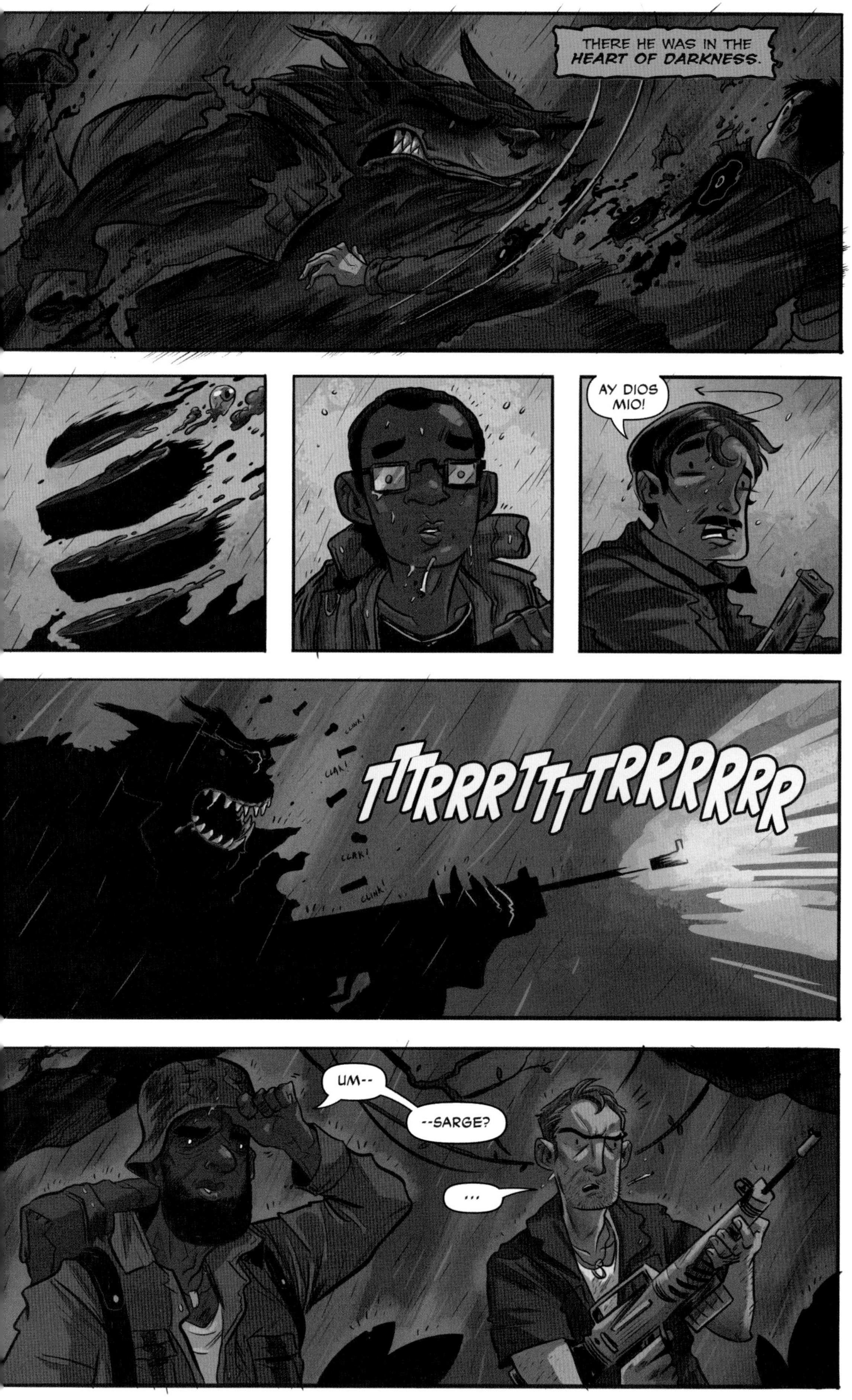
THERE HE WAS IN THE *HEART OF DARKNESS.*
AY DIOS MIO!
CLINK!
CLAK!
TTTRRRTTTTRRRRRR
CLAK!
CLINK!
UM--
--SARGE?
...

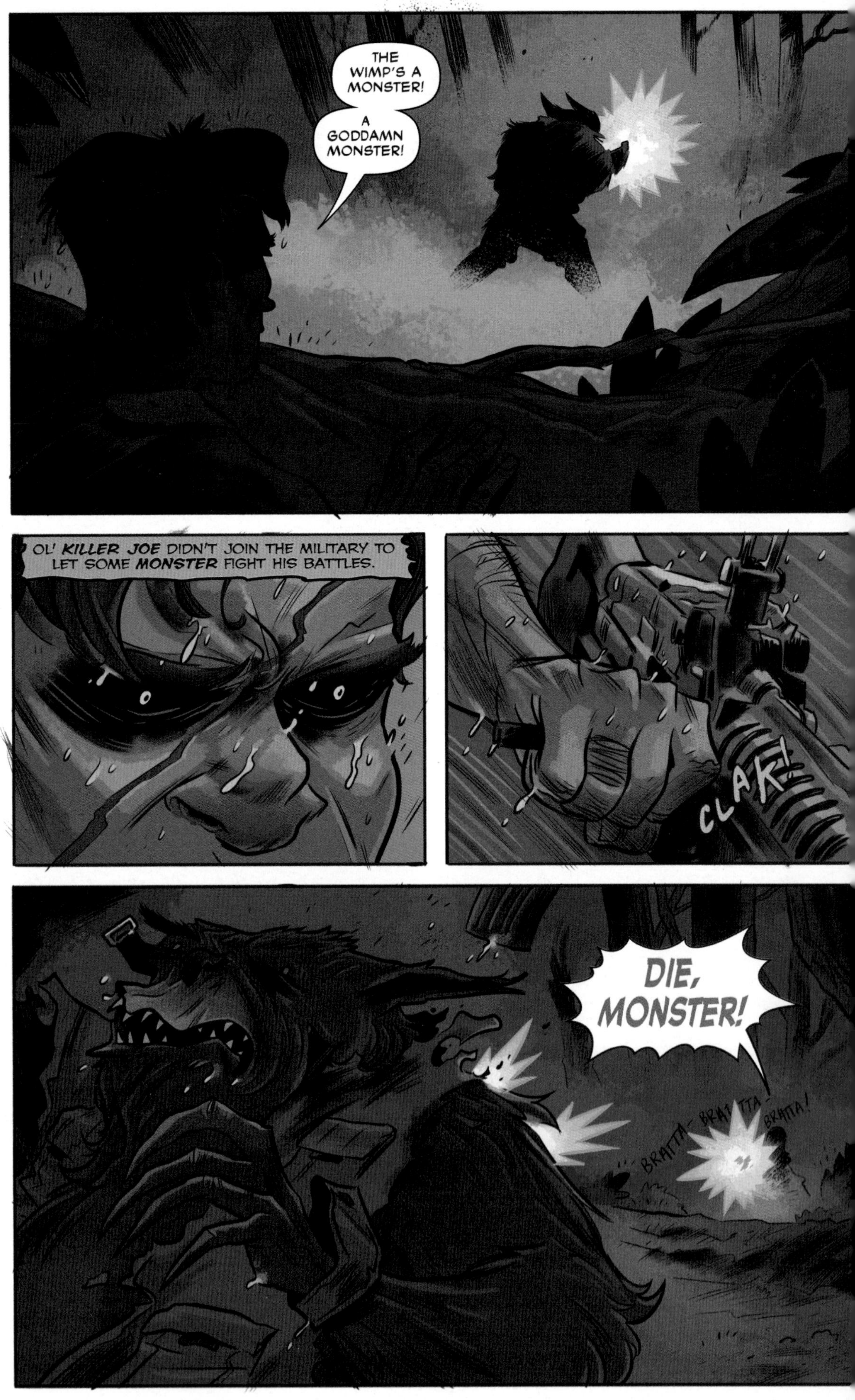
THE WIMP'S A MONSTER!
A GODDAMN MONSTER!
OL' KILLER JOE DIDN'T JOIN THE MILITARY TO LET SOME MONSTER FIGHT HIS BATTLES.
CLAK!
DIE, MONSTER!
BRATTA- BRATTA- BRATTA!

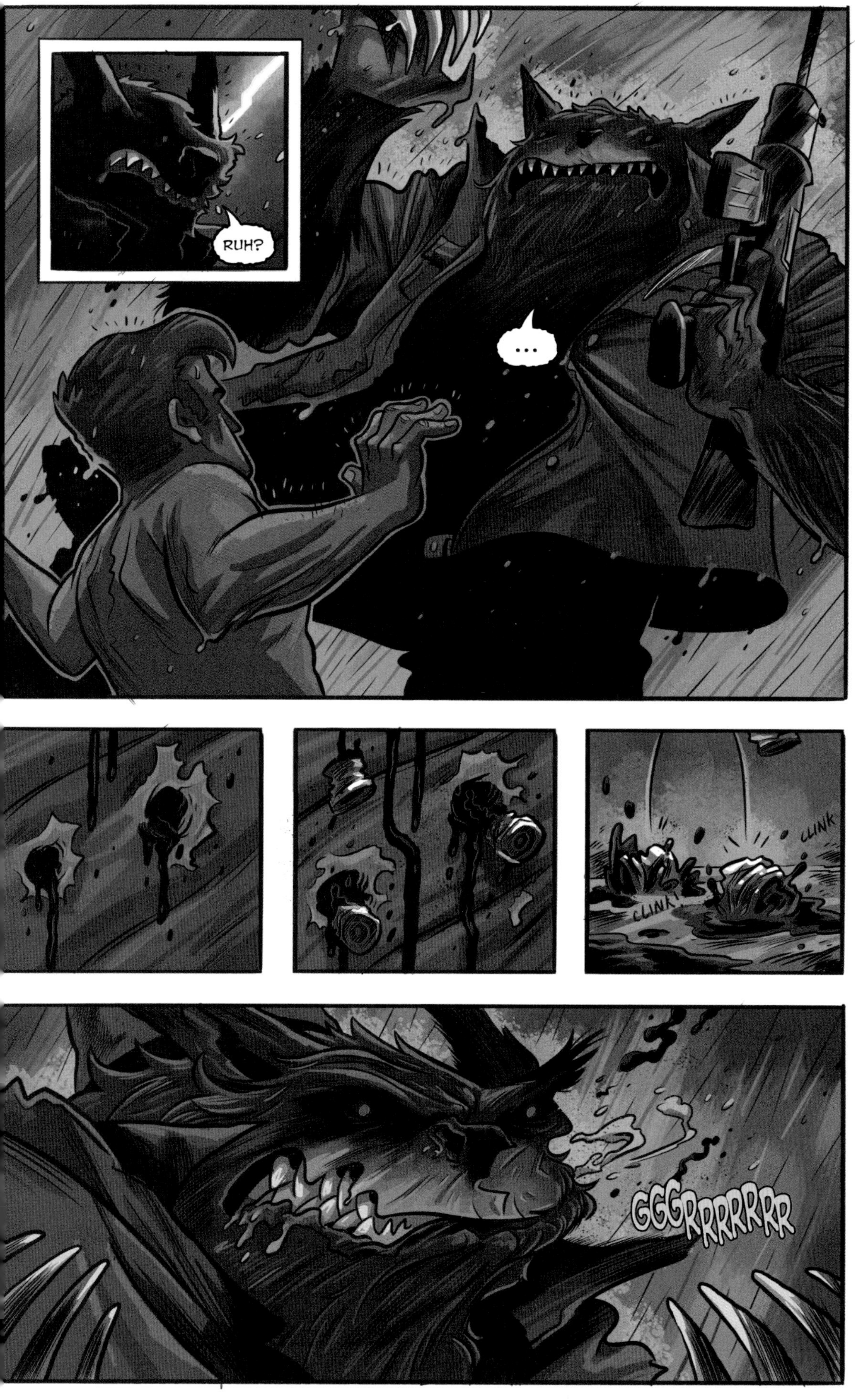
RUH?
...
CLINK!
CLINK
GGGRRRRRRR

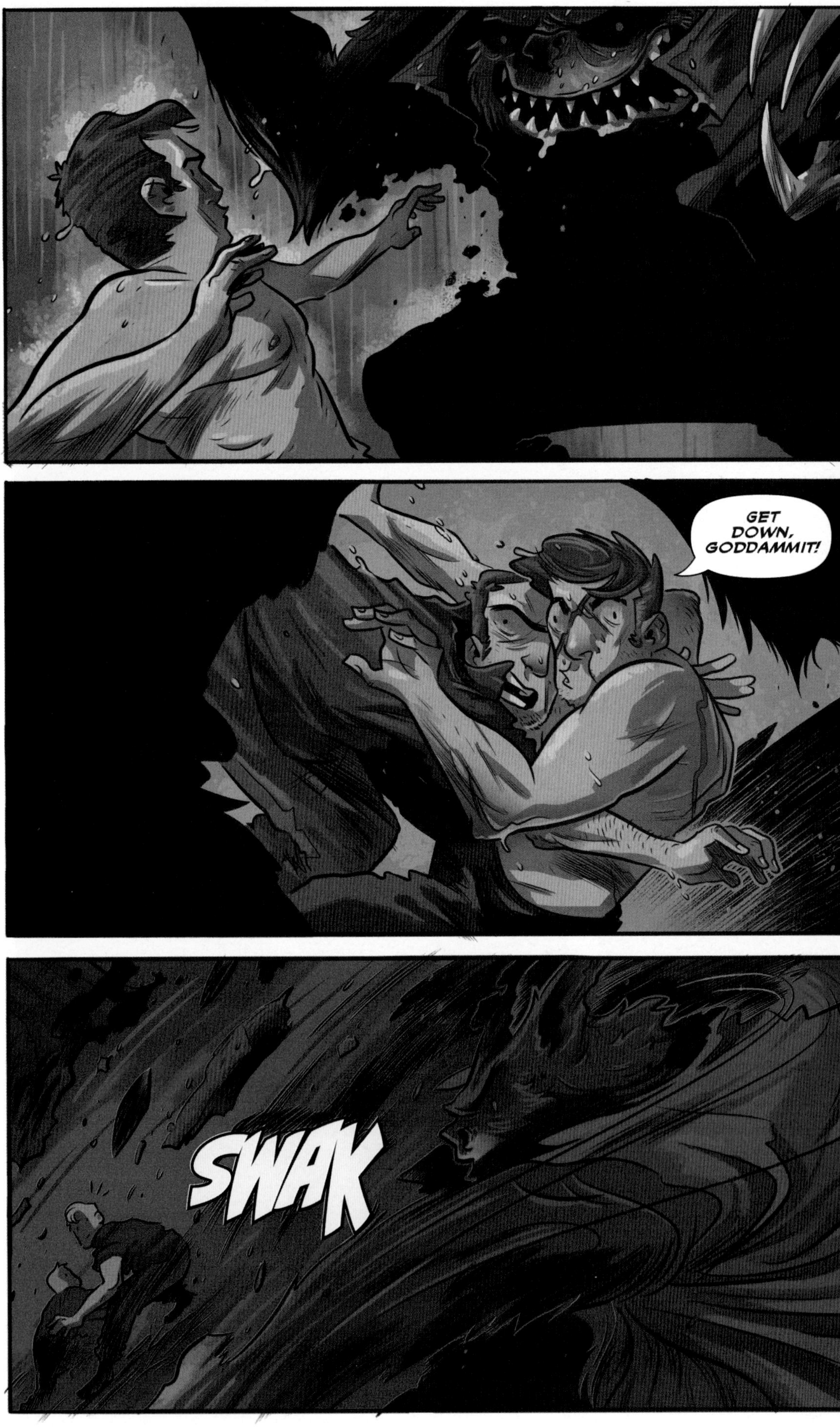
GET DOWN, GODDAMMIT!
SWAK

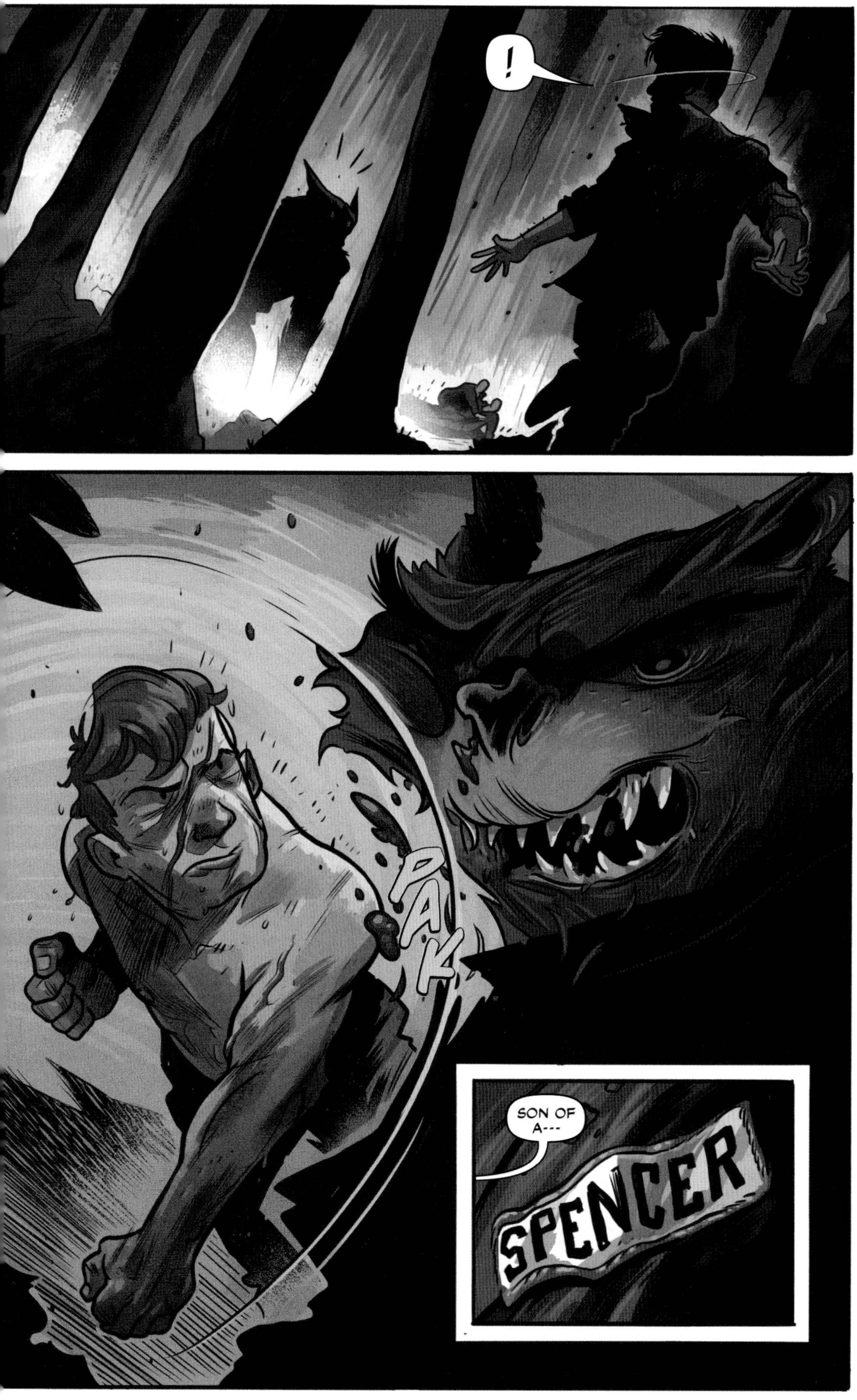
!
PAK
SON OF A---
SPENCER

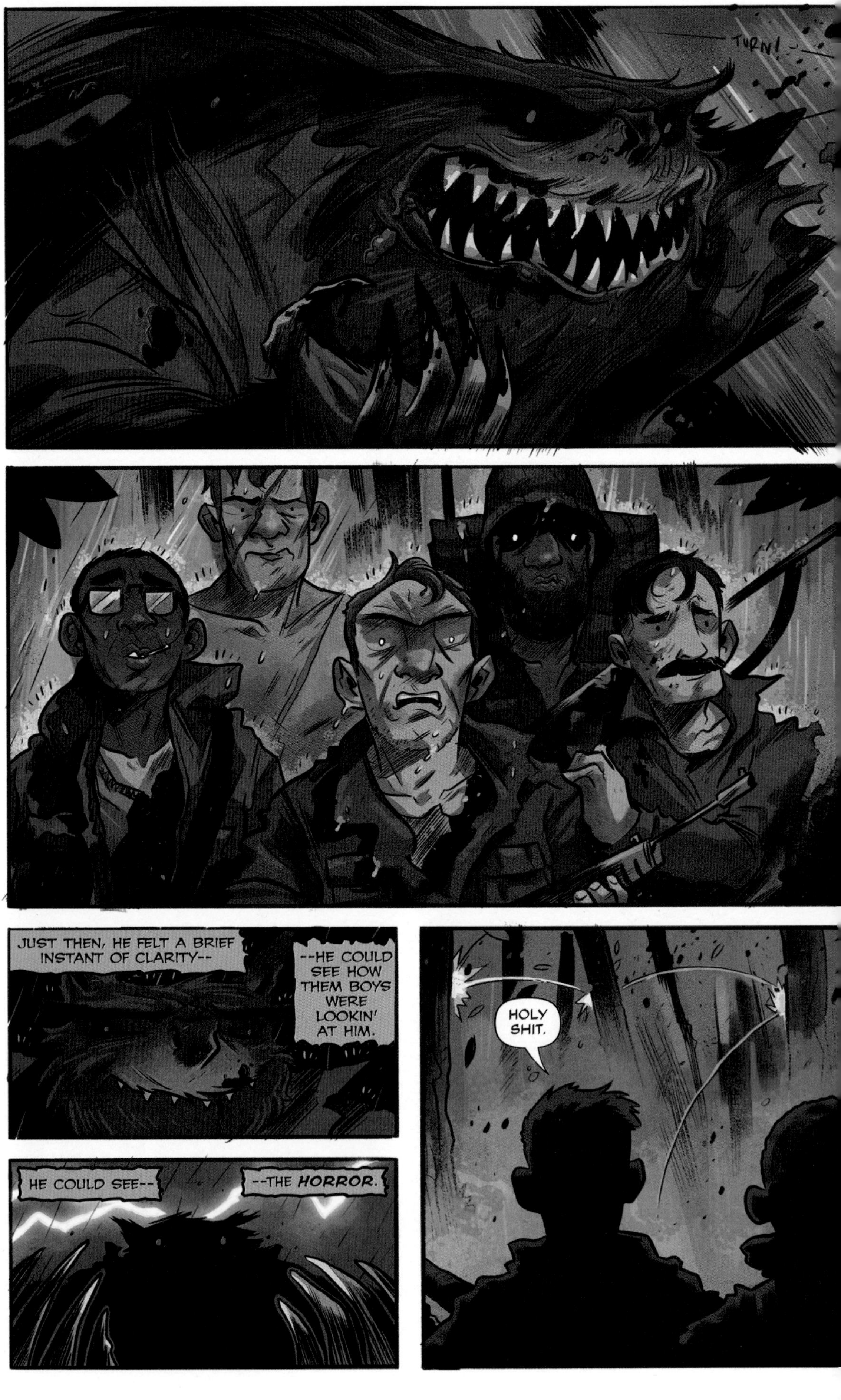
TURN!
JUST THEN, HE FELT A BRIEF INSTANT OF CLARITY--
--HE COULD SEE HOW THEM BOYS WERE LOOKIN' AT HIM.
HE COULD SEE--
--THE HORROR.
HOLY SHIT.

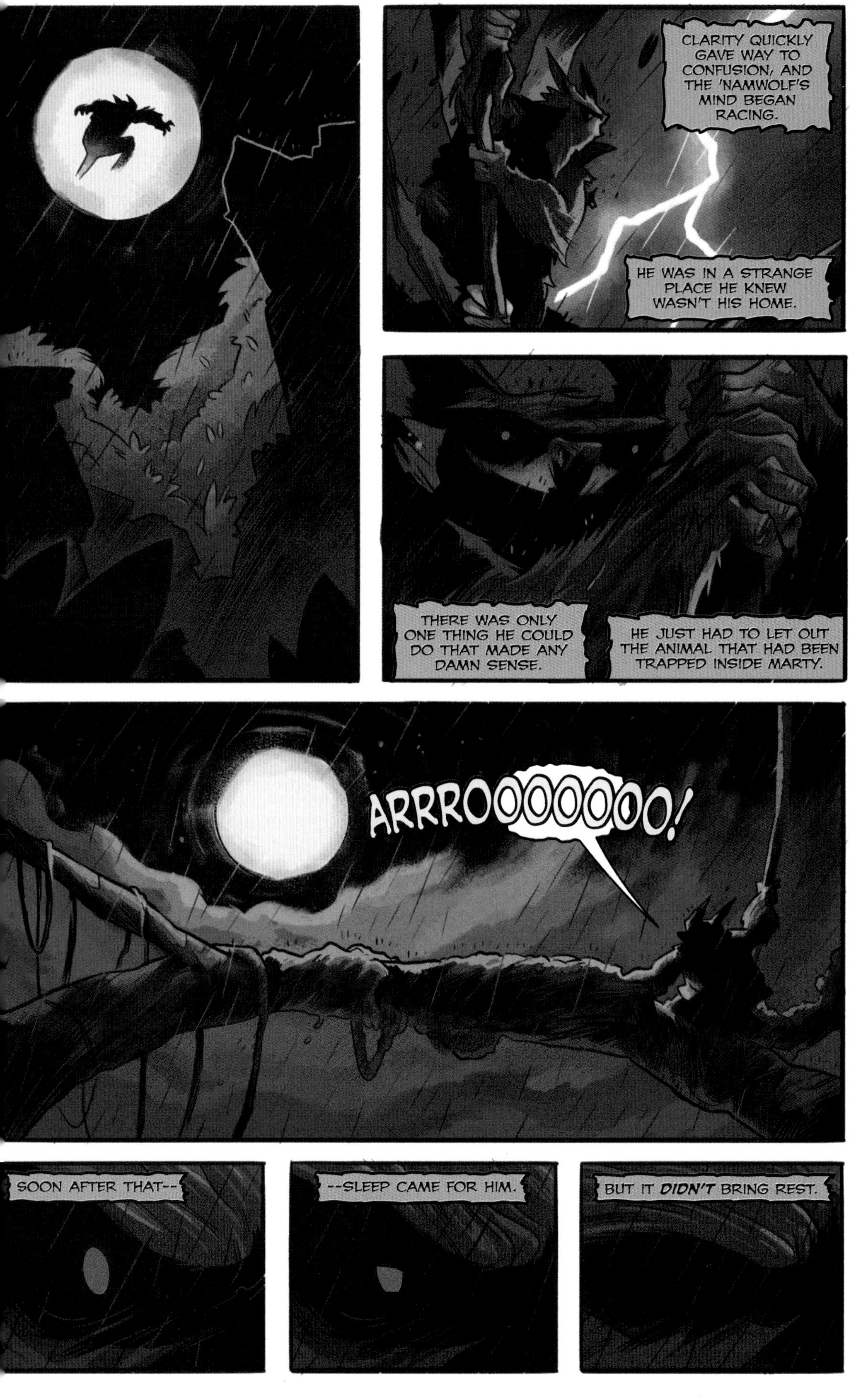
CLARITY QUICKLY GAVE WAY TO CONFUSION, AND THE 'NAMWOLF'S MIND BEGAN RACING.
HE WAS IN A STRANGE PLACE HE KNEW WASN'T HIS HOME.
THERE WAS ONLY ONE THING HE COULD DO THAT MADE ANY DAMN SENSE.
HE JUST HAD TO LET OUT THE ANIMAL THAT HAD BEEN TRAPPED INSIDE MARTY.
ARRROOOOOOOO!
SOON AFTER THAT--
--SLEEP CAME FOR HIM.
BUT IT *DIDN'T* BRING REST.

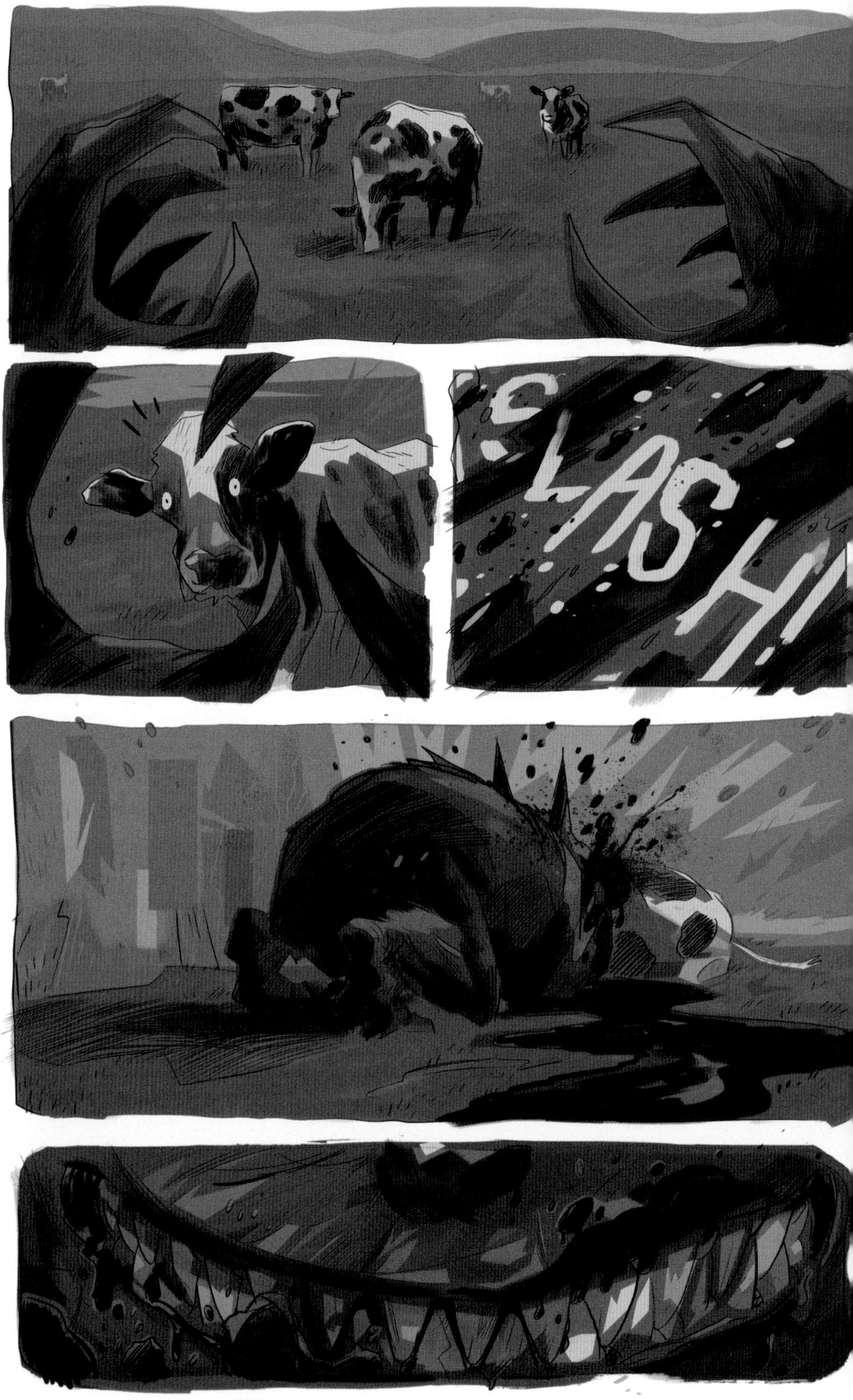
SLASH!

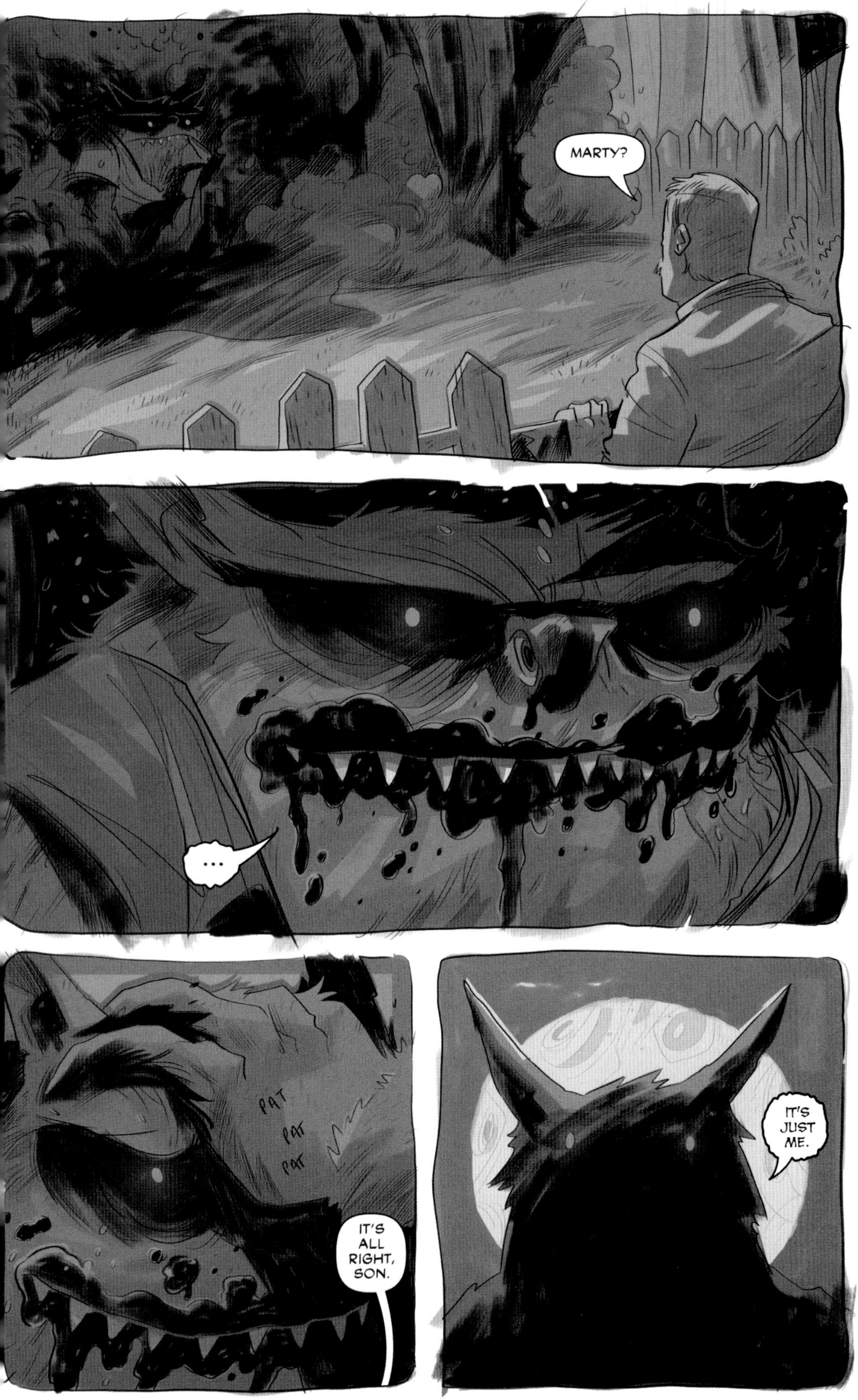
MARTY?
...
PAT
PAT
PAT
IT'S ALL RIGHT, SON.
IT'S JUST ME.

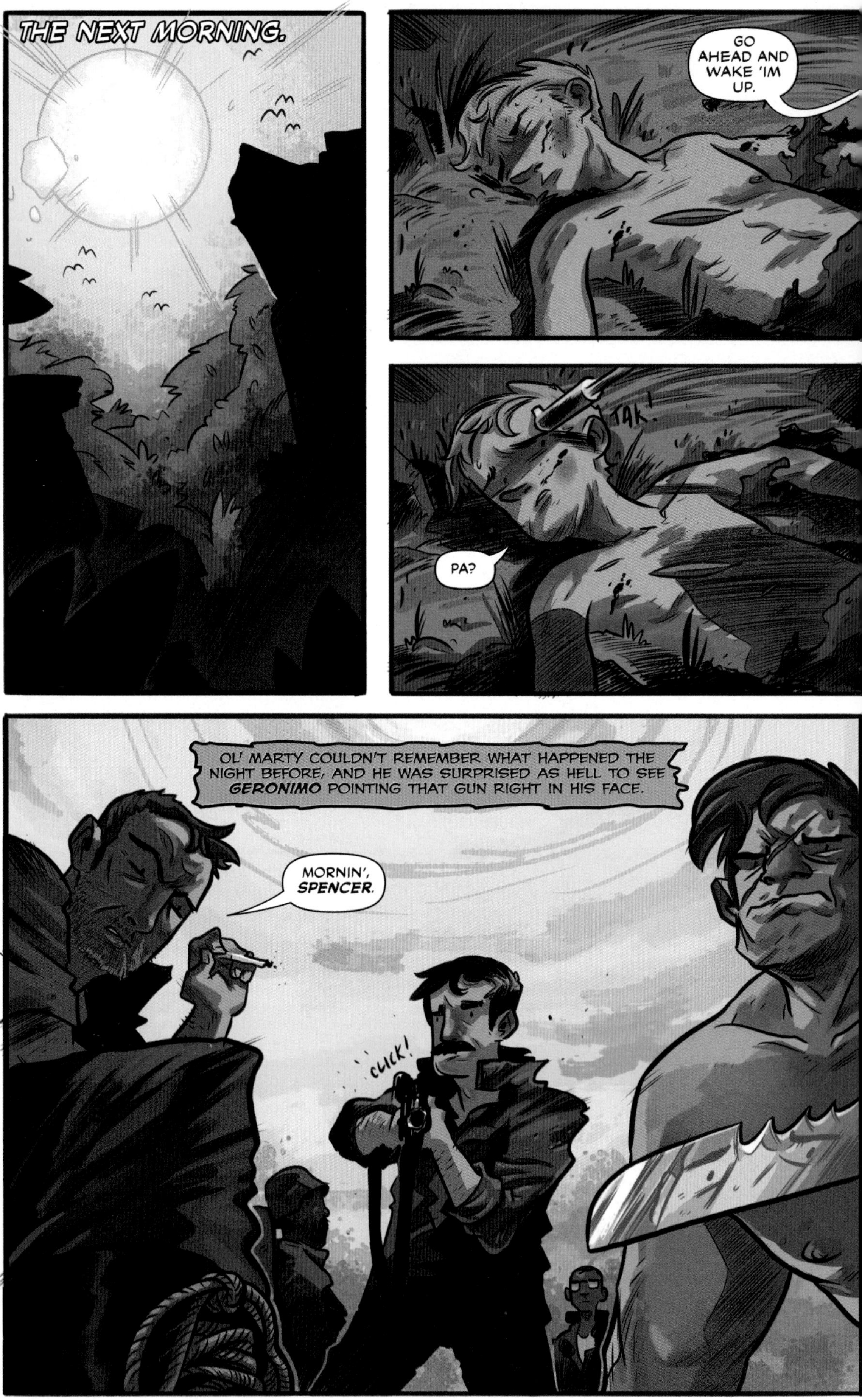
THE NEXT MORNING.
GO AHEAD AND WAKE 'IM UP.
TAK!
PA?
OL' MARTY COULDN'T REMEMBER WHAT HAPPENED THE NIGHT BEFORE, AND HE WAS SURPRISED AS HELL TO SEE GERONIMO POINTING THAT GUN RIGHT IN HIS FACE.
MORNIN', SPENCER.
CLICK!

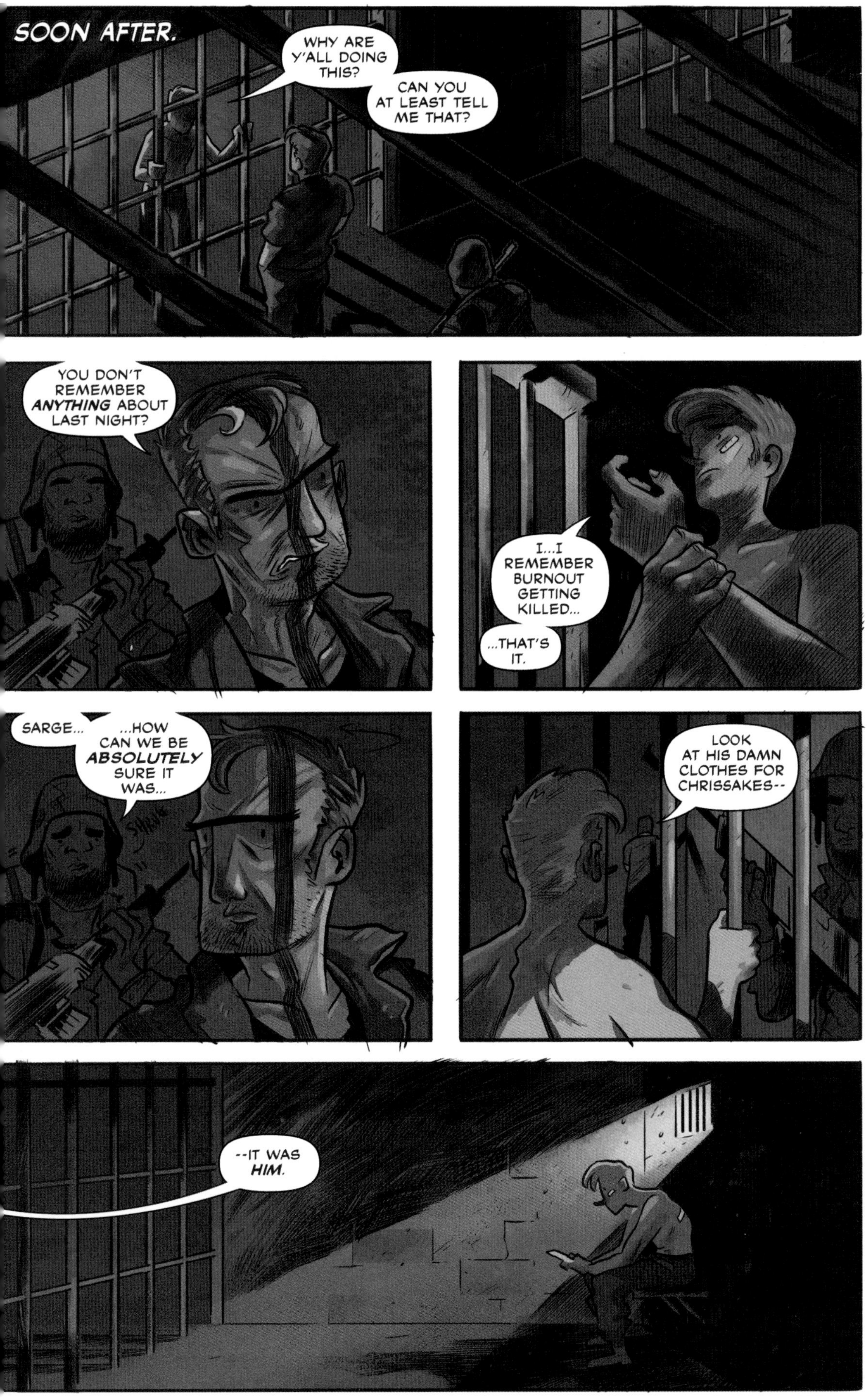
SOON AFTER.
WHY ARE Y'ALL DOING THIS?
CAN YOU AT LEAST TELL ME THAT?
YOU DON'T REMEMBER **ANYTHING** ABOUT LAST NIGHT?
I...I REMEMBER BURNOUT GETTING KILLED...
...THAT'S IT.
SARGE...
...HOW CAN WE BE **ABSOLUTELY** SURE IT WAS...
LOOK AT HIS DAMN CLOTHES FOR CHRISSAKES--
--IT WAS **HIM**.

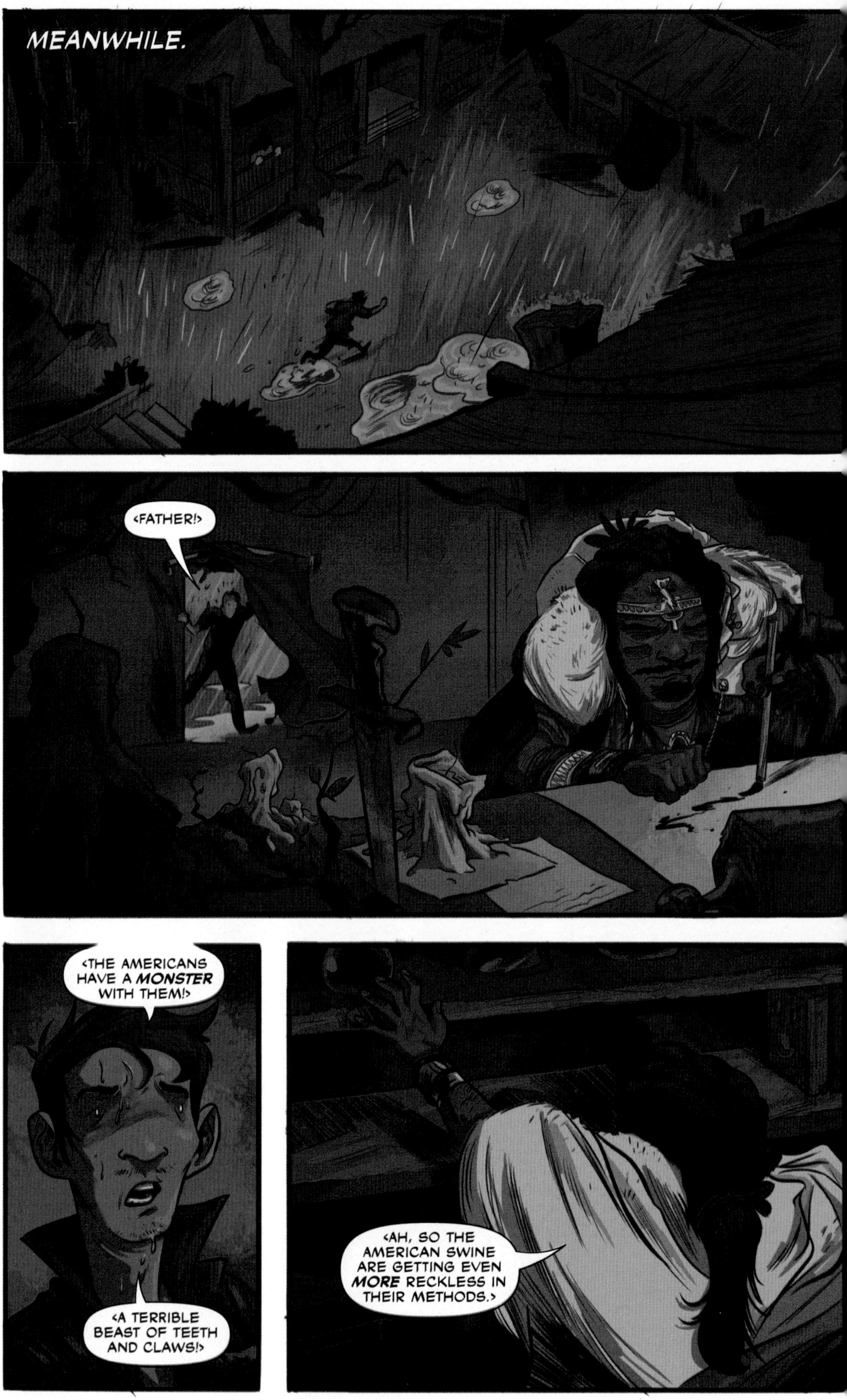
MEANWHILE.
<FATHER!>
<THE AMERICANS HAVE A MONSTER WITH THEM!>
<A TERRIBLE BEAST OF TEETH AND CLAWS!>
<AH, SO THE AMERICAN SWINE ARE GETTING EVEN MORE RECKLESS IN THEIR METHODS.>

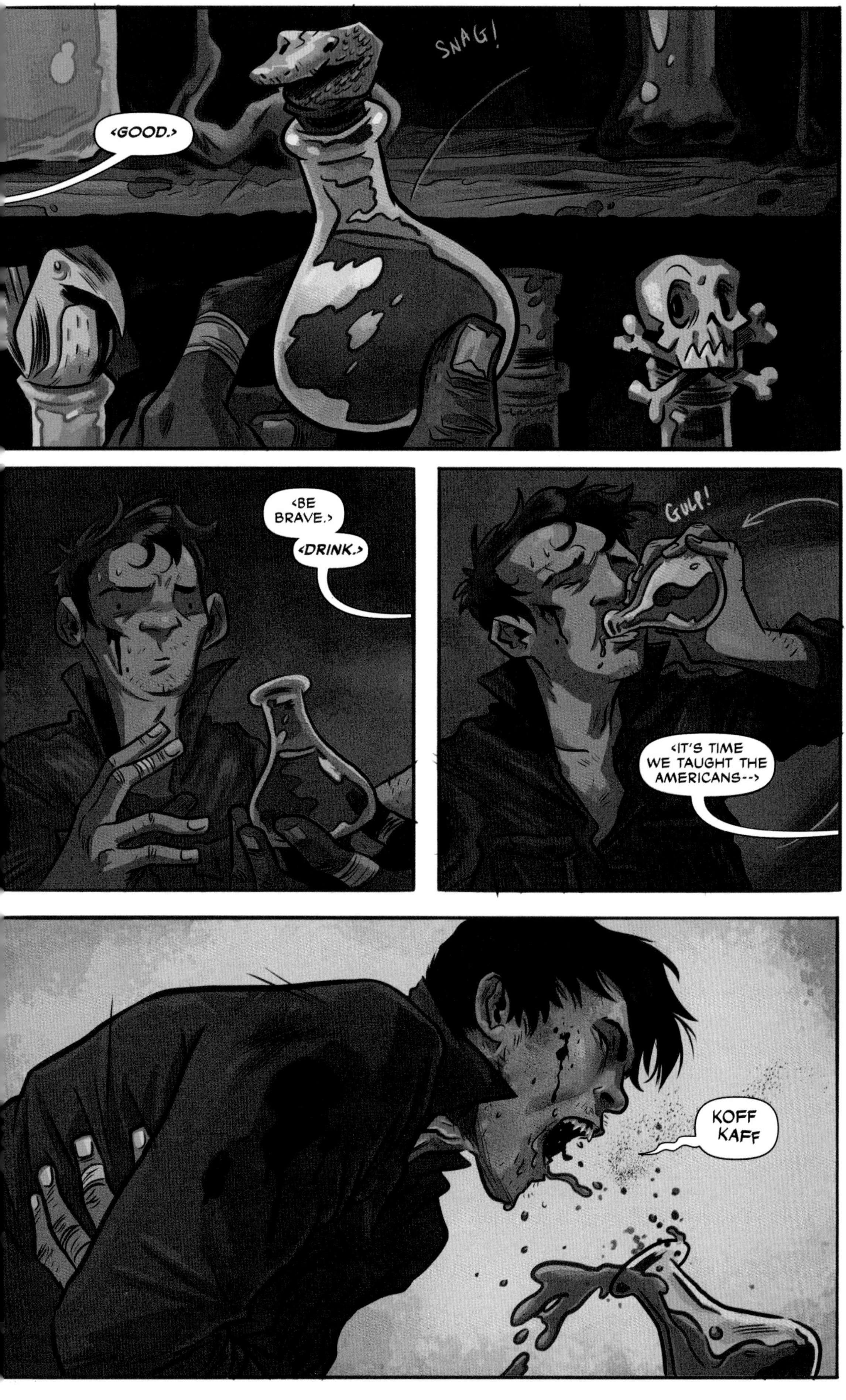
SNAG!
<GOOD.>
<BE BRAVE.>
<DRINK.>
GULP!
<IT'S TIME WE TAUGHT THE AMERICANS-->
KOFF KAFF

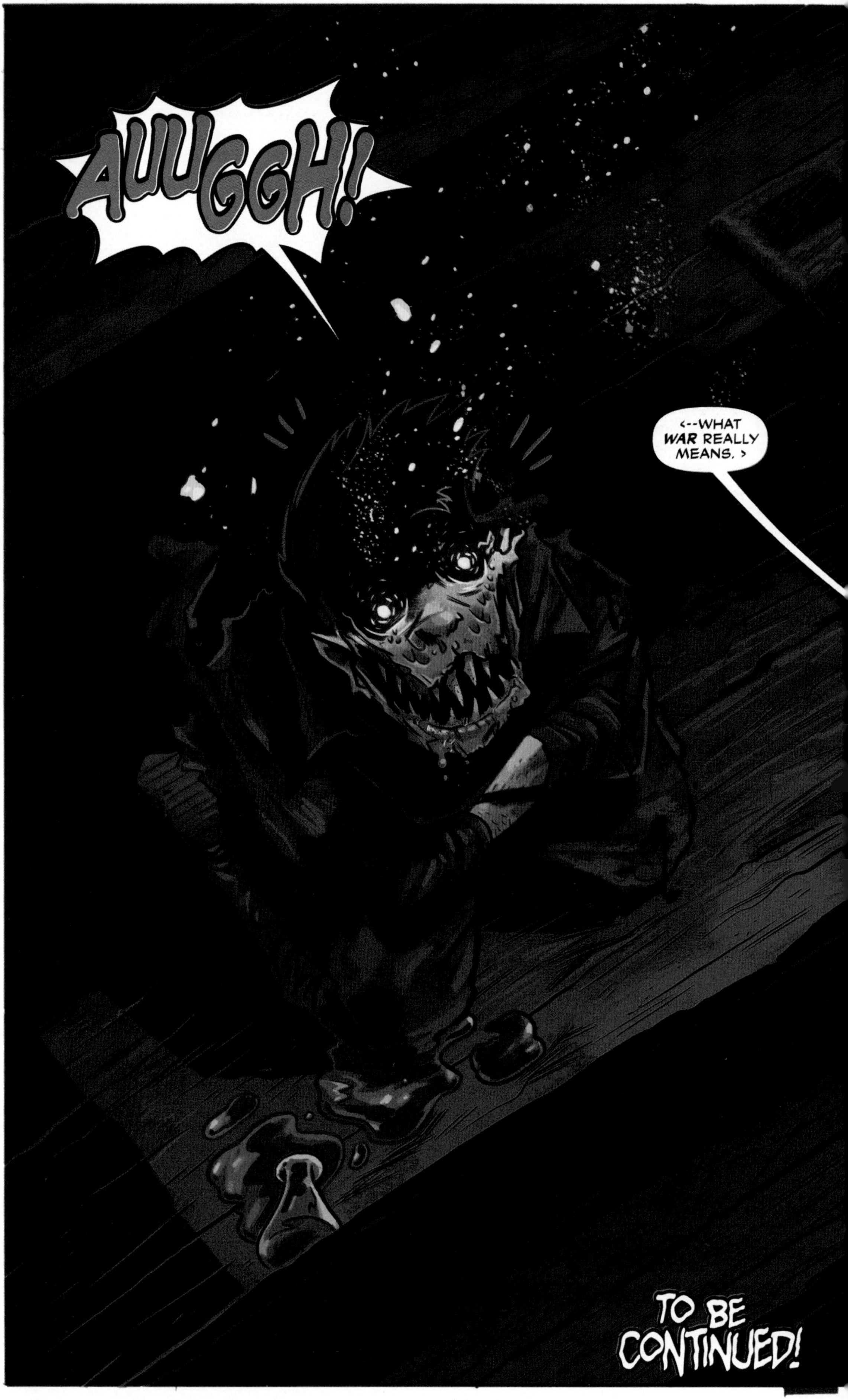
AUUGGH!
<--WHAT WAR REALLY MEANS.>
TO BE CONTINUED!

# CHAPTER TWO

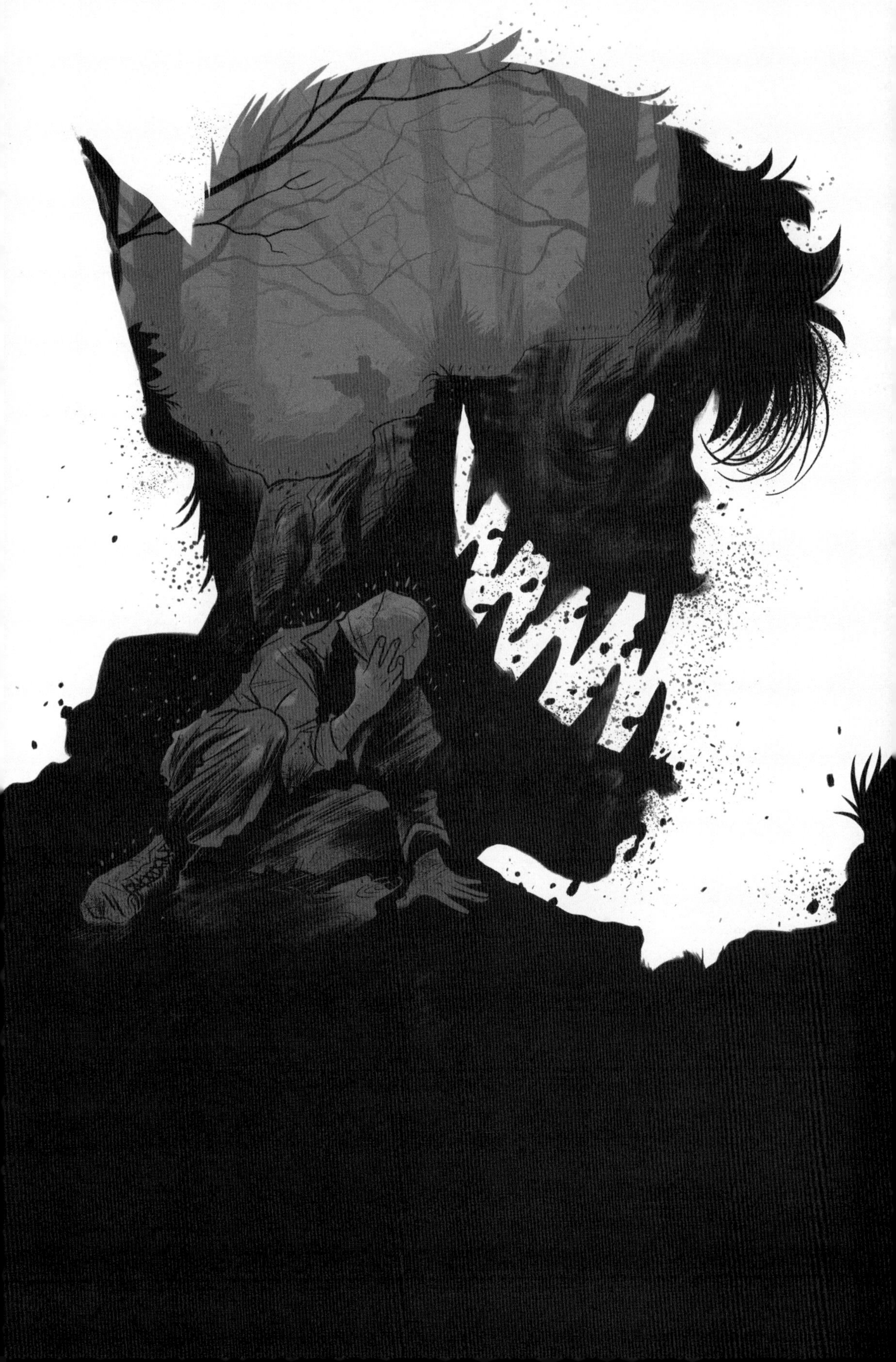

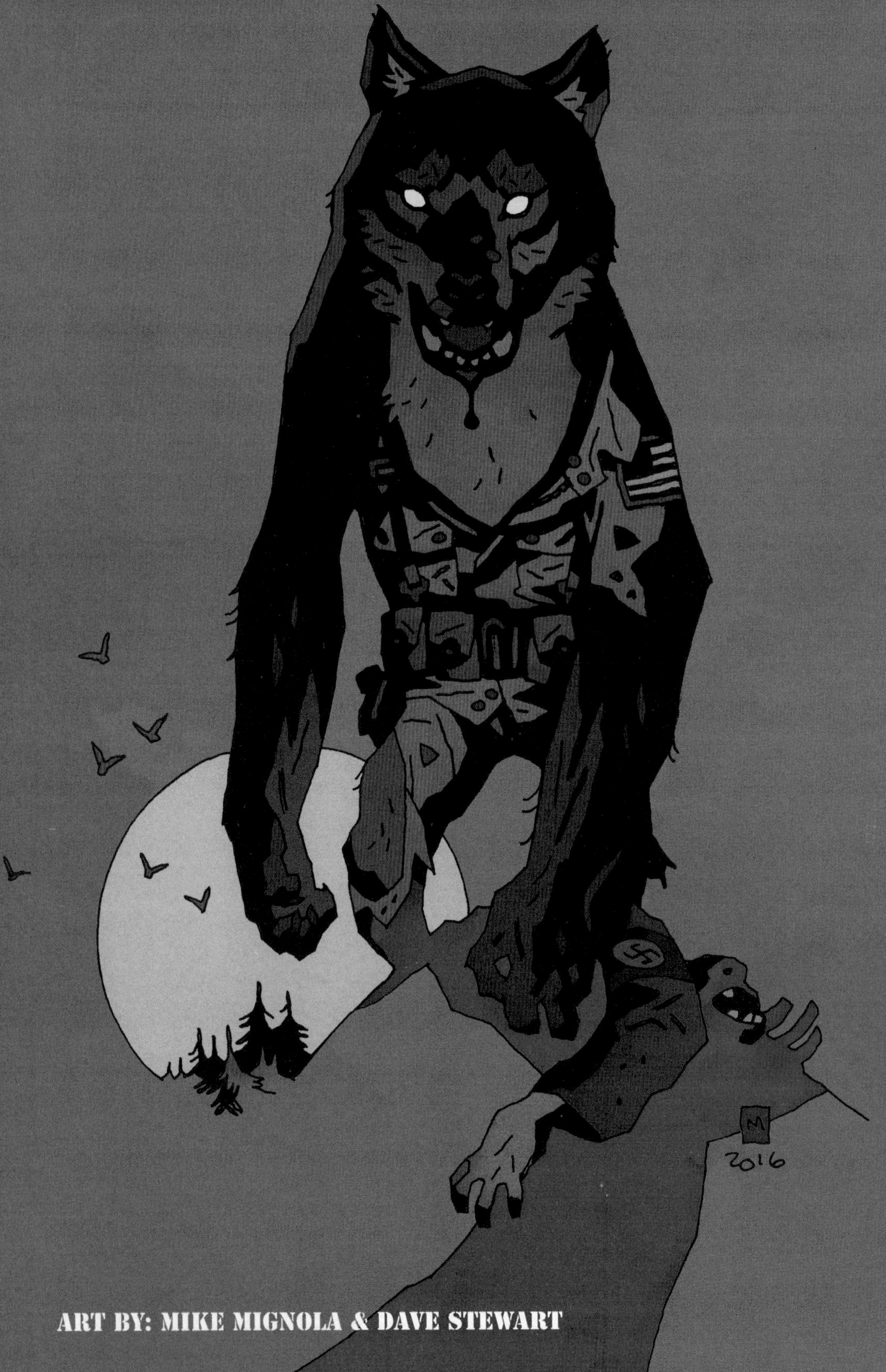
2016

ART BY: MIKE MIGNOLA & DAVE STEWART

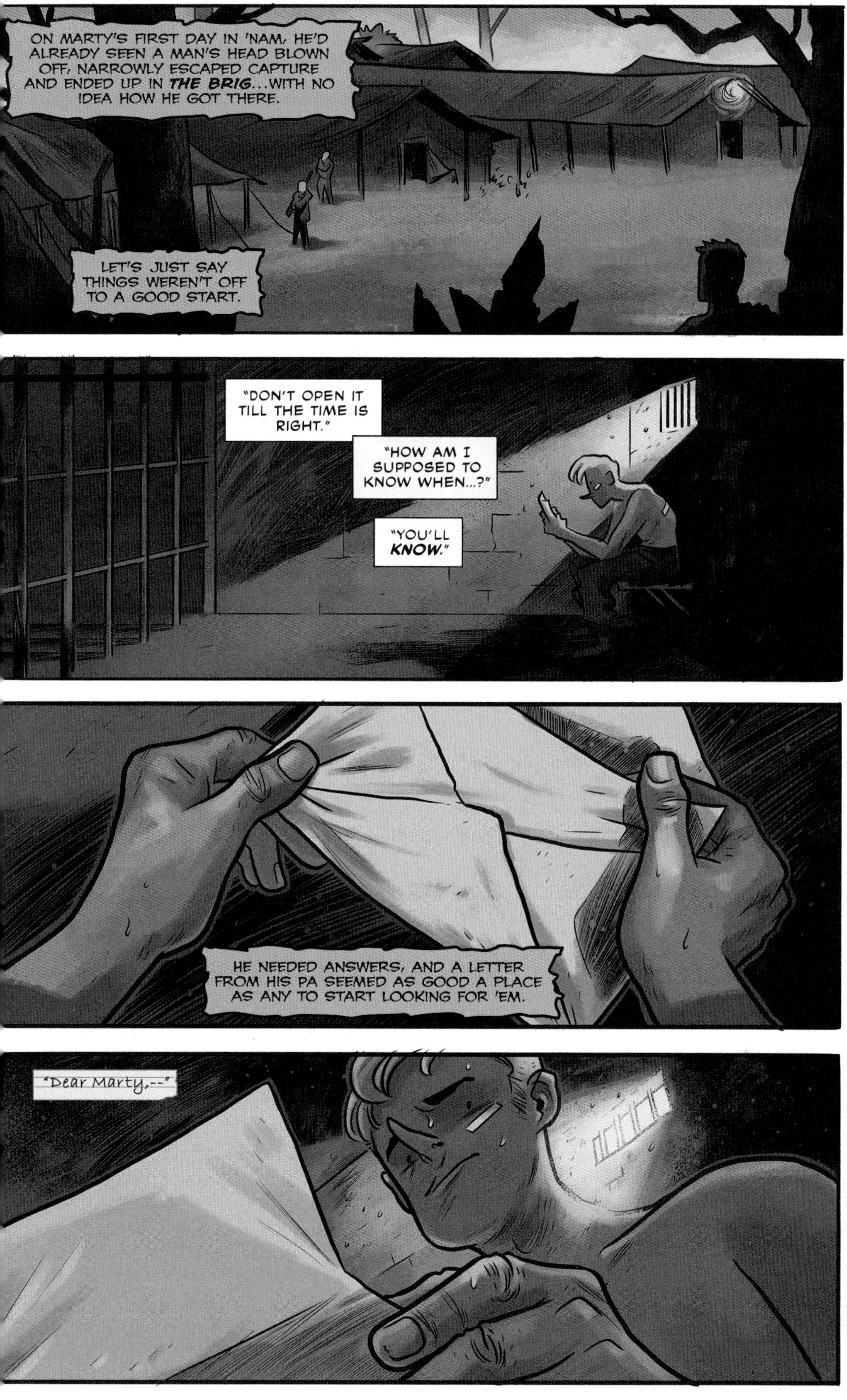
ON MARTY'S FIRST DAY IN 'NAM, HE'D ALREADY SEEN A MAN'S HEAD BLOWN OFF, NARROWLY ESCAPED CAPTURE AND ENDED UP IN ***THE BRIG***...WITH NO IDEA HOW HE GOT THERE.
LET'S JUST SAY THINGS WEREN'T OFF TO A GOOD START.
"DON'T OPEN IT TILL THE TIME IS RIGHT."
"HOW AM I SUPPOSED TO KNOW WHEN...?"
"YOU'LL ***KNOW.***"
HE NEEDED ANSWERS, AND A LETTER FROM HIS PA SEEMED AS GOOD A PLACE AS ANY TO START LOOKING FOR 'EM.
"Dear Marty,--"

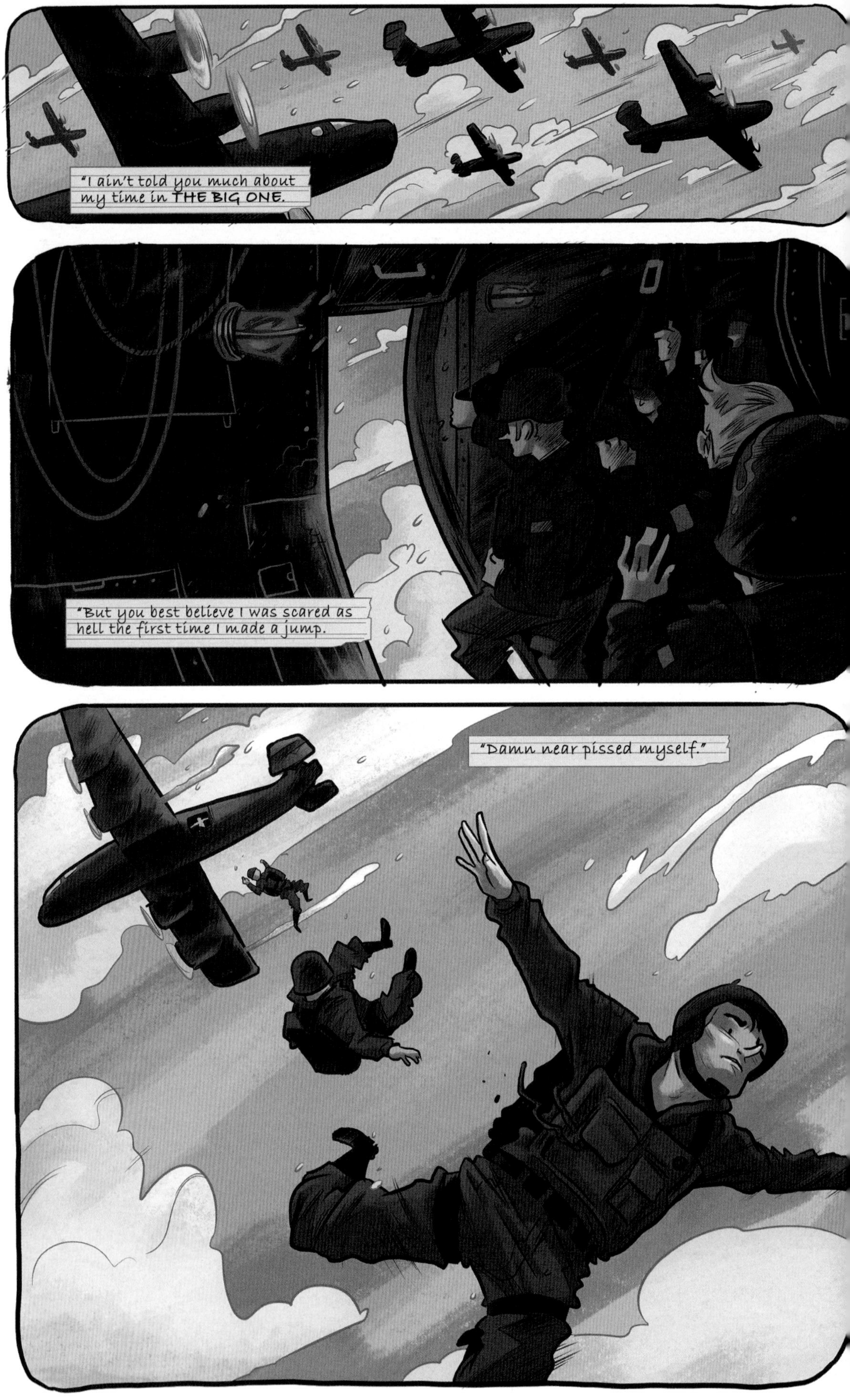
"I ain't told you much about my time in THE BIG ONE.
"But you best believe I was scared as hell the first time I made a jump.
"Damn near pissed myself."

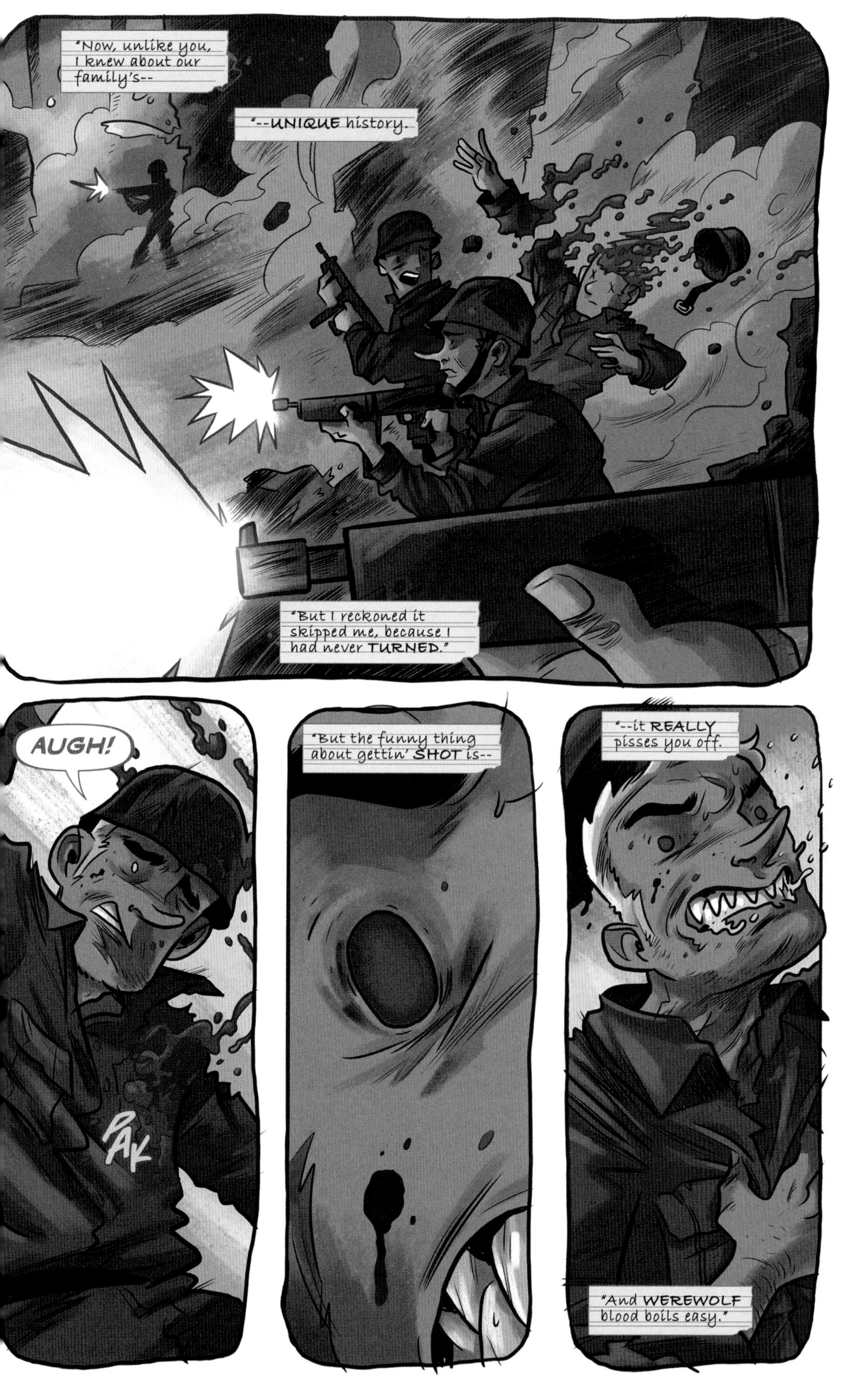
"Now, unlike you, I knew about our family's--
"--UNIQUE history.
"But I reckoned it skipped me, because I had never TURNED."
AUGH!
PAK
"But the funny thing about gettin' SHOT is--
"--it REALLY pisses you off.
"And WEREWOLF blood boils easy."

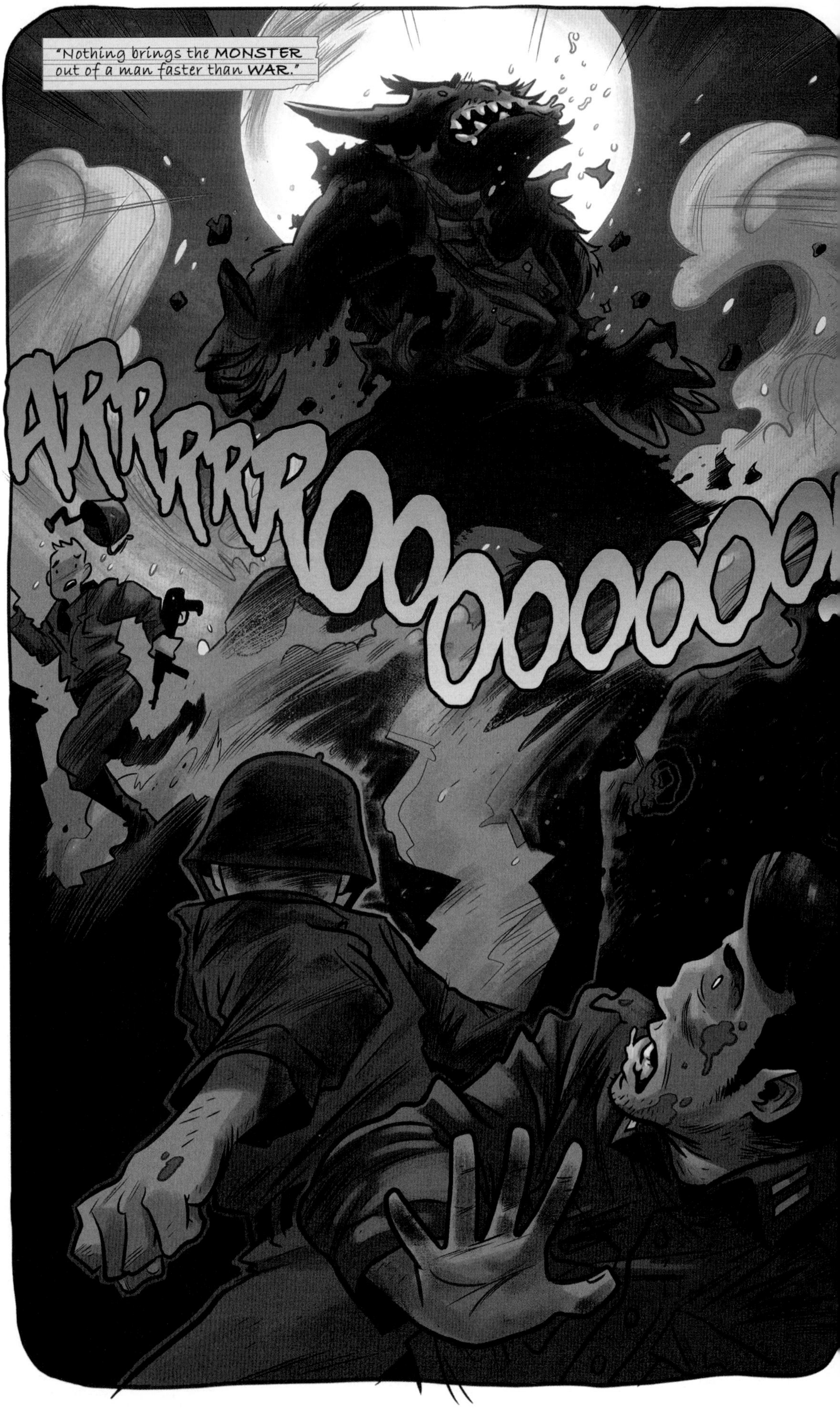
"Nothing brings the MONSTER out of a man faster than WAR."
ARRRRRROOOOOOOOO

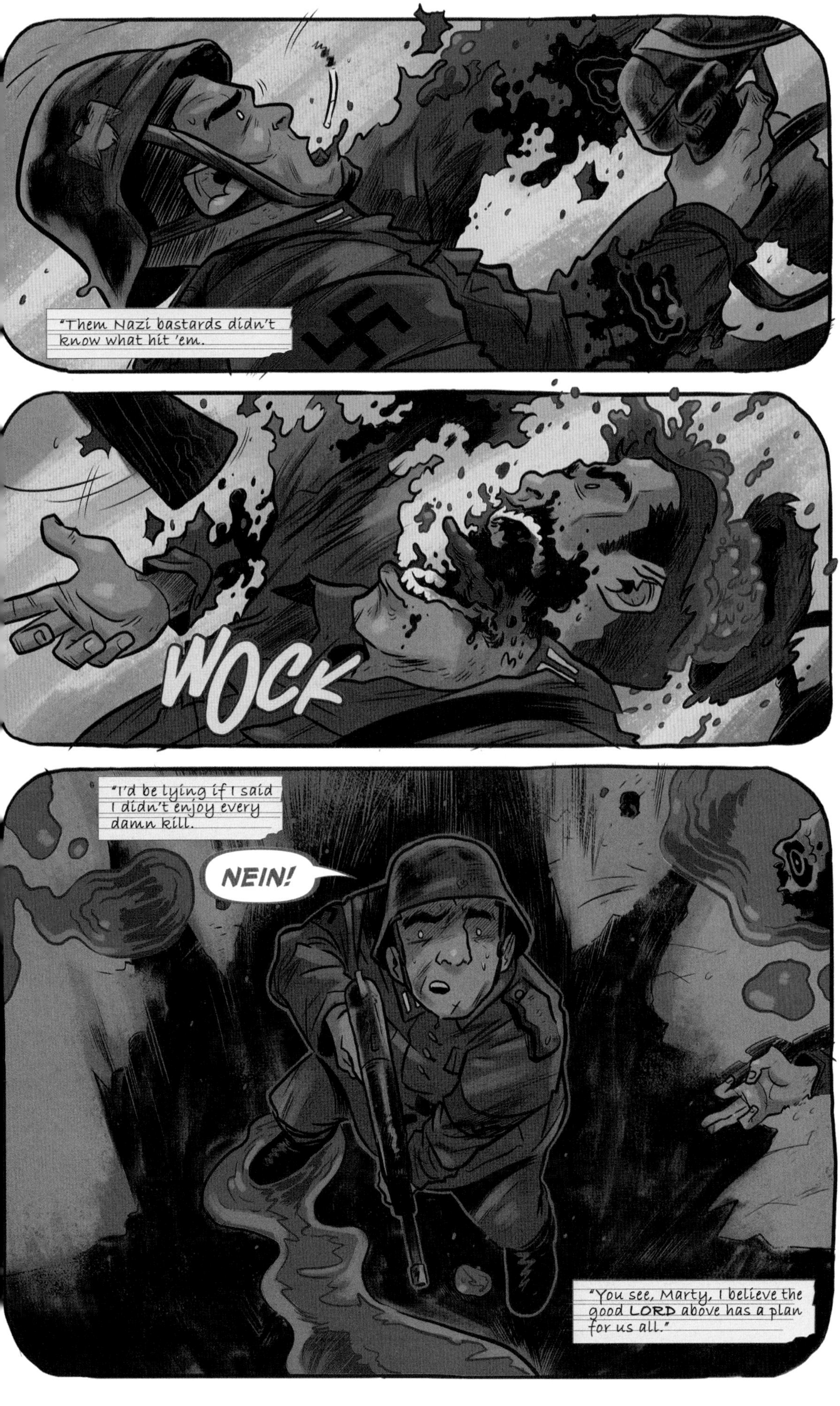
"Them Nazi bastards didn't know what hit 'em.
WOCK
"I'd be lying if I said I didn't enjoy every damn kill.
NEIN!
"You see, Marty, I believe the good LORD above has a plan for us all."

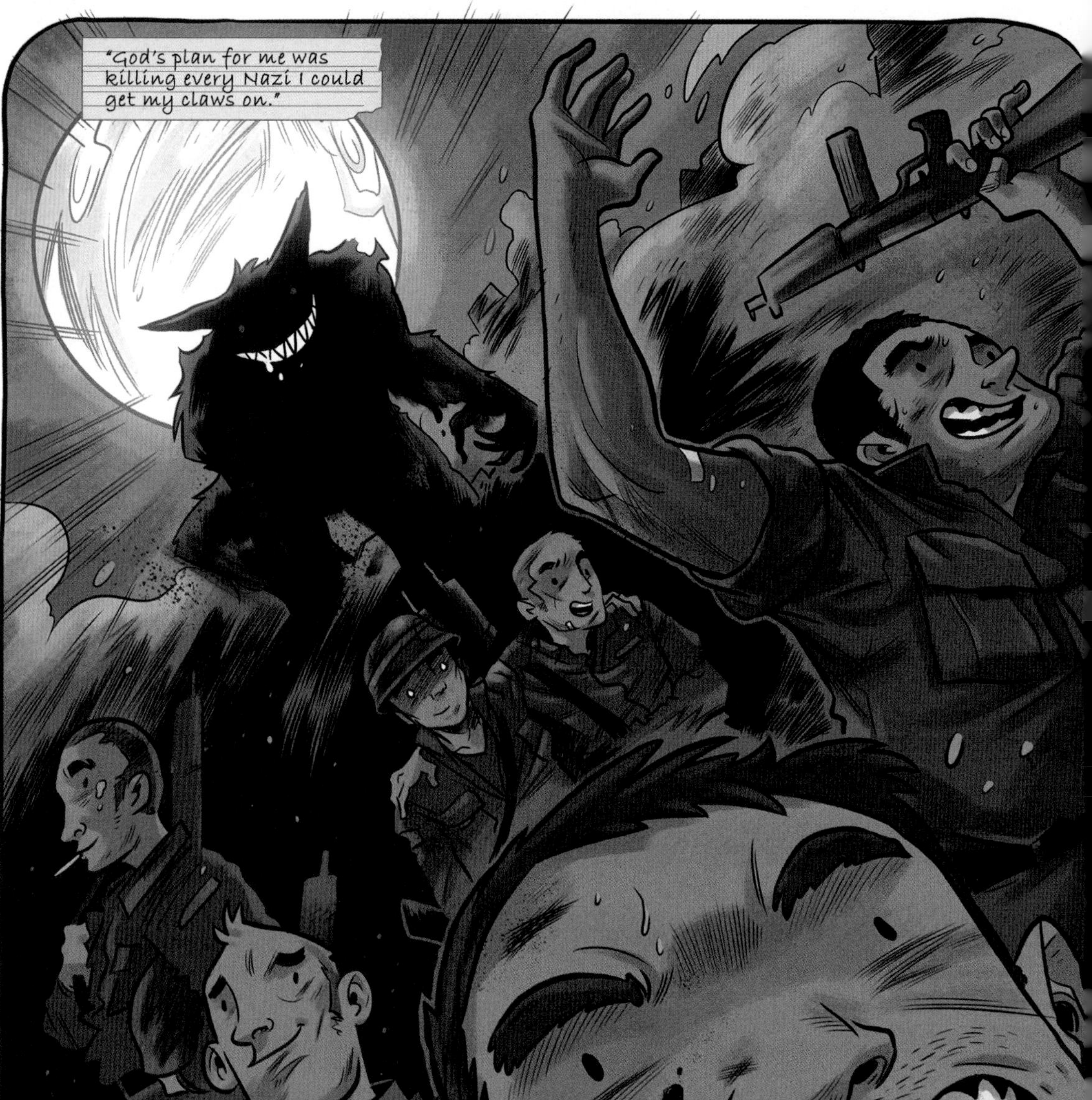
"God's plan for me was killing every Nazi I could get my claws on."

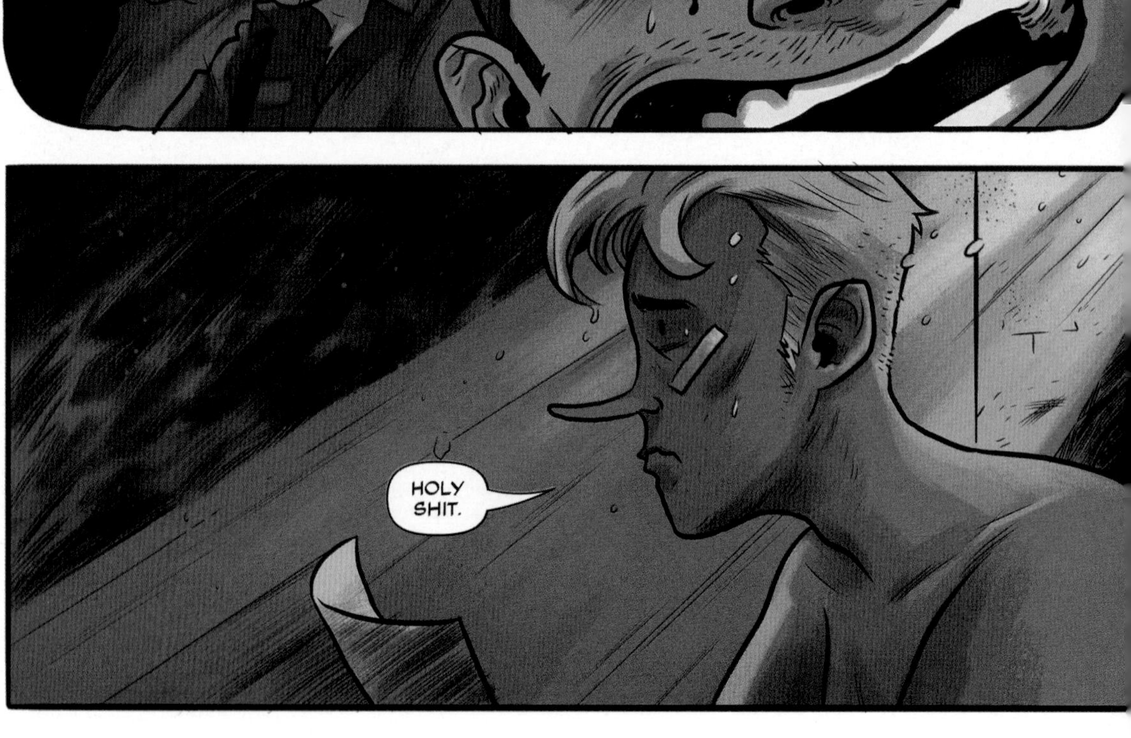
HOLY SHIT.

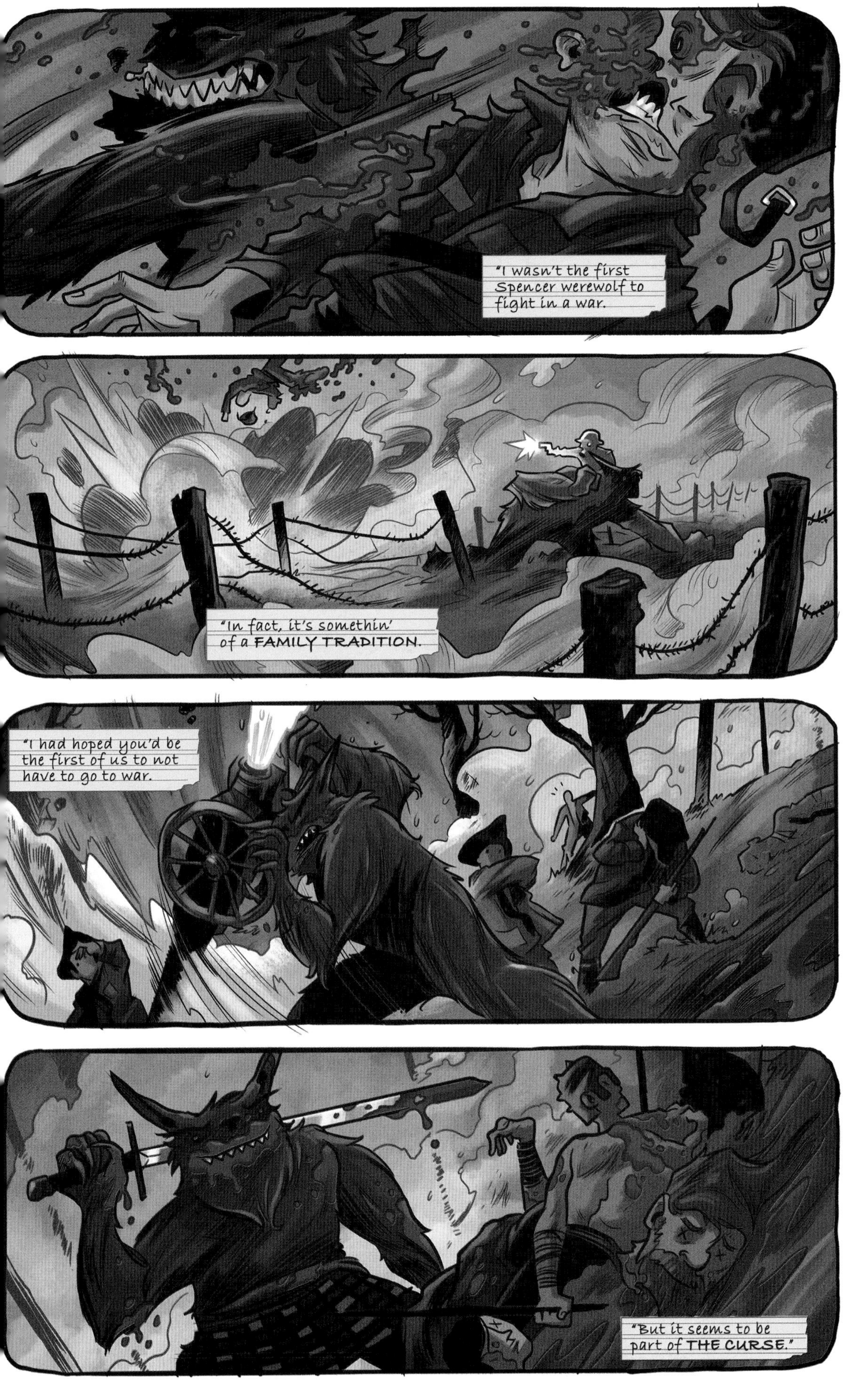
"I wasn't the first Spencer werewolf to fight in a war.
"In fact, it's somethin' of a FAMILY TRADITION.
"I had hoped you'd be the first of us to not have to go to war.
"But it seems to be part of THE CURSE."

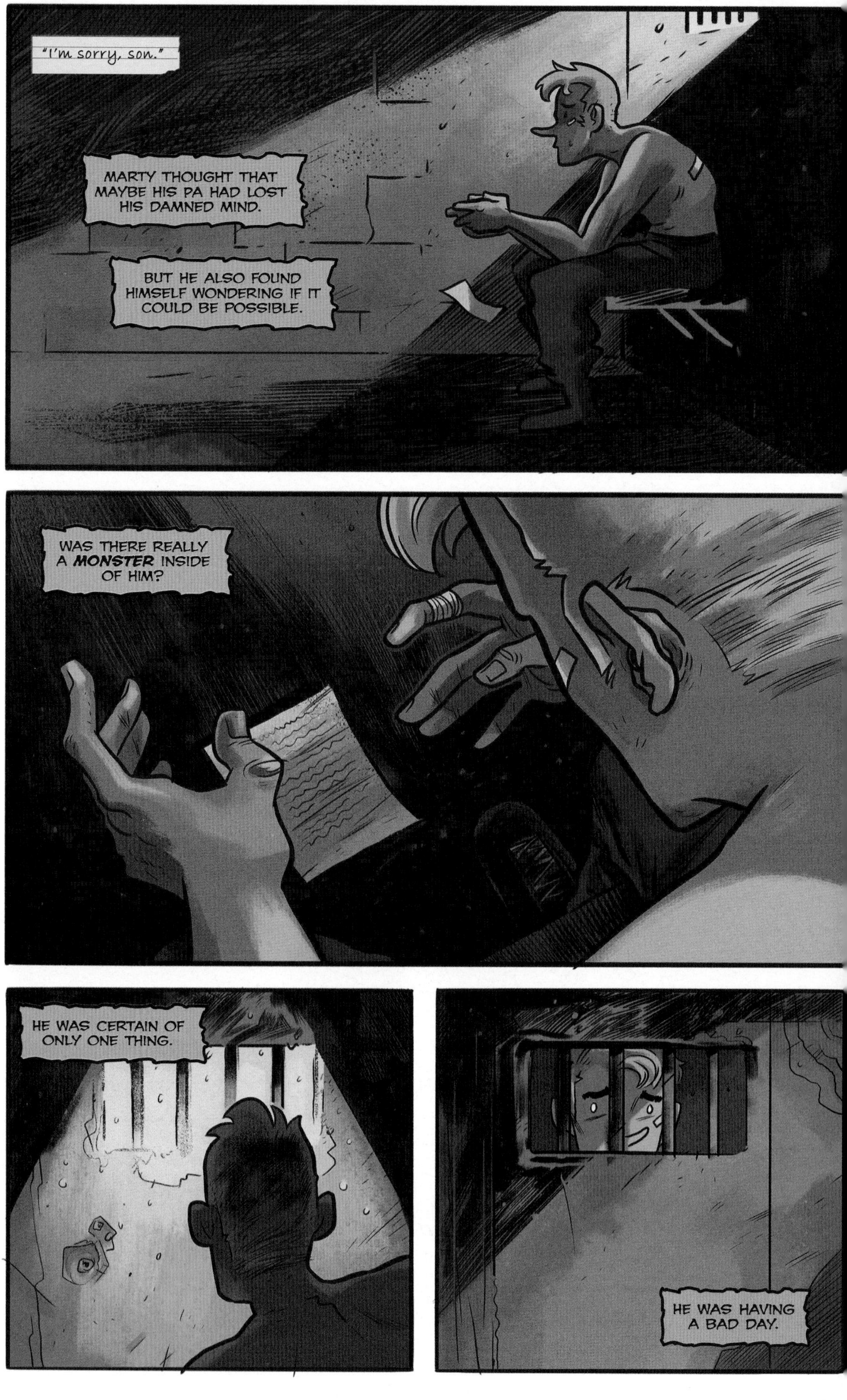
"I'm sorry, son."
MARTY THOUGHT THAT MAYBE HIS PA HAD LOST HIS DAMNED MIND.
BUT HE ALSO FOUND HIMSELF WONDERING IF IT COULD BE POSSIBLE.
WAS THERE REALLY A MONSTER INSIDE OF HIM?
HE WAS CERTAIN OF ONLY ONE THING.
HE WAS HAVING A BAD DAY.

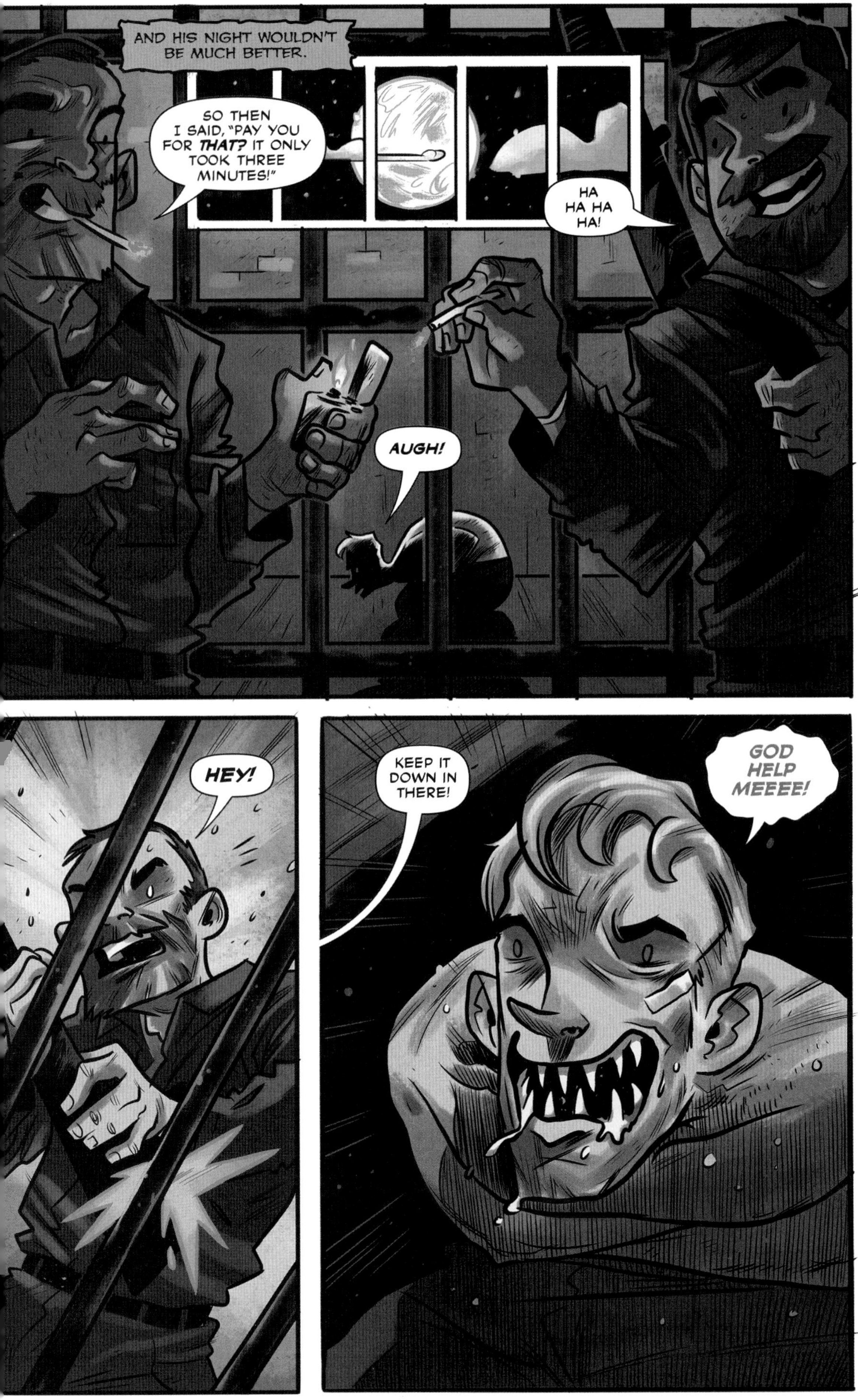
AND HIS NIGHT WOULDN'T BE MUCH BETTER.
SO THEN I SAID, "PAY YOU FOR *THAT?* IT ONLY TOOK THREE MINUTES!"
HA HA HA HA!
AUGH!
HEY!
KEEP IT DOWN IN THERE!
GOD HELP MEEEE!

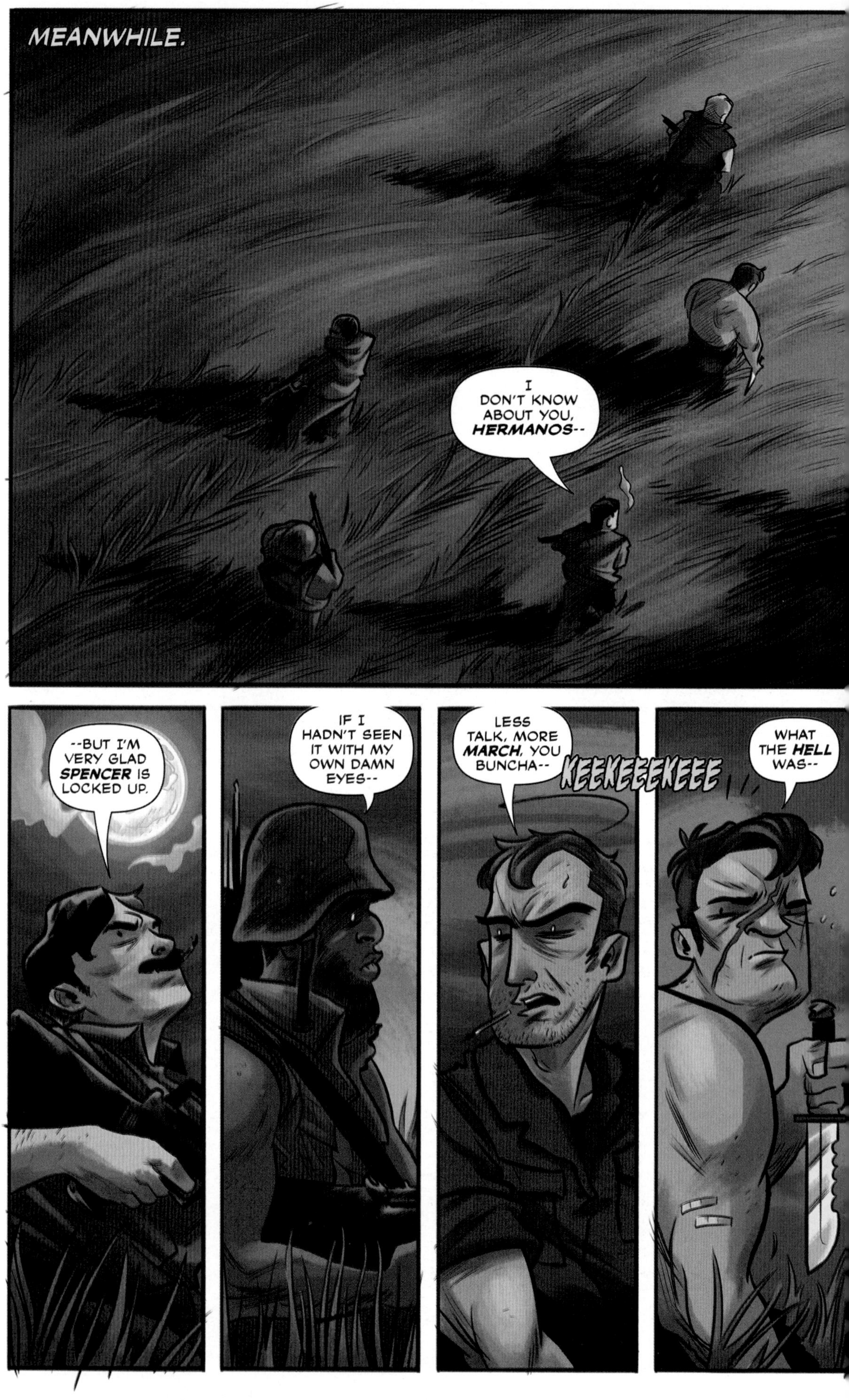
MEANWHILE.
I DON'T KNOW ABOUT YOU, HERMANOS--
--BUT I'M VERY GLAD SPENCER IS LOCKED UP.
IF I HADN'T SEEN IT WITH MY OWN DAMN EYES--
LESS TALK, MORE MARCH, YOU BUNCHA--
KEEKEEEKEEE
WHAT THE HELL WAS--

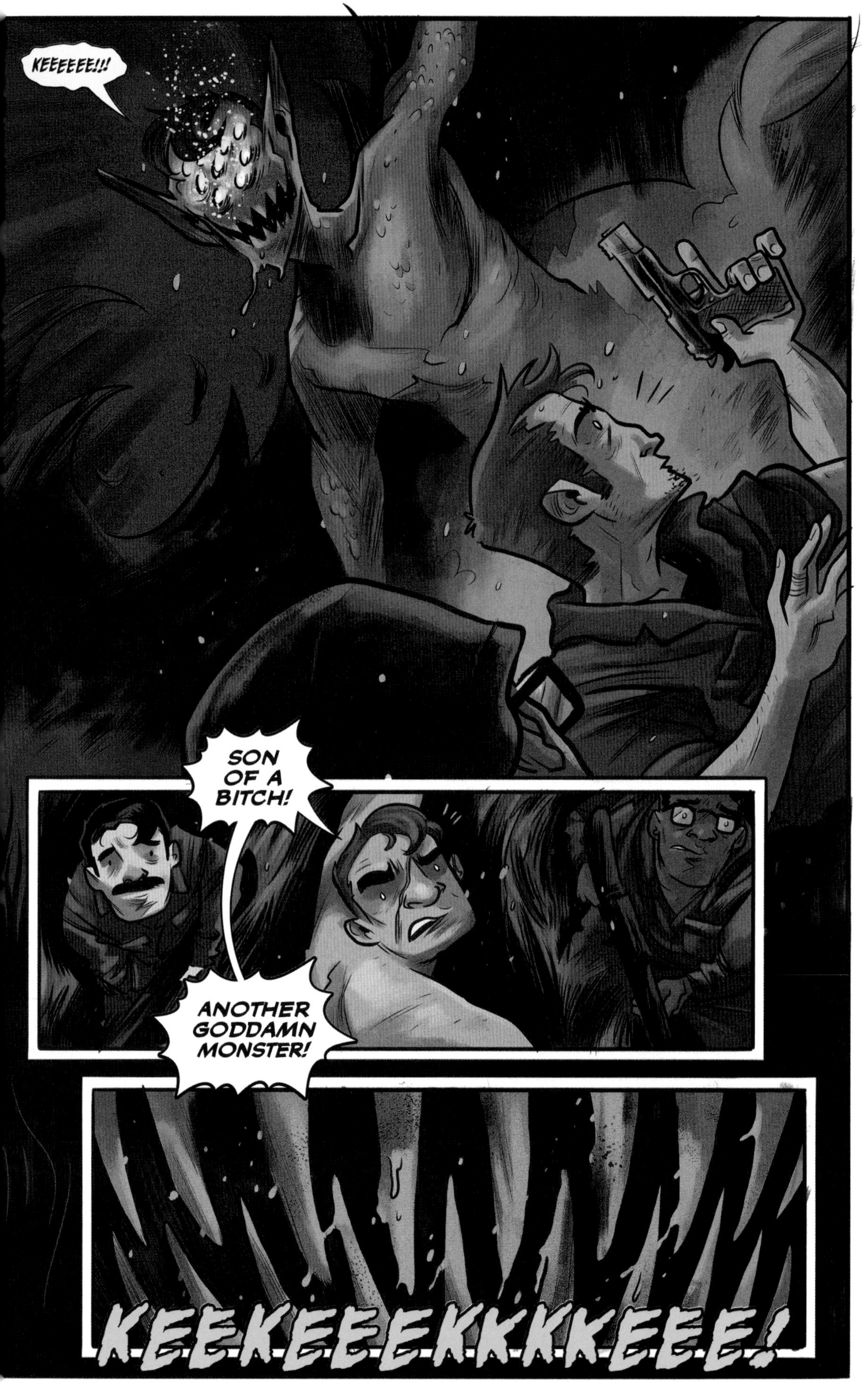
KEEEEEE!!!
SON OF A BITCH!
ANOTHER GODDAMN MONSTER!
KEEKEEEEKKKKEEE!

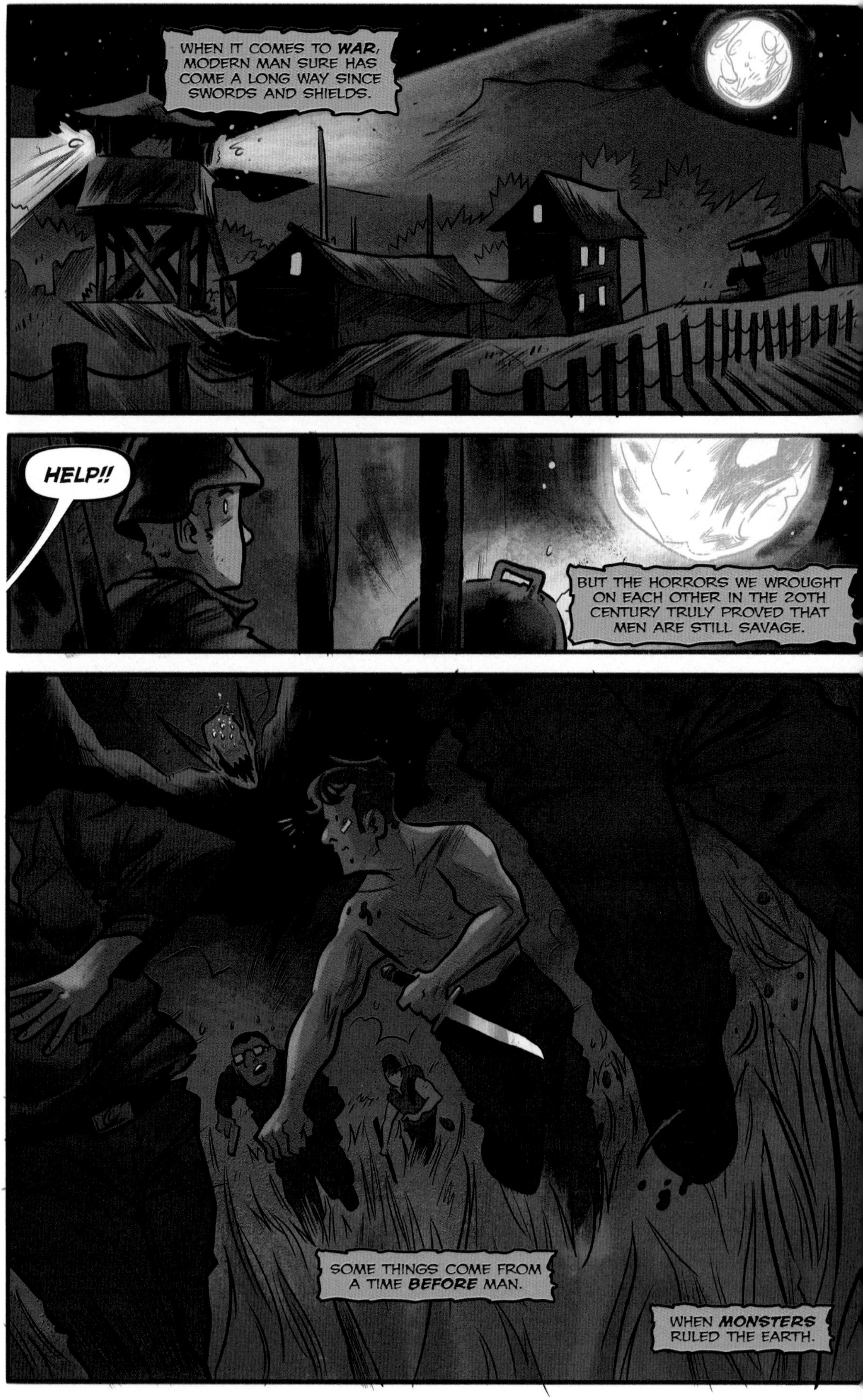
WHEN IT COMES TO WAR, MODERN MAN SURE HAS COME A LONG WAY SINCE SWORDS AND SHIELDS.
HELP!!
BUT THE HORRORS WE WROUGHT ON EACH OTHER IN THE 20TH CENTURY TRULY PROVED THAT MEN ARE STILL SAVAGE.
SOME THINGS COME FROM A TIME BEFORE MAN.
WHEN MONSTERS RULED THE EARTH.

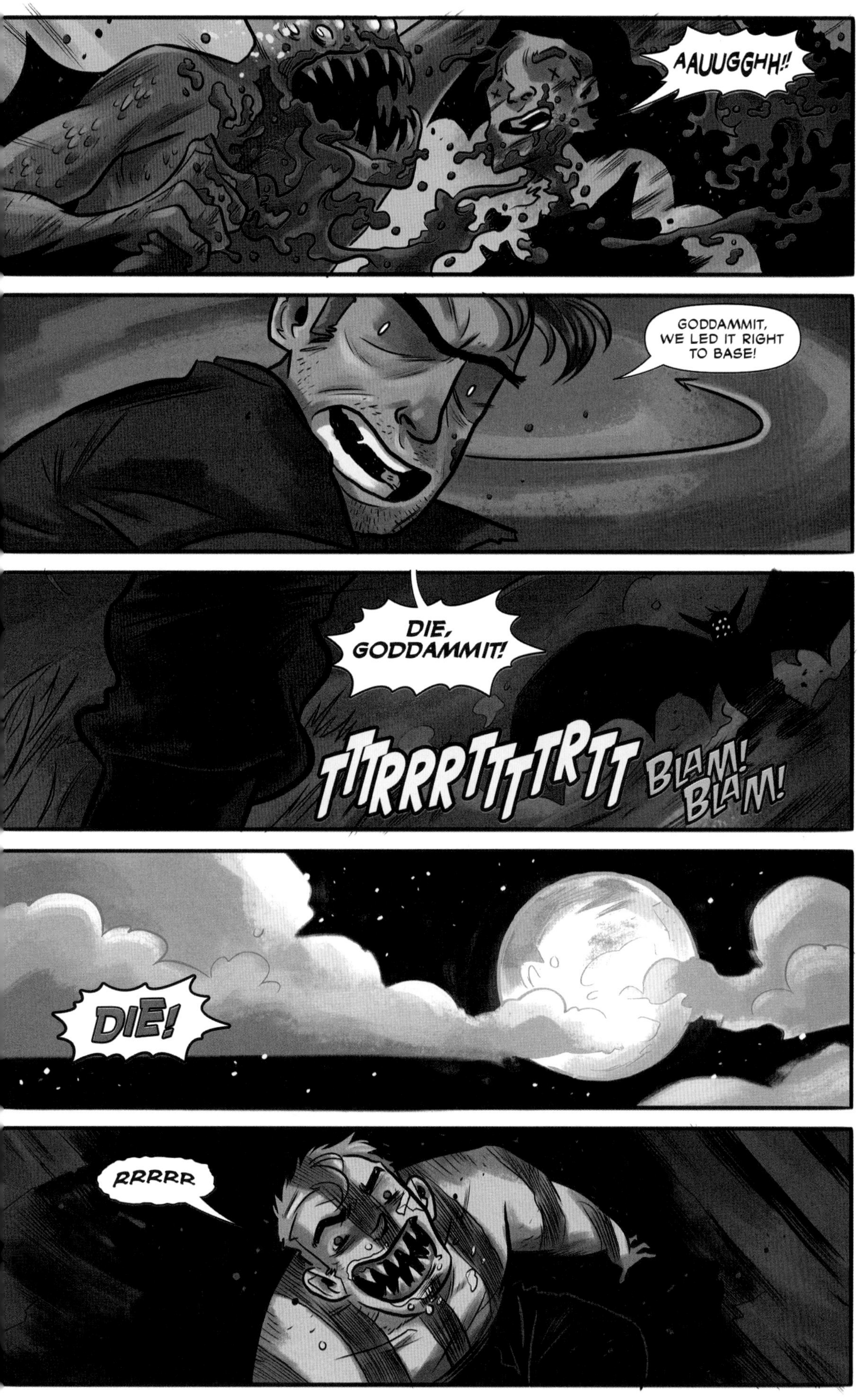
AAUUGGHH!!
GODDAMMIT, WE LED IT RIGHT TO BASE!
DIE, GODDAMMIT!
TTTRRRTTTTRTT
BLAM! BLAM!
DIE!
RRRRR

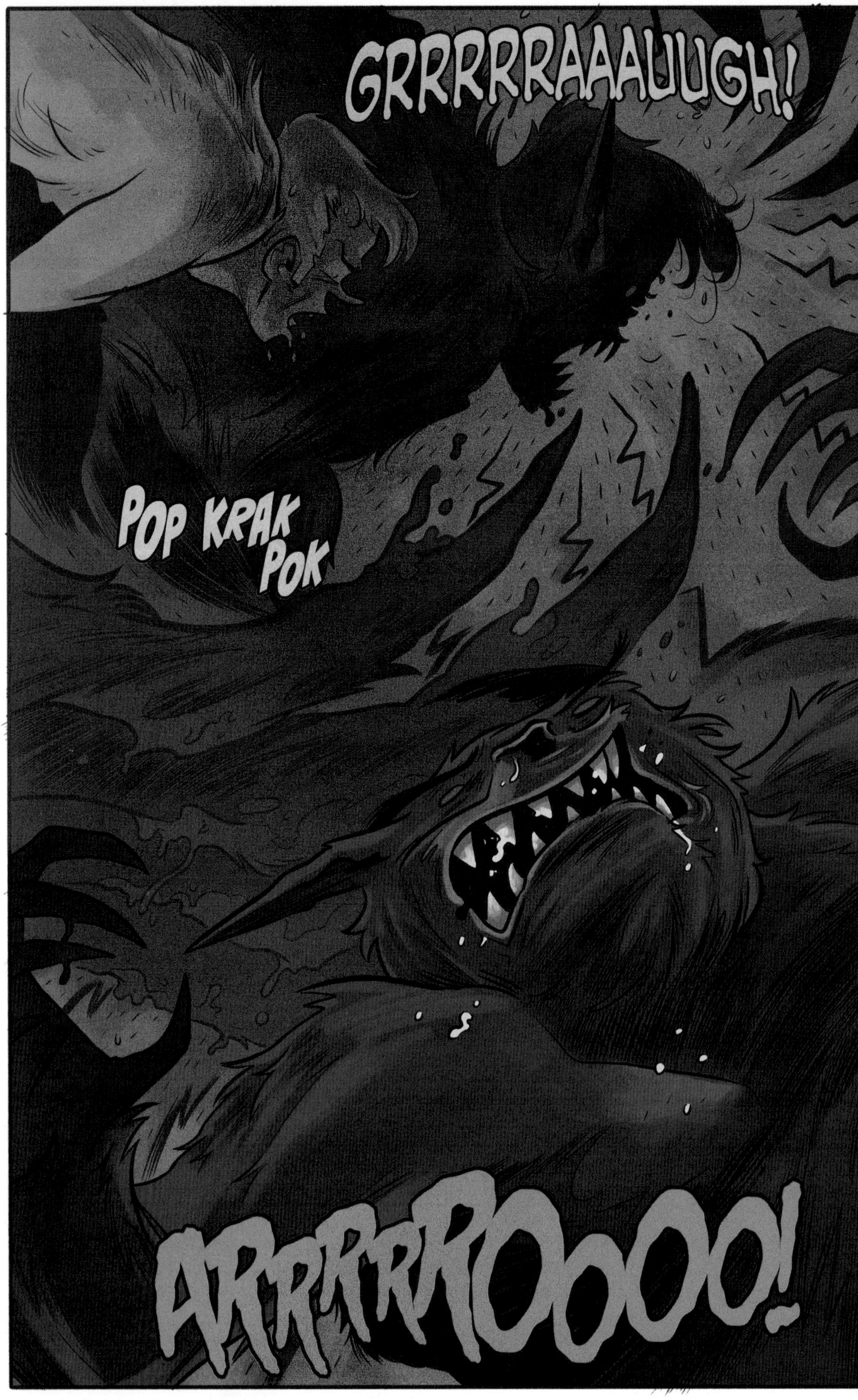
GRRRRRAAAUUGH!
POP KRAK POK
ARRRRROOOOO!

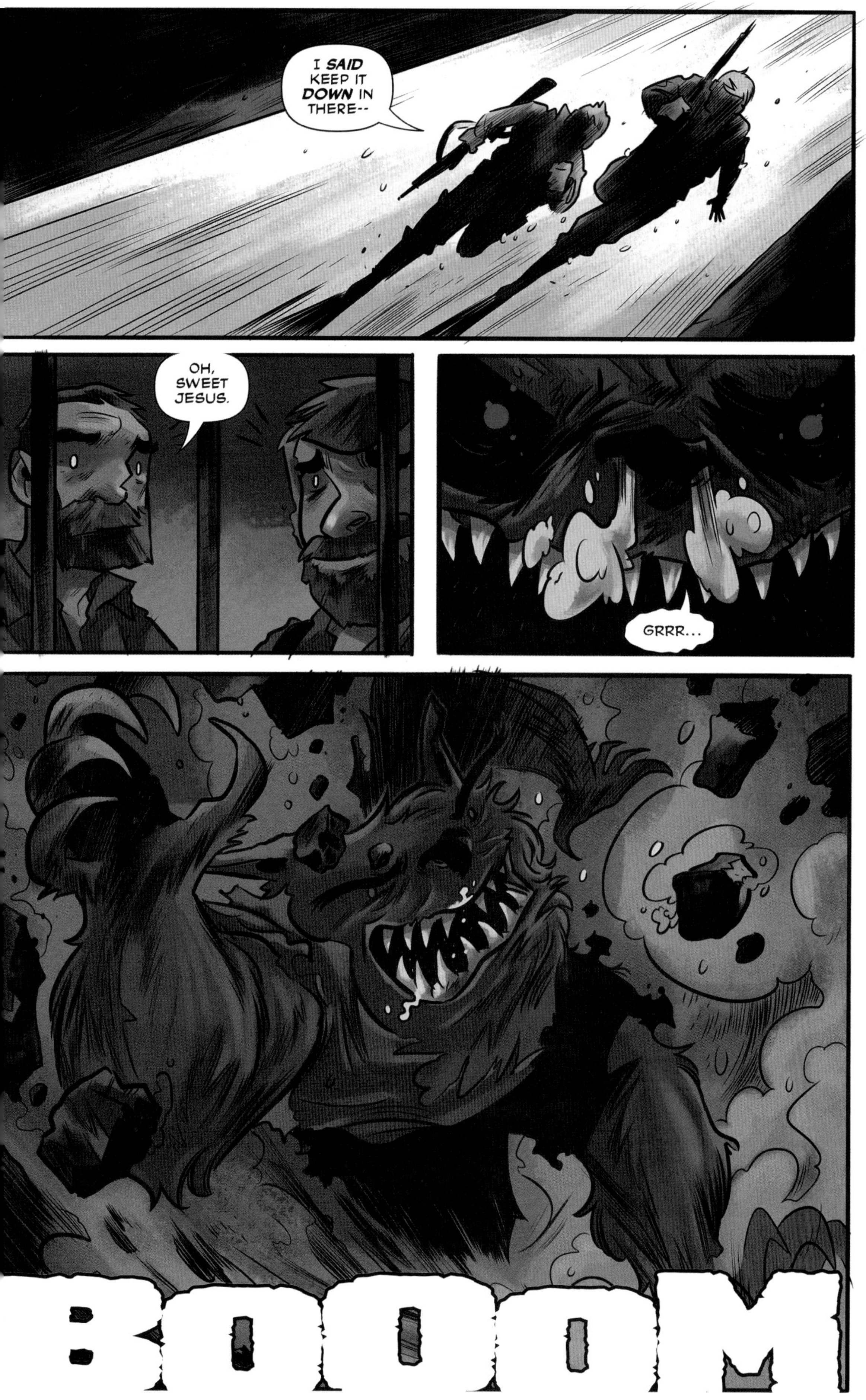
I SAID KEEP IT DOWN IN THERE--
OH, SWEET JESUS.
GRRR...
BOOOOM

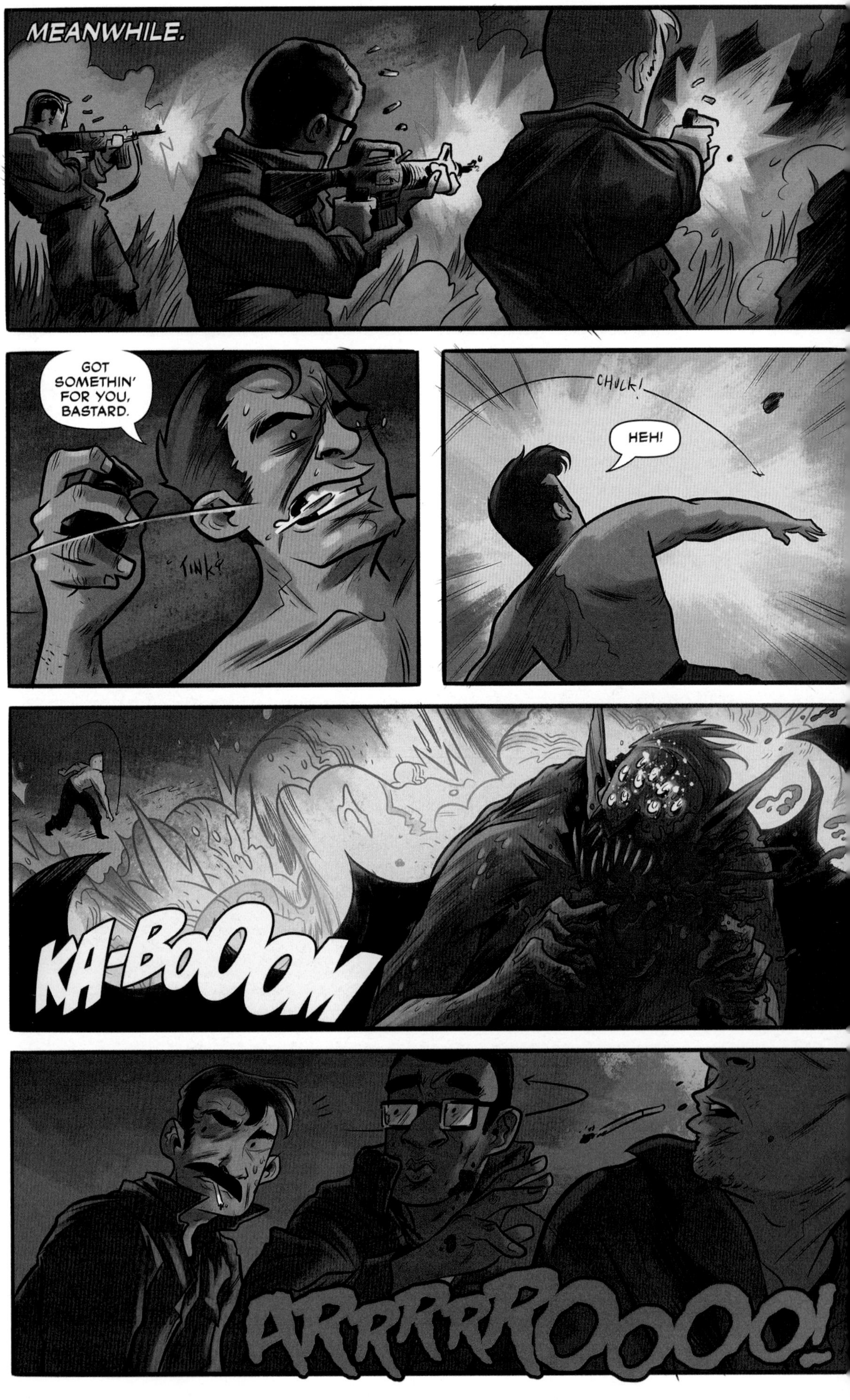
MEANWHILE.
GOT SOMETHIN' FOR YOU, BASTARD.
TINK!
CHULK!
HEH!
KA-BOOOOM
ARRRRROOOOO!

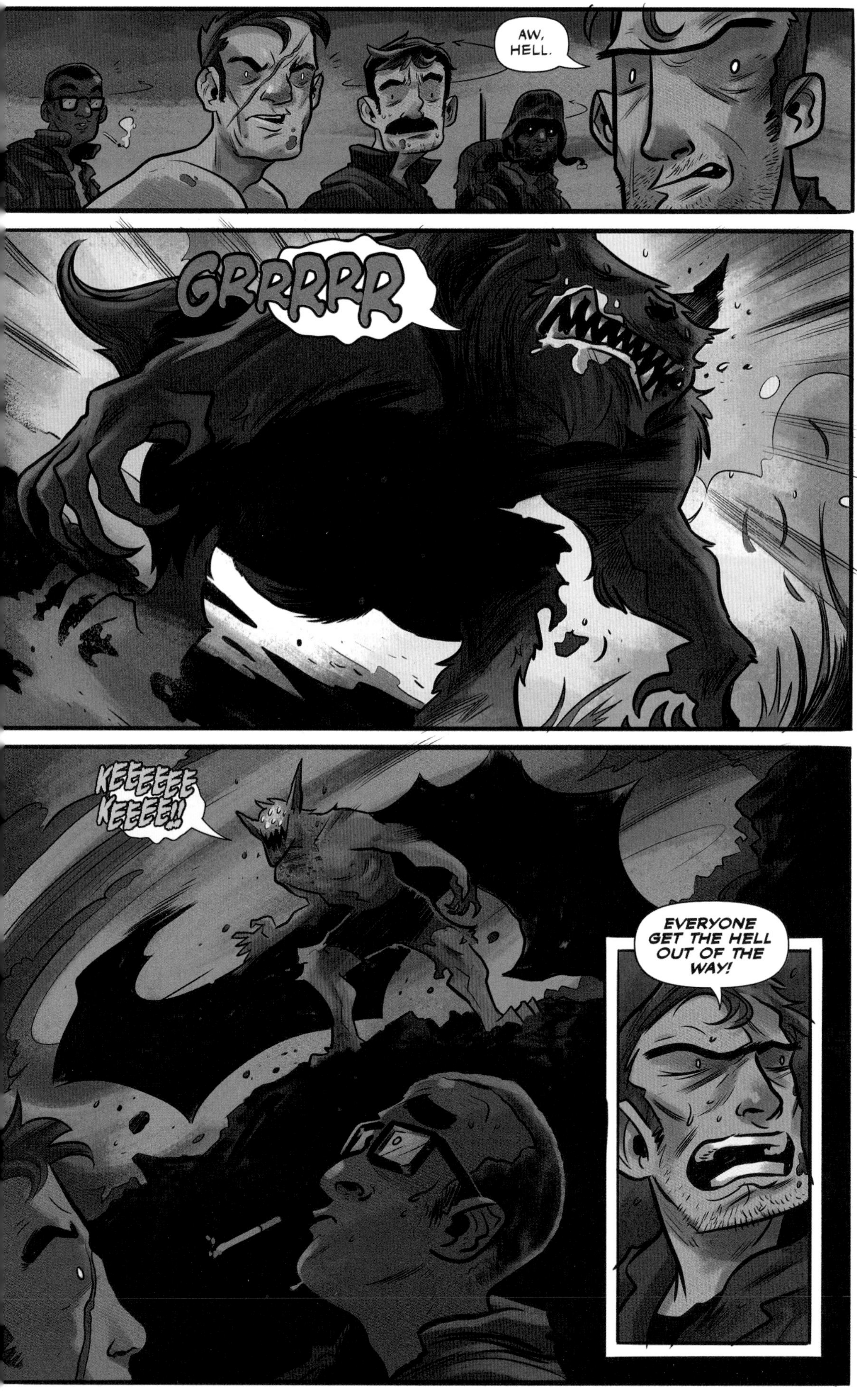
AW, HELL.
GRRRRR
KEEEEEE KEEEEE!!
EVERYONE GET THE HELL OUT OF THE WAY!

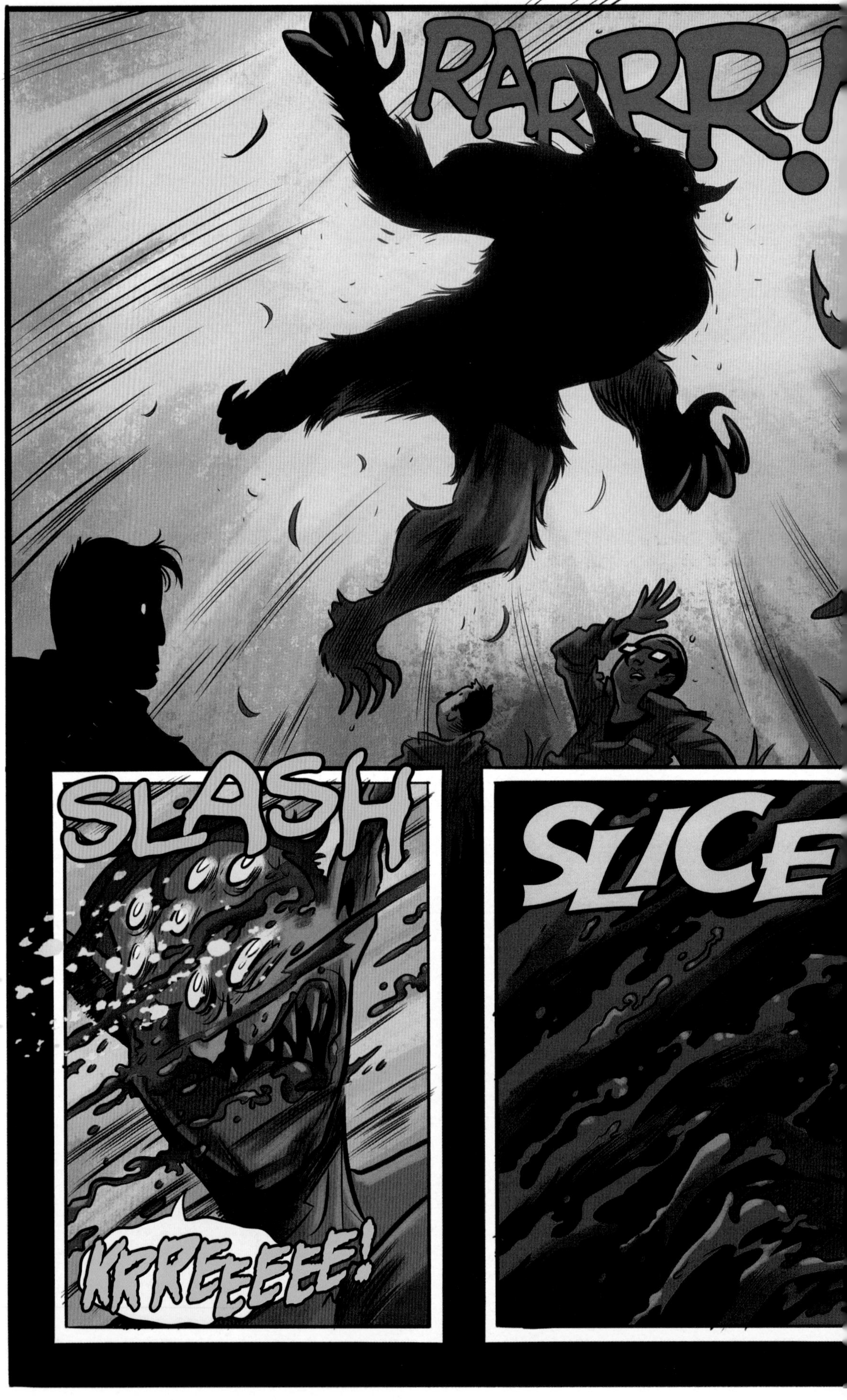
RARRRR!
SLASH
KRREEEEEE!
SLICE

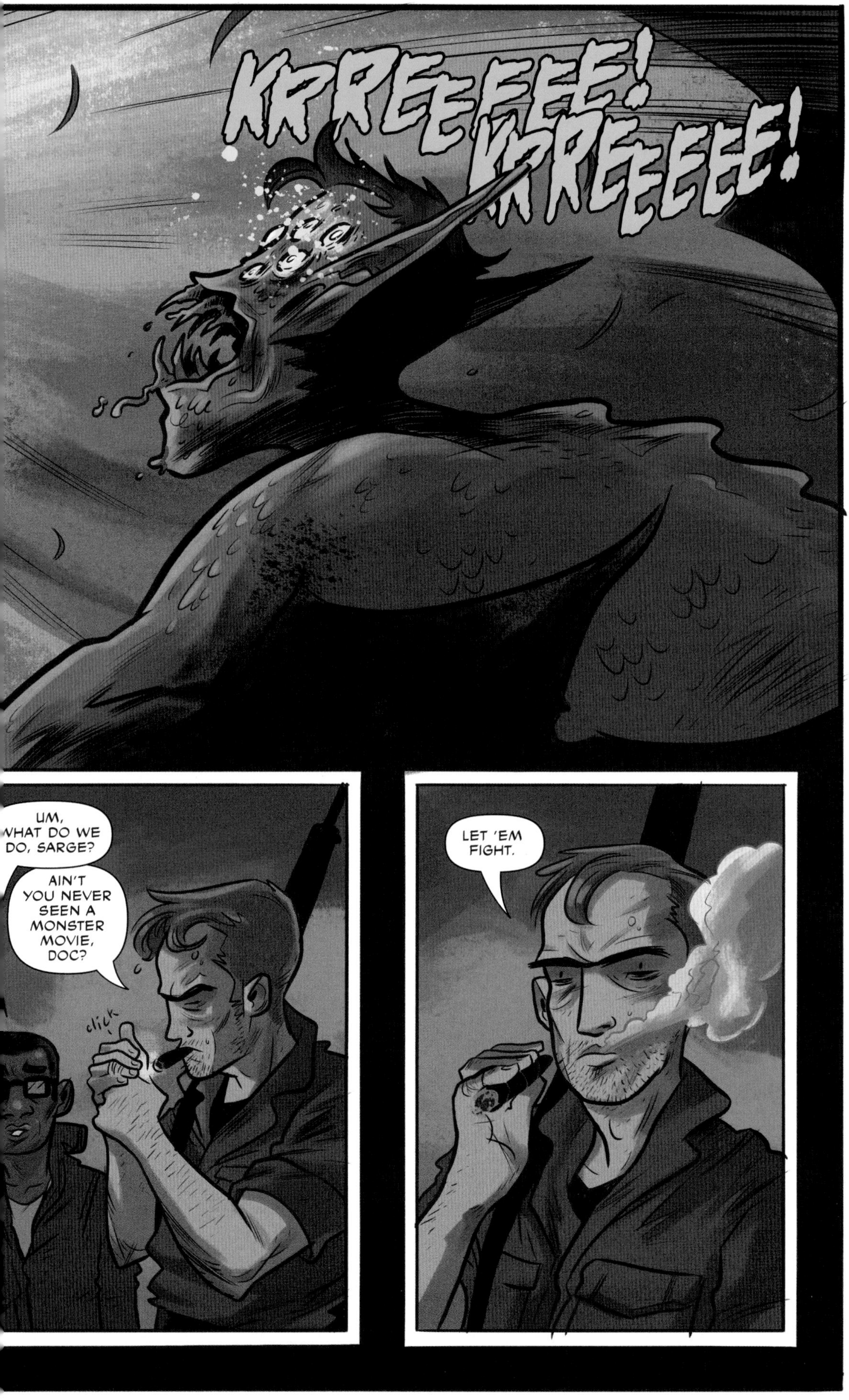
KRREEEEE! KRREEEEE!
UM, WHAT DO WE DO, SARGE?
AIN'T YOU NEVER SEEN A MONSTER MOVIE, DOC?
click
LET 'EM FIGHT.

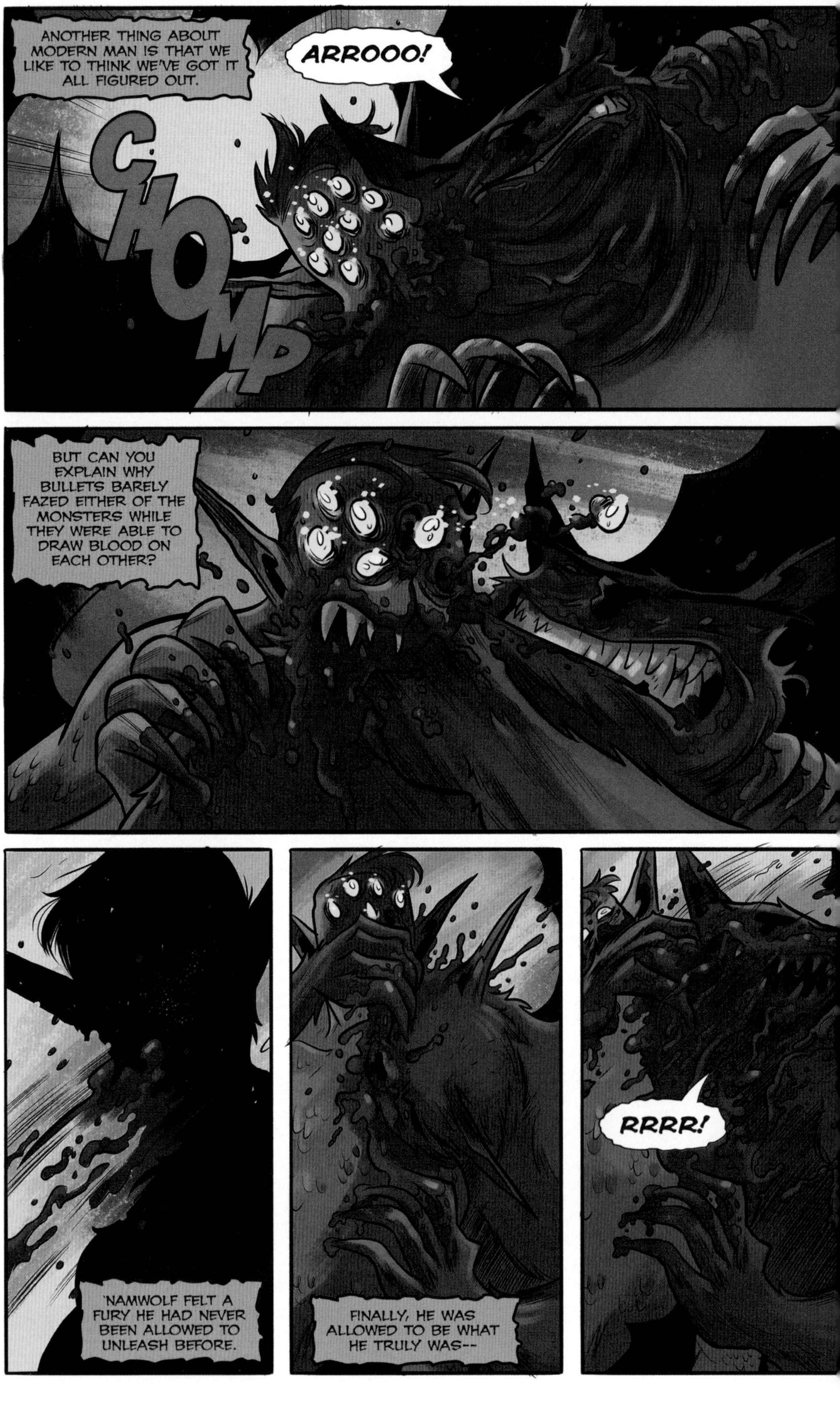
ANOTHER THING ABOUT MODERN MAN IS THAT WE LIKE TO THINK WE'VE GOT IT ALL FIGURED OUT.
ARROOO!
CHOMP
BUT CAN YOU EXPLAIN WHY BULLETS BARELY FAZED EITHER OF THE MONSTERS WHILE THEY WERE ABLE TO DRAW BLOOD ON EACH OTHER?
'NAMWOLF FELT A FURY HE HAD NEVER BEEN ALLOWED TO UNLEASH BEFORE.
FINALLY, HE WAS ALLOWED TO BE WHAT HE TRULY WAS--
RRRR!

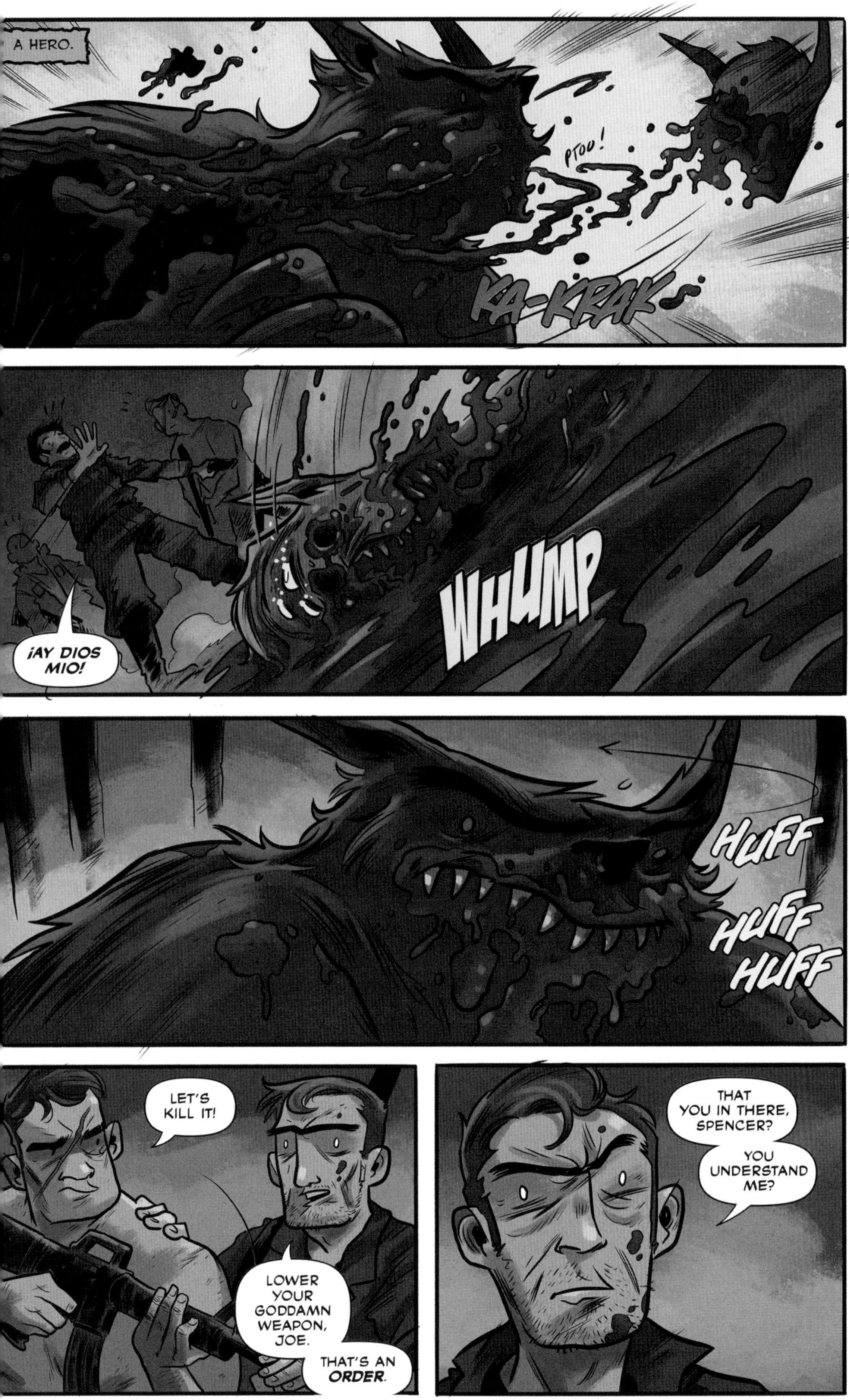
A HERO.
PTOO!
KA-KRAK
¡AY DIOS MIO!
WHUMP
HUFF
HUFF
HUFF
LET'S KILL IT!
LOWER YOUR GODDAMN WEAPON, JOE.
THAT'S AN ORDER.
THAT YOU IN THERE, SPENCER?
YOU UNDERSTAND ME?

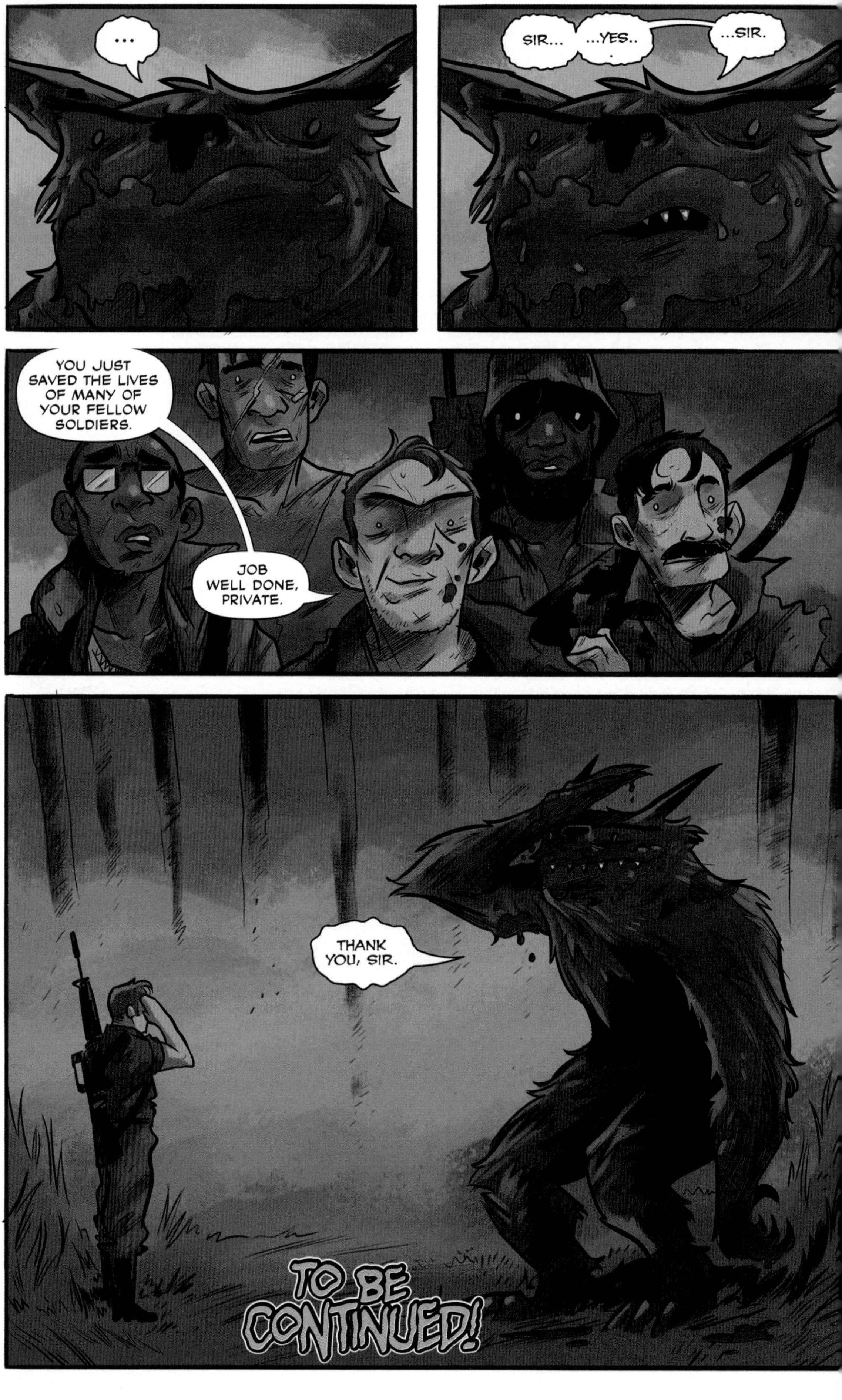
...
SIR...
...YES..
...SIR.
YOU JUST SAVED THE LIVES OF MANY OF YOUR FELLOW SOLDIERS.
JOB WELL DONE, PRIVATE.
THANK YOU, SIR.
TO BE CONTINUED!

# CHAPTER THREE

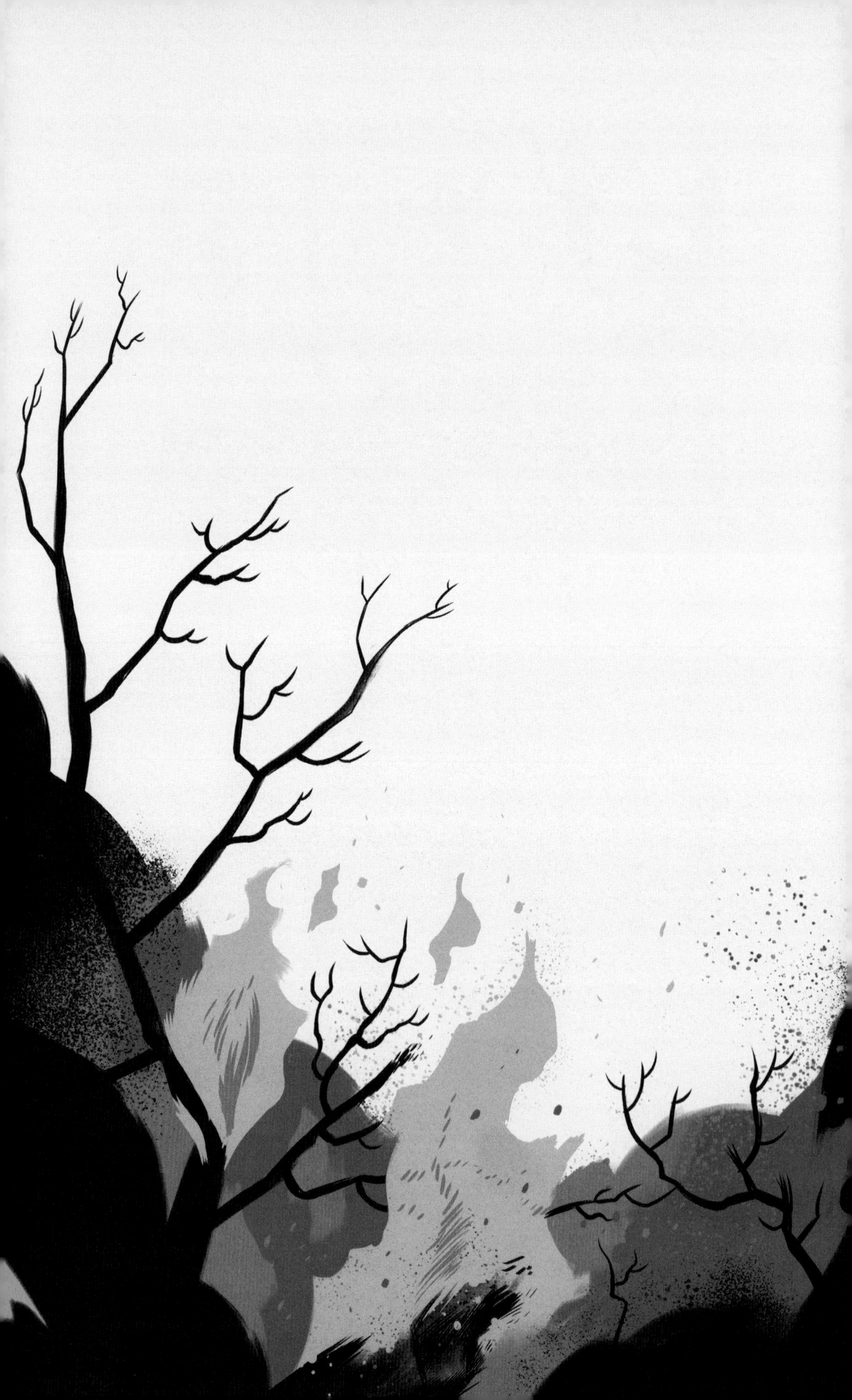

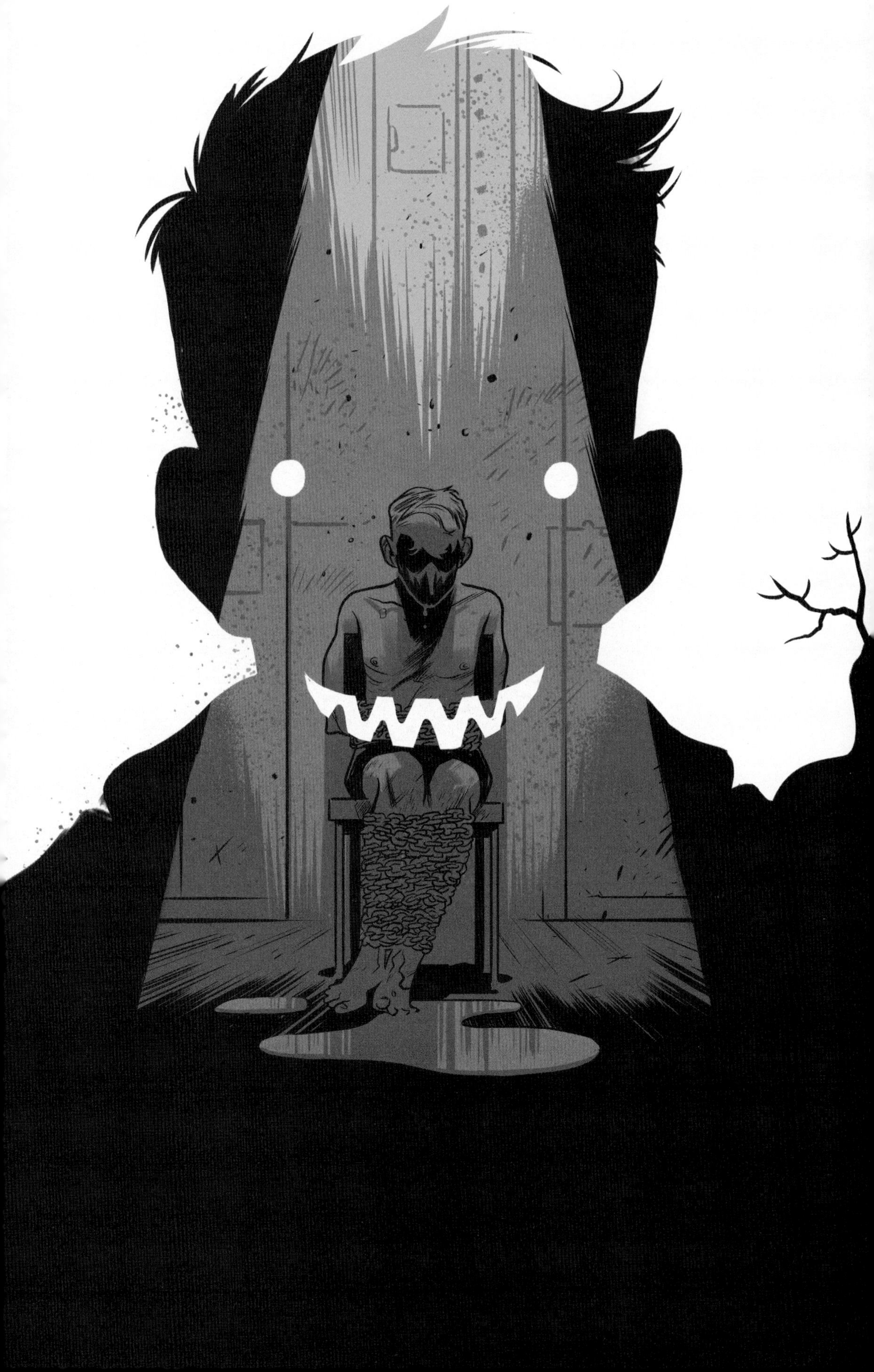

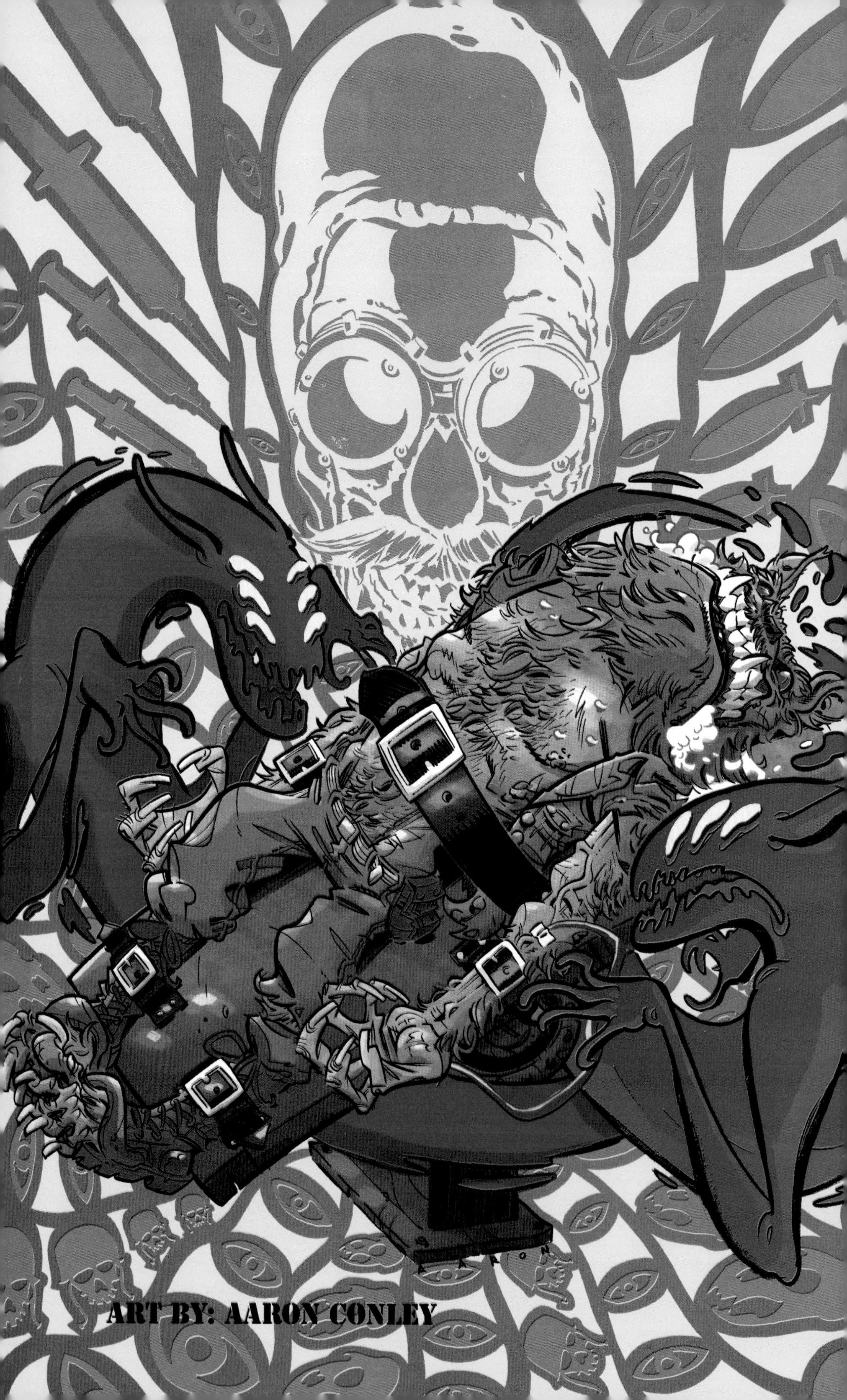

ART BY: AARON CONLEY

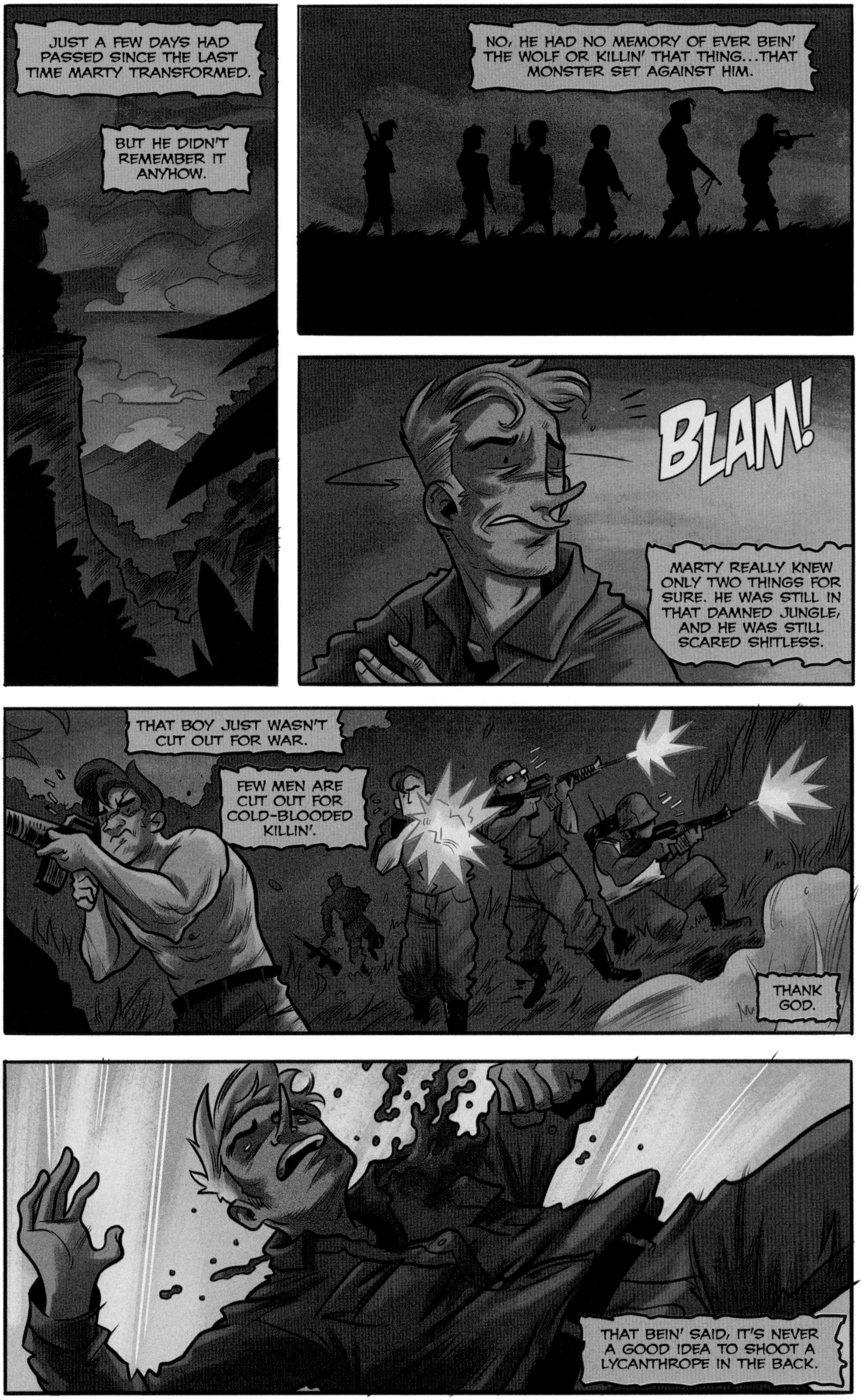

JUST A FEW DAYS HAD PASSED SINCE THE LAST TIME MARTY TRANSFORMED.
BUT HE DIDN'T REMEMBER IT ANYHOW.
NO, HE HAD NO MEMORY OF EVER BEIN' THE WOLF OR KILLIN' THAT THING...THAT MONSTER SET AGAINST HIM.
BLAM!
MARTY REALLY KNEW ONLY TWO THINGS FOR SURE. HE WAS STILL IN THAT DAMNED JUNGLE, AND HE WAS STILL SCARED SHITLESS.
THAT BOY JUST WASN'T CUT OUT FOR WAR.
FEW MEN ARE CUT OUT FOR COLD-BLOODED KILLIN'.
THANK GOD.
THAT BEIN' SAID, IT'S NEVER A GOOD IDEA TO SHOOT A LYCANTHROPE IN THE BACK.

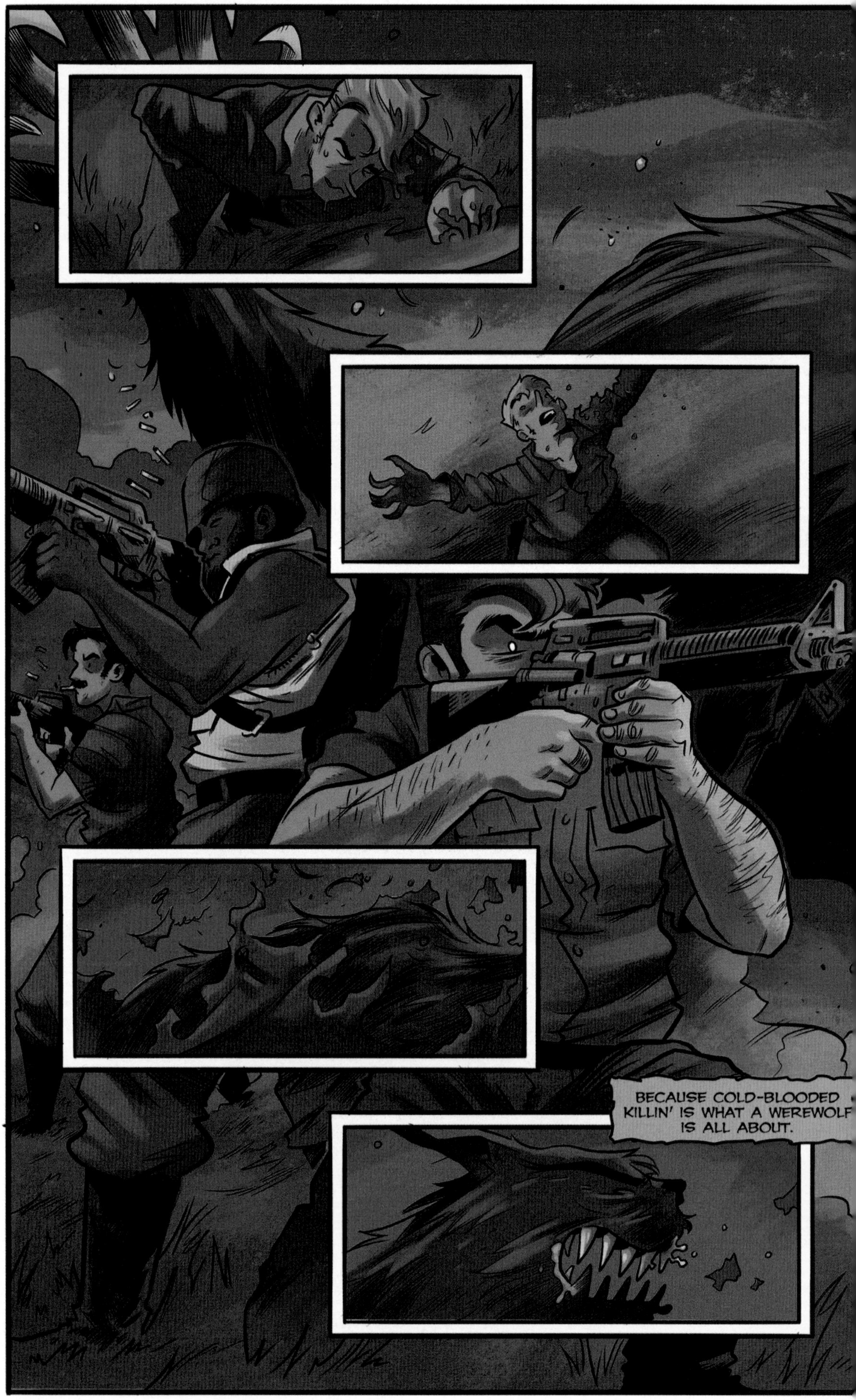
BECAUSE COLD-BLOODED KILLIN' IS WHAT A WEREWOLF IS ALL ABOUT.

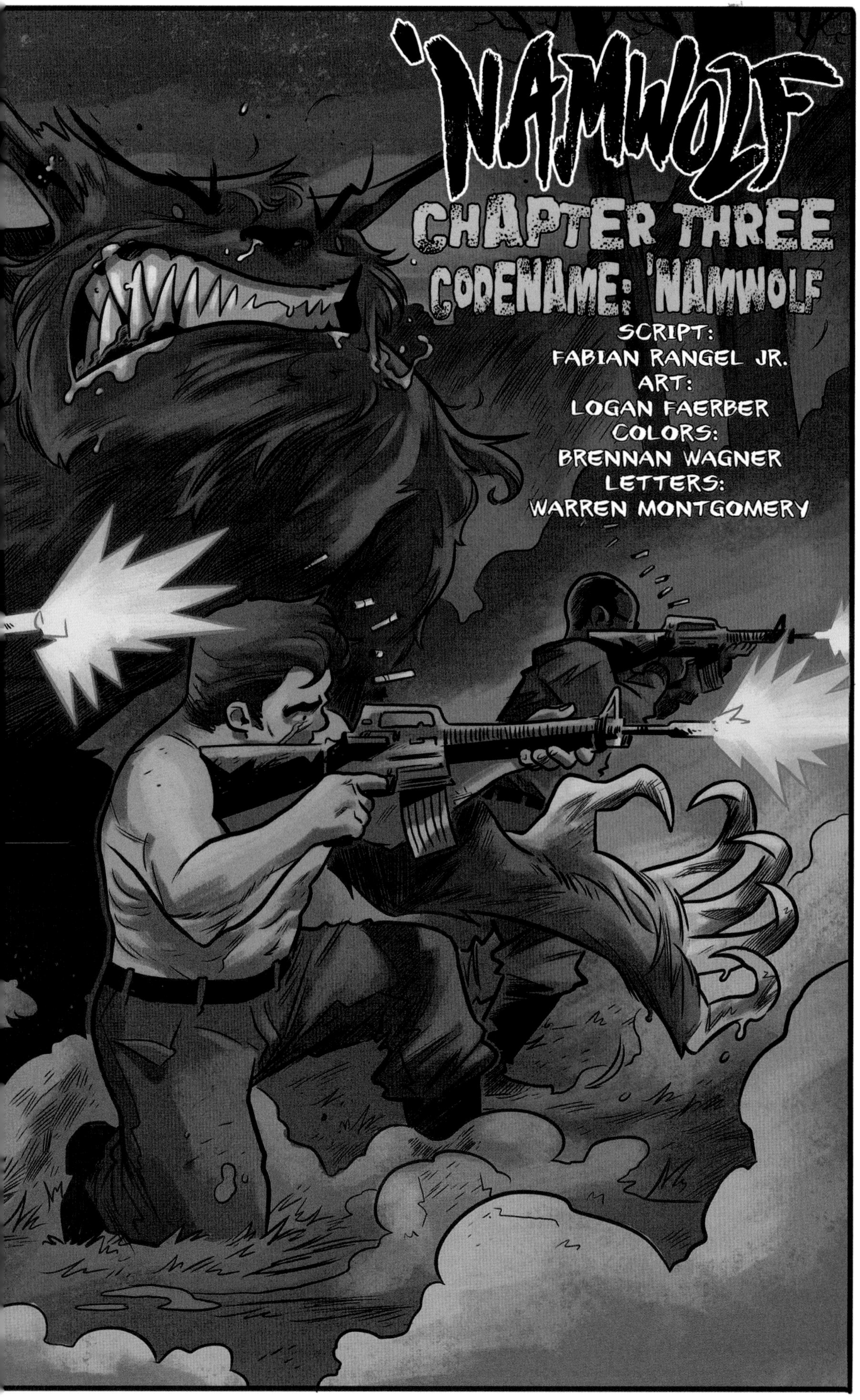
'NAMWOLF
CHAPTER THREE
CODENAME: 'NAMWOLF
SCRIPT:
FABIAN RANGEL JR.
ART:
LOGAN FAERBER
COLORS:
BRENNAN WAGNER
LETTERS:
WARREN MONTGOMERY

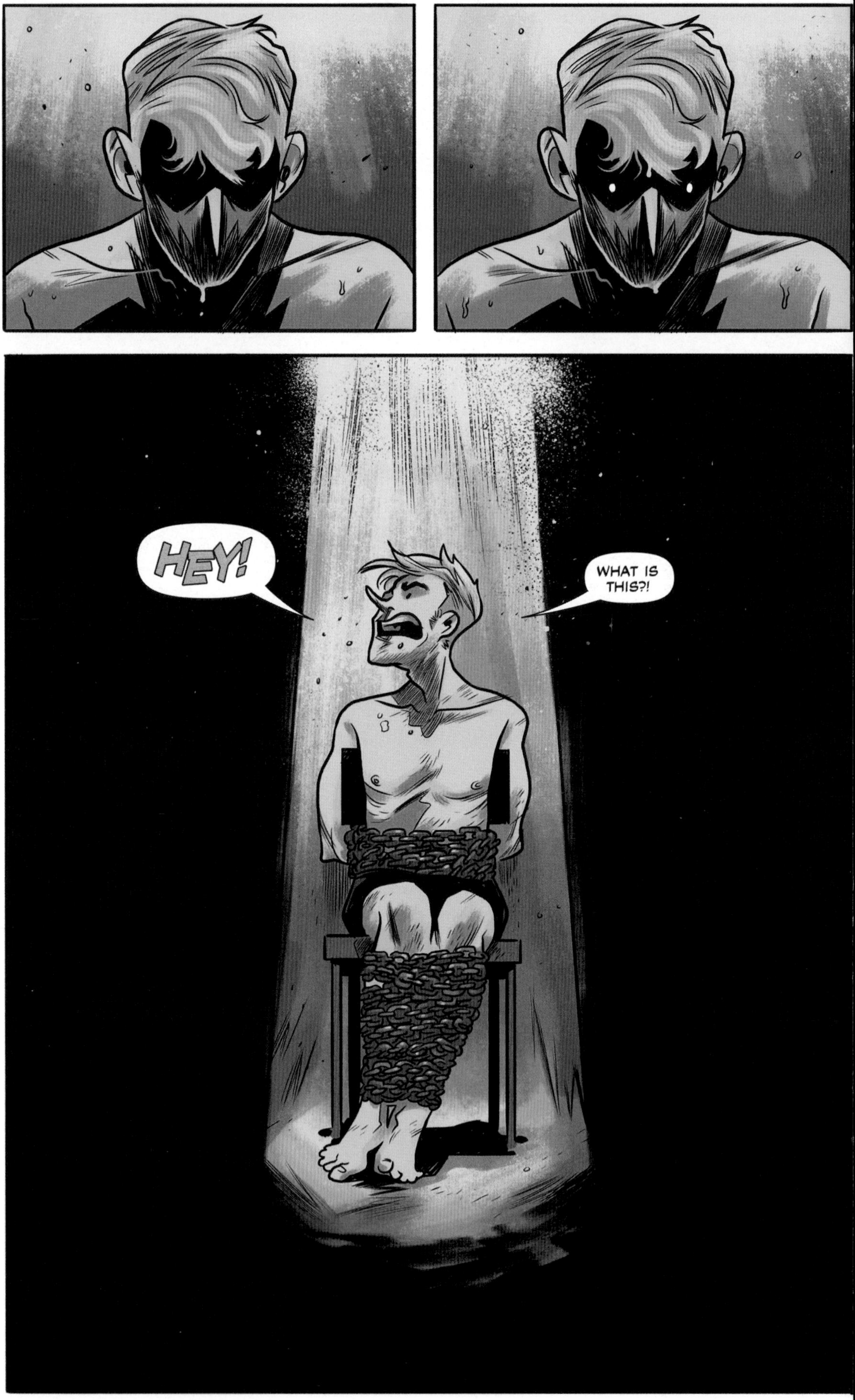
HEY!
WHAT IS THIS?!

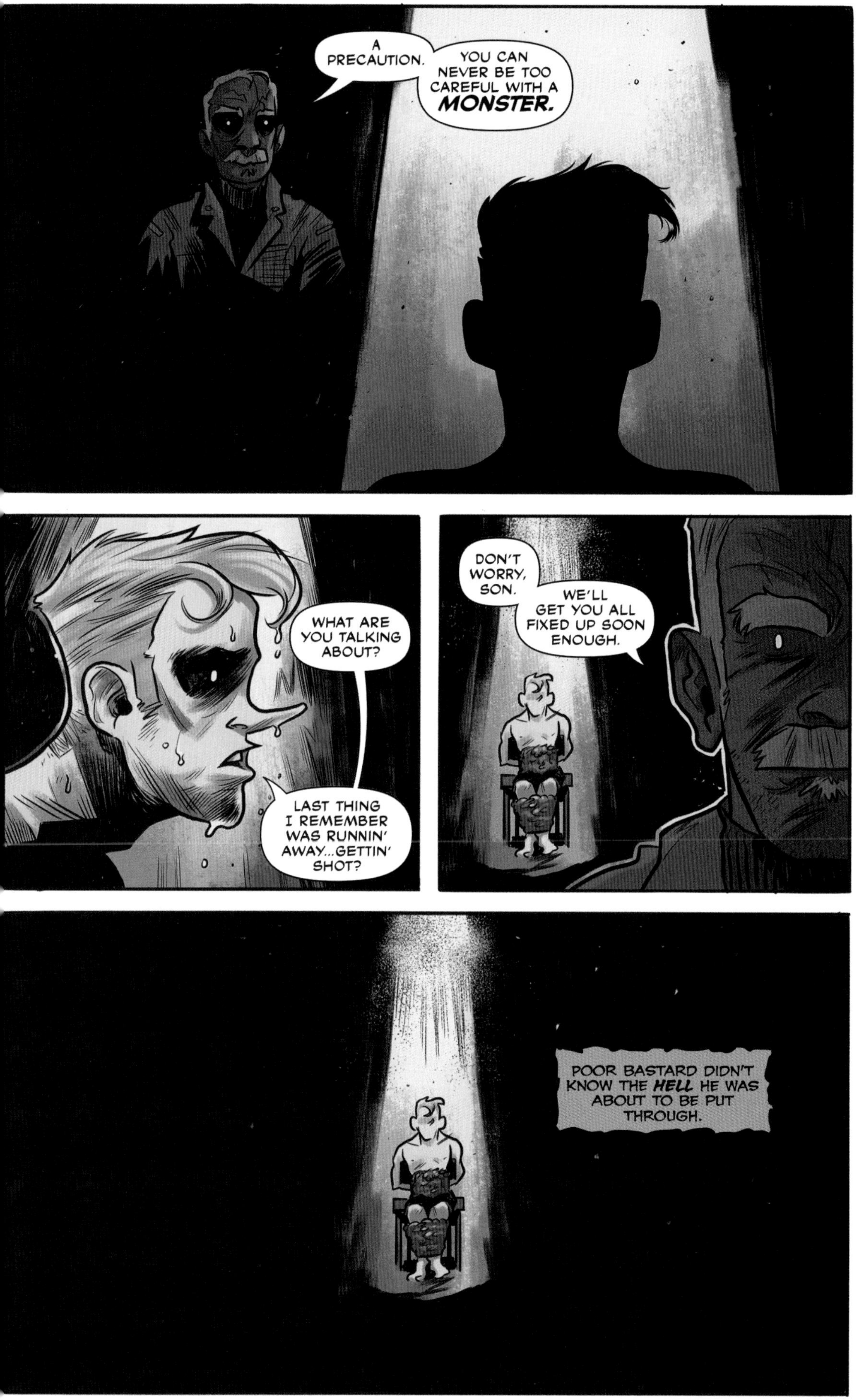
A PRECAUTION.
YOU CAN NEVER BE TOO CAREFUL WITH A MONSTER.
WHAT ARE YOU TALKING ABOUT?
LAST THING I REMEMBER WAS RUNNIN' AWAY...GETTIN' SHOT?
DON'T WORRY, SON.
WE'LL GET YOU ALL FIXED UP SOON ENOUGH.
POOR BASTARD DIDN'T KNOW THE HELL HE WAS ABOUT TO BE PUT THROUGH.

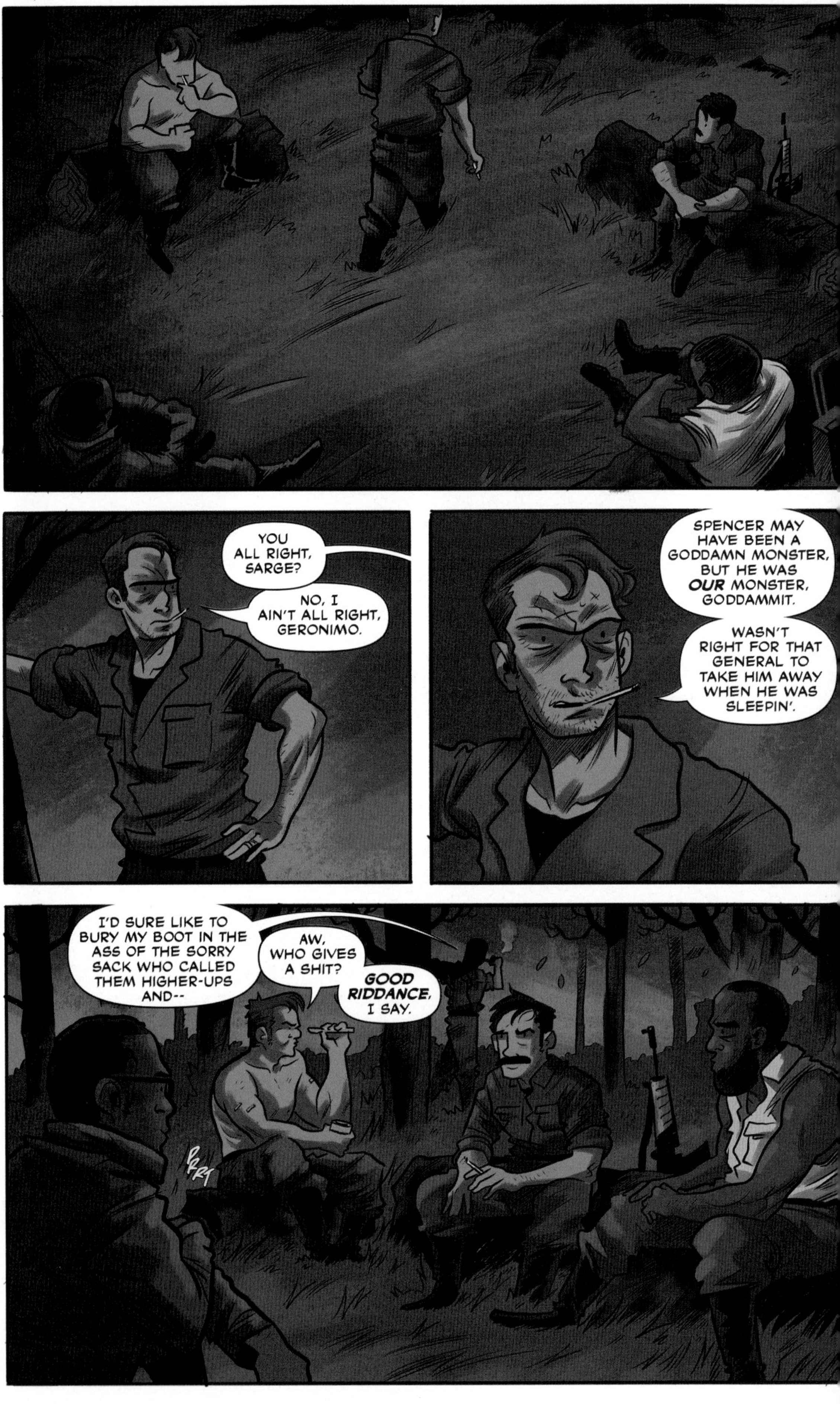
YOU ALL RIGHT, SARGE?
NO, I AIN'T ALL RIGHT, GERONIMO.
SPENCER MAY HAVE BEEN A GODDAMN MONSTER, BUT HE WAS ***OUR*** MONSTER, GODDAMMIT.
WASN'T RIGHT FOR THAT GENERAL TO TAKE HIM AWAY WHEN HE WAS SLEEPIN'.
I'D SURE LIKE TO BURY MY BOOT IN THE ASS OF THE SORRY SACK WHO CALLED THEM HIGHER-UPS AND--
AW, WHO GIVES A SHIT?
***GOOD RIDDANCE,*** I SAY.

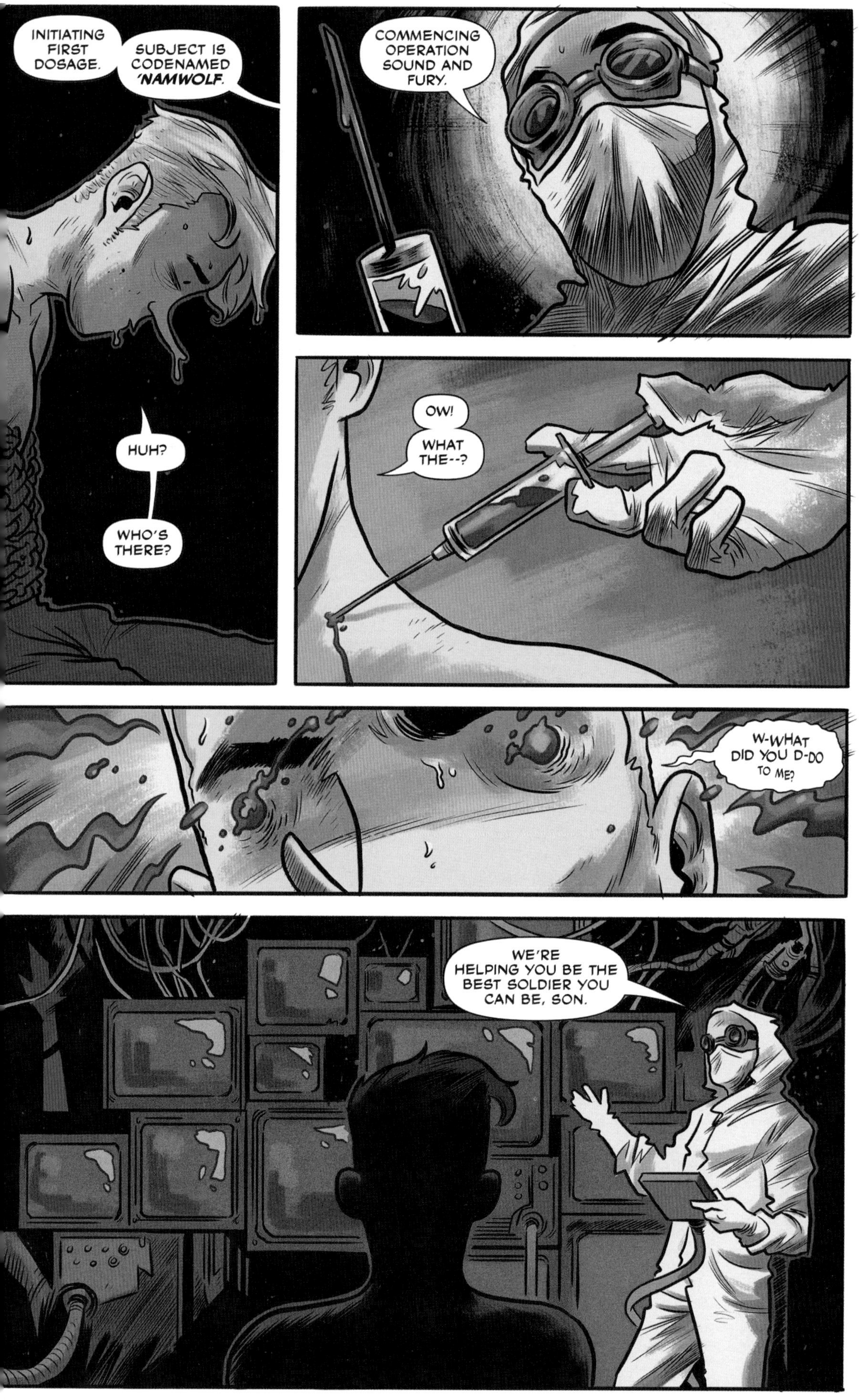
INITIATING FIRST DOSAGE.
SUBJECT IS CODENAMED 'NAMWOLF.
COMMENCING OPERATION SOUND AND FURY.
HUH?
WHO'S THERE?
OW!
WHAT THE--?
W-WHAT DID YOU D-DO TO ME?
WE'RE HELPING YOU BE THE BEST SOLDIER YOU CAN BE, SON.

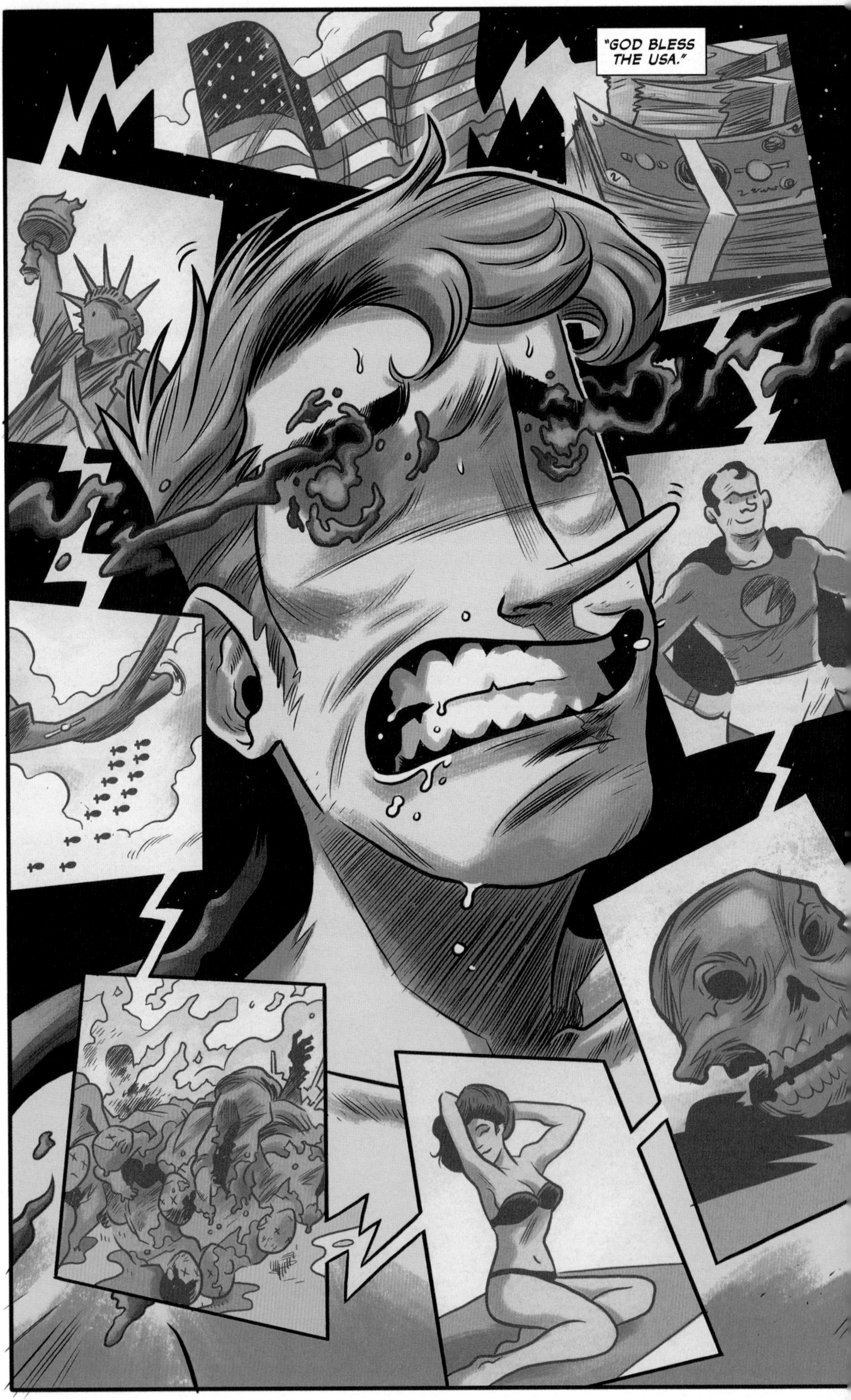
"GOD BLESS THE USA."

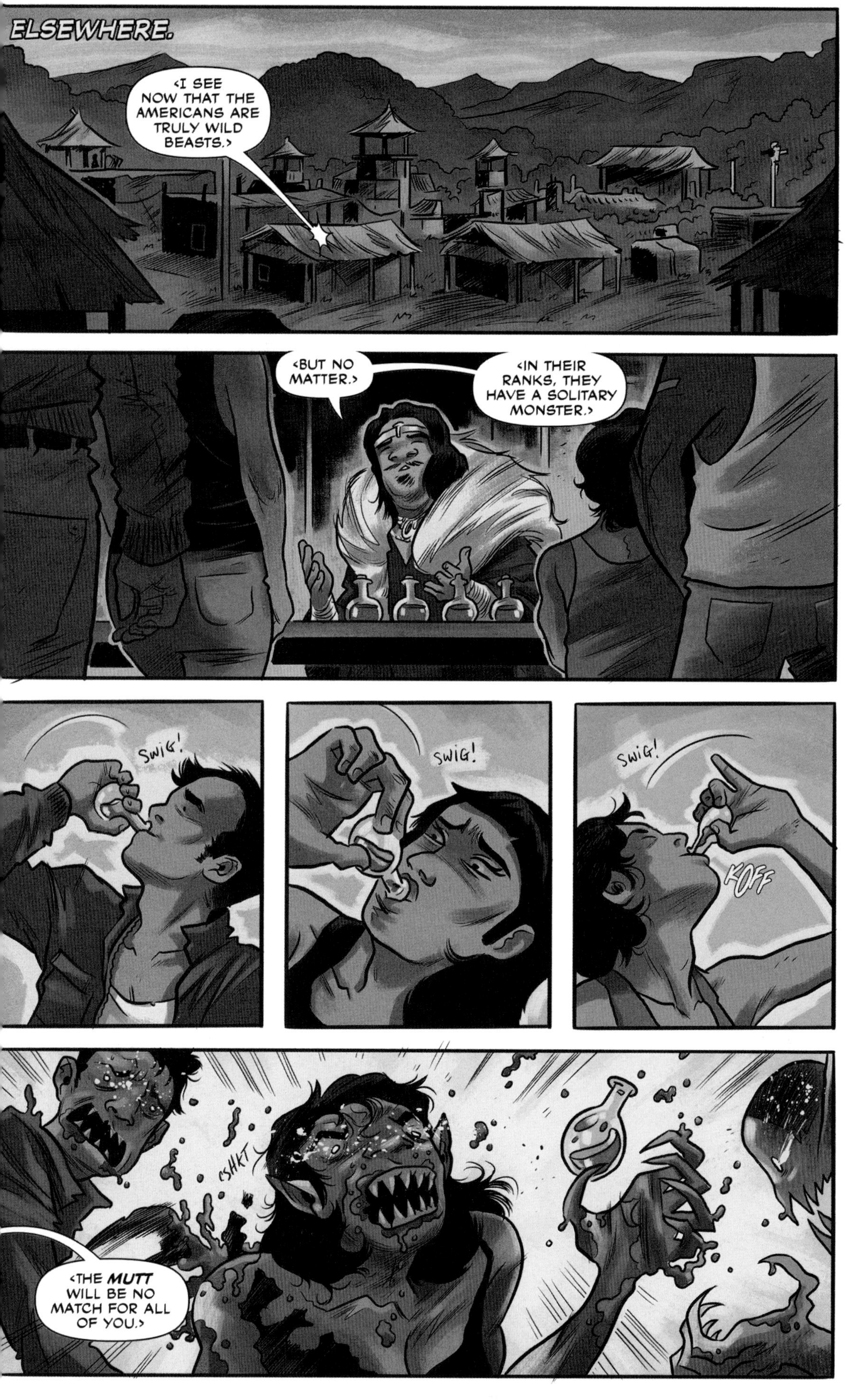
ELSEWHERE.
<I SEE NOW THAT THE AMERICANS ARE TRULY WILD BEASTS.>
<BUT NO MATTER.>
<IN THEIR RANKS, THEY HAVE A SOLITARY MONSTER.>
SWIG!
SWIG!
SWIG!
KOFF
CSHKT
<THE MUTT WILL BE NO MATCH FOR ALL OF YOU.>

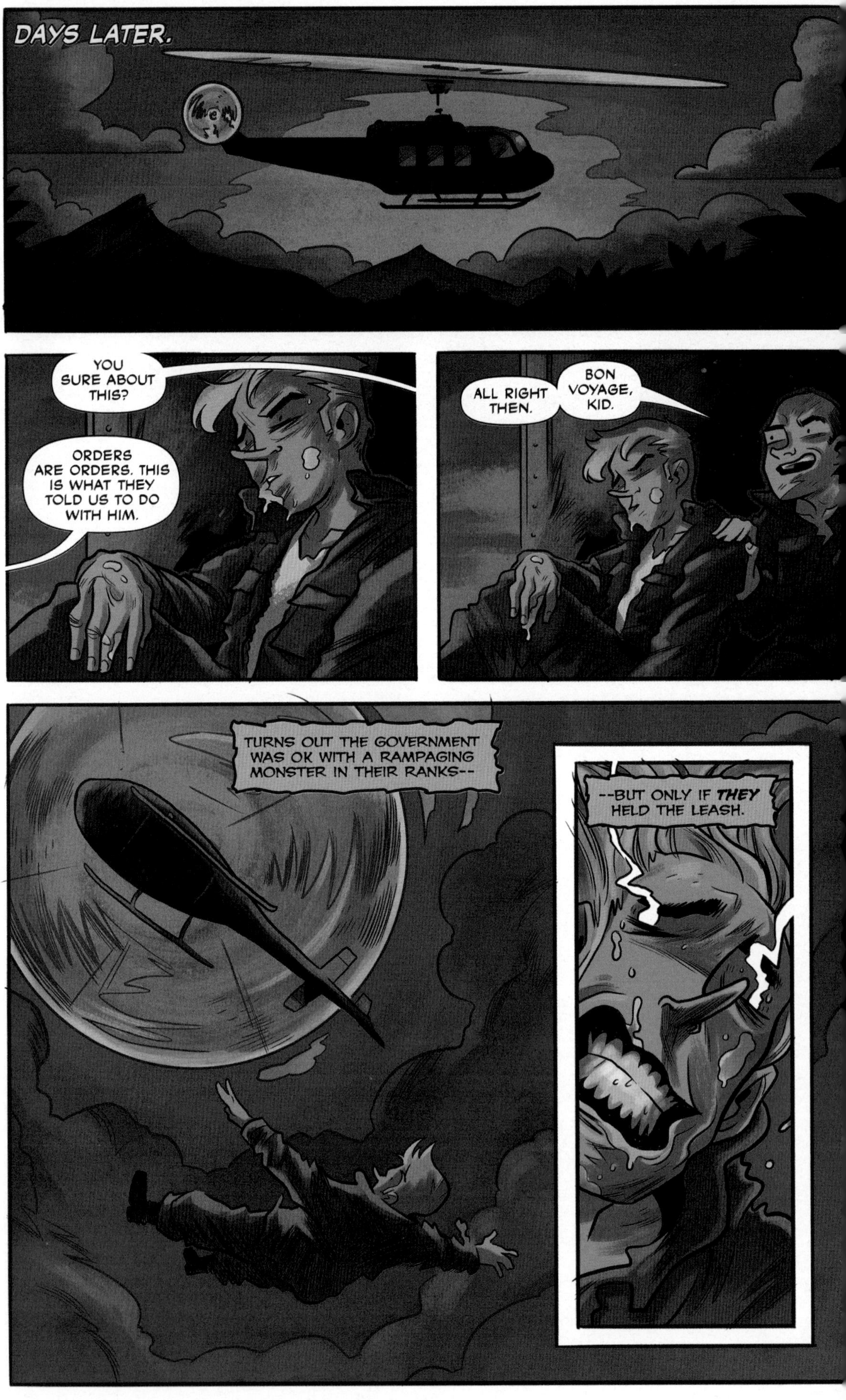
DAYS LATER.
YOU SURE ABOUT THIS?
ORDERS ARE ORDERS. THIS IS WHAT THEY TOLD US TO DO WITH HIM.
ALL RIGHT THEN.
BON VOYAGE, KID.
TURNS OUT THE GOVERNMENT WAS OK WITH A RAMPAGING MONSTER IN THEIR RANKS--
--BUT ONLY IF *THEY* HELD THE LEASH.

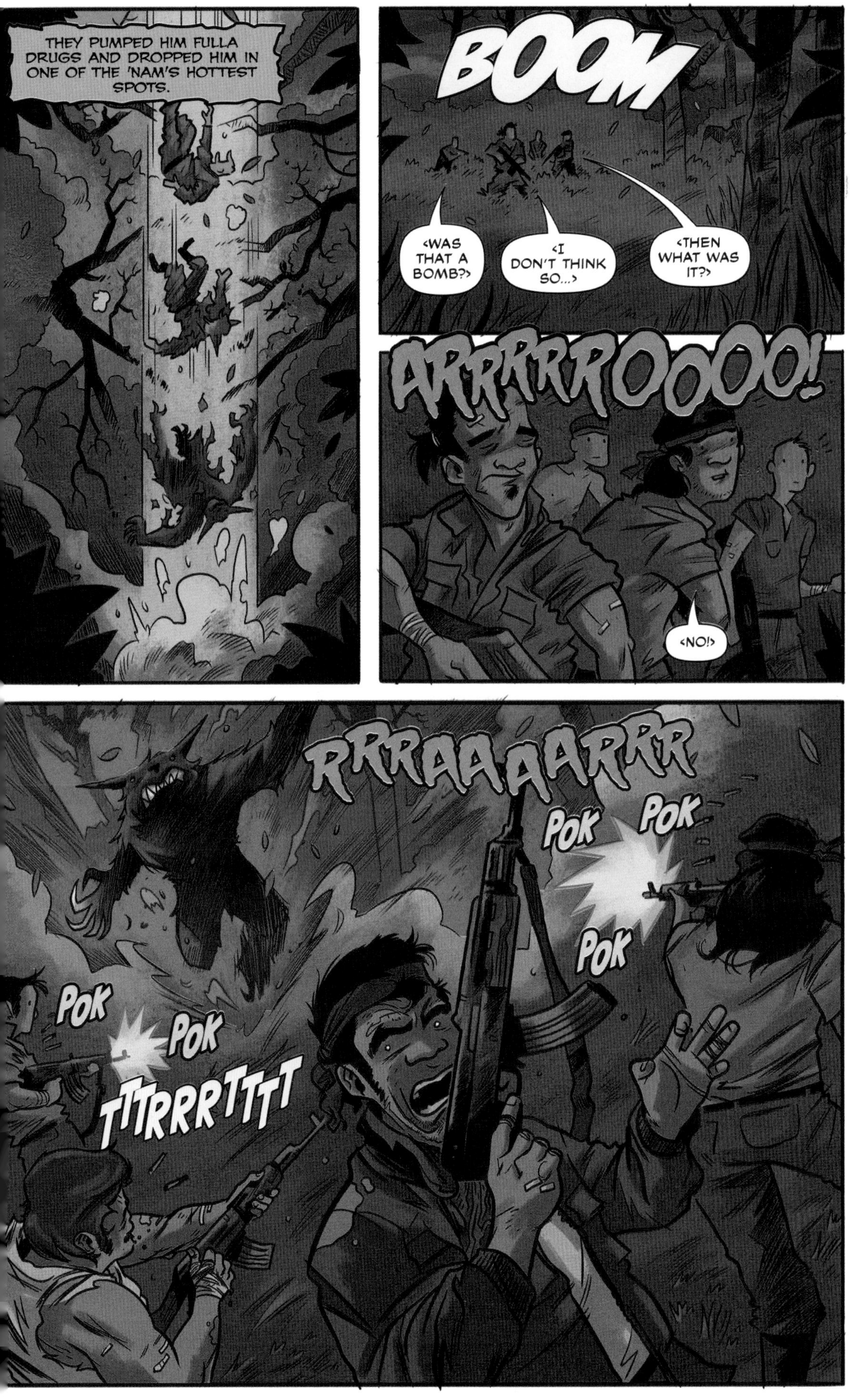
THEY PUMPED HIM FULLA DRUGS AND DROPPED HIM IN ONE OF THE 'NAM'S HOTTEST SPOTS.
BOOM
<WAS THAT A BOMB?>
<I DON'T THINK SO...>
<THEN WHAT WAS IT?>
ARRRRRROOOO!
<NO!>
RRRAAAARRR
POK
POK
POK
POK
POK
TTTRRRTTTT

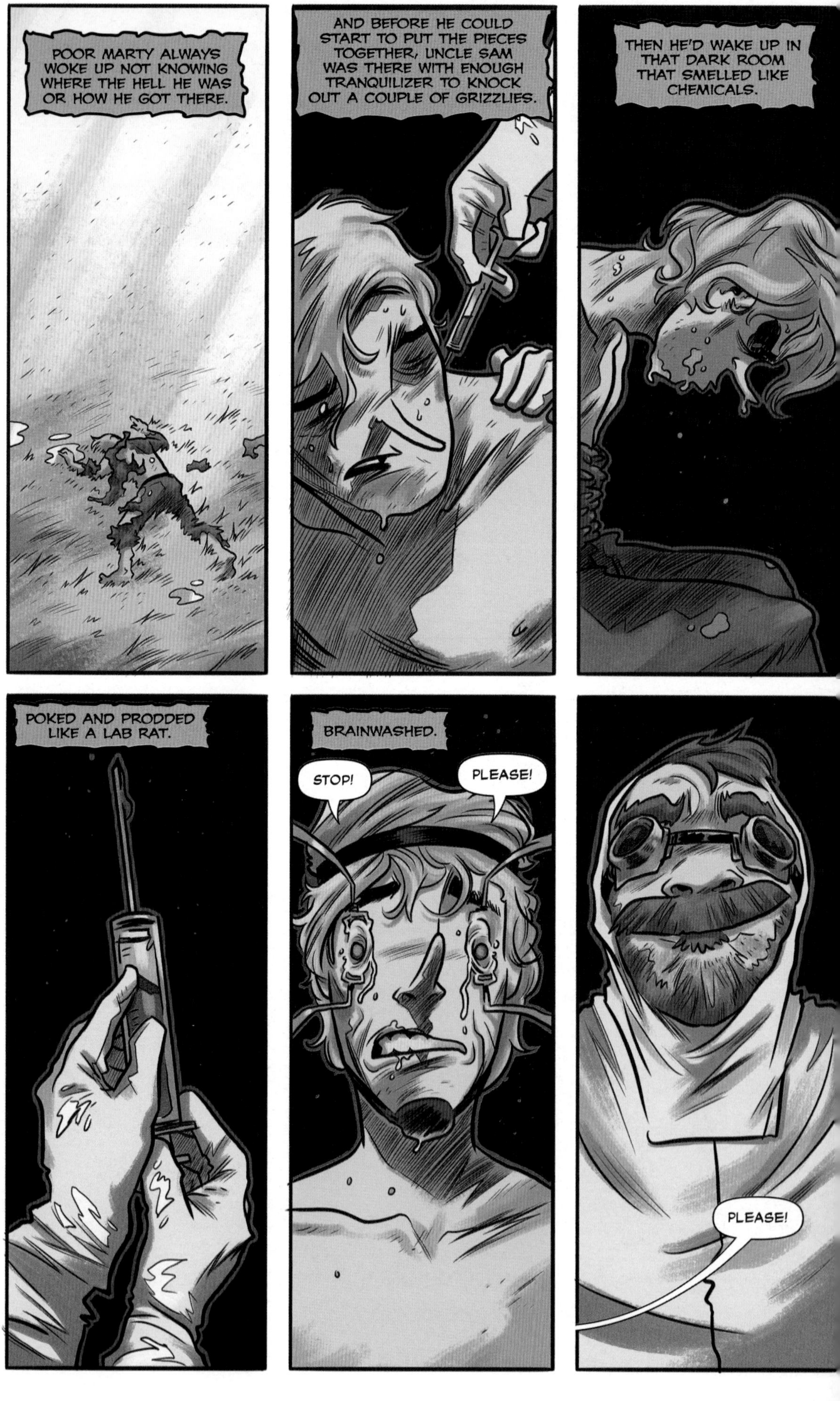
POOR MARTY ALWAYS WOKE UP NOT KNOWING WHERE THE HELL HE WAS OR HOW HE GOT THERE.
AND BEFORE HE COULD START TO PUT THE PIECES TOGETHER, UNCLE SAM WAS THERE WITH ENOUGH TRANQUILIZER TO KNOCK OUT A COUPLE OF GRIZZLIES.
THEN HE'D WAKE UP IN THAT DARK ROOM THAT SMELLED LIKE CHEMICALS.
POKED AND PRODDED LIKE A LAB RAT.
BRAINWASHED.
STOP!
PLEASE!
PLEASE!

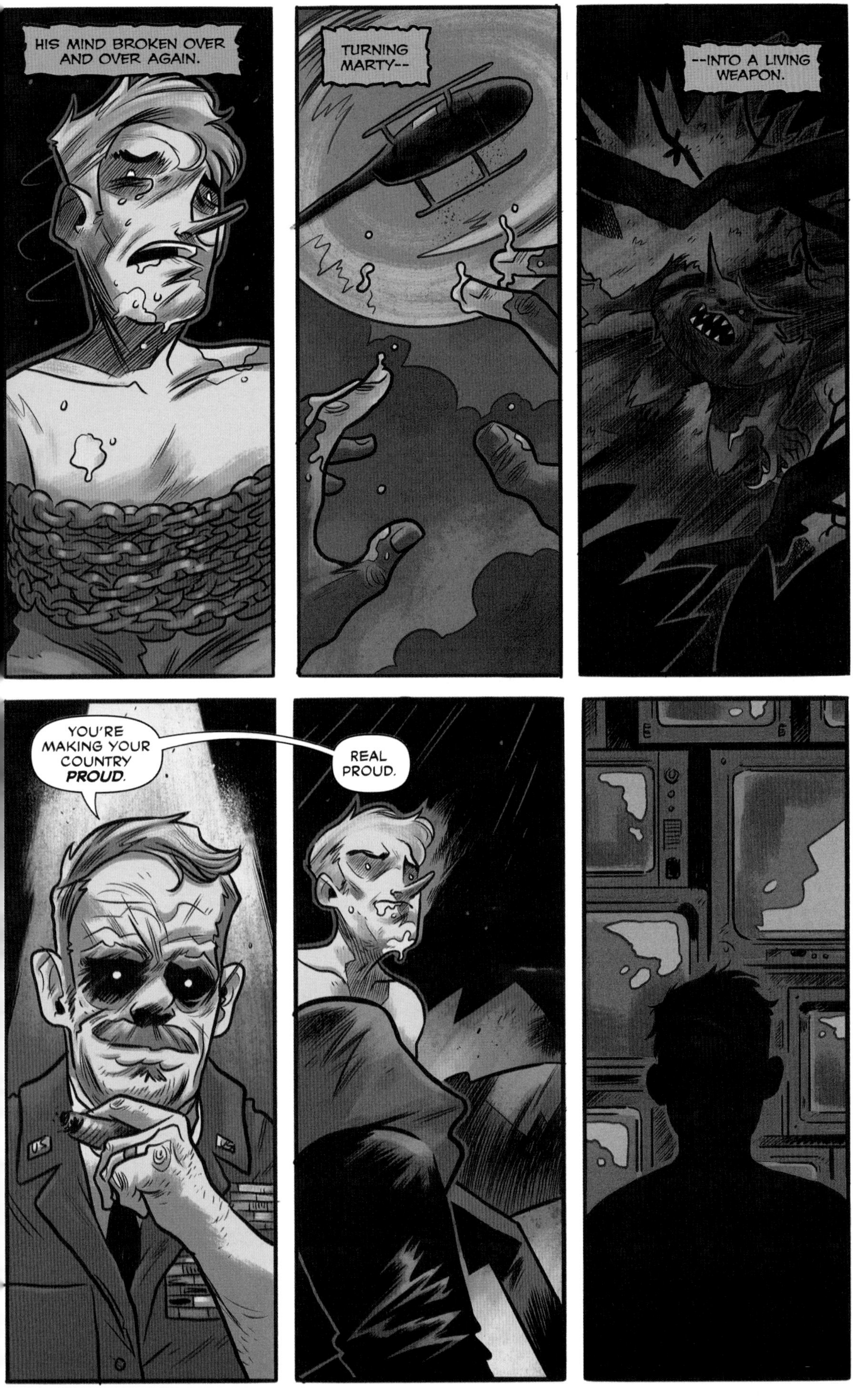
HIS MIND BROKEN OVER AND OVER AGAIN.
TURNING MARTY--
--INTO A LIVING WEAPON.
YOU'RE MAKING YOUR COUNTRY **PROUD**.
REAL PROUD.

MEANWHILE.

WHAT THE HELL HAPPENED HERE?

HOWDY, BOYS.

I'M **SERGEANT WHITEHILL.** SORRY TO SAY YOU MISSED ALL THE FUN.

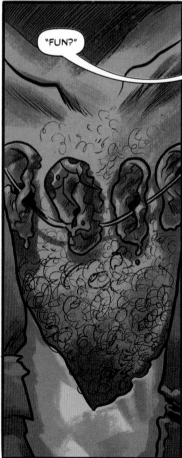

"FUN?"

KEE KEE KEE

WHAT WAS THAT?

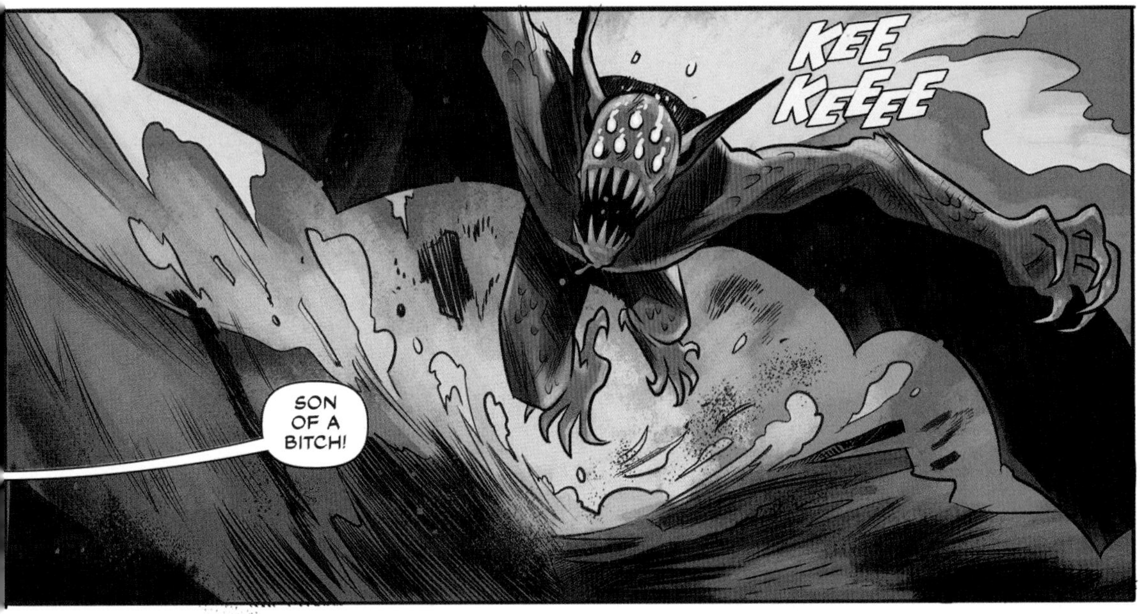
KEE KEEEEE
SON OF A BITCH!

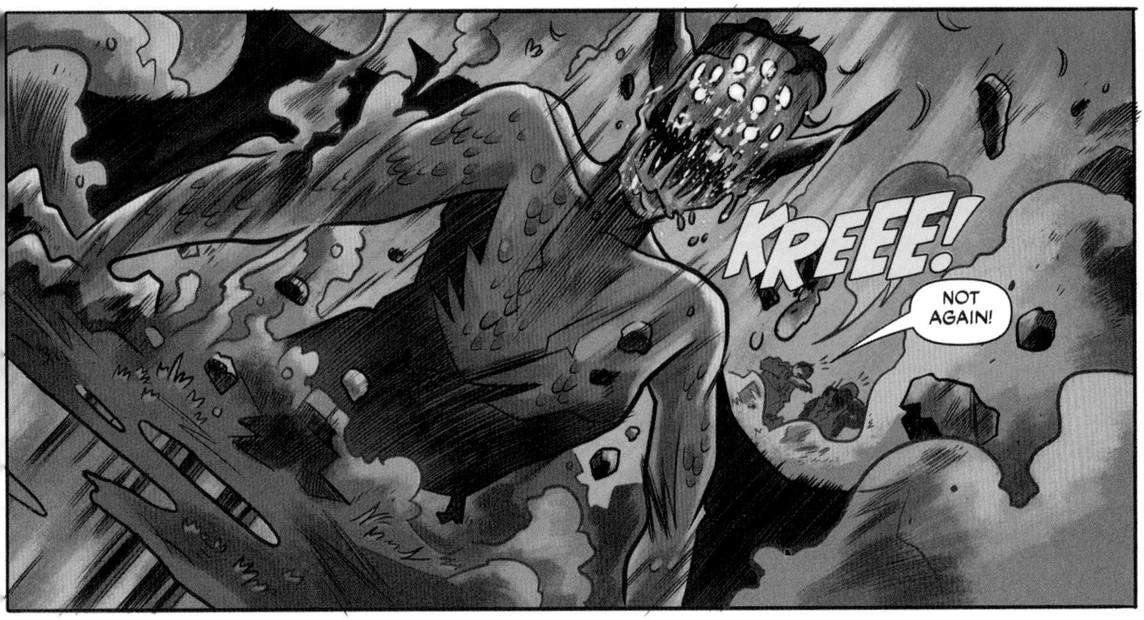
KREEE!
NOT AGAIN!

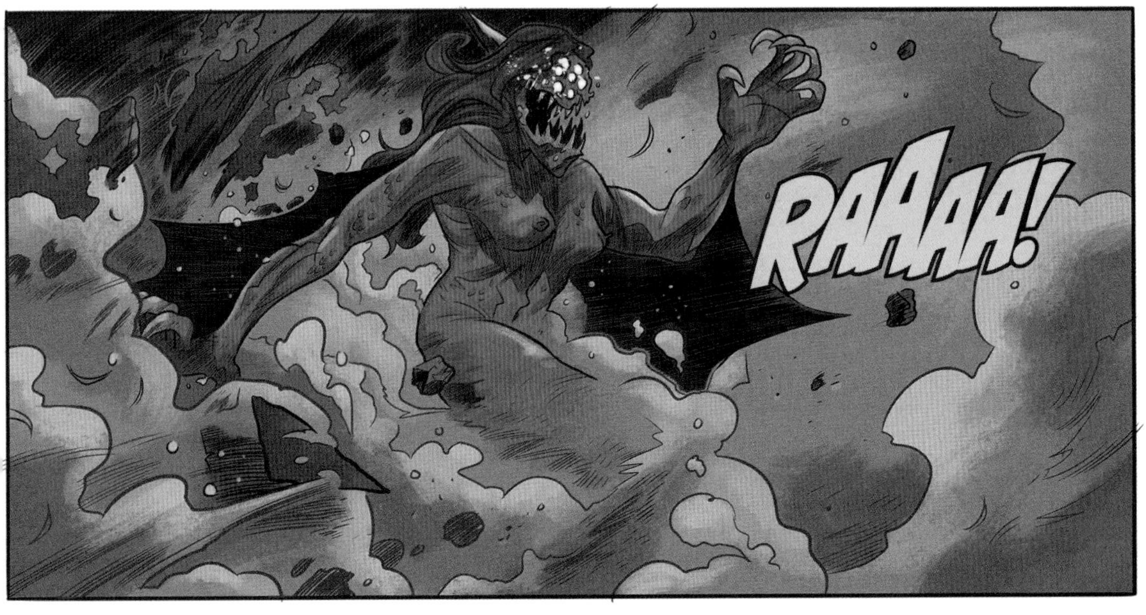
RAAAA!

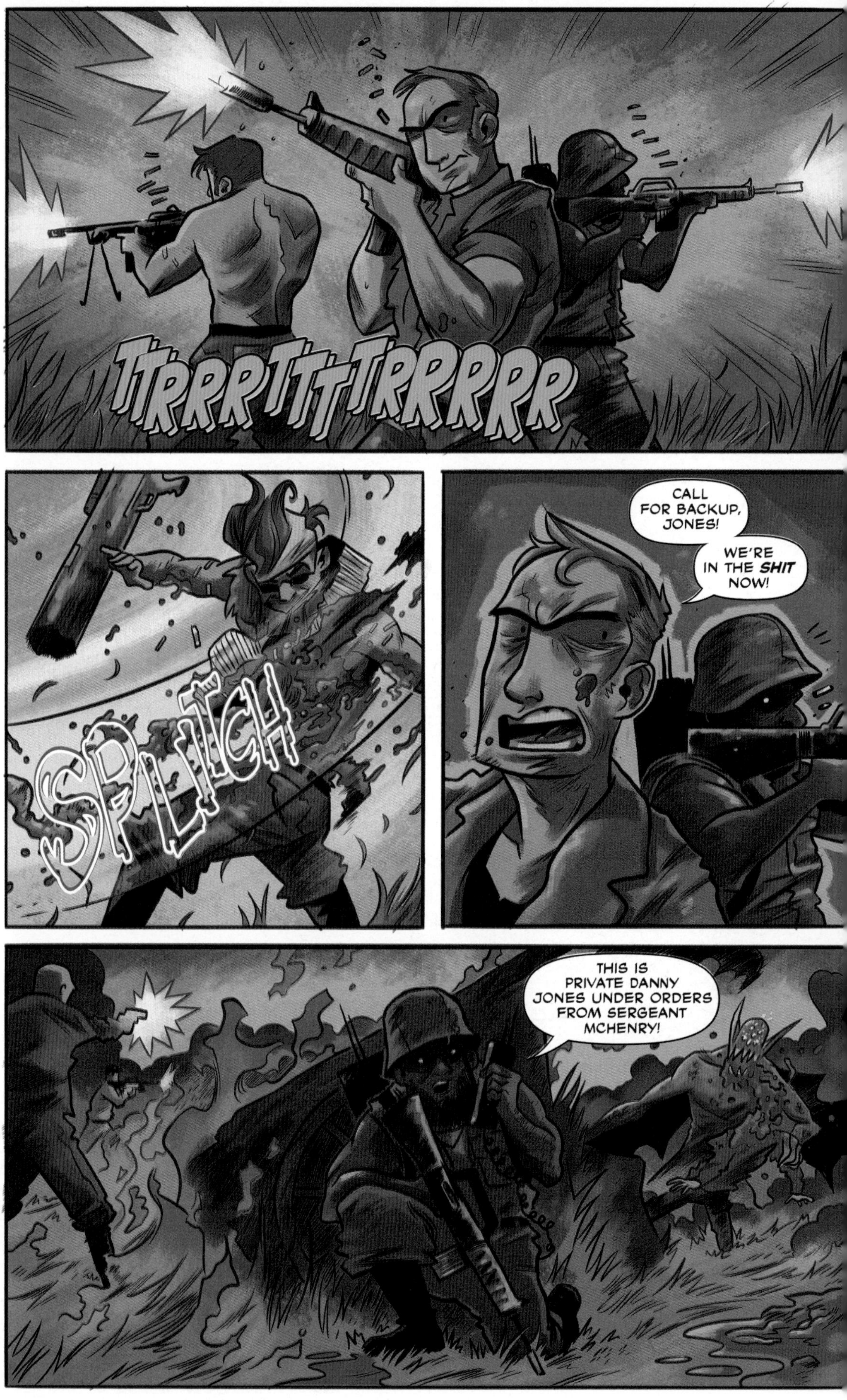
TTRRRTTTTRRRRRR
SPLITCH
CALL FOR BACKUP, JONES!
WE'RE IN THE SHIT NOW!
THIS IS PRIVATE DANNY JONES UNDER ORDERS FROM SERGEANT MCHENRY!

MARTY MAY HAVE BEEN OUT OF HIS MIND ON DRUGS--

WE'RE UNDER ATTACK BY A BUNCH OF FUCKIN' *MONSTERS!*

I REPEAT, THIS IS DANNY *JONES*--

--BUT RADIO'S VOICE CUT THROUGH THAT HAZE LIKE A KNIFE.

--REQUESTING IMMEDIATE ASSISTANCE!

HIS FRIENDS WERE IN DANGER.

AND HE WAS THE ONLY ONE WHO COULD DO ANYTHING ABOUT IT.

WE'RE RIGHT OVER THAT...

SHOULD WE--?

LEMME OUT...

*NO!*

WE GOT ORDERS TO BRING THE CARGO TO A DIFFERENT SPOT.

THEM BOYS ARE ON THEIR OWN.

SO FOR THE FIRST TIME, HE TOOK CONTROL OF THE BEAST INSIDE HIM.

LET--

--ME--

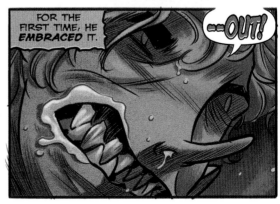

FOR THE FIRST TIME, HE *EMBRACED* IT.

*--OUT!*

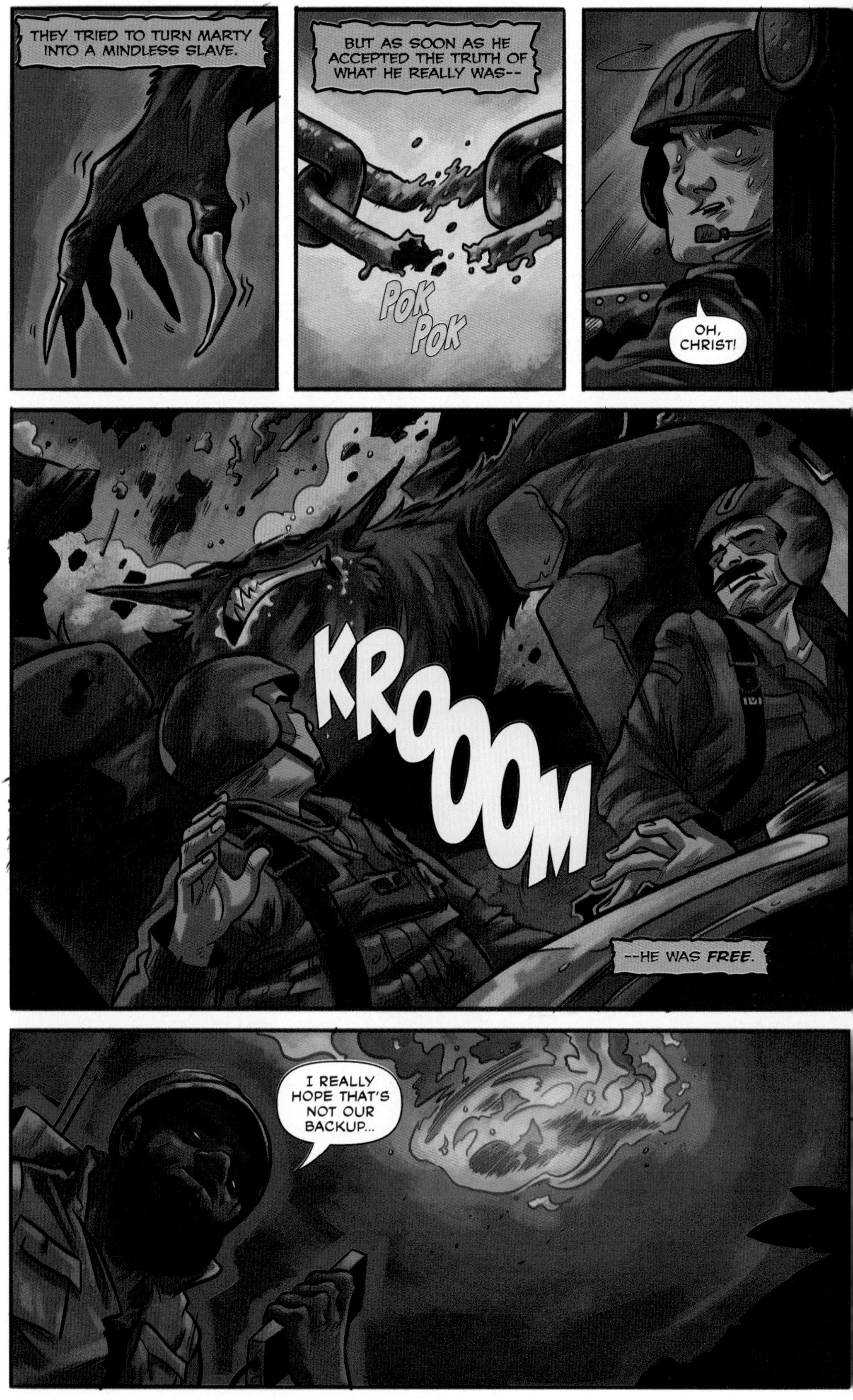
THEY TRIED TO TURN MARTY INTO A MINDLESS SLAVE.
BUT AS SOON AS HE ACCEPTED THE TRUTH OF WHAT HE REALLY WAS--
POK POK
OH, CHRIST!
KROOOM
--HE WAS FREE.
I REALLY HOPE THAT'S NOT OUR BACKUP...

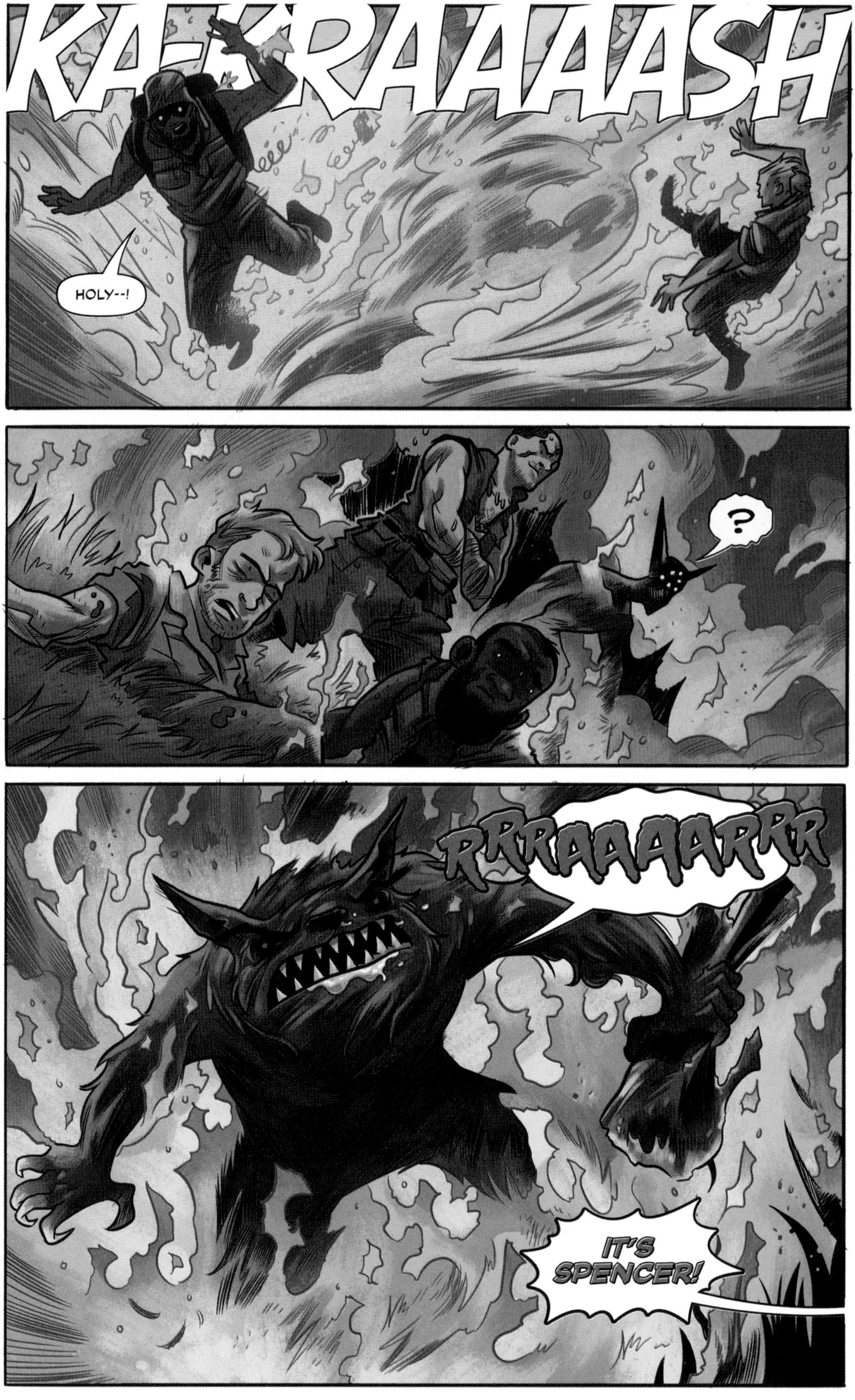
KA-KRAAAAASH
HOLY--!
?
RRRAAAAARRR
IT'S SPENCER!

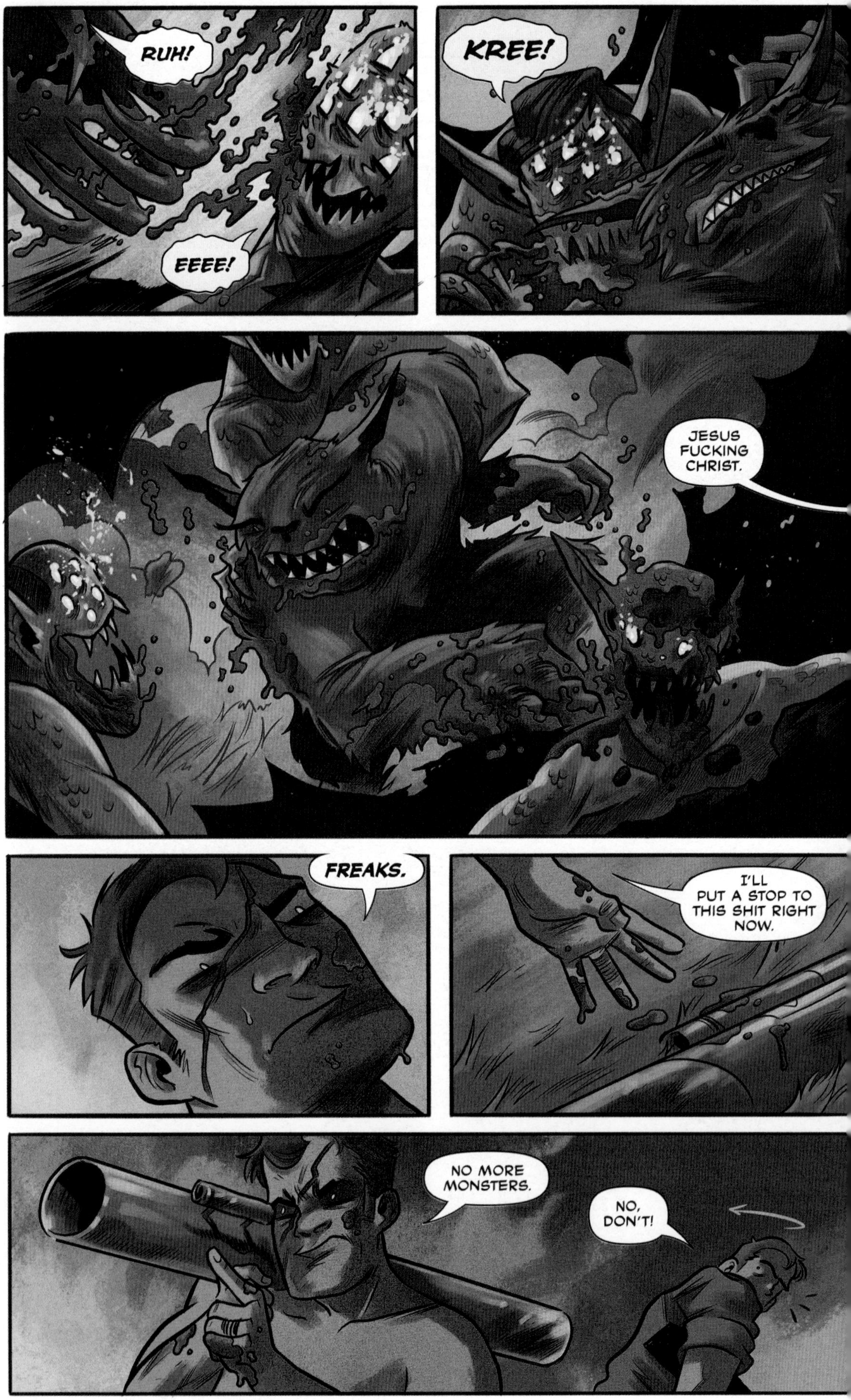
RUH!
EEEE!
KREE!
JESUS FUCKING CHRIST.
FREAKS.
I'LL PUT A STOP TO THIS SHIT RIGHT NOW.
NO MORE MONSTERS.
NO, DON'T!

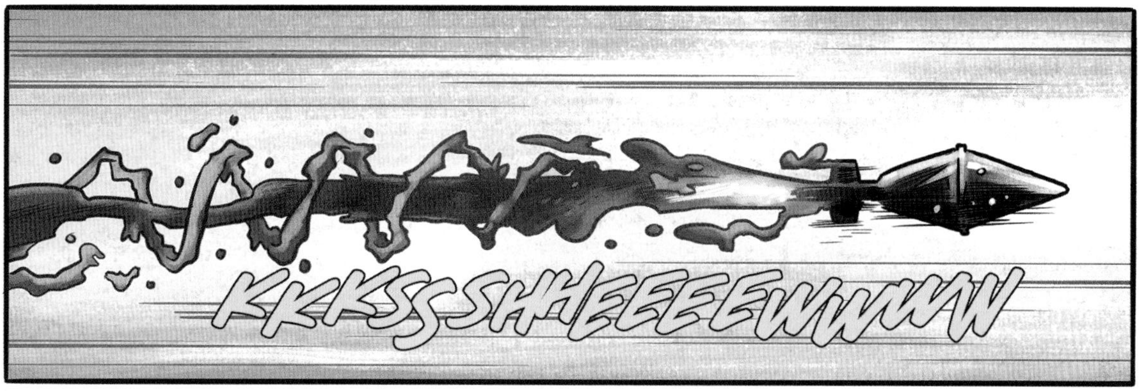
KKKSSSHHEEEEEWWWWW

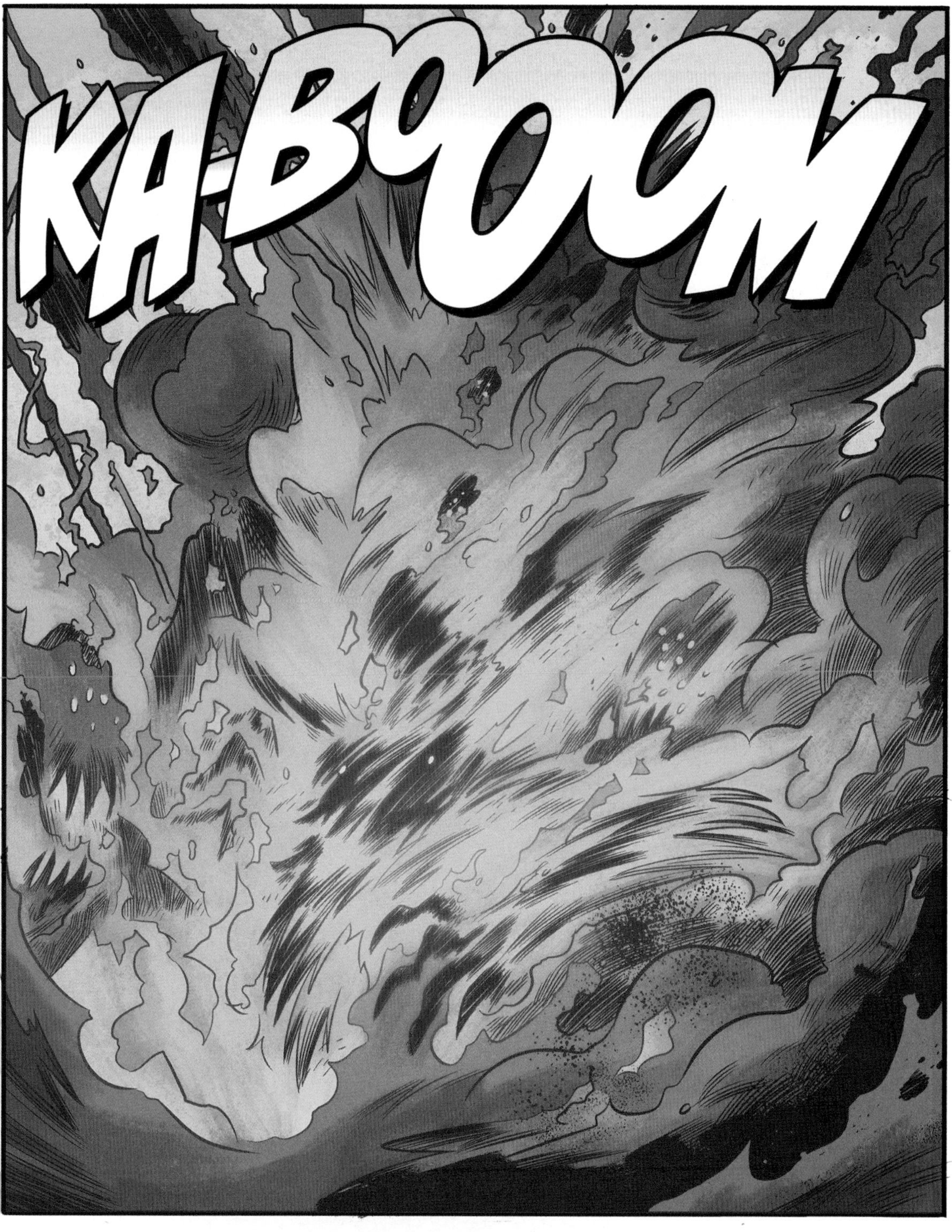
KA-BOOOM

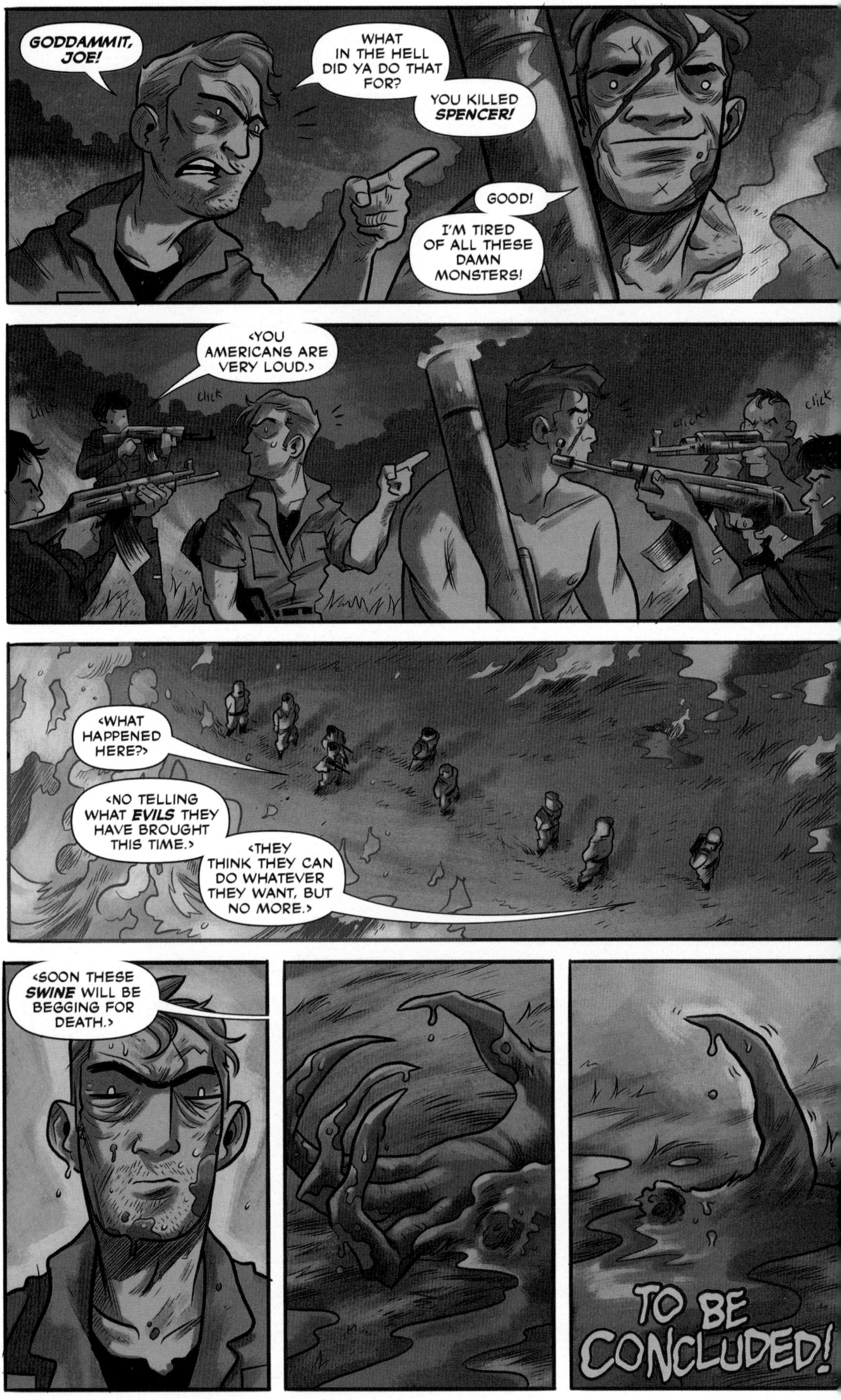
GODDAMMIT, JOE!
WHAT IN THE HELL DID YA DO THAT FOR?
YOU KILLED SPENCER!
GOOD!
I'M TIRED OF ALL THESE DAMN MONSTERS!
‹YOU AMERICANS ARE VERY LOUD.›
‹WHAT HAPPENED HERE?›
‹NO TELLING WHAT EVILS THEY HAVE BROUGHT THIS TIME.›
‹THEY THINK THEY CAN DO WHATEVER THEY WANT, BUT NO MORE.›
‹SOON THESE SWINE WILL BE BEGGING FOR DEATH.›
TO BE CONCLUDED!

# CHAPTER FOUR

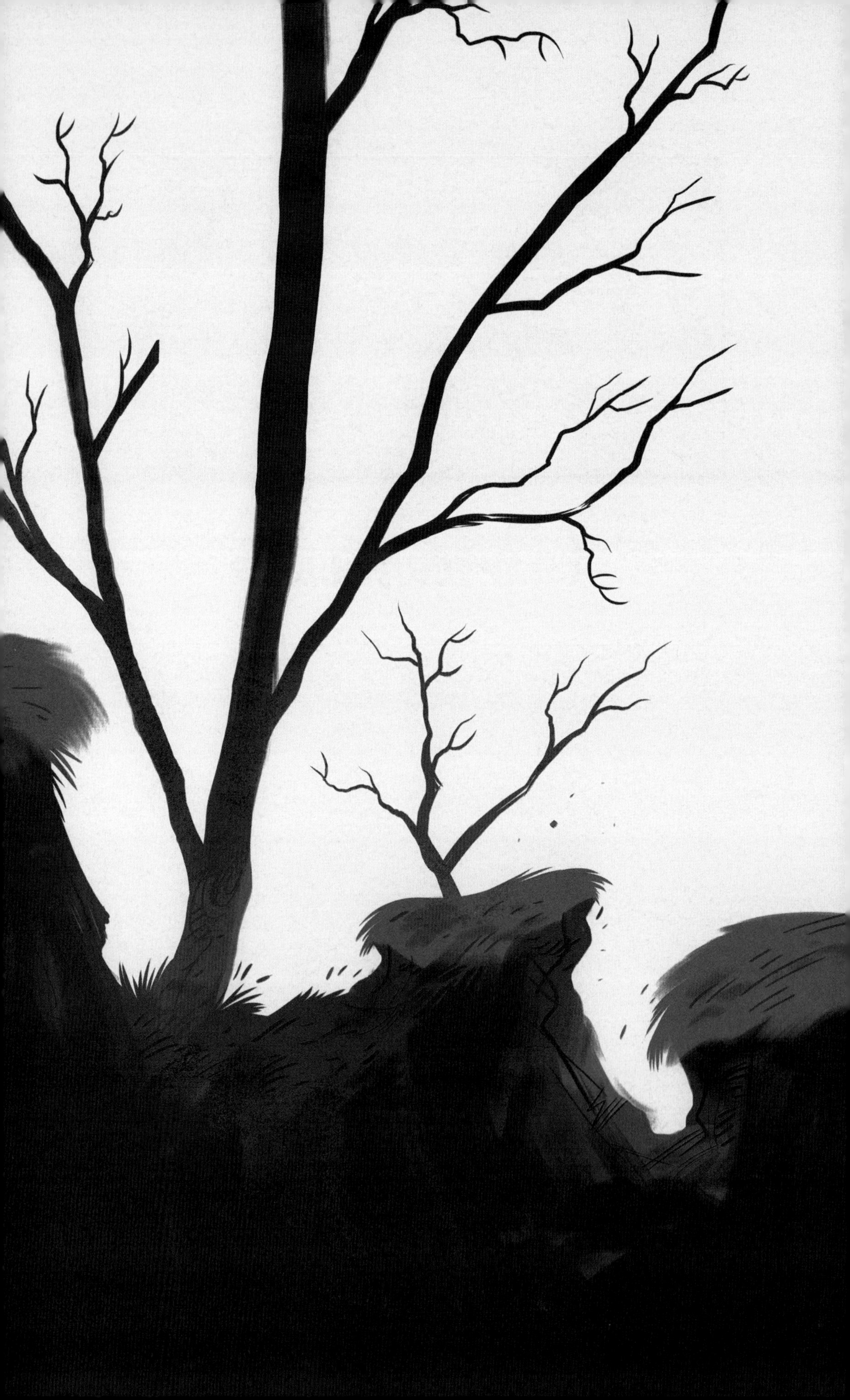

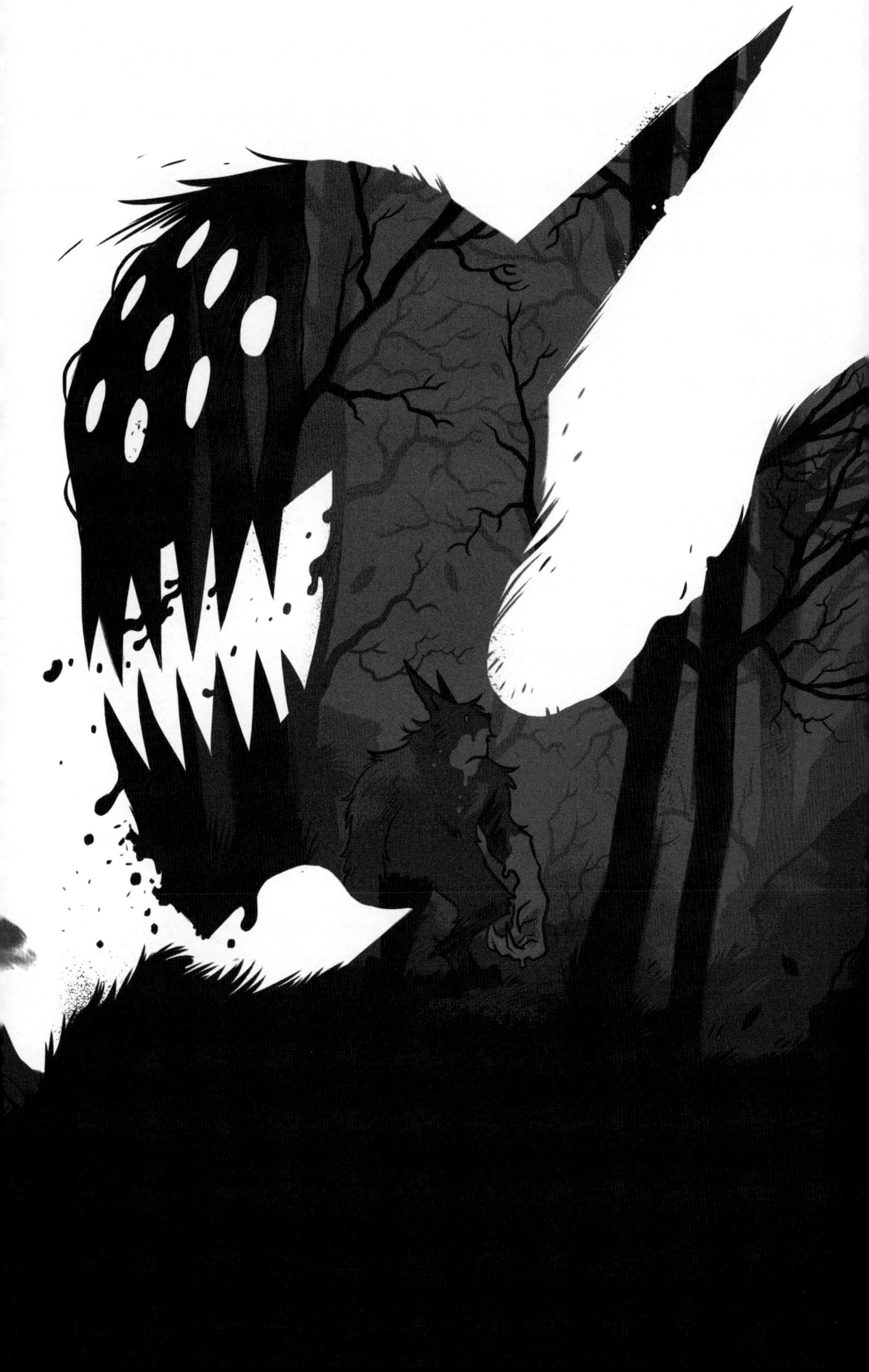

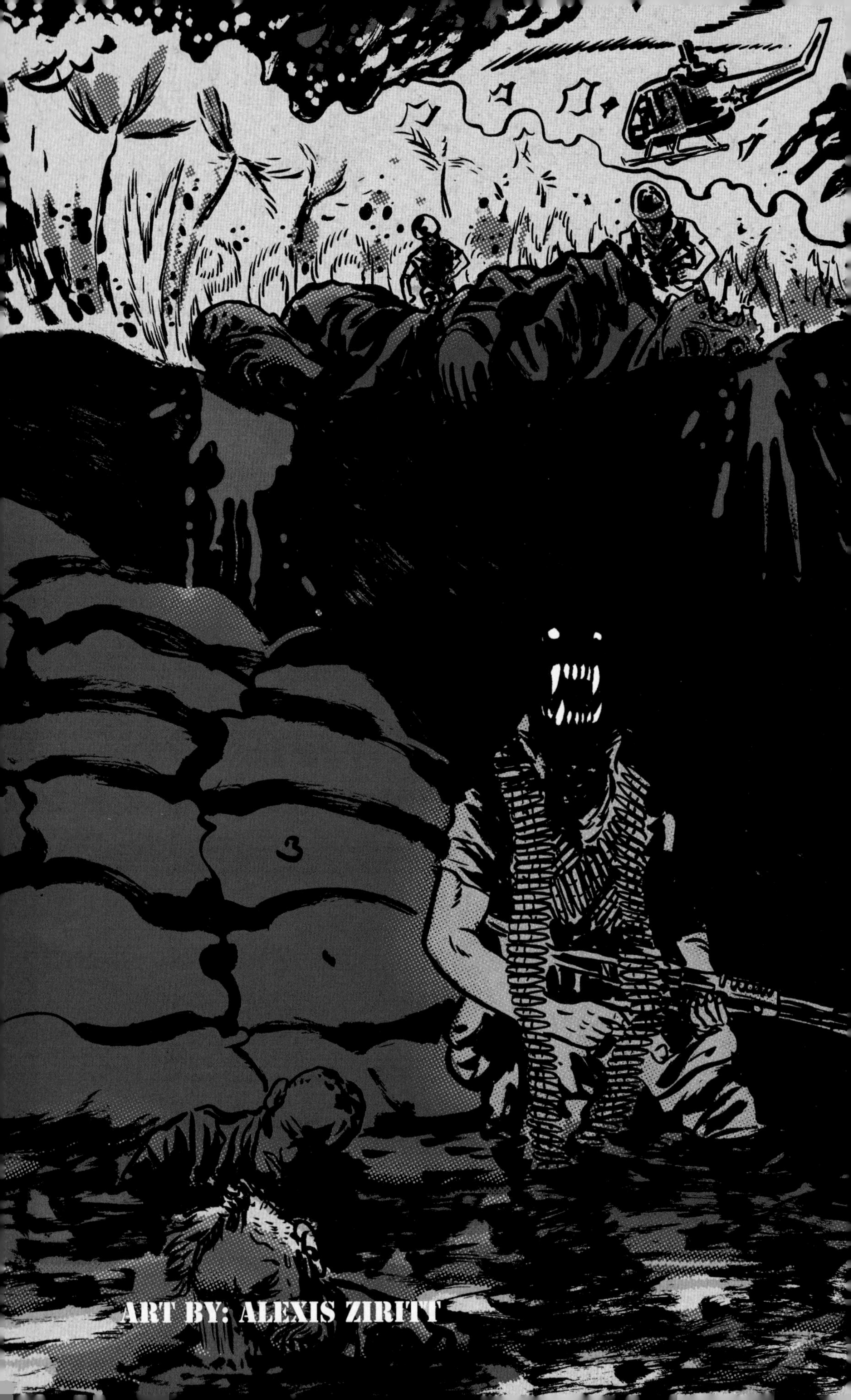
ART BY: ALEXIS ZIRITT

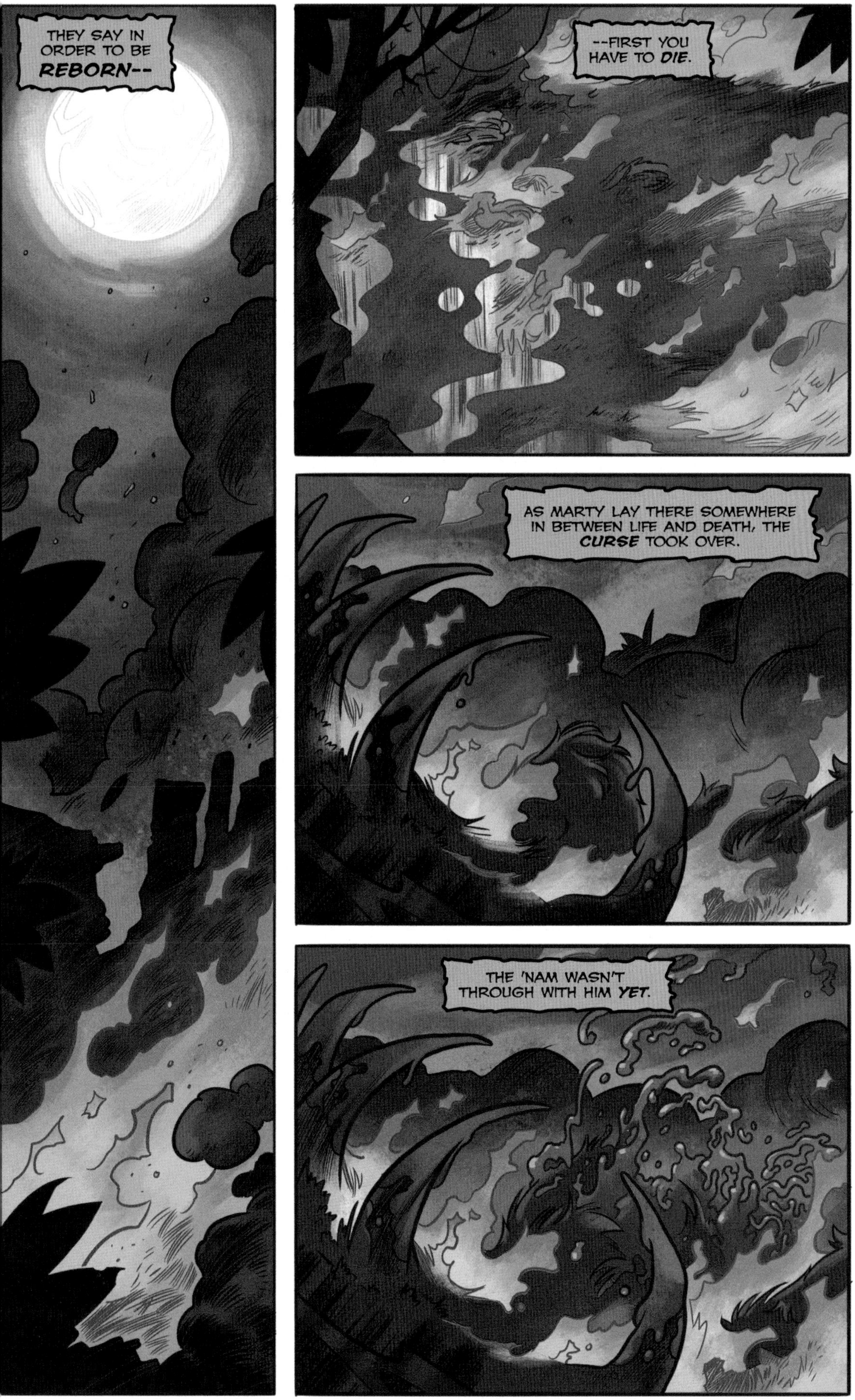
THEY SAY IN ORDER TO BE REBORN--
--FIRST YOU HAVE TO DIE.
AS MARTY LAY THERE SOMEWHERE IN BETWEEN LIFE AND DEATH, THE CURSE TOOK OVER.
THE 'NAM WASN'T THROUGH WITH HIM YET.

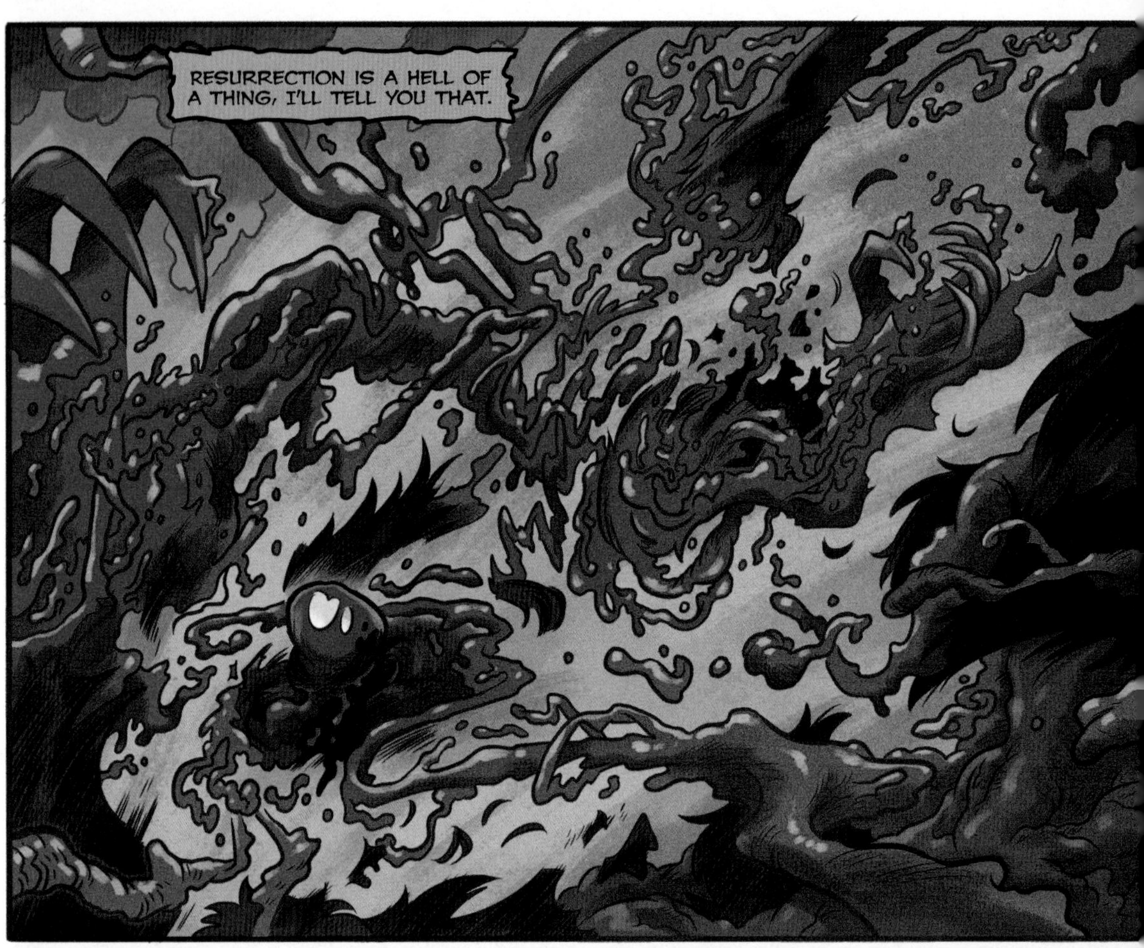
RESURRECTION IS A HELL OF A THING, I'LL TELL YOU THAT.

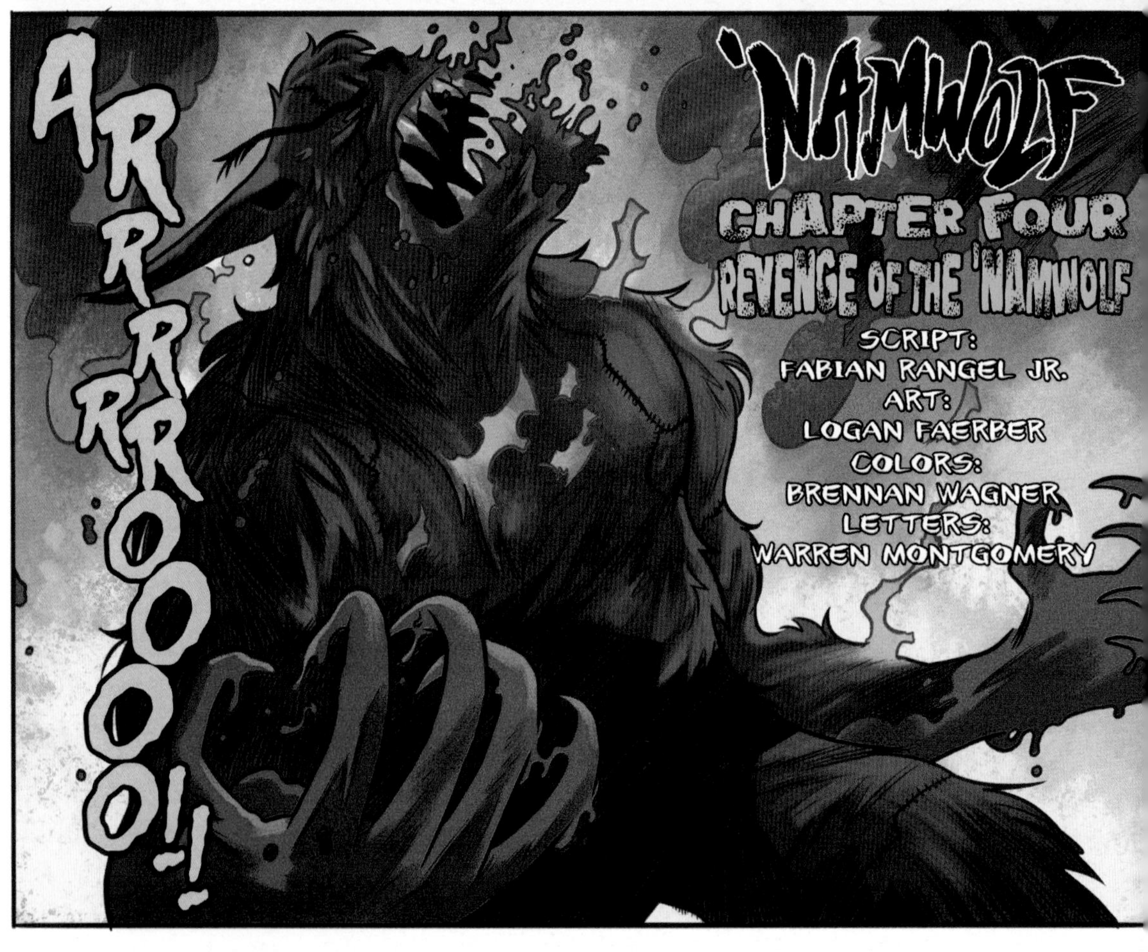
ARRRRROOOOO!!!
'NAMWOLF
CHAPTER FOUR
REVENGE OF THE 'NAMWOLF
SCRIPT:
FABIAN RANGEL JR.
ART:
LOGAN FAERBER
COLORS:
BRENNAN WAGNER
LETTERS:
WARREN MONTGOMERY

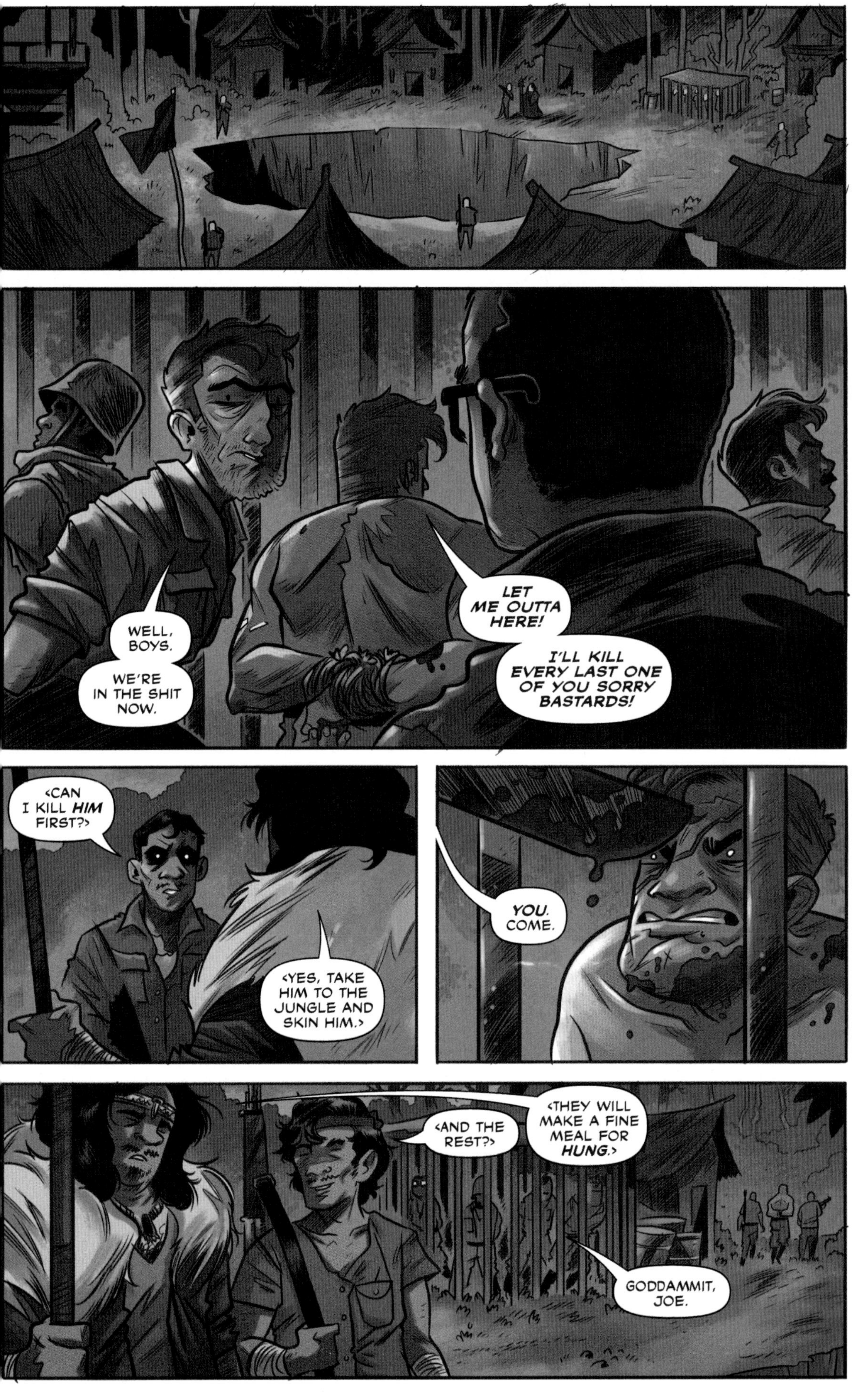
WELL, BOYS.
WE'RE IN THE SHIT NOW.
LET ME OUTTA HERE!
I'LL KILL EVERY LAST ONE OF YOU SORRY BASTARDS!
<CAN I KILL HIM FIRST?>
<YES, TAKE HIM TO THE JUNGLE AND SKIN HIM.>
YOU. COME.
<AND THE REST?>
<THEY WILL MAKE A FINE MEAL FOR HUNG.>
GODDAMMIT, JOE.

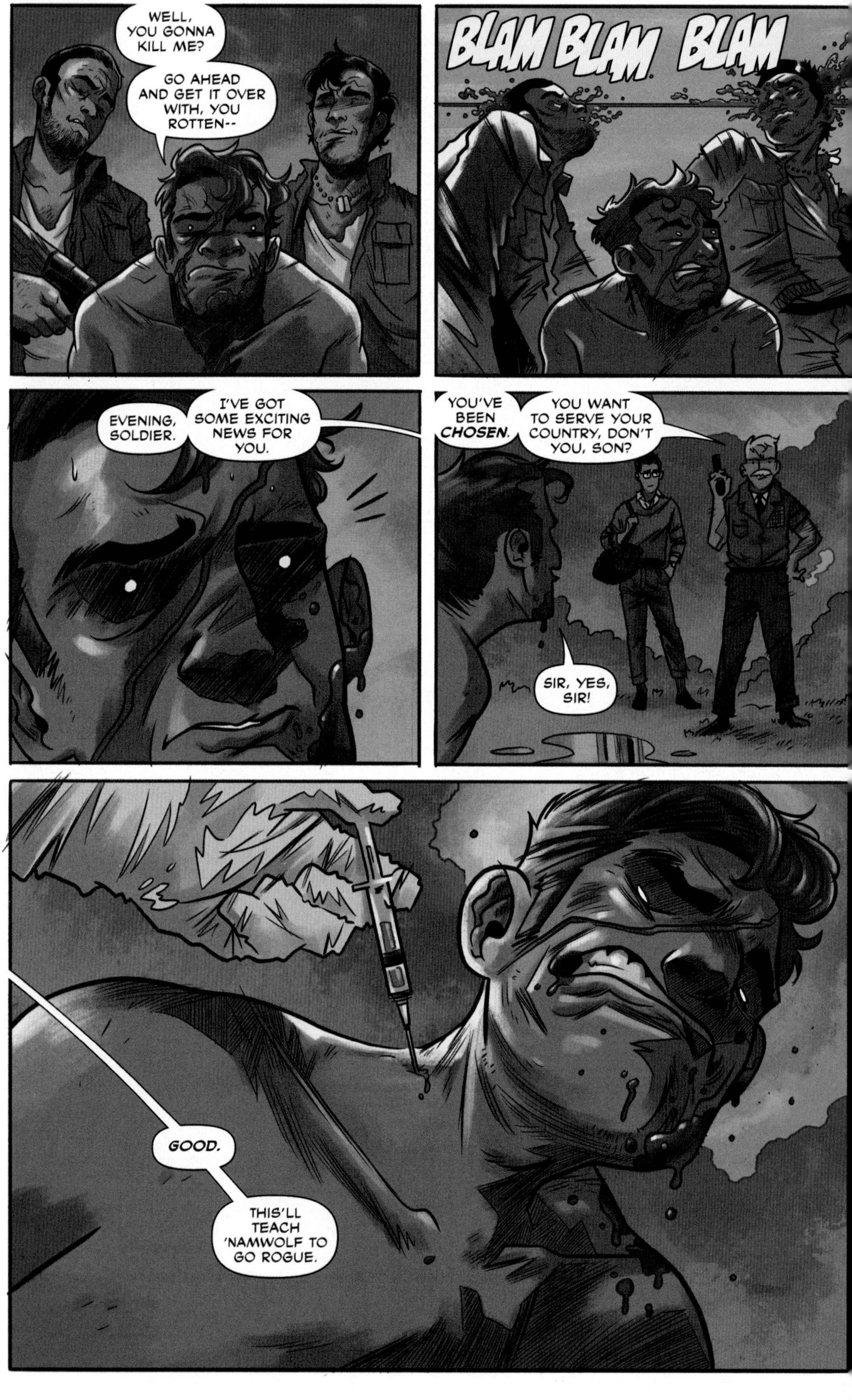
WELL, YOU GONNA KILL ME?
GO AHEAD AND GET IT OVER WITH, YOU ROTTEN--
BLAM BLAM BLAM
EVENING, SOLDIER.
I'VE GOT SOME EXCITING NEWS FOR YOU.
YOU'VE BEEN *CHOSEN*.
YOU WANT TO SERVE YOUR COUNTRY, DON'T YOU, SON?
SIR, YES, SIR!
*GOOD.*
THIS'LL TEACH 'NAMWOLF TO GO ROGUE.

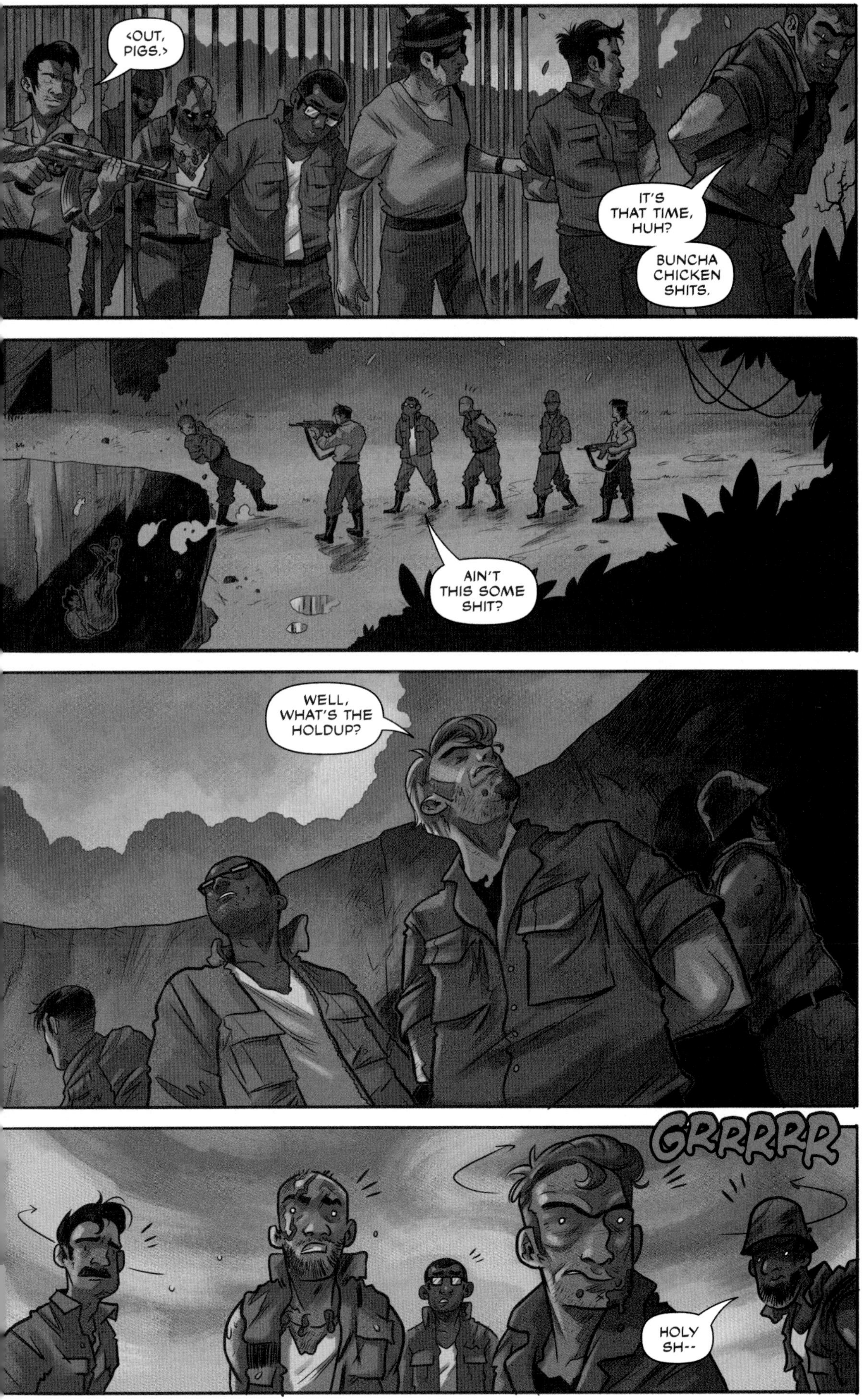
<OUT, PIGS.>
IT'S THAT TIME, HUH?
BUNCHA CHICKEN SHITS.
AIN'T THIS SOME SHIT?
WELL, WHAT'S THE HOLDUP?
GRRRRR
HOLY SH--

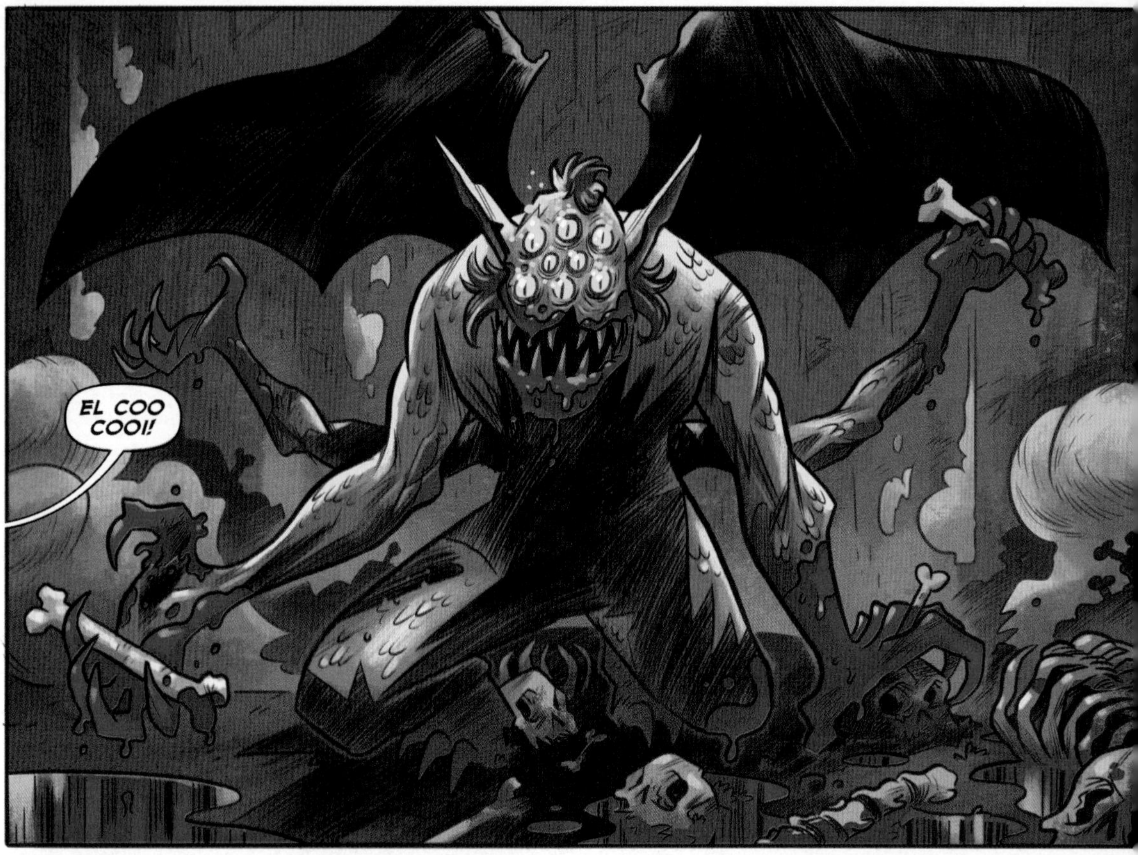
EL COO COO!!

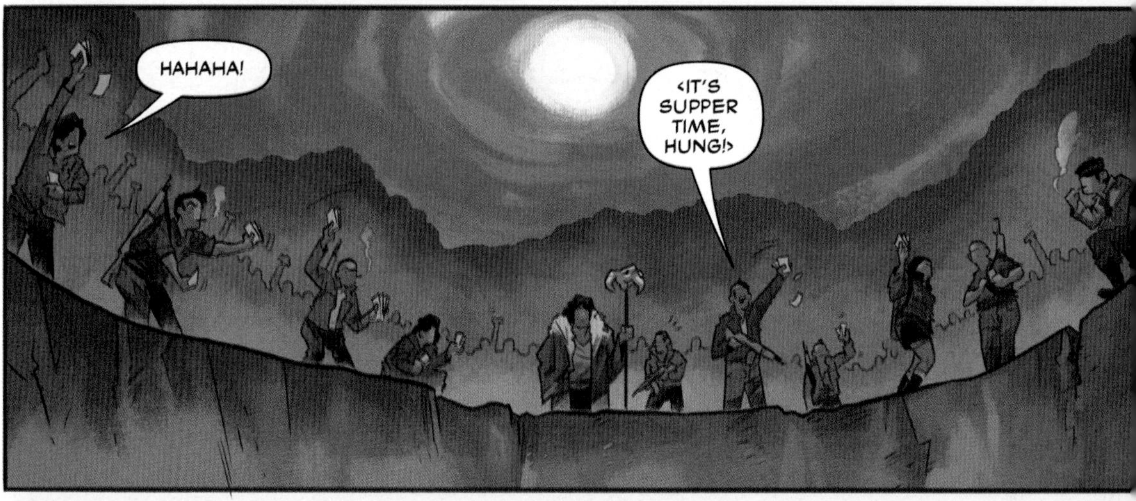
HAHAHA!
‹IT'S SUPPER TIME, HUNG!›

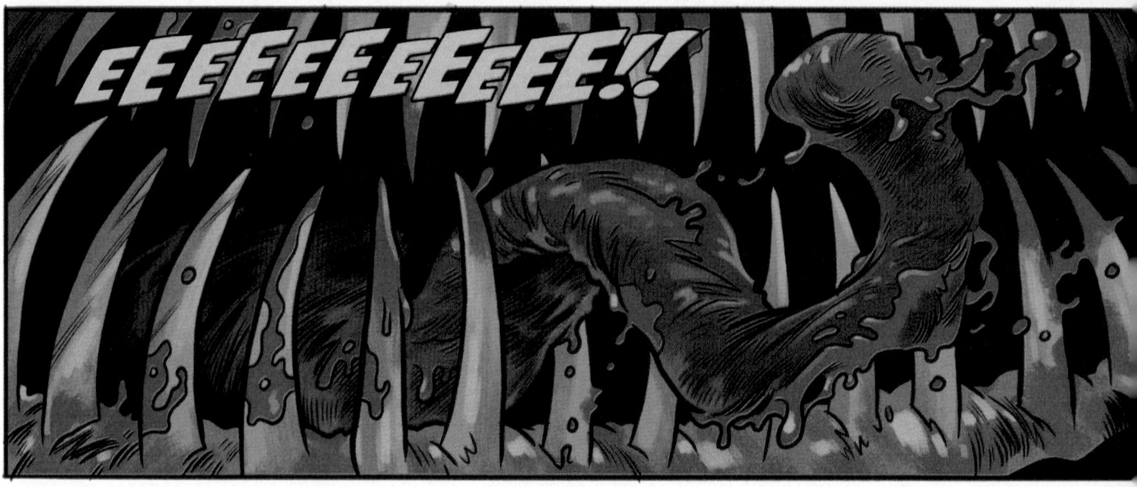
EEEEEEEEEEEE!!

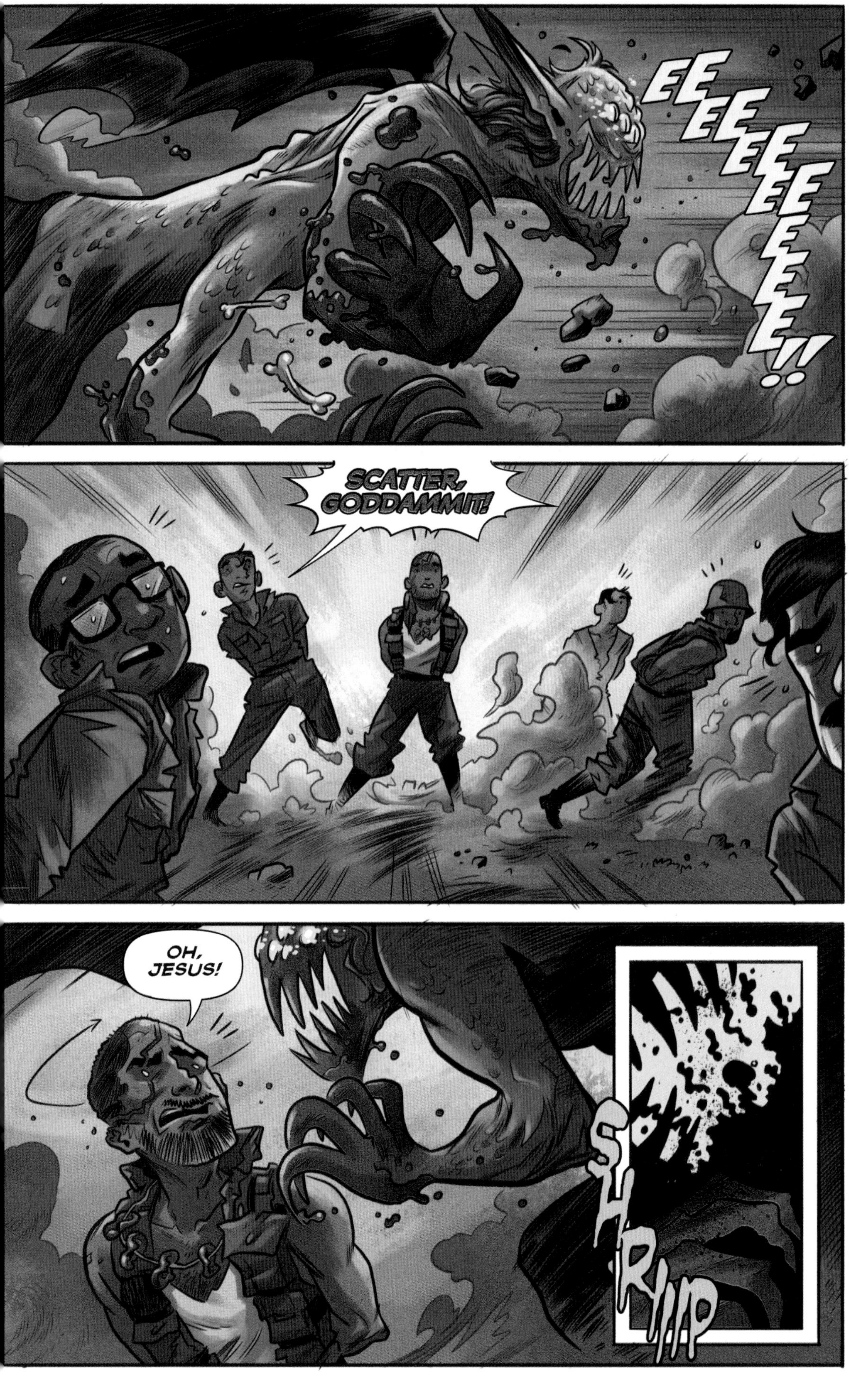
EEEEEEEEEEE!!
SCATTER, GODDAMMIT!
OH, JESUS!
SHRIIP

'NAMWOLF STARTED LOOKING FOR HIS PLATOON, KNOWING THAT SOMETHIN' BAD WAS ABOUT TO GO DOWN.

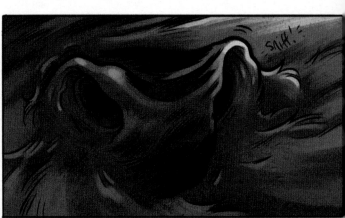

SNIFF!

AND THAT HE HAD TO *HURRY*.

AAUUGGGGHH!

RRR?

IF HE WAS GONNA SAVE THEM BOYS, HE NEEDED TO HAUL ASS.

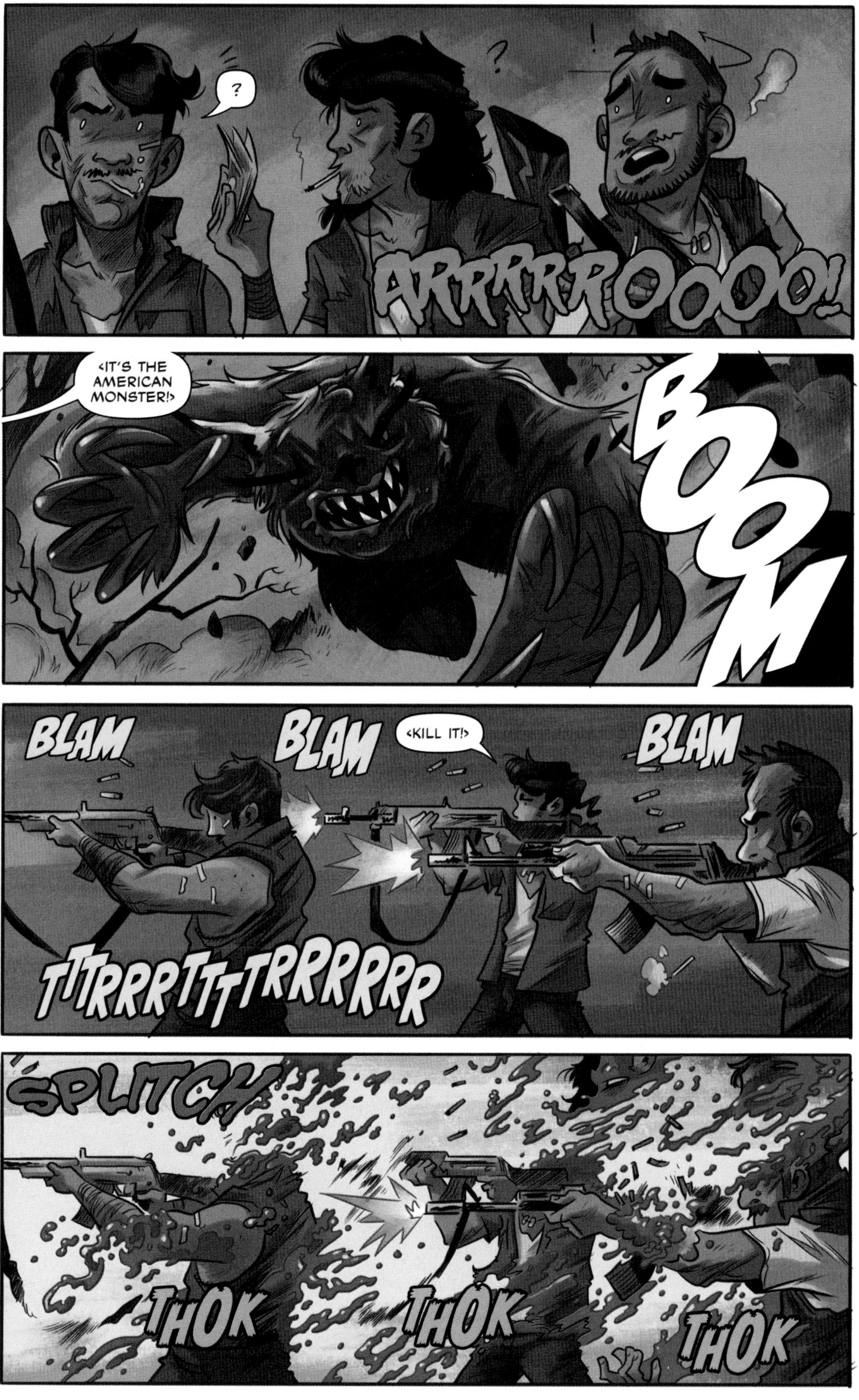
?
?
!
ARRRRRROOOO!
<IT'S THE AMERICAN MONSTER!>
BOOOM
BLAM
BLAM
<KILL IT!>
BLAM
TTTRRRTTTTRRRRRR
SPLITCH
THOK
THOK
THOK

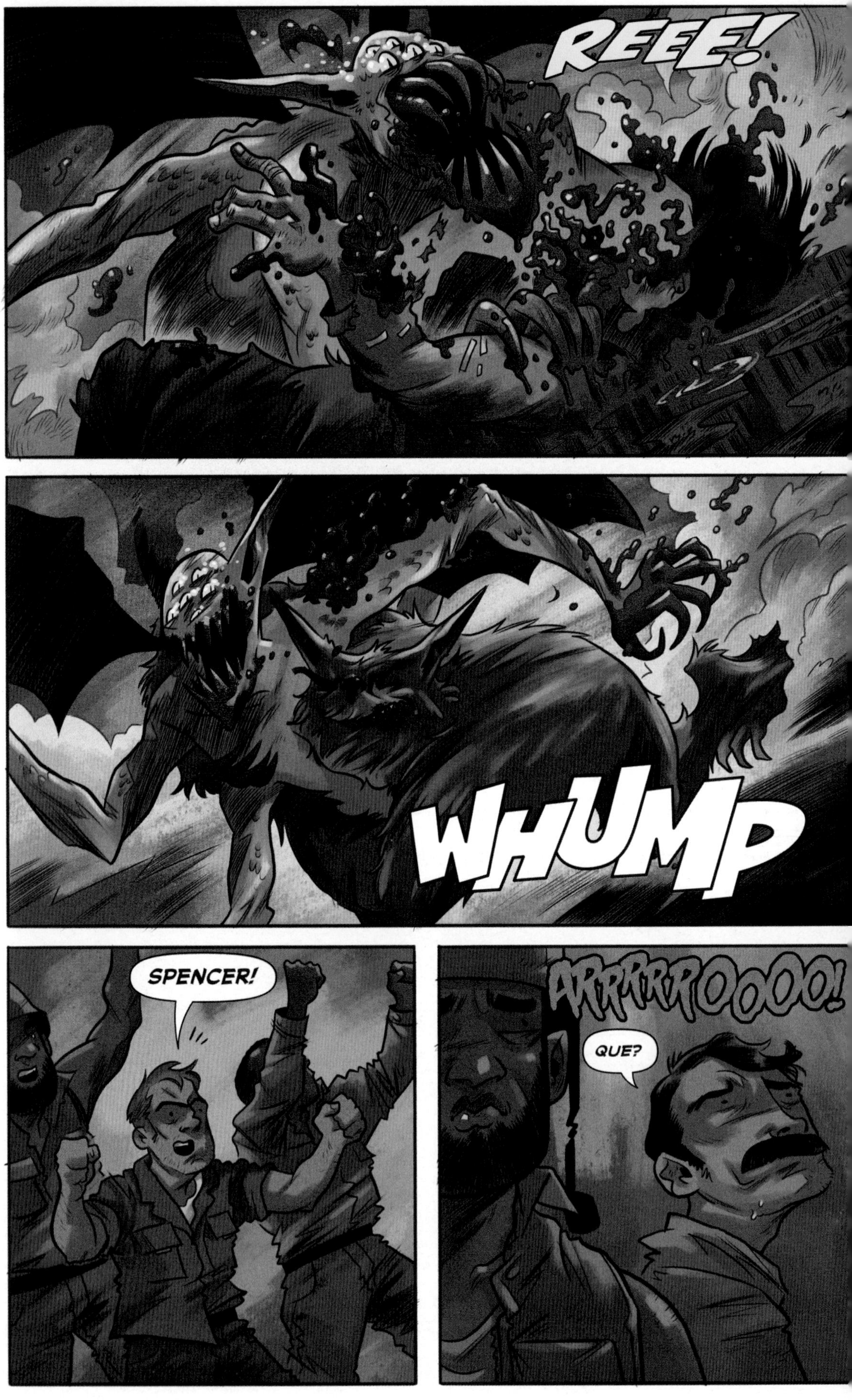
REEE!
WHUMP
SPENCER!
ARRRRRROOOO!
QUE?

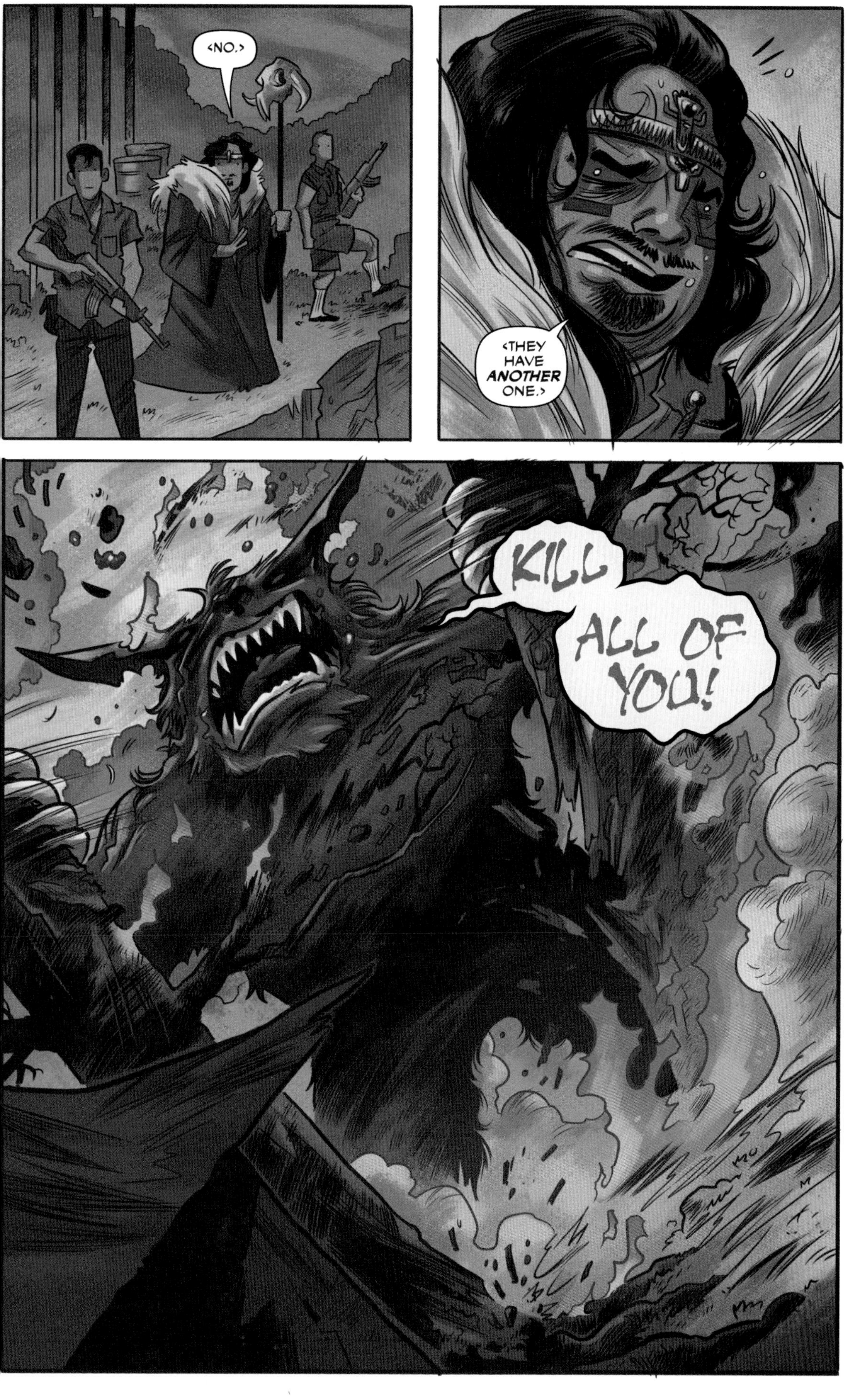
<NO.>
<THEY HAVE **ANOTHER** ONE.>
KILL
ALL OF YOU!

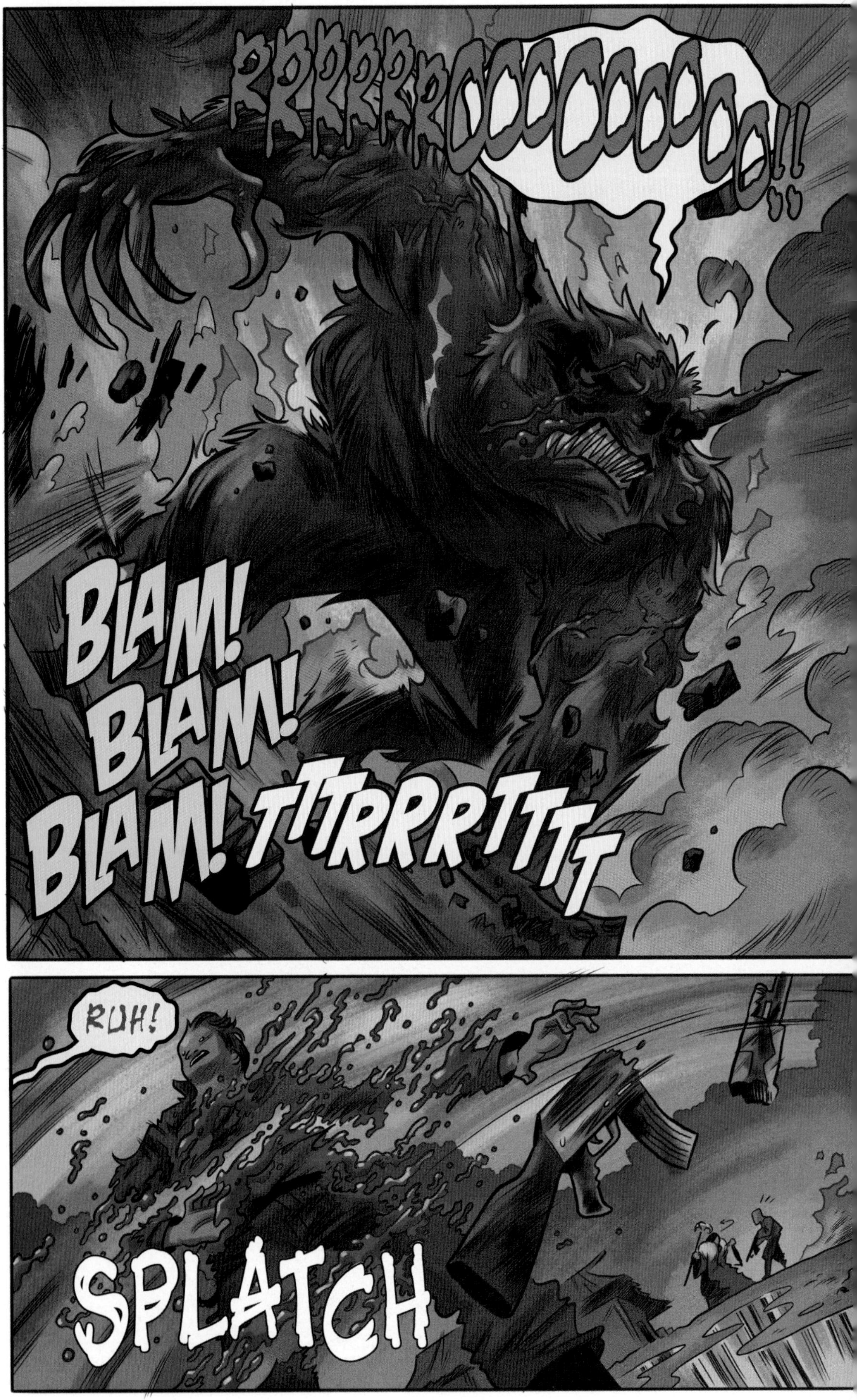
RRRRRROOOOOOOOO!!
BLAM! BLAM! BLAM!
TTTRRRTTTT
RUH!
SPLATCH

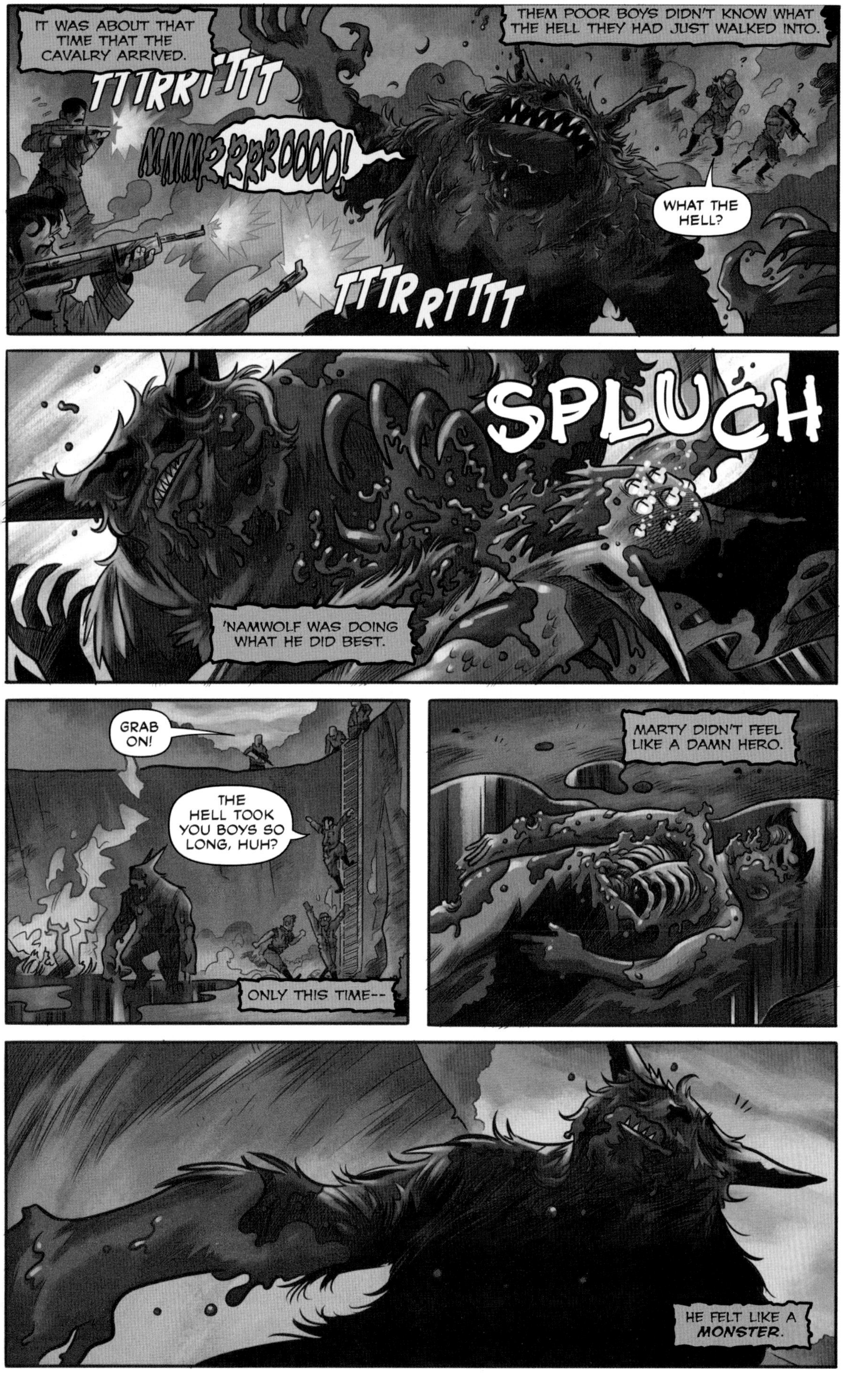
IT WAS ABOUT THAT TIME THAT THE CAVALRY ARRIVED.
THEM POOR BOYS DIDN'T KNOW WHAT THE HELL THEY HAD JUST WALKED INTO.
TTTRRTTTT
MNNNRRRROOOO!
WHAT THE HELL?
TTTR RTTTT
SPLUCH
'NAMWOLF WAS DOING WHAT HE DID BEST.
GRAB ON!
THE HELL TOOK YOU BOYS SO LONG, HUH?
ONLY THIS TIME--
MARTY DIDN'T FEEL LIKE A DAMN HERO.
HE FELT LIKE A *MONSTER*.

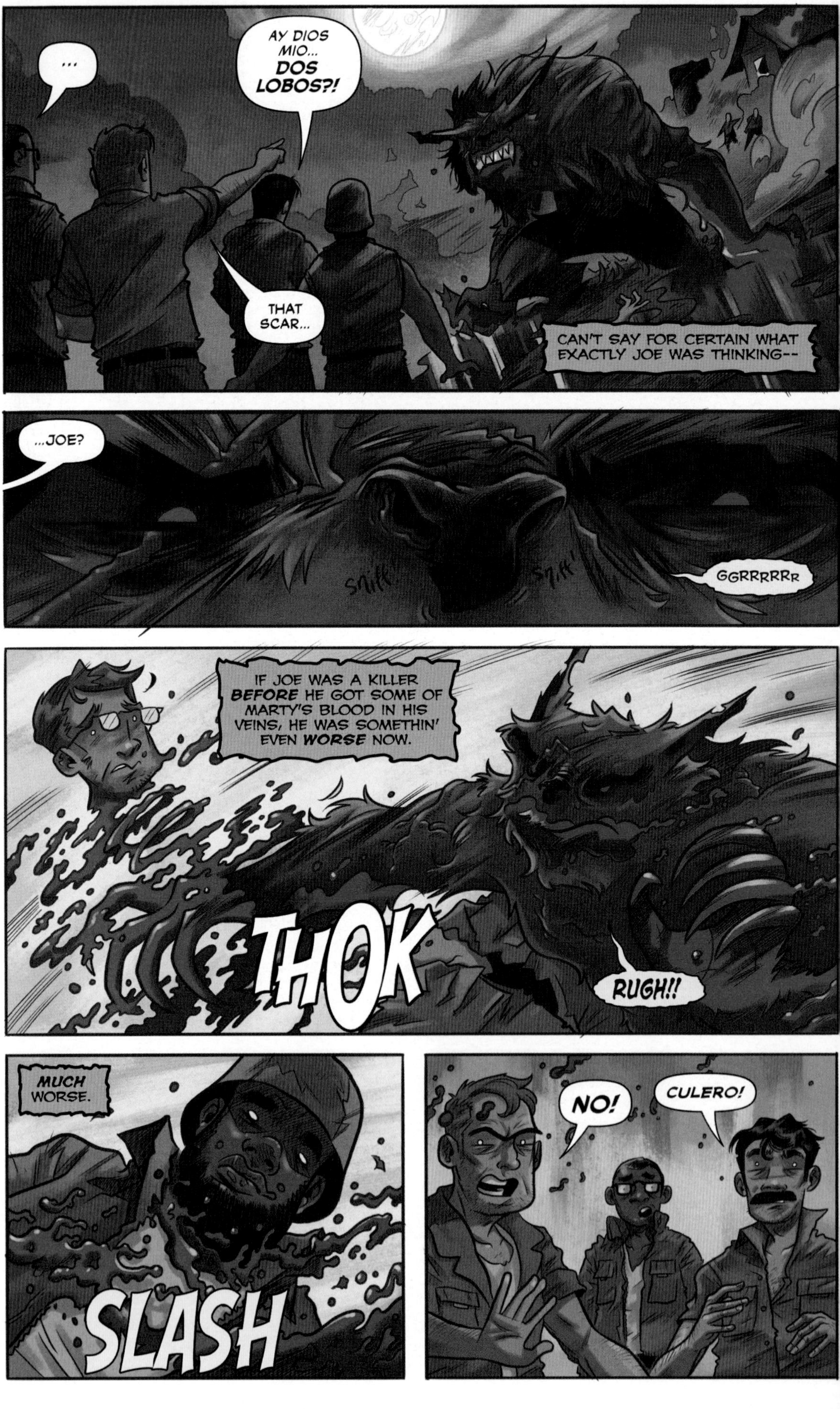
...
AY DIOS MIO... DOS LOBOS?!
THAT SCAR...
CAN'T SAY FOR CERTAIN WHAT EXACTLY JOE WAS THINKING--
...JOE?
GGRRRRRR
IF JOE WAS A KILLER BEFORE HE GOT SOME OF MARTY'S BLOOD IN HIS VEINS, HE WAS SOMETHIN' EVEN WORSE NOW.
THOK
RUGH!!
MUCH WORSE.
SLASH
NO!
CULERO!

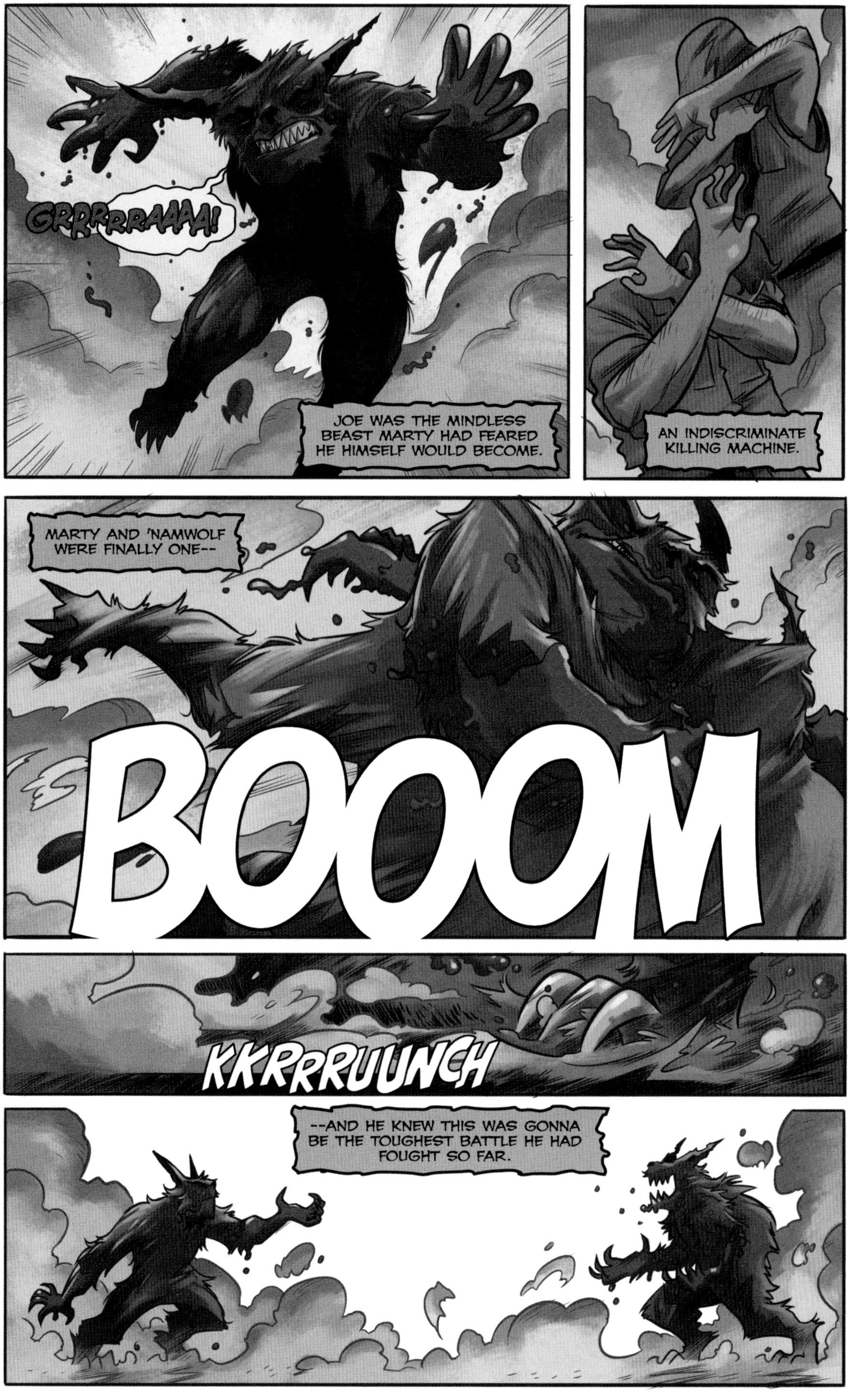
GRRRRRAAAA!
JOE WAS THE MINDLESS BEAST MARTY HAD FEARED HE HIMSELF WOULD BECOME.
AN INDISCRIMINATE KILLING MACHINE.
MARTY AND 'NAMWOLF WERE FINALLY ONE--
BOOOM
KKRRRUUNCH
--AND HE KNEW THIS WAS GONNA BE THE TOUGHEST BATTLE HE HAD FOUGHT SO FAR.

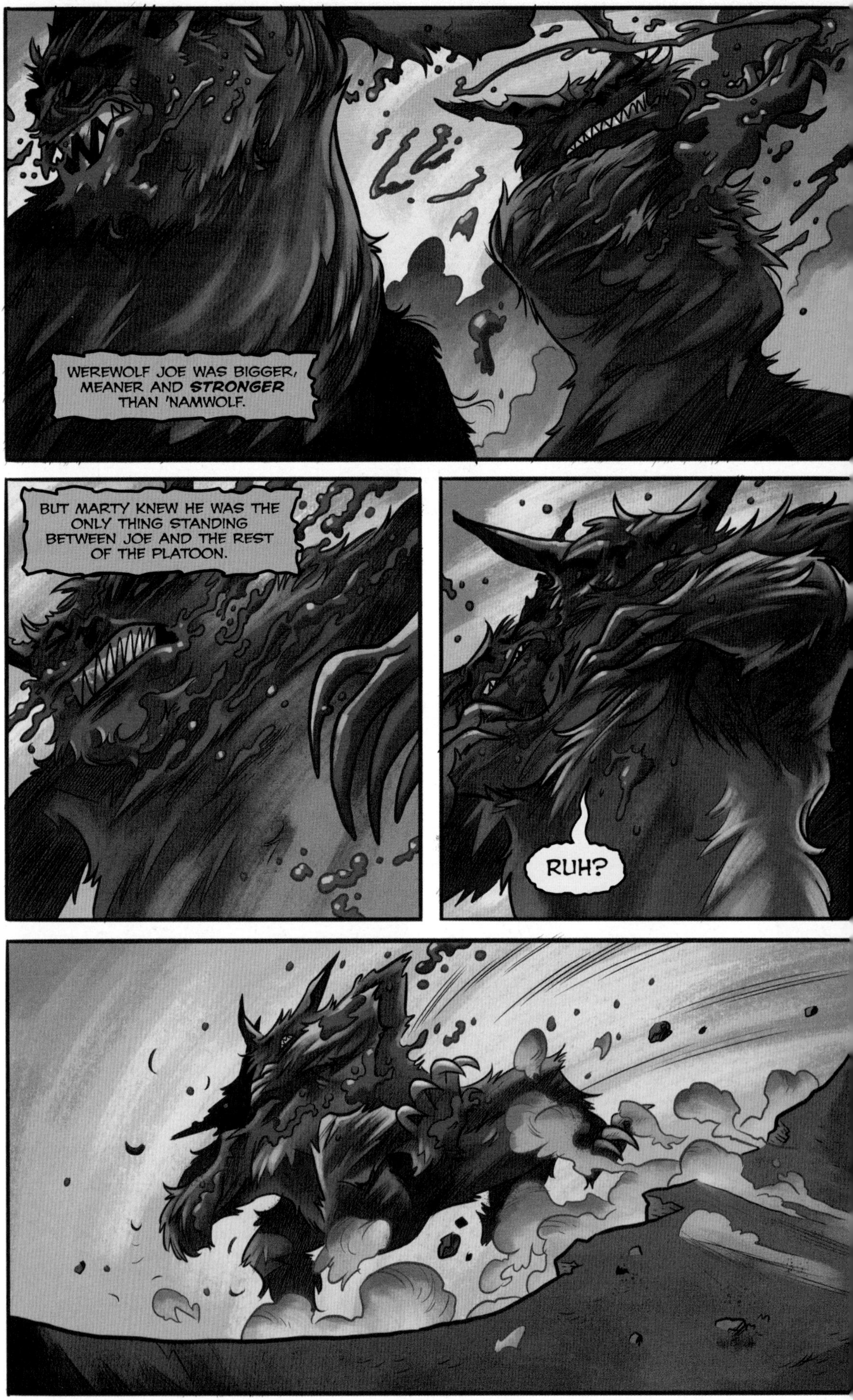
WEREWOLF JOE WAS BIGGER, MEANER AND STRONGER THAN 'NAMWOLF.
BUT MARTY KNEW HE WAS THE ONLY THING STANDING BETWEEN JOE AND THE REST OF THE PLATOON.
RUH?

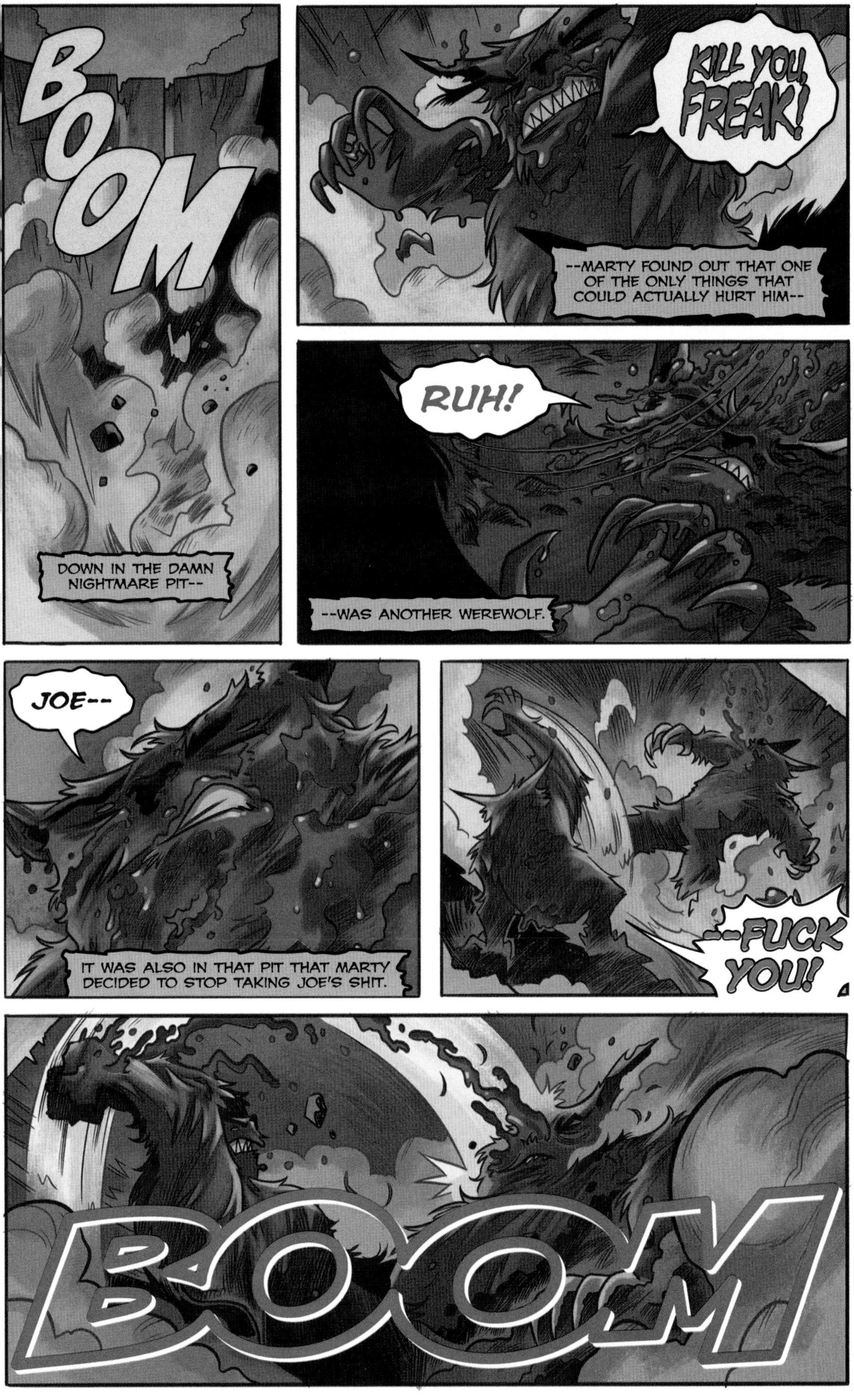
BOOM
DOWN IN THE DAMN NIGHTMARE PIT--
KILL YOU, FREAK!
--MARTY FOUND OUT THAT ONE OF THE ONLY THINGS THAT COULD ACTUALLY HURT HIM--
RUH!
--WAS ANOTHER WEREWOLF.
JOE--
IT WAS ALSO IN THAT PIT THAT MARTY DECIDED TO STOP TAKING JOE'S SHIT.
--FUCK YOU!
BOOM

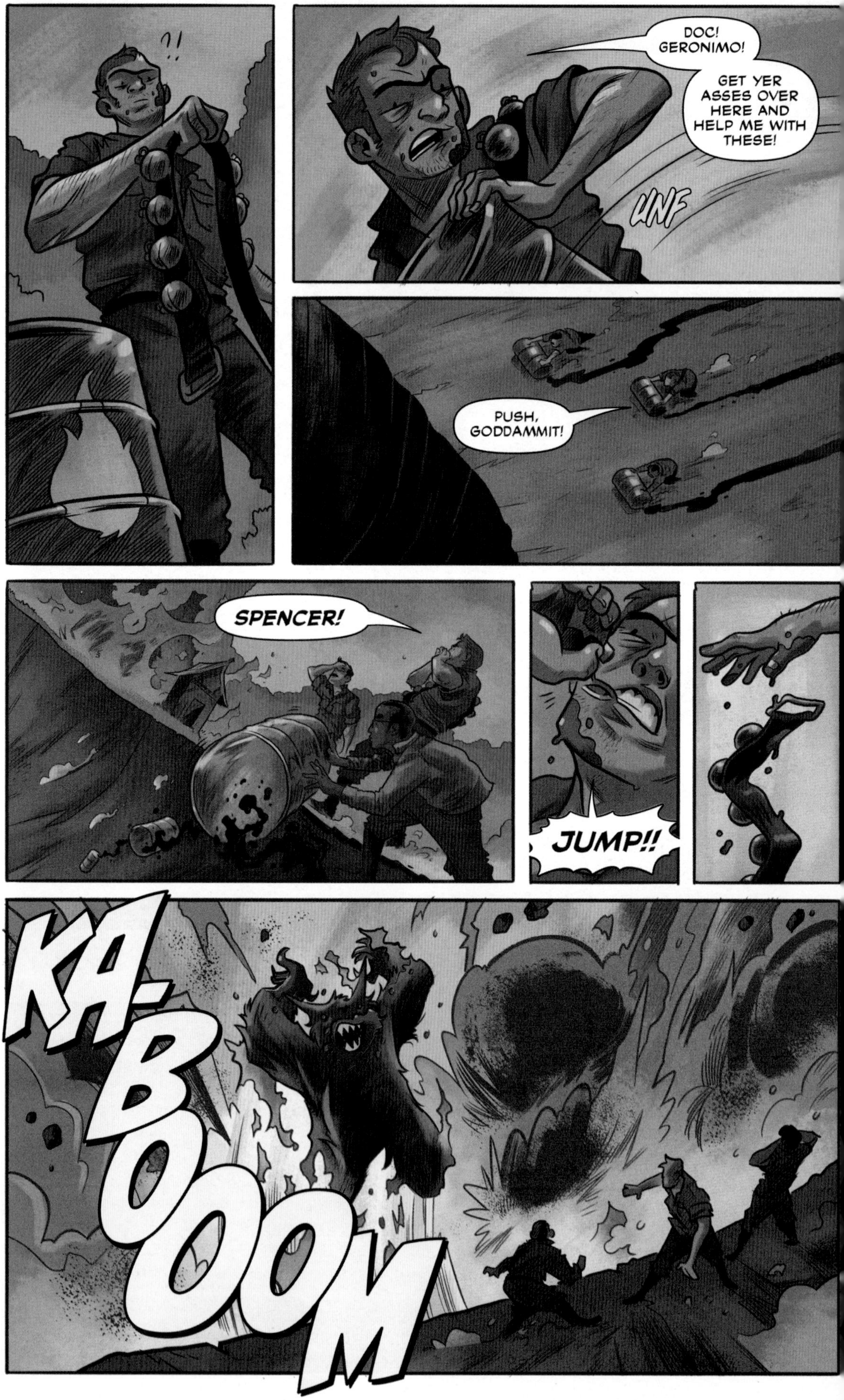
?!
DOC! GERONIMO!
GET YER ASSES OVER HERE AND HELP ME WITH THESE!
UNF
PUSH, GODDAMMIT!
SPENCER!
JUMP!!
KA-BOOOOM

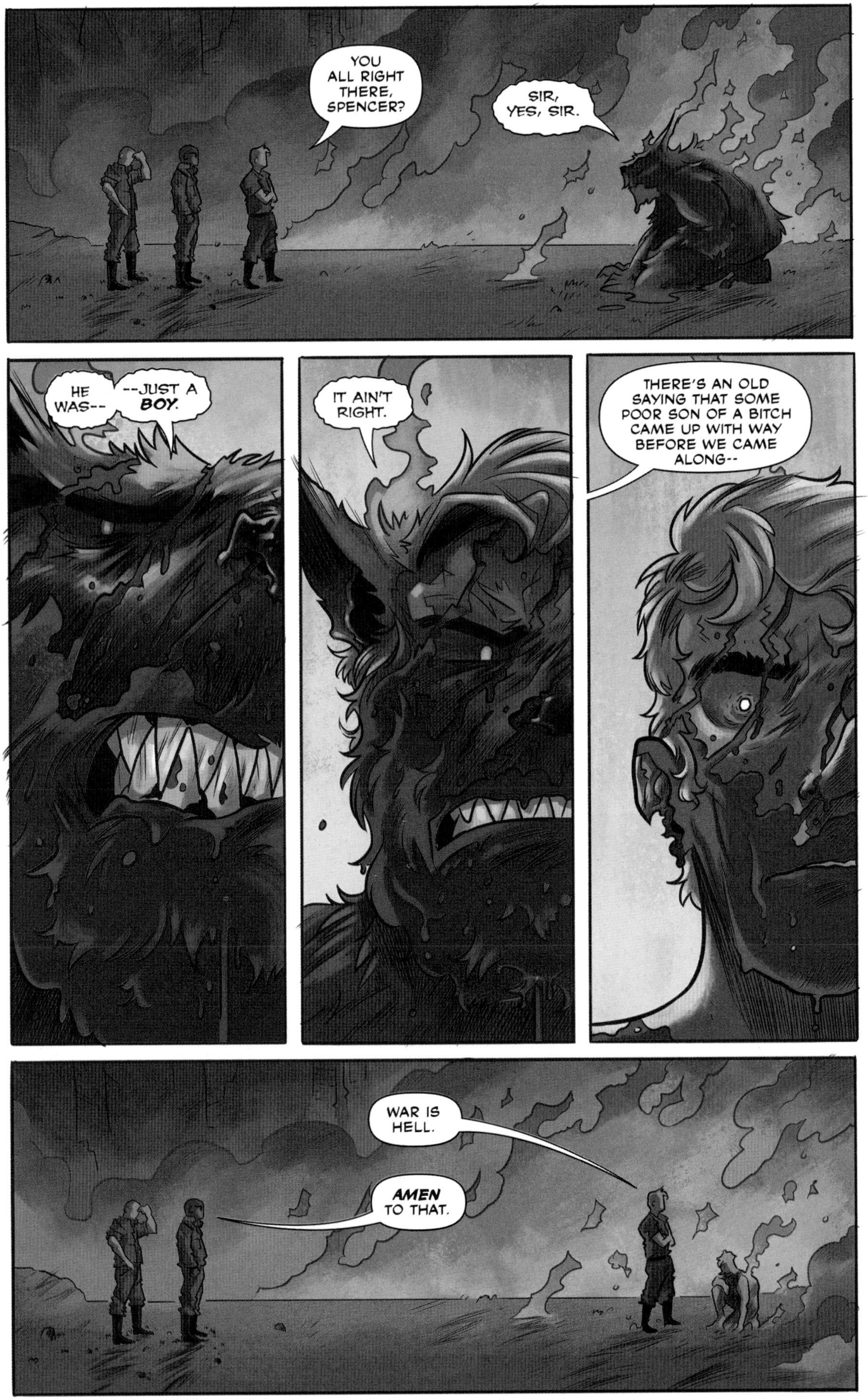
YOU ALL RIGHT THERE, SPENCER?
SIR, YES, SIR.
HE WAS--
--JUST A *BOY*.
IT AIN'T RIGHT.
THERE'S AN OLD SAYING THAT SOME POOR SON OF A BITCH CAME UP WITH WAY BEFORE WE CAME ALONG--
WAR IS HELL.
*AMEN* TO THAT.

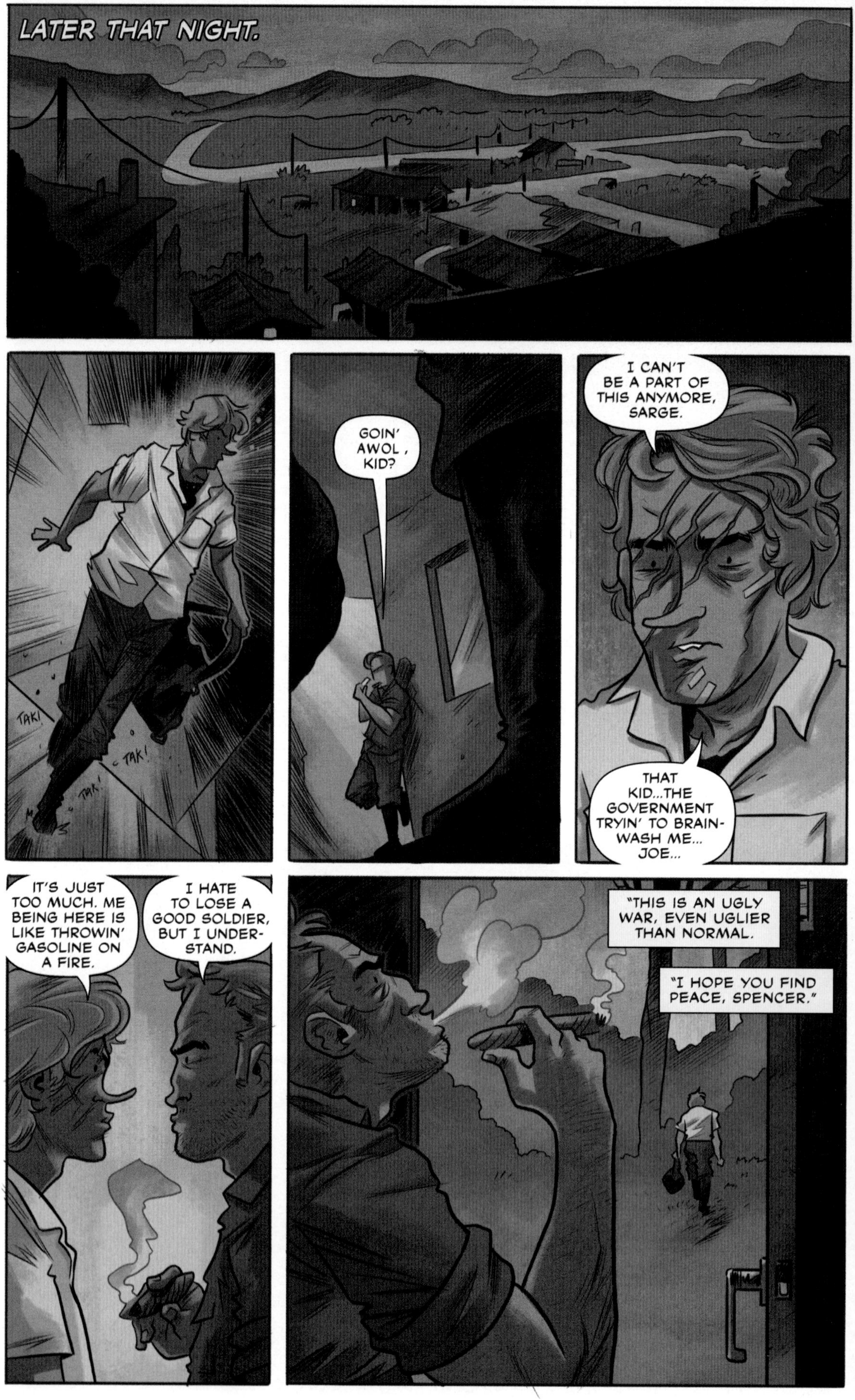
LATER THAT NIGHT.
TAK!
TAK!
TAK!
GOIN' AWOL, KID?
I CAN'T BE A PART OF THIS ANYMORE, SARGE.
THAT KID...THE GOVERNMENT TRYIN' TO BRAIN-WASH ME... JOE...
IT'S JUST TOO MUCH. ME BEING HERE IS LIKE THROWIN' GASOLINE ON A FIRE.
I HATE TO LOSE A GOOD SOLDIER, BUT I UNDER-STAND.
"THIS IS AN UGLY WAR, EVEN UGLIER THAN NORMAL.
"I HOPE YOU FIND PEACE, SPENCER."

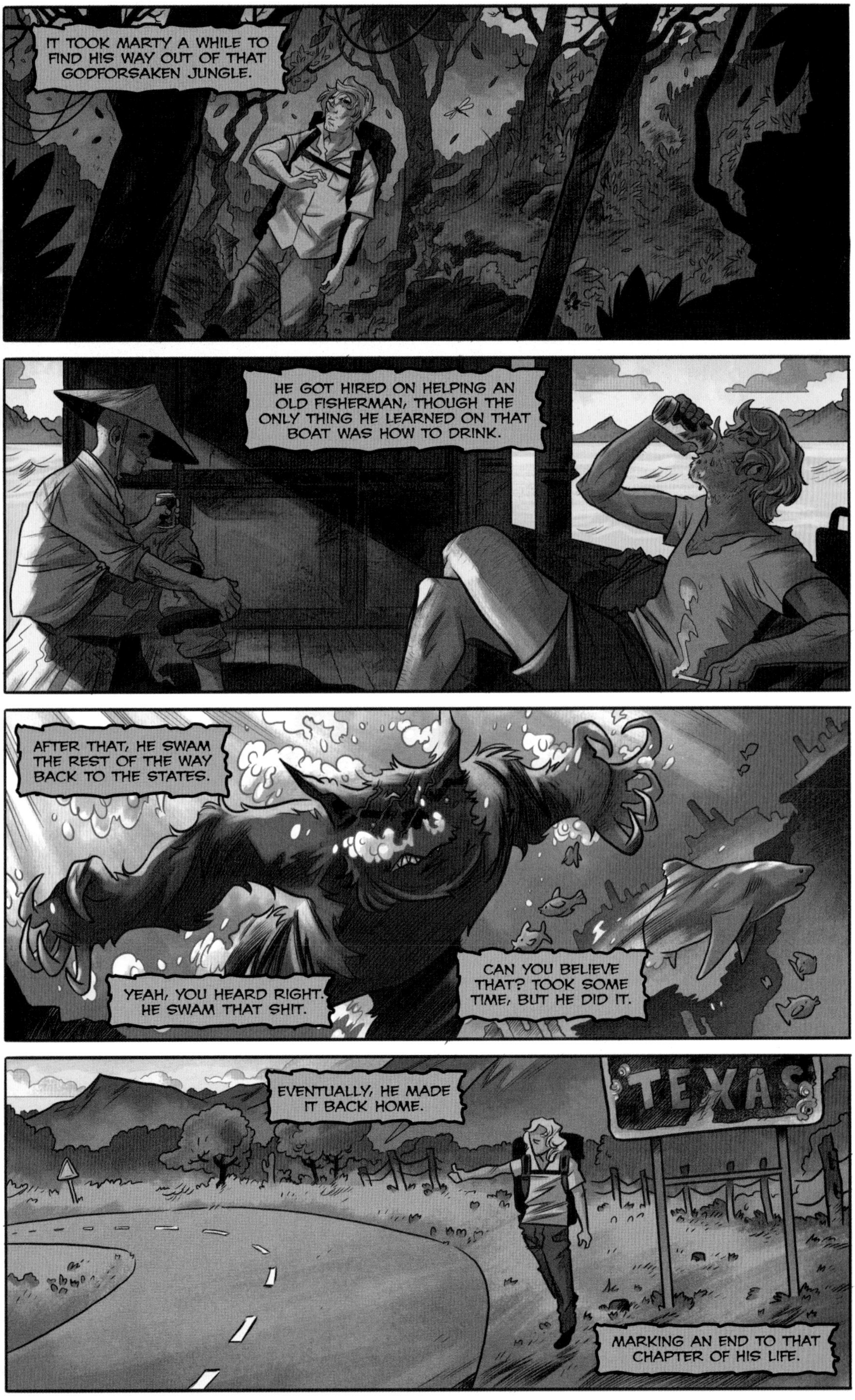
IT TOOK MARTY A WHILE TO FIND HIS WAY OUT OF THAT GODFORSAKEN JUNGLE.
HE GOT HIRED ON HELPING AN OLD FISHERMAN, THOUGH THE ONLY THING HE LEARNED ON THAT BOAT WAS HOW TO DRINK.
AFTER THAT, HE SWAM THE REST OF THE WAY BACK TO THE STATES.
YEAH, YOU HEARD RIGHT. HE SWAM THAT SHIT.
CAN YOU BELIEVE THAT? TOOK SOME TIME, BUT HE DID IT.
EVENTUALLY, HE MADE IT BACK HOME.
TEXAS
MARKING AN END TO THAT CHAPTER OF HIS LIFE.

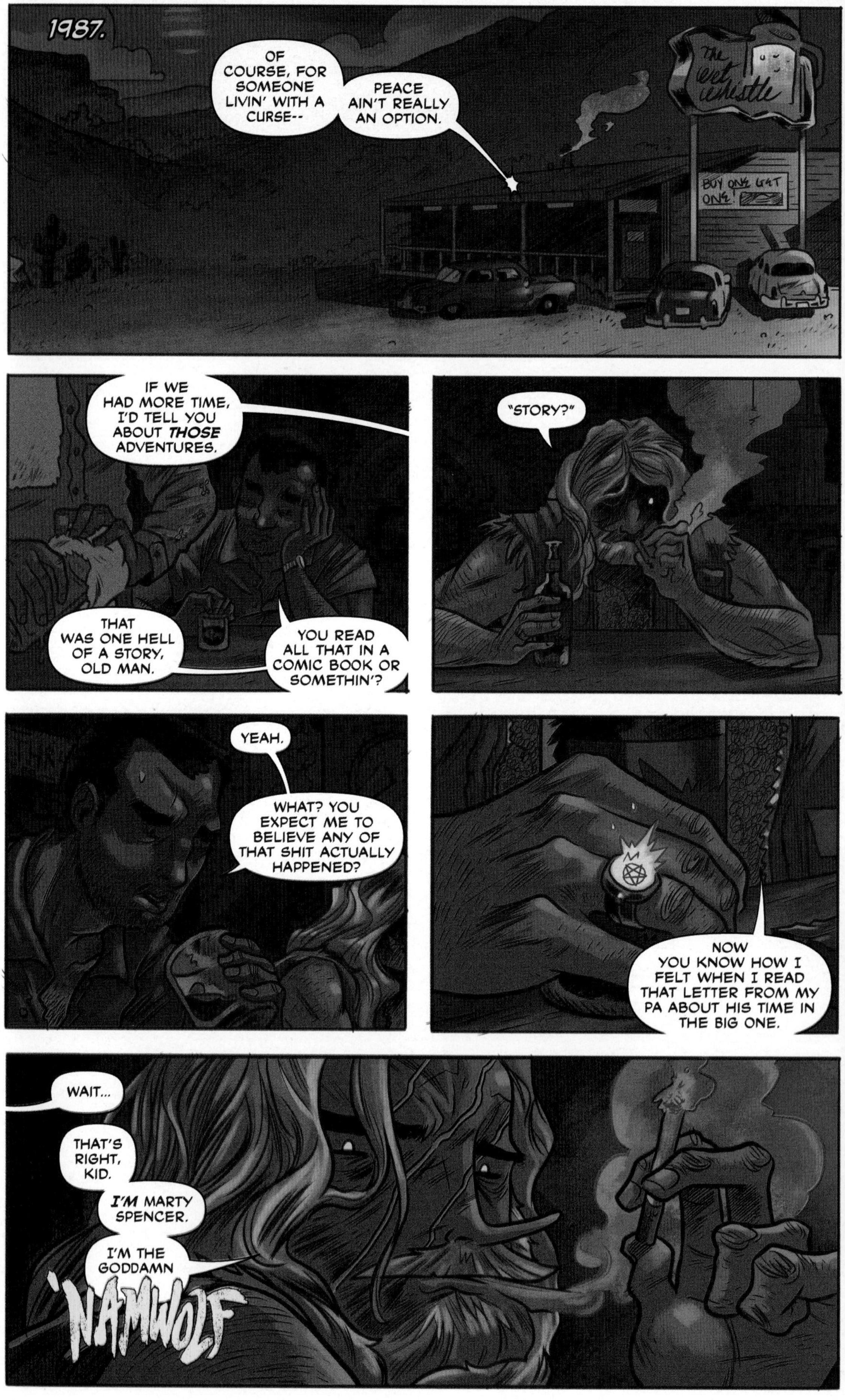
1987.
OF COURSE, FOR SOMEONE LIVIN' WITH A CURSE--
PEACE AIN'T REALLY AN OPTION.
The wet whistle
BUY ONE GET ONE
IF WE HAD MORE TIME, I'D TELL YOU ABOUT *THOSE* ADVENTURES.
THAT WAS ONE HELL OF A STORY, OLD MAN.
YOU READ ALL THAT IN A COMIC BOOK OR SOMETHIN'?
"STORY?"
YEAH.
WHAT? YOU EXPECT ME TO BELIEVE ANY OF THAT SHIT ACTUALLY HAPPENED?
NOW YOU KNOW HOW I FELT WHEN I READ THAT LETTER FROM MY PA ABOUT HIS TIME IN THE BIG ONE.
WAIT...
THAT'S RIGHT, KID.
*I'M* MARTY SPENCER.
I'M THE GODDAMN
'NAMWOLF

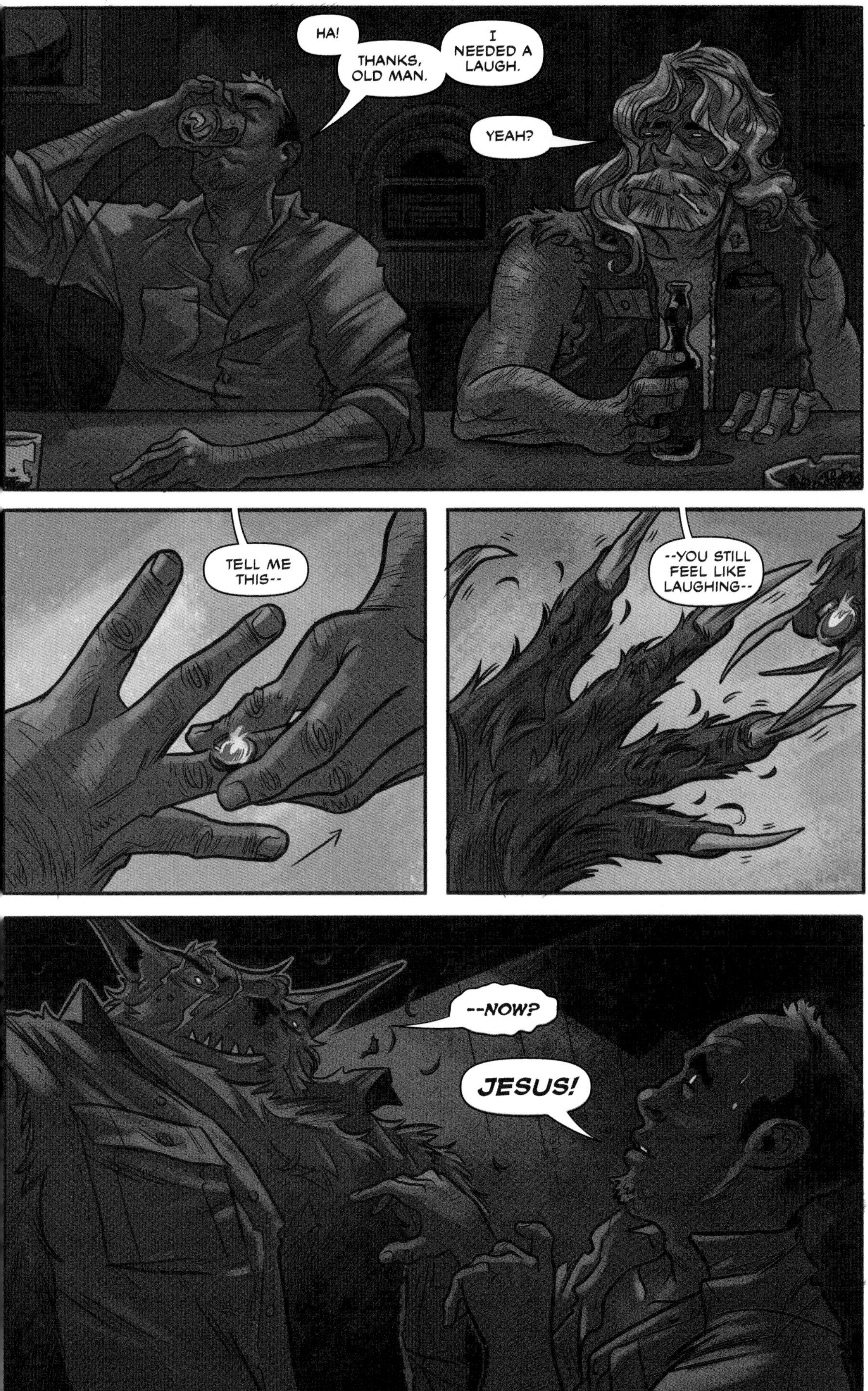
HA!
THANKS, OLD MAN.
I NEEDED A LAUGH.
YEAH?
TELL ME THIS--
--YOU STILL FEEL LIKE LAUGHING--
--NOW?
JESUS!

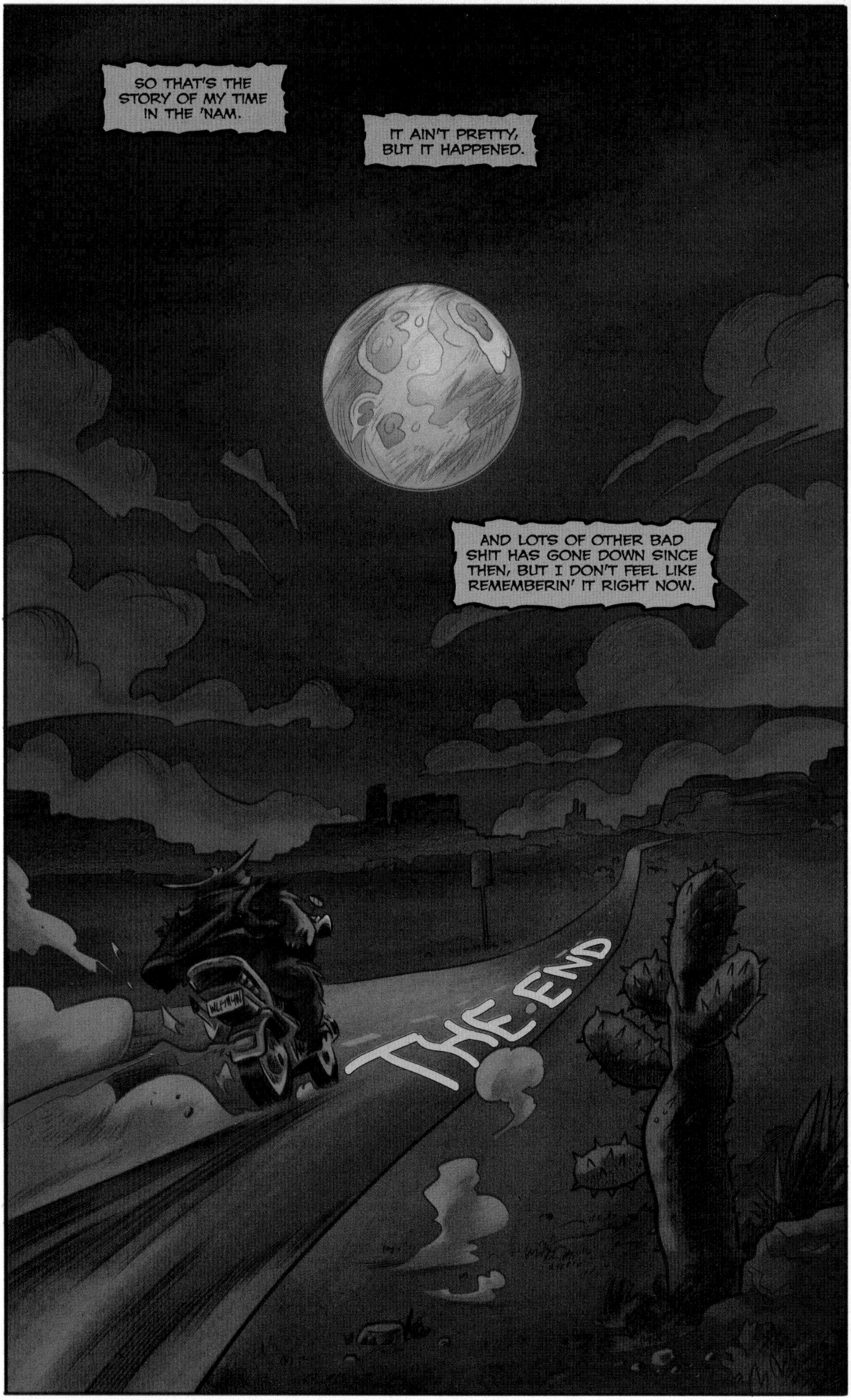
SO THAT'S THE STORY OF MY TIME IN THE 'NAM.
IT AIN'T PRETTY, BUT IT HAPPENED.
AND LOTS OF OTHER BAD SHIT HAS GONE DOWN SINCE THEN, BUT I DON'T FEEL LIKE REMEMBERIN' IT RIGHT NOW.
THE END

# THE ORIGINAL 'NAMWOLF PITCH

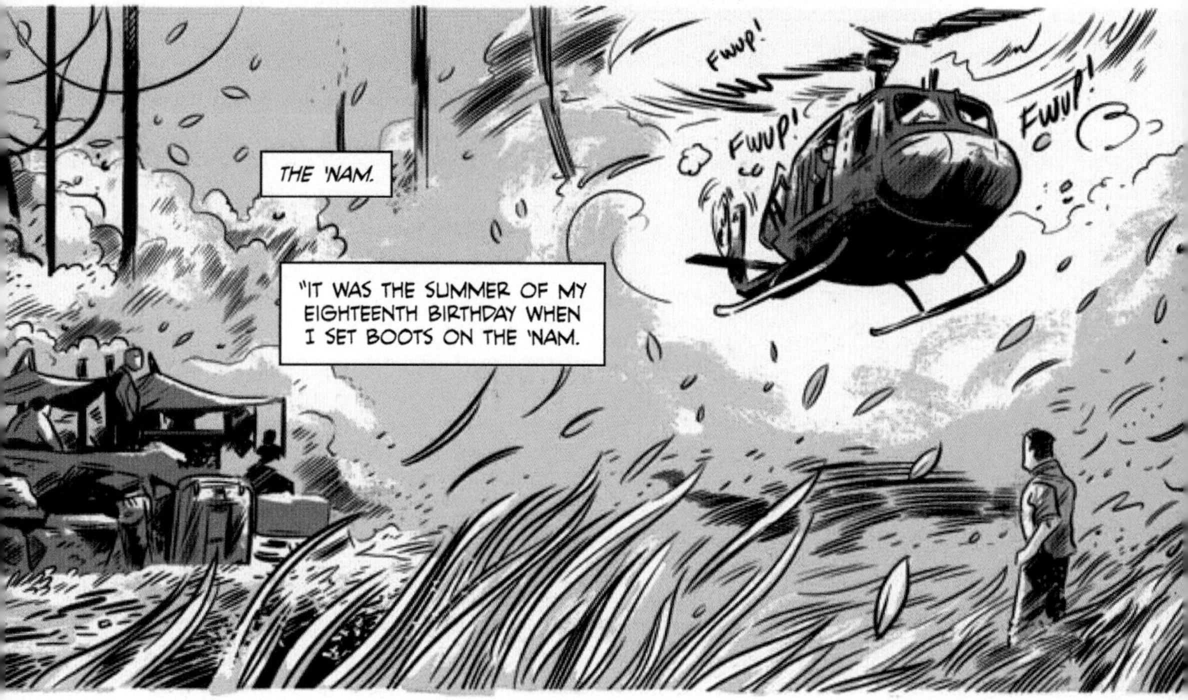
THE 'NAM.
"IT WAS THE SUMMER OF MY EIGHTEENTH BIRTHDAY WHEN I SET BOOTS ON THE 'NAM.
FWUP!
FWUP!
FWUP!

What follows is the original 'Namwolf pitch. Back at HeroesCon 2014, I was tabling with Alexis Ziritt, and we were next to Logan [Faerber]. Logan and I were chatting and getting to know each other. We started talking about movies we liked, and I could have sworn I heard him say "American Werewolf in Vietnam." We thought that was funny and cool. We tossed some ideas back and forth jokingly, but after the con, I couldn't get the idea out of my head. I came up with the name 'Namwolf and asked Logan if he wanted to try and actually make the comic. He said yes, and we did these pages. Fast forward a couple of years—after rejections from publishers and an ashcan—to me reading that Eric [Powell] would be publishing other people's comics through Albatross. I had a feeling he would dig 'Namwolf.

And at HeroesCon 2016, we made it official.

I chose the name Marty for the protagonist because of Back to the Future, since Michael J. Fox had played Teen Wolf, and because Fox was also in Casualties of War. At first, Marty's last name was Powell, because I'd recently rediscovered a piece Eric had done for one of my older comics, Doc Unknown. When we eventually pitched 'Namwolf to Eric, he dug the pitch but asked us to change Marty's last name, assuming people would think he was some kind of controlling egomaniac who demanded we name the main character after him. So I went on Twitter and saw Kirk Spencer was on, a guy who has bought every comic I've ever done. I gave Marty his last name as a thank-you.

- Fabian Rangel Jr.

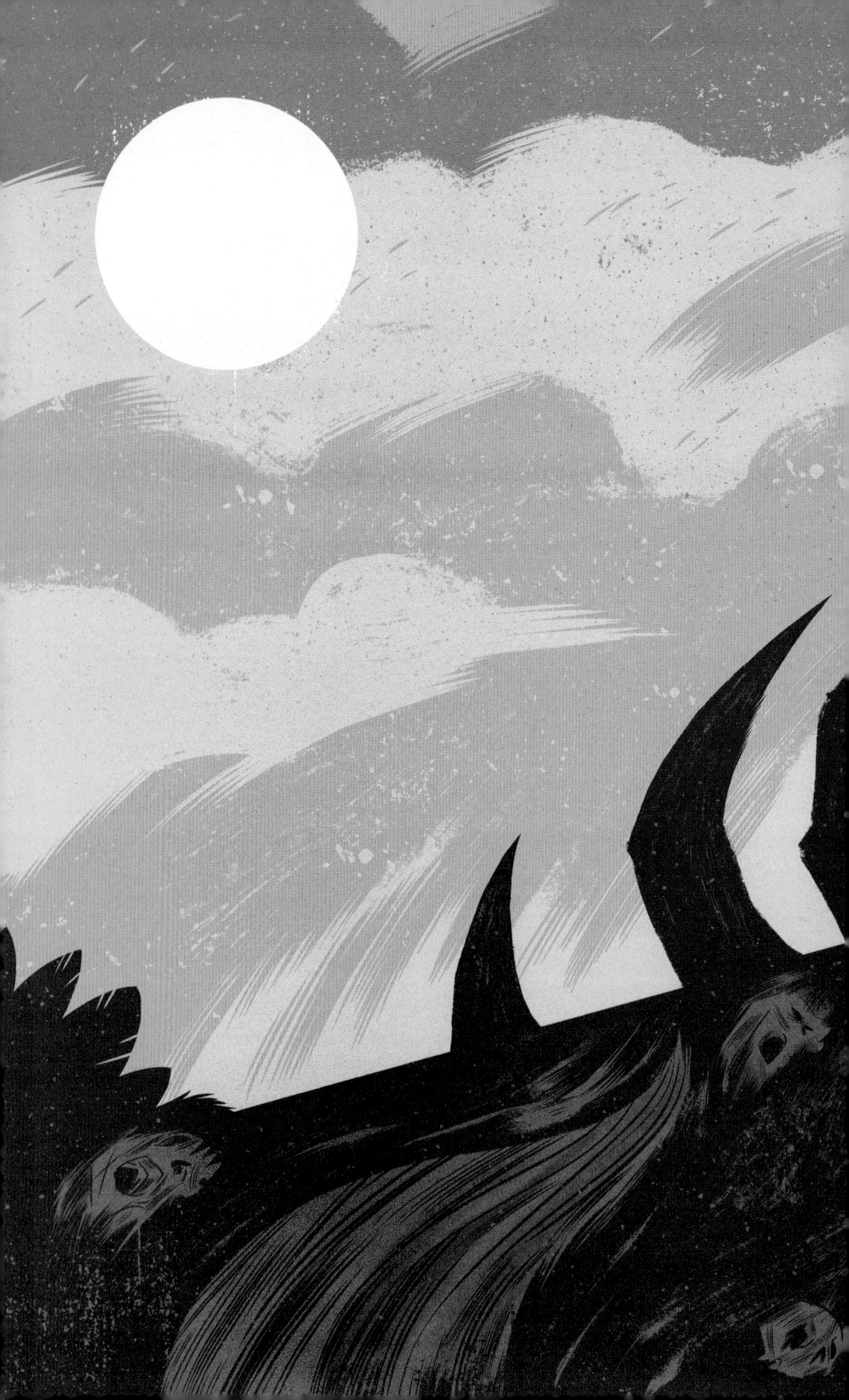

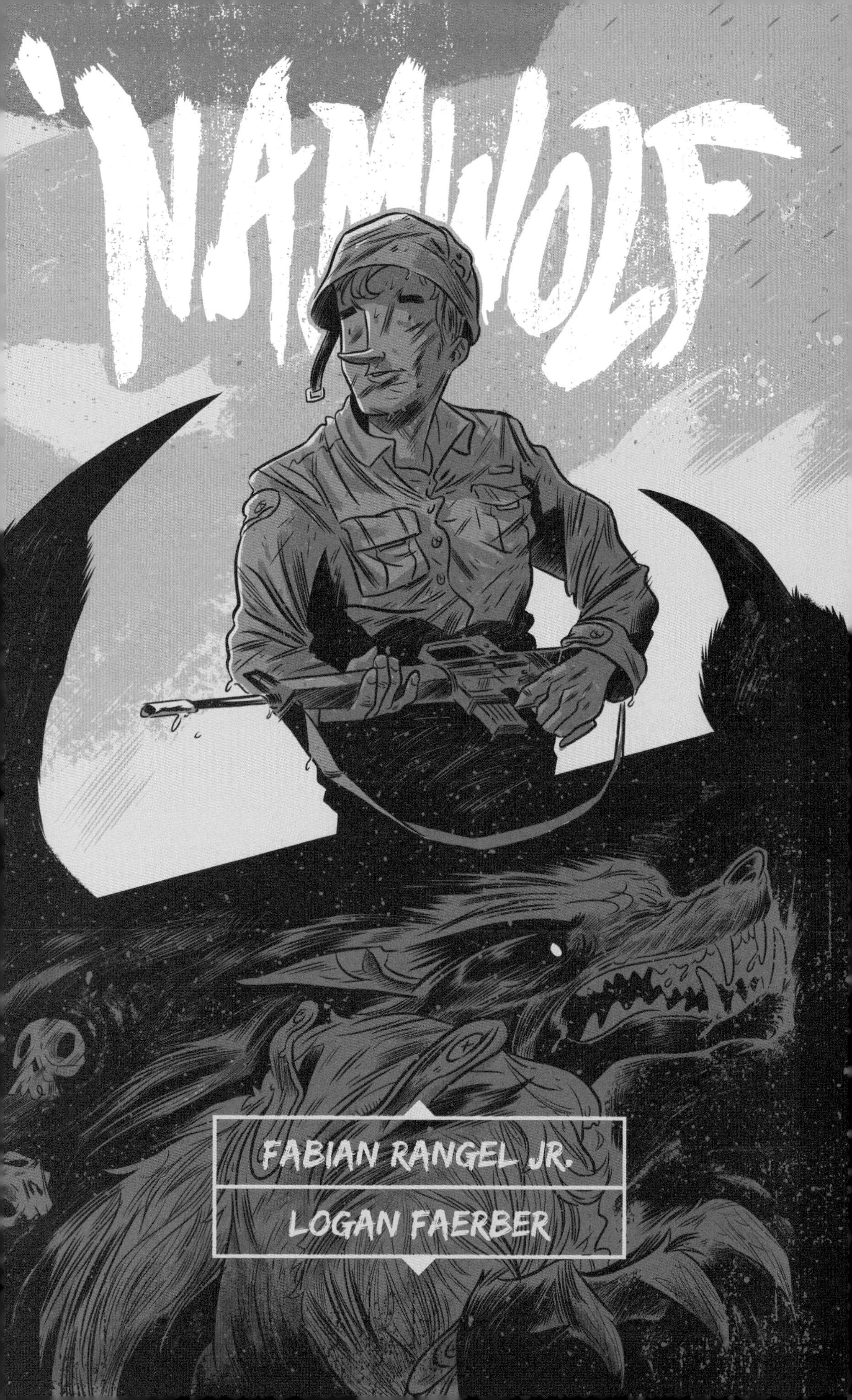
'NAMWOLF
FABIAN RANGEL JR.
LOGAN FAERBER

# 'NAMWOLF

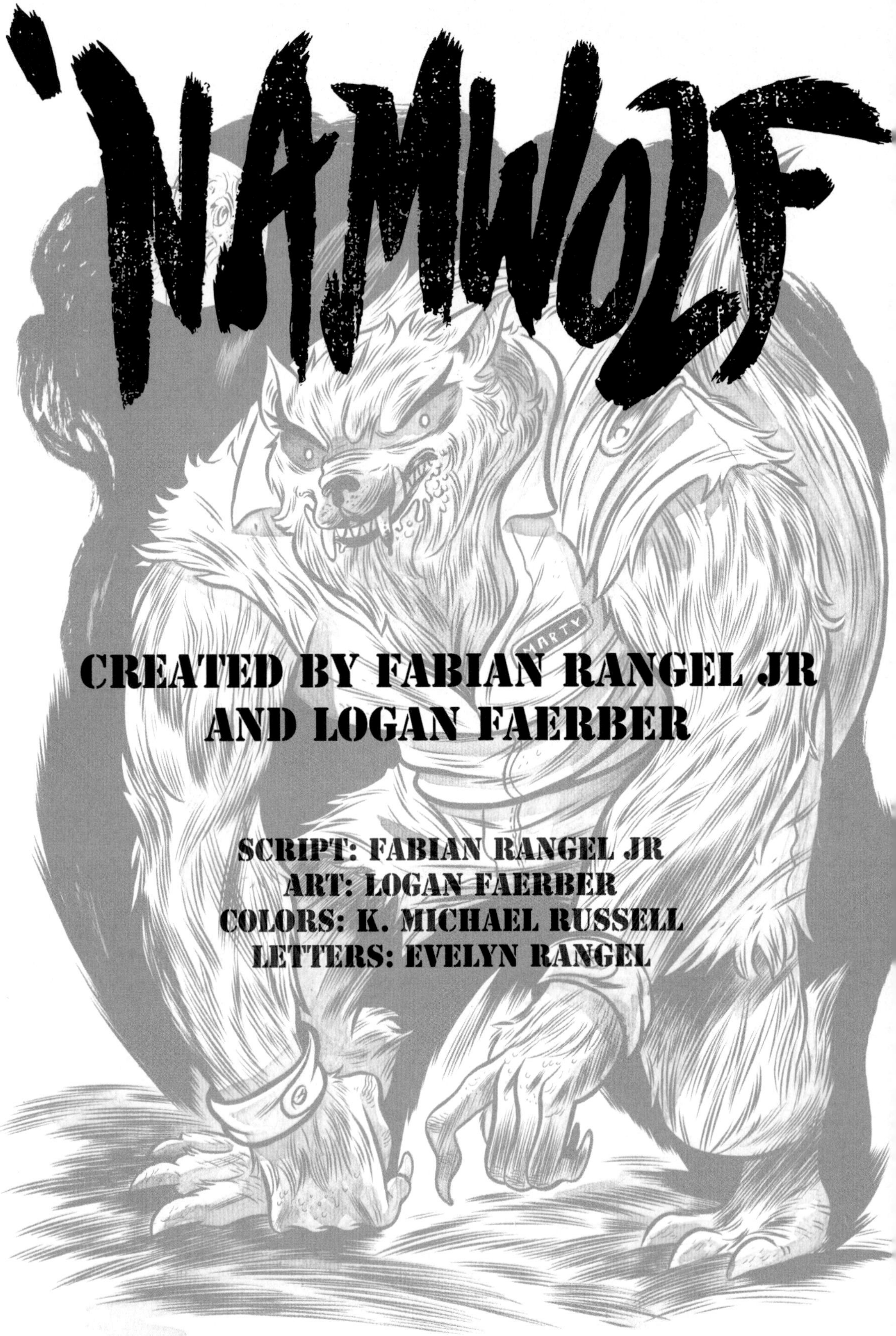
MARTY

**CREATED BY FABIAN RANGEL JR
AND LOGAN FAERBER**

**SCRIPT: FABIAN RANGEL JR
ART: LOGAN FAERBER
COLORS: K. MICHAEL RUSSELL
LETTERS: EVELYN RANGEL**

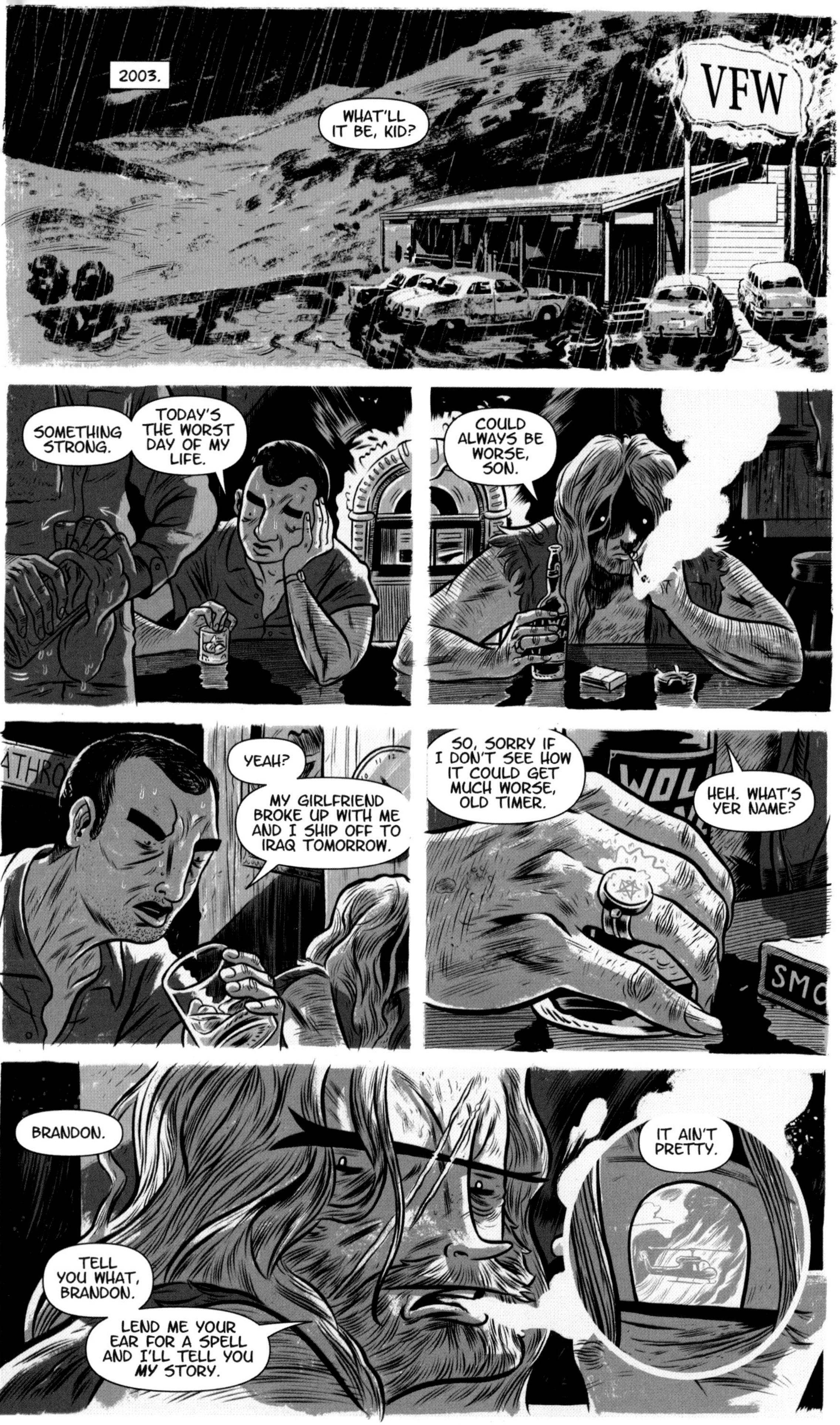
2003.
VFW
WHAT'LL IT BE, KID?
SOMETHING STRONG.
TODAY'S THE WORST DAY OF MY LIFE.
COULD ALWAYS BE WORSE, SON.
YEAH?
MY GIRLFRIEND BROKE UP WITH ME AND I SHIP OFF TO IRAQ TOMORROW.
SO, SORRY IF I DON'T SEE HOW IT COULD GET MUCH WORSE, OLD TIMER.
HEH. WHAT'S YER NAME?
BRANDON.
IT AIN'T PRETTY.
TELL YOU WHAT, BRANDON.
LEND ME YOUR EAR FOR A SPELL AND I'LL TELL YOU *MY* STORY.

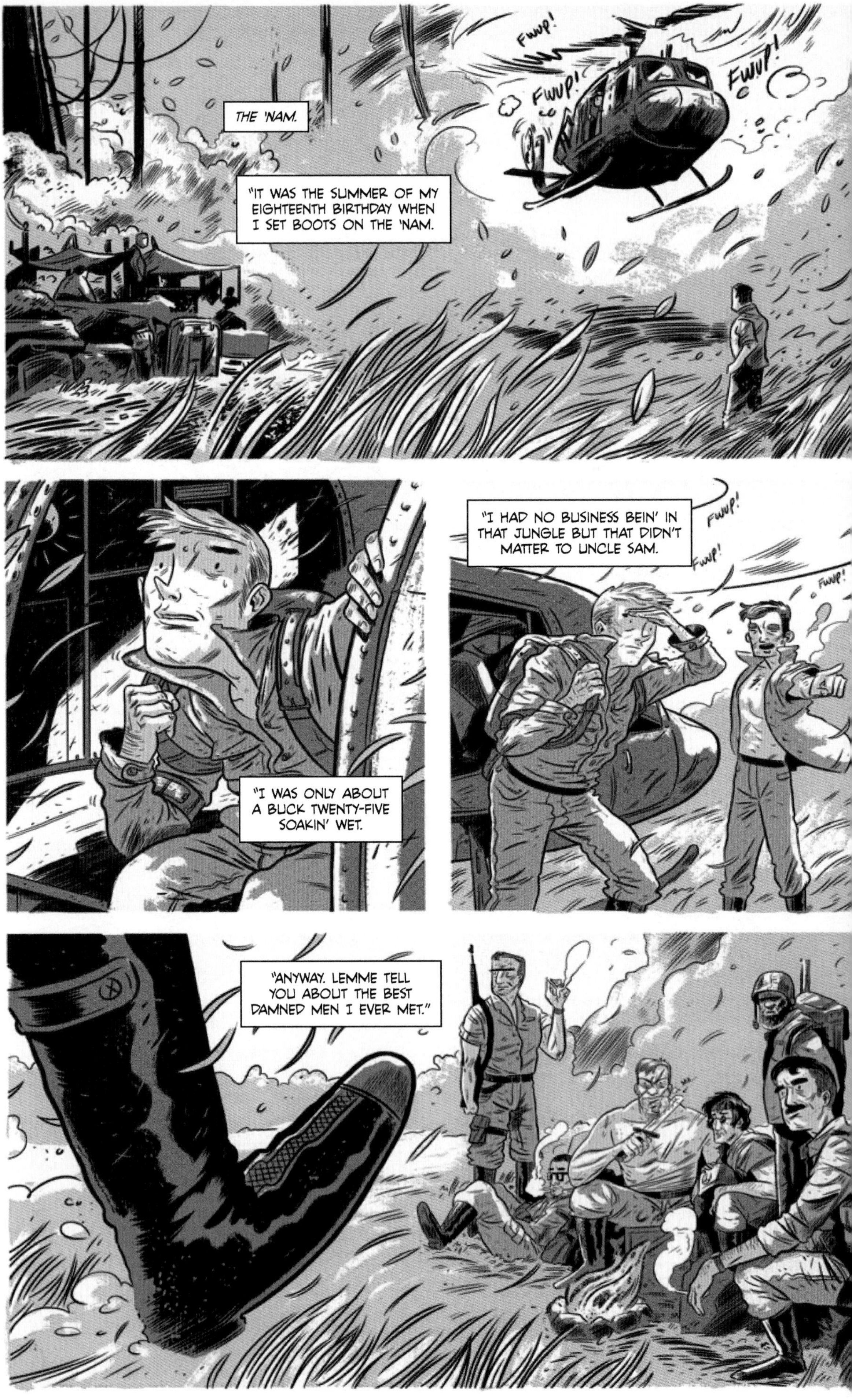
FWUP!
FWUP!
FWUP!
THE 'NAM.
"IT WAS THE SUMMER OF MY EIGHTEENTH BIRTHDAY WHEN I SET BOOTS ON THE 'NAM.
"I WAS ONLY ABOUT A BUCK TWENTY-FIVE SOAKIN' WET.
"I HAD NO BUSINESS BEIN' IN THAT JUNGLE BUT THAT DIDN'T MATTER TO UNCLE SAM.
FWUP!
FWUP!
FWUP!
"ANYWAY. LEMME TELL YOU ABOUT THE BEST DAMNED MEN I EVER MET."

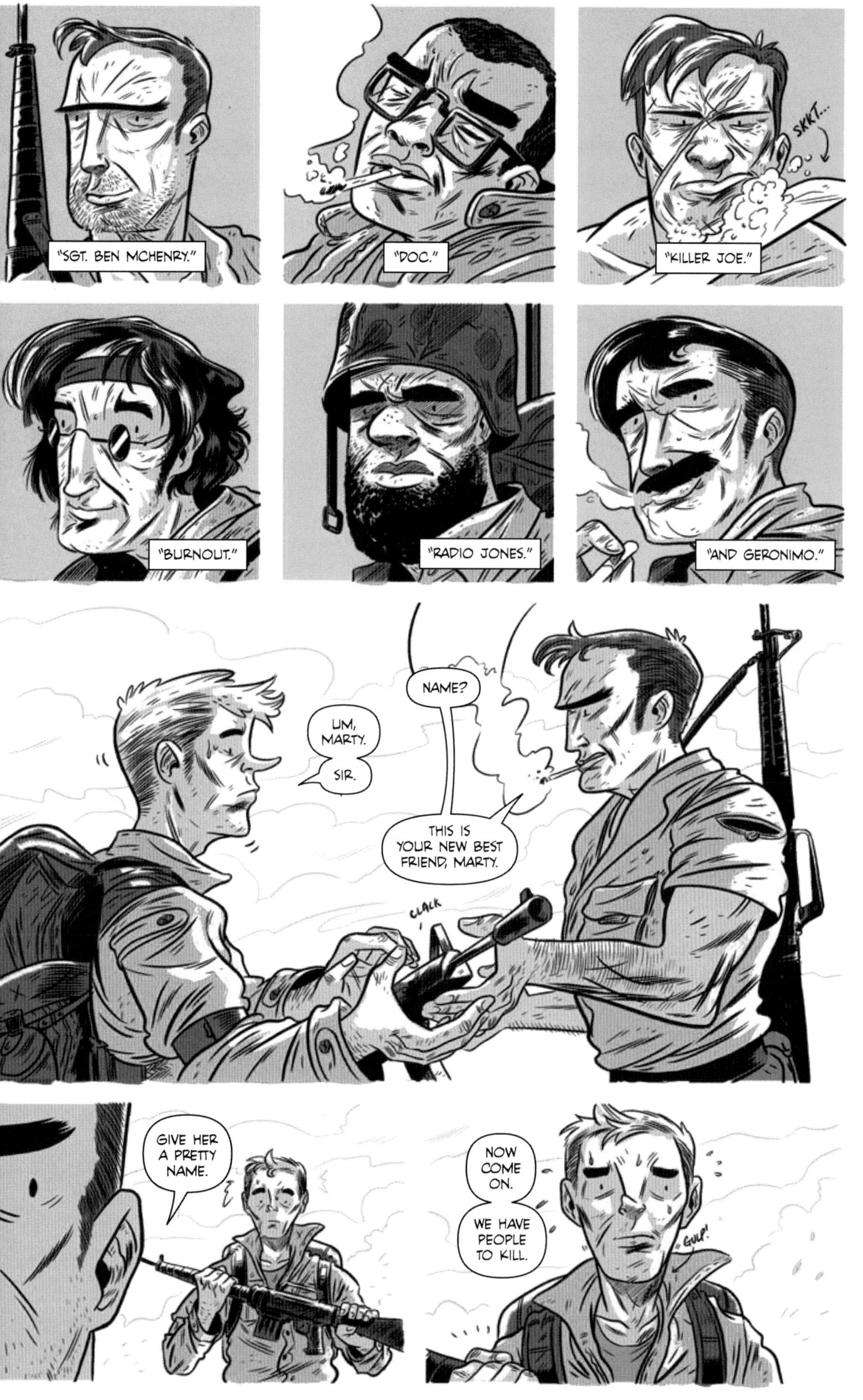
"SGT. BEN MCHENRY."
"DOC."
SKKT...
"KILLER JOE."
"BURNOUT."
"RADIO JONES."
"AND GERONIMO."
NAME?
UM, MARTY.
SIR.
THIS IS YOUR NEW BEST FRIEND, MARTY.
CLACK
GIVE HER A PRETTY NAME.
NOW COME ON.
WE HAVE PEOPLE TO KILL.
GULP!

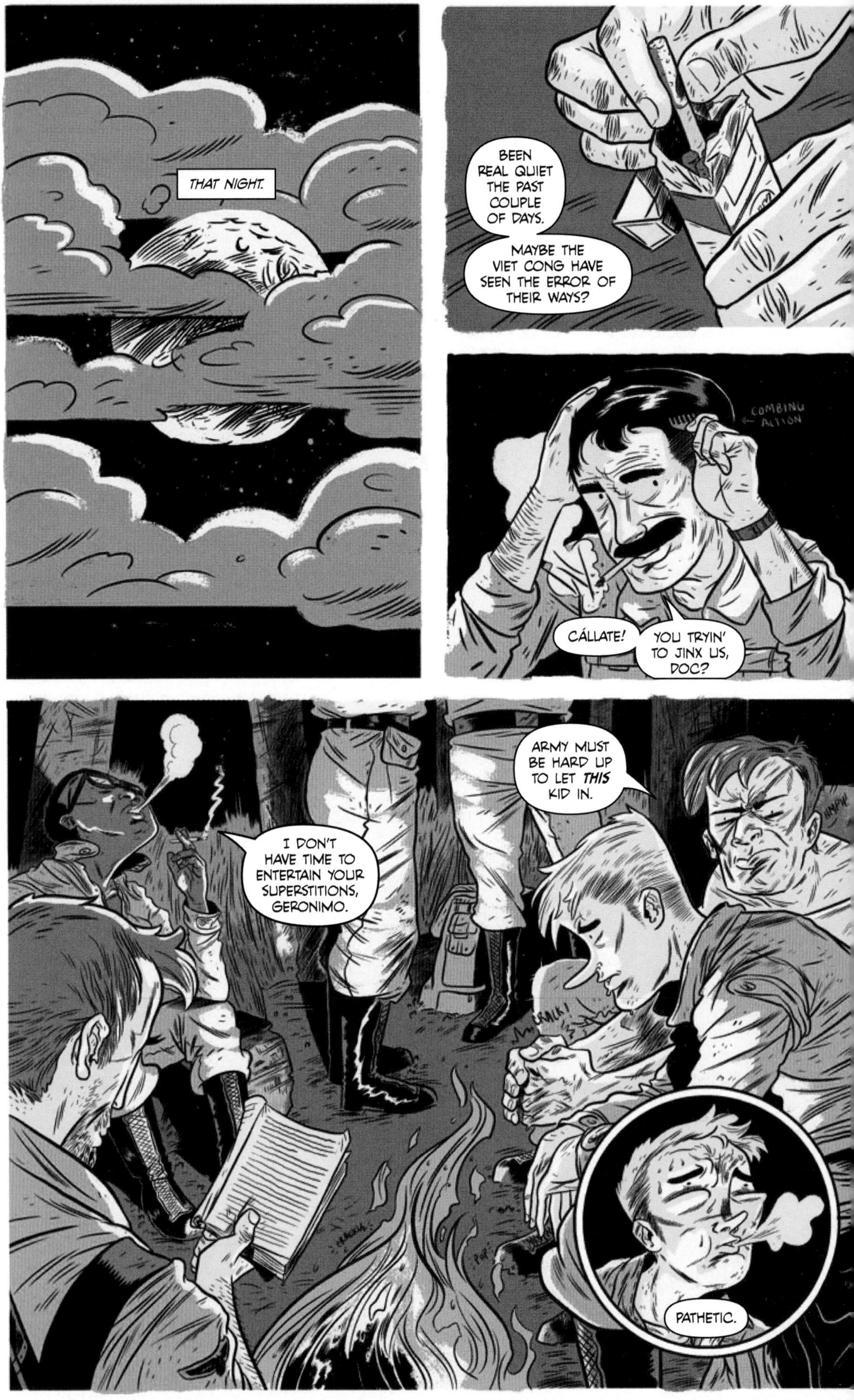
THAT NIGHT.
BEEN REAL QUIET THE PAST COUPLE OF DAYS.
MAYBE THE VIET CONG HAVE SEEN THE ERROR OF THEIR WAYS?
COMBING ACTION
CÁLLATE!
YOU TRYIN' TO JINX US, DOC?
I DON'T HAVE TIME TO ENTERTAIN YOUR SUPERSTITIONS, GERONIMO.
ARMY MUST BE HARD UP TO LET *THIS* KID IN.
PATHETIC.

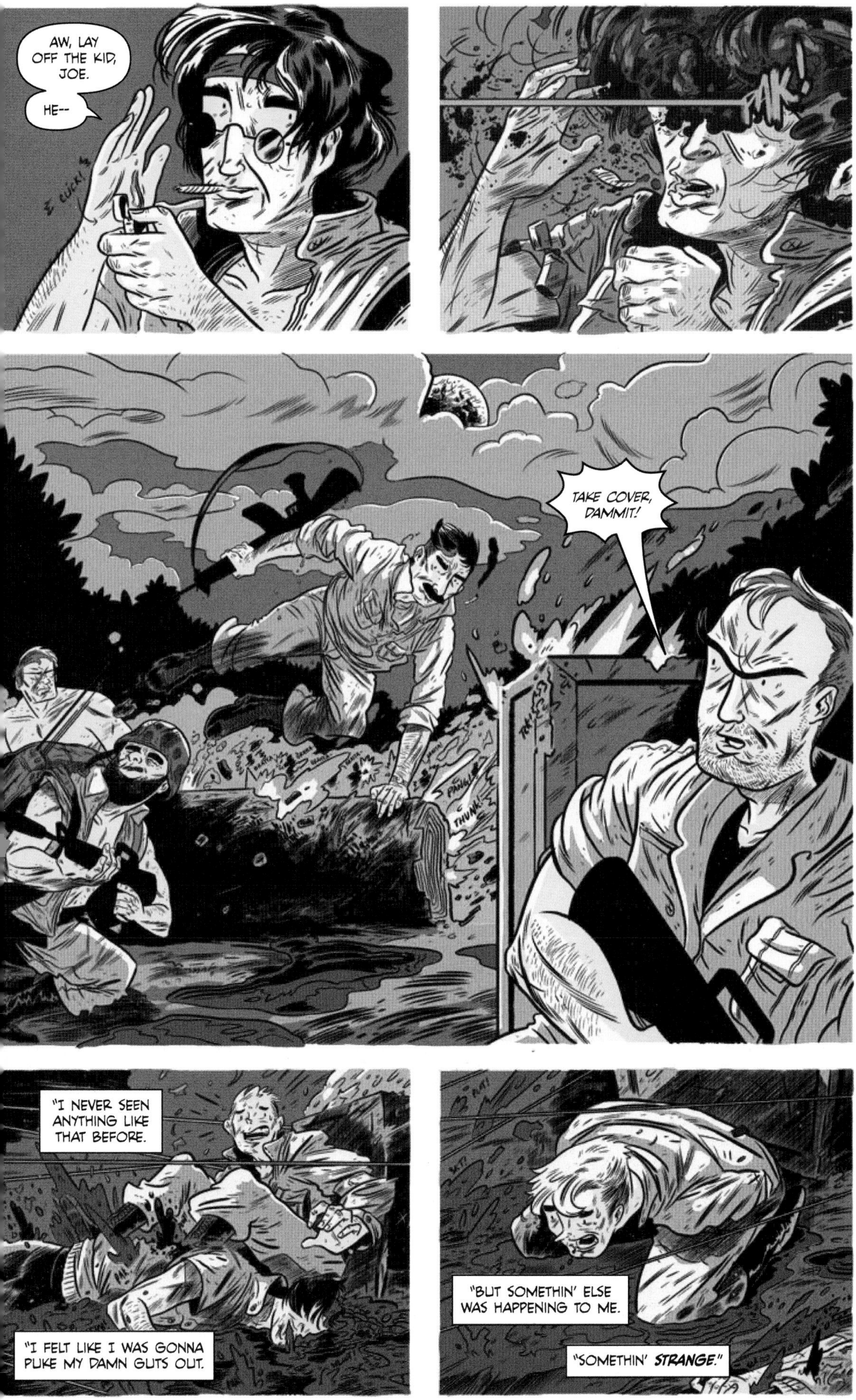
AW, LAY OFF THE KID, JOE.
HE--
CLICK!
PAK!
TAKE COVER, DAMMIT!
THUNK
"I NEVER SEEN ANYTHING LIKE THAT BEFORE.
"I FELT LIKE I WAS GONNA PUKE MY DAMN GUTS OUT.
"BUT SOMETHIN' ELSE WAS HAPPENING TO ME.
"SOMETHIN' ***STRANGE.***"

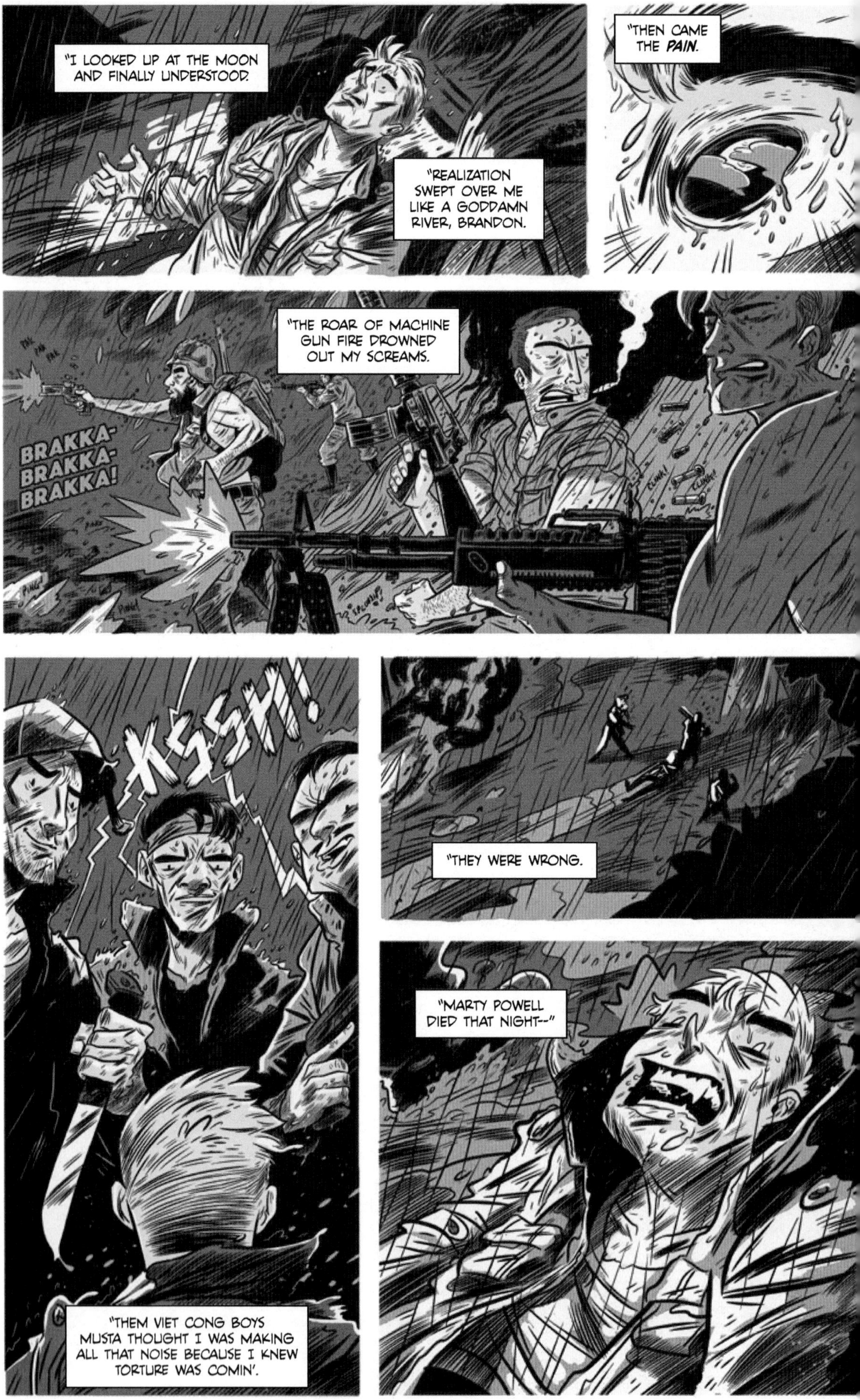
"I LOOKED UP AT THE MOON AND FINALLY UNDERSTOOD.
"REALIZATION SWEPT OVER ME LIKE A GODDAMN RIVER, BRANDON.
"THEN CAME THE *PAIN*.
"THE ROAR OF MACHINE GUN FIRE DROWNED OUT MY SCREAMS.
BRAKKA-BRAKKA-BRAKKA!
KSSH!!
"THEM VIET CONG BOYS MUSTA THOUGHT I WAS MAKING ALL THAT NOISE BECAUSE I KNEW TORTURE WAS COMIN'.
"THEY WERE WRONG.
"MARTY POWELL DIED THAT NIGHT--"

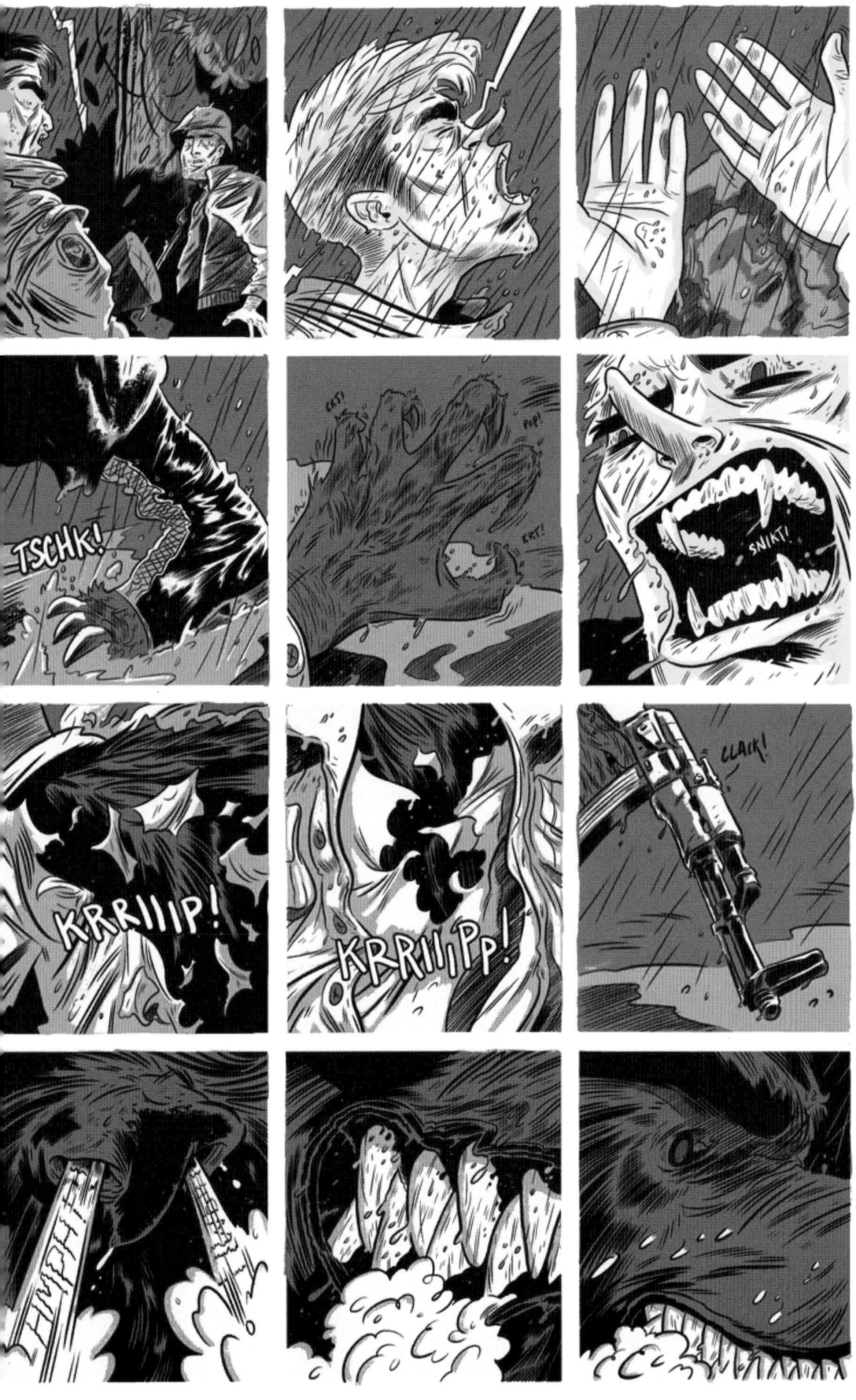
TSCHK!
POP!
KRT!
SNIKT!
KRRIIIP!
KRRIIIPP!
CLACK!
HMPHH!

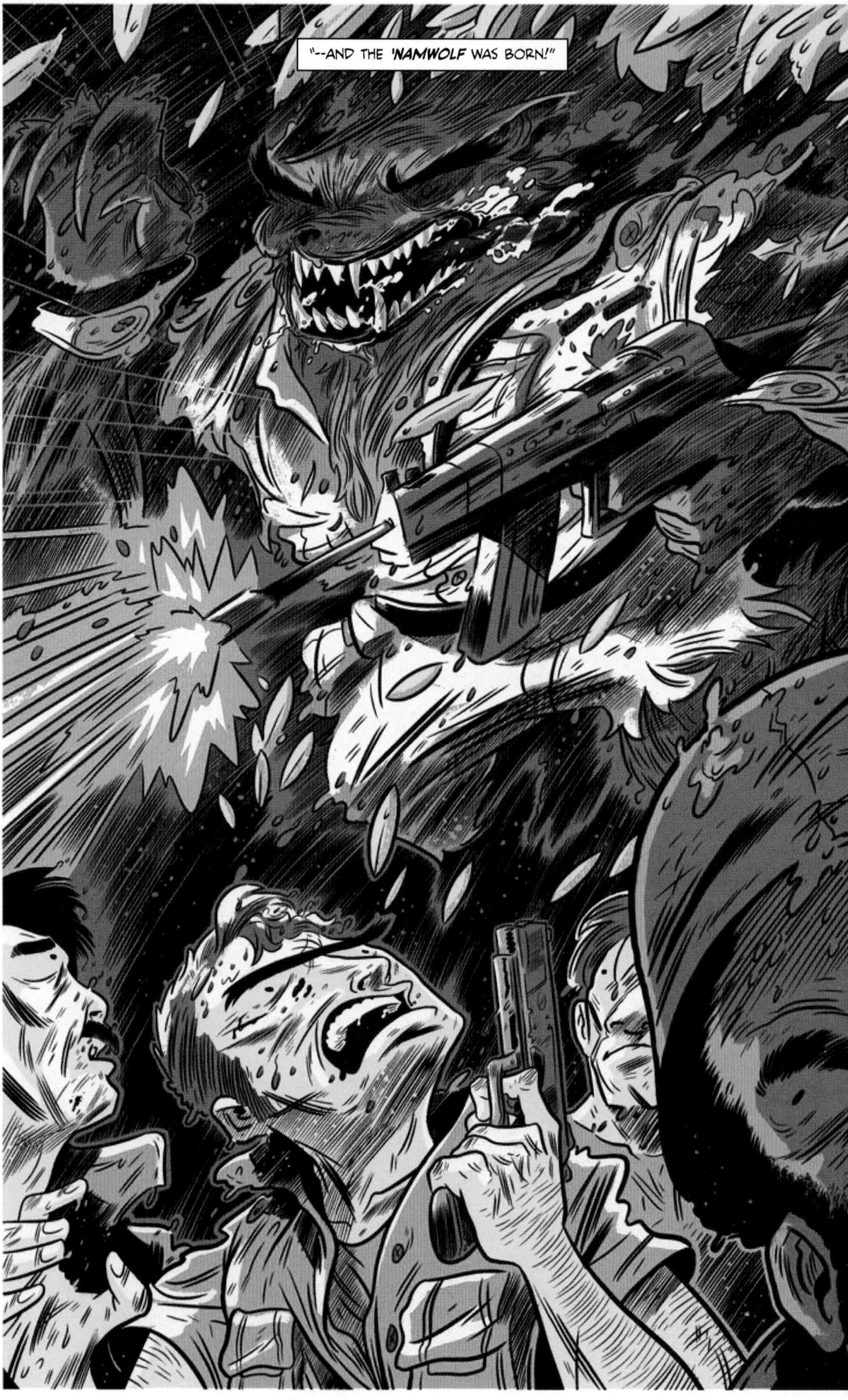
"--AND THE 'NAMWOLF WAS BORN!"

# SKETCHBOOK

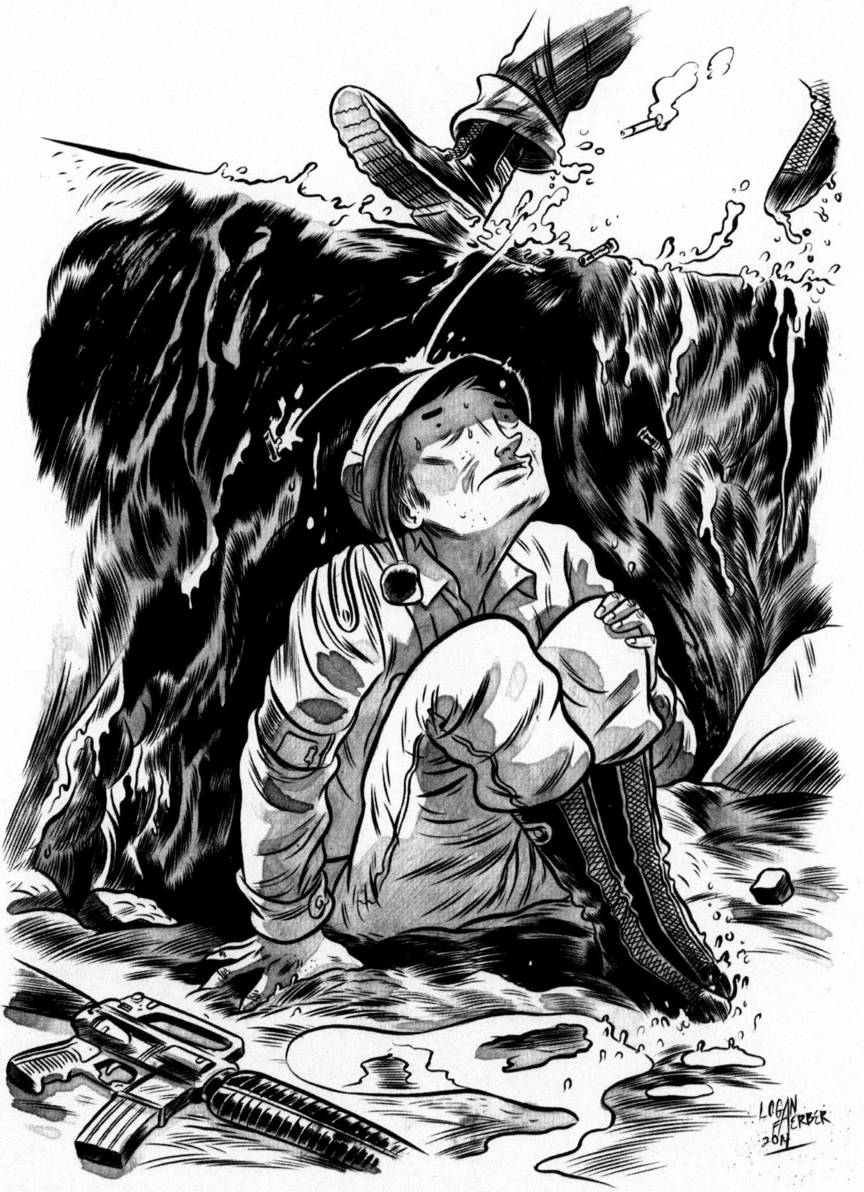
LOGAN FAERBER 2014

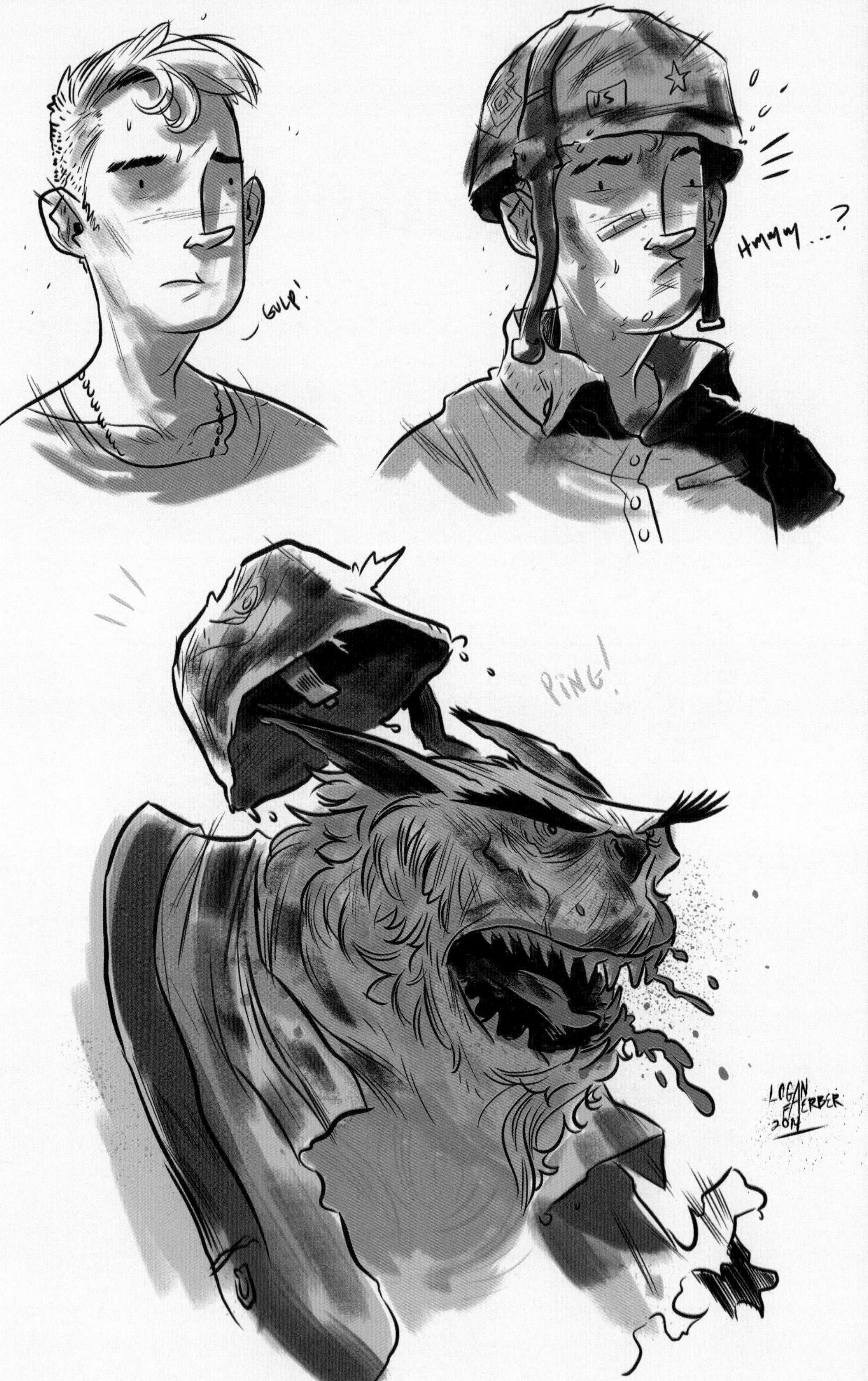
GULP!
HMMM...?
PING!
LOGAN FAERBER 2014

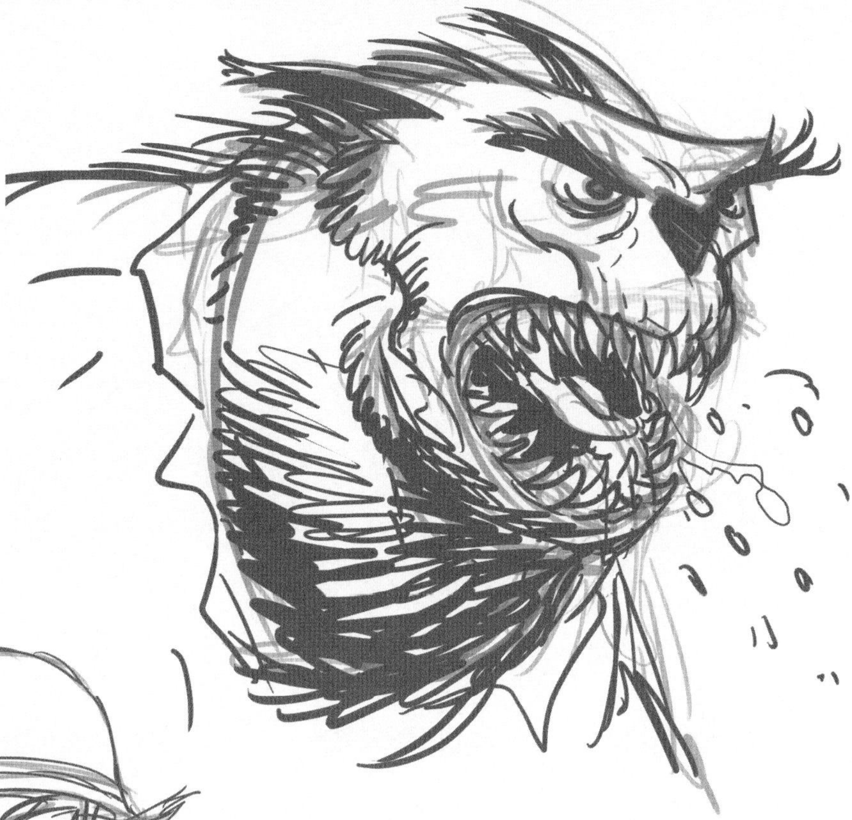
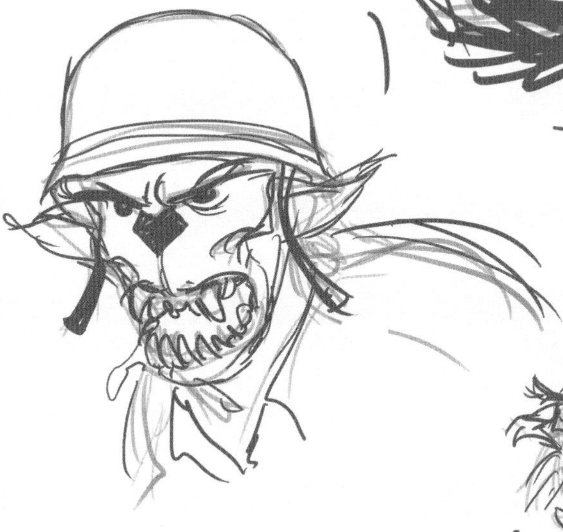
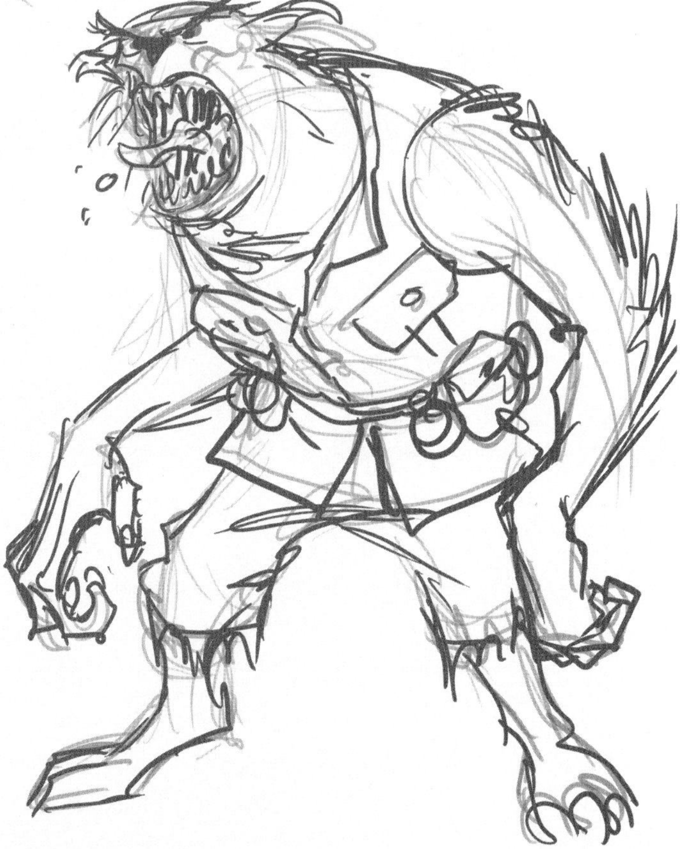

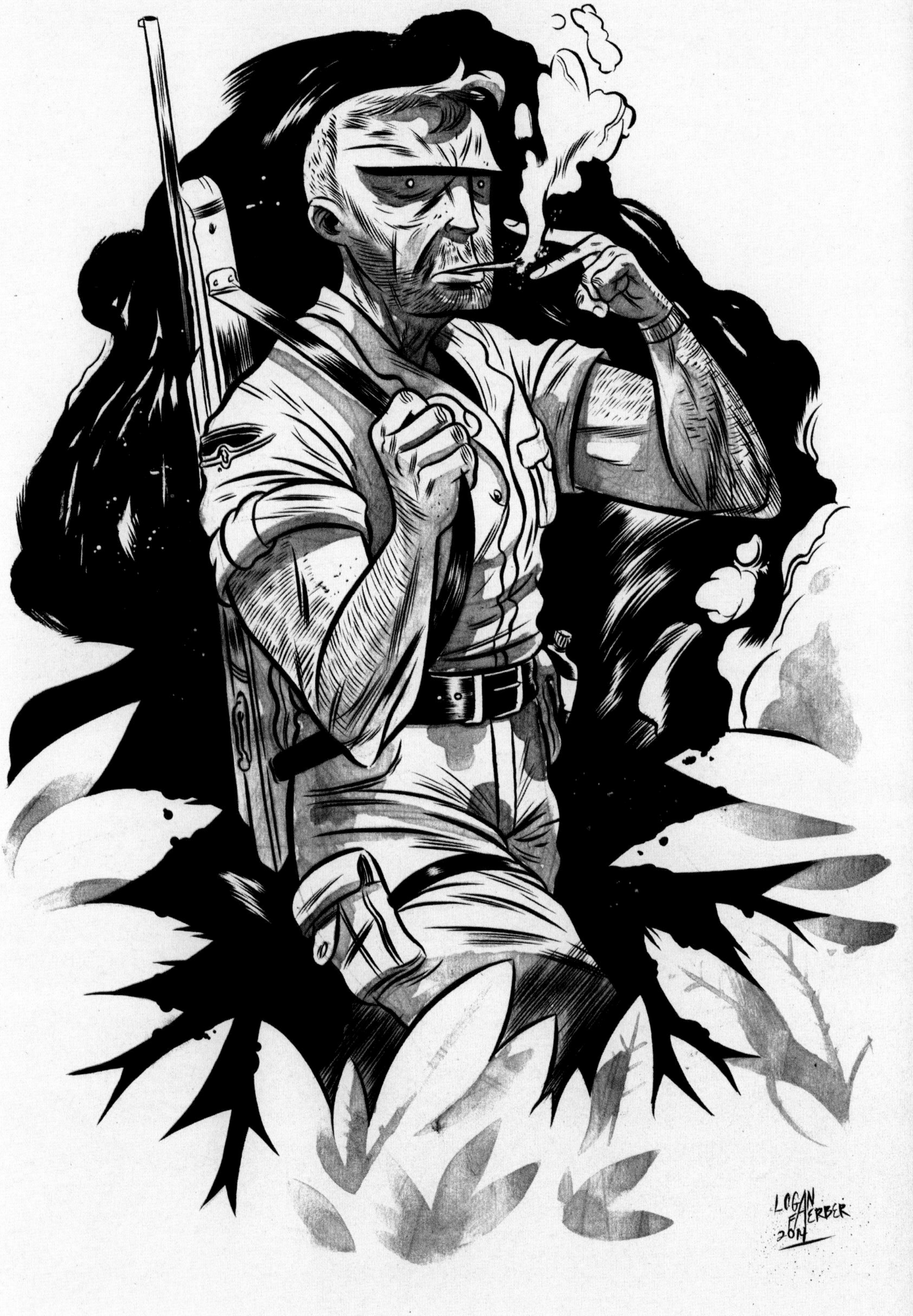
LOGAN
FAERBER
2014

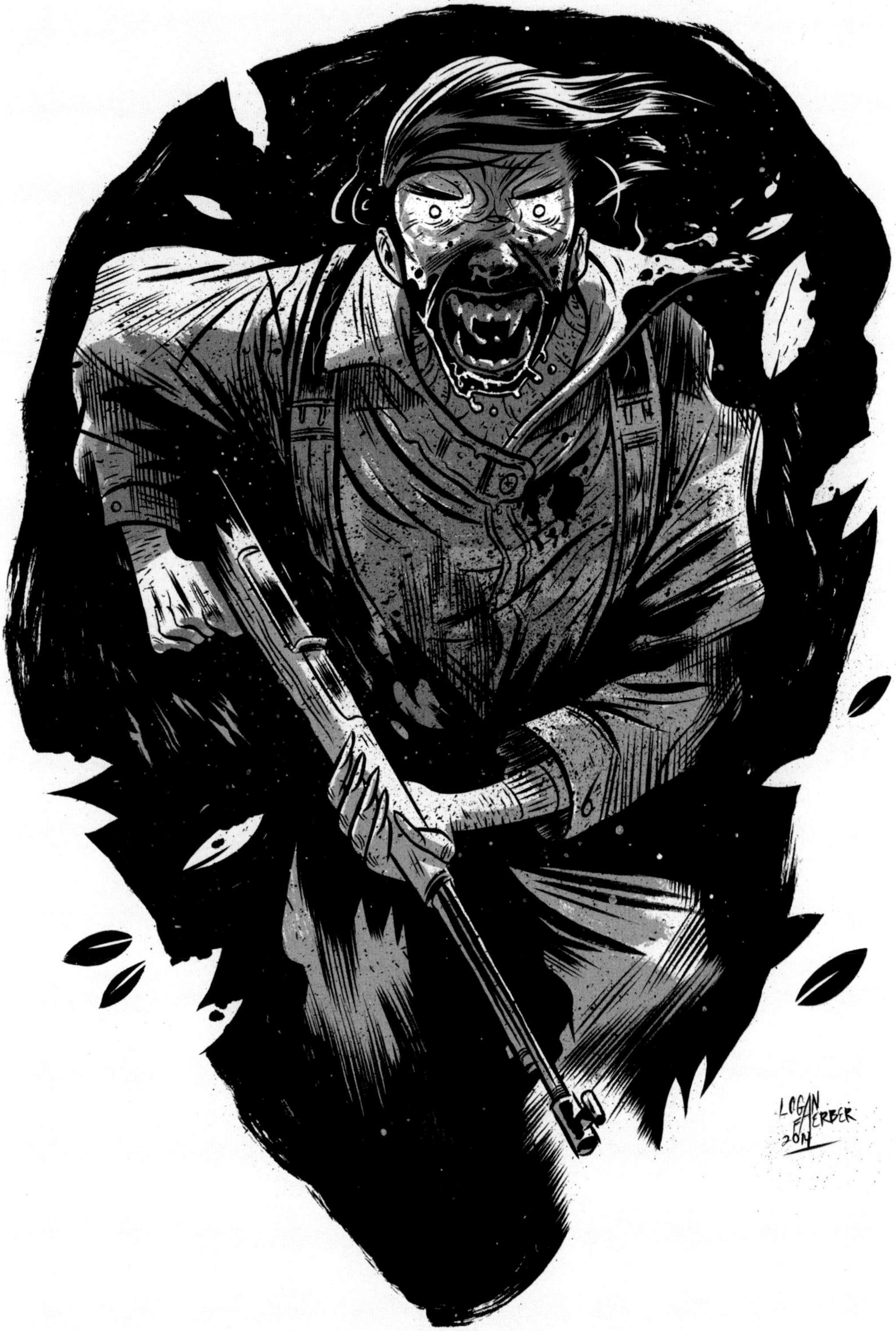
LOGAN FAERBER 2014

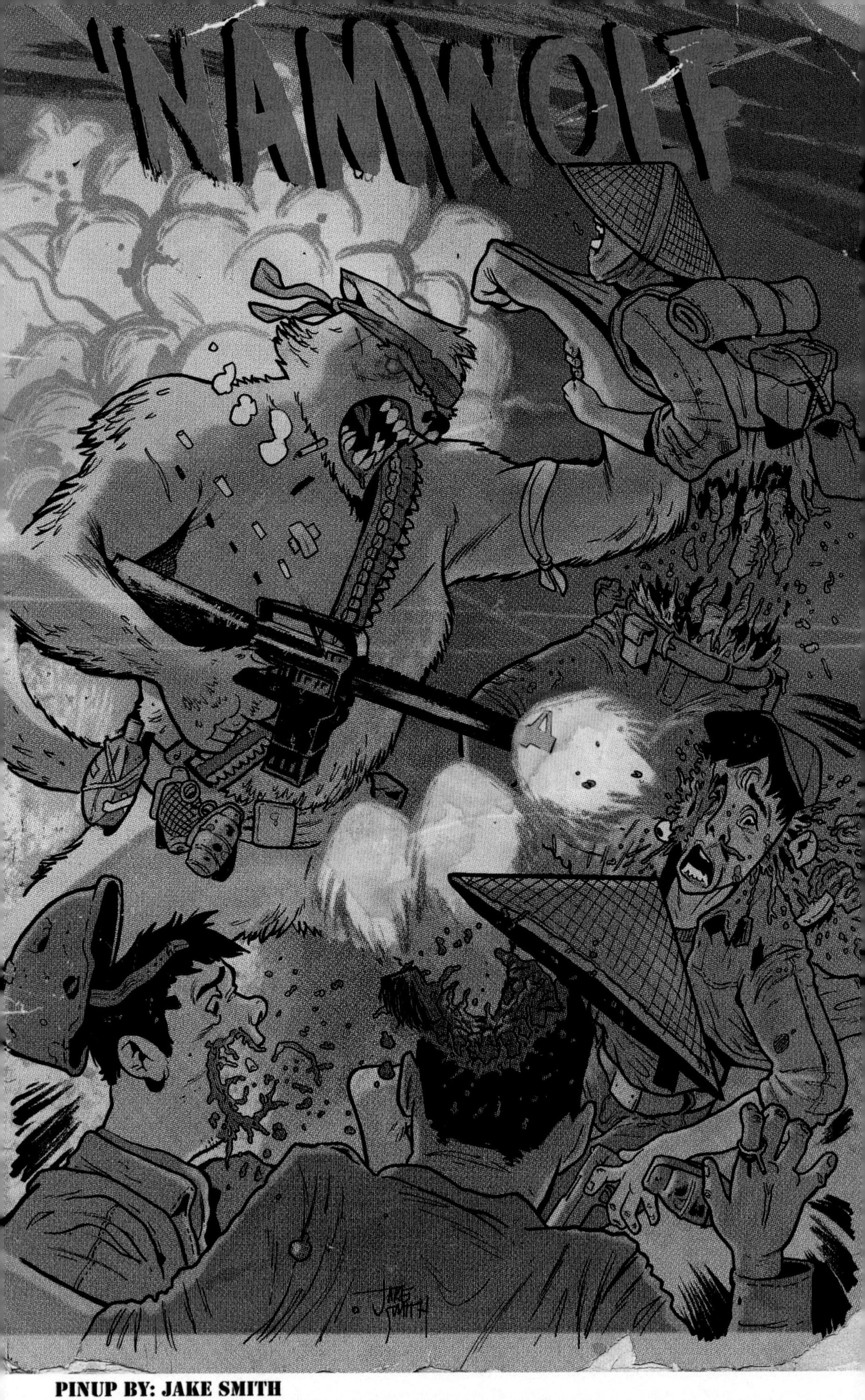
'NAMWOLF
JAKE SMITH

PINUP BY: JAKE SMITH

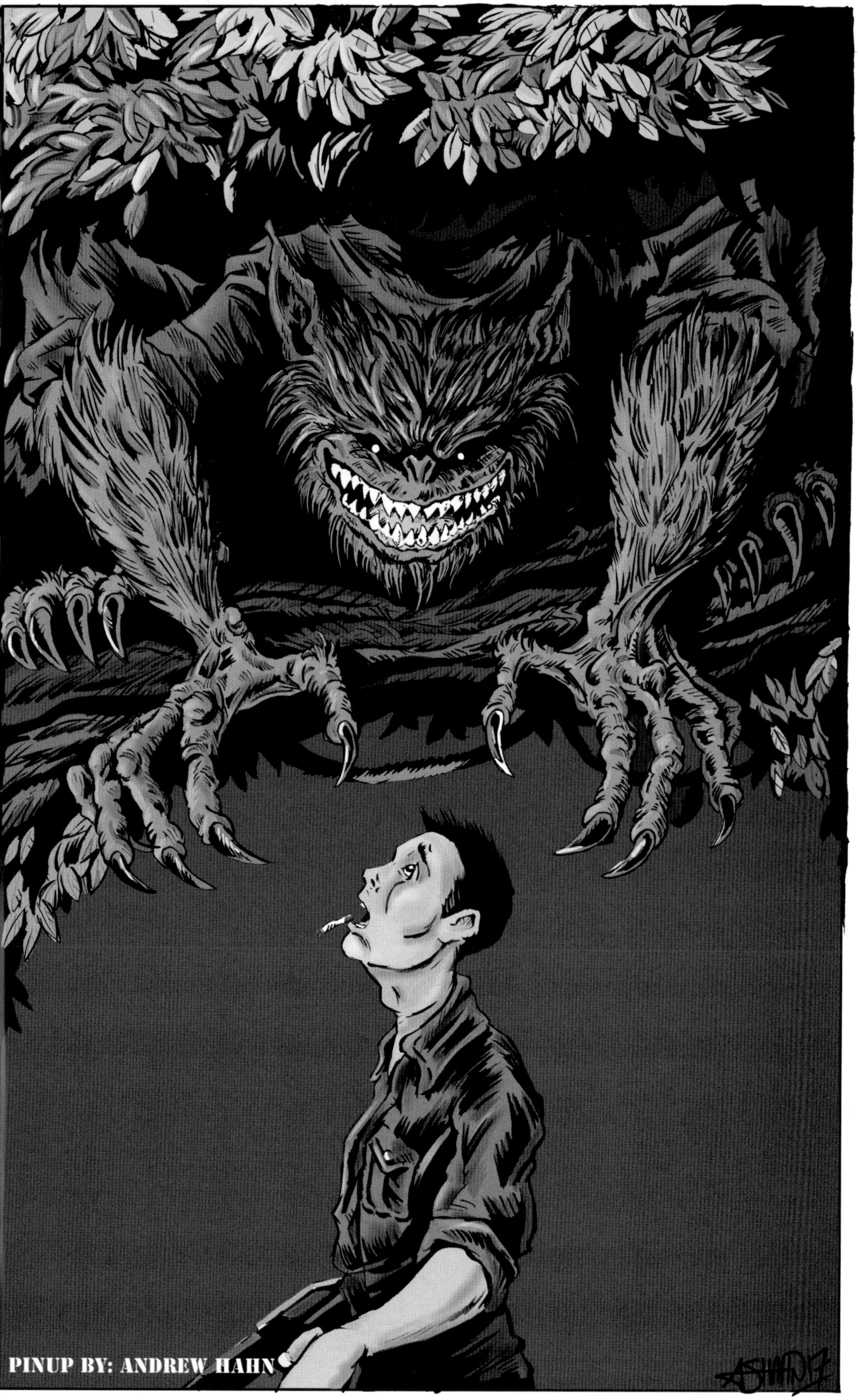
PINUP BY: ANDREW HAHN

Hillbilly
BY
ERIC POWELL
VOLUME ONE

**HILLBILLY: VOLUME ONE**
**ISBN: 978-0-9983792-0-3**
**$17.99**

Hillbilly
BY
ERIC
POWELL
VOLUME TWO

**HILLBILLY: VOLUME TWO**
**ISBN: 978-0-9983792-3-4**
**$17.99**

SCARY STORIES FOR KIDS!
SPOOK
HOUSE
KEEP OUT!
CHOCOLATE!

**SPOOK HOUSE: VOLUME ONE**
**ISBN: 978-0-9983792-1-0**
**$17.99**

'NAMWOLF

**'NAMWOLF: HEART OF DARKNESS**
**ISBN: 978-0-9983792-2-7**
**$17.99**

# BUILD YOUR ALBATROSS FUNNYBOOKS LIBRARY!

ALBATROSS

www.albatrossfunnybooks.com

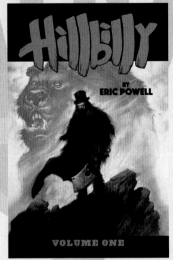

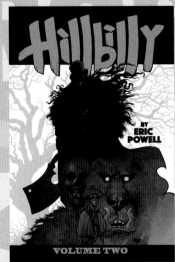

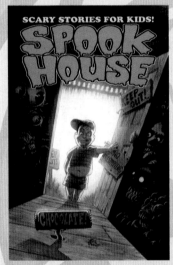

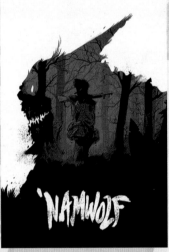

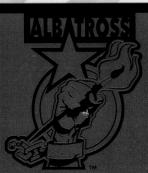